Jeff Christopherson writes *Once You See* from a unique vantage point, as someone who has led the largest church-planting network in North America and is now leading a denomination in Canada. What is presented here as missiological fiction is close to our future reality, especially as it pertains to the urgency of our mission in North America. This is captivating storytelling that masterfully weaves the themes required to lead the church into the future.

—**ED STETZER**, dean and professor, Wheaton College, Illinois

Jeff Christopherson has an unusual capacity to see things others miss. He relentlessly gets to the root of the problem. His conclusions may shock, enlighten, inspire, or offend you, but once you read this captivating book, you will never view the church the same way again.

—**RICHARD BLACKABY**, president, Blackaby Ministries International, Atlanta; author, *Experiencing God* and *The Ways of God*

Jeff Christopherson shows us what it looks like to resist the temptations of the Western church and live instead as kingdom people under the beautiful reign of Christ. Presented in a lively narrative, *Once You See* is a book about kingdom ethics for those who need to see what it could look like, not just read the theory. The list of seven temptations and kingdom correctives are worth the price of admission alone.

—**MICHAEL FROST**, Morling College, Sydney

In *Once You See*, Jeff Christopherson uses the intriguing medium of story to encourage, instruct, and admonish the Western church to reconsider how it functions and how it intends to move forward in this global era. Fascinating! I loved this book! I could hardly put it down.

—**LINDA BERGQUIST**, church planting catalyst, North American Mission Board; author and coauthor of three books and two ebooks

Once You See is one of those rare books where you anticipate the finish, but you don't want it to end. In a heart-grabbing, present-day story, with roots two thousand years old, Jeff Christopherson blends prophetic imagination, rebuke, hope, and redemption into a vision-bearing narrative that skillfully unwraps Jesus' intention for his church and then makes you want to become part of the story.

—**LANCE FORD**, author, *UnLeader* and *The Starfish and The Spirit*

In the subversive form of a novel, Jeff Christopherson artfully unmasks the temptations of the Christendom forms of church and demonstrates why these have inevitably led to the corruption of the church that Jesus truly intended. Given his long experience as a church planter and a senior denominational and agency leader, along with significant academic reflections on the topic of missional forms of church, this book delivers a much-needed prophetic call to awaken readers to their own participation in these collective sins and, from there, move them to *metanoia* and paradigm shift. A worthy read.

—**ALAN HIRSCH**, author of numerous books on missional leadership, organization, and spirituality; founder of Movement Leaders Collective, Forge Missional Training Network, and 5Q Collective

Jesus came to show us the kingdom. In fact, he was kingdom-obsessed. It was his frame of reference, the lens through which he saw everything. He spent his entire life helping people get a glimpse of it for themselves because he knew that once you see it, you cannot unsee it. Jeff's creative and convicting novel challenges the church to move from creating church-centric consumers to kingdom-centric followers of the Way.

—**REGGIE MCNEAL**, best-selling author, *Kingdom Come* and *Kingdom Collaborators*

Jeff Christopherson is one of the leading missiologists of our day who carries a depth of understanding and passion for the kingdom of God. His life's message of calling the church to recapture its purpose of multiplying disciples and churches is desperately needed in this critical hour. *Once You See* might be Christopherson's most accessible and heart-shifting work yet. I highly recommend it!

—**VANCE PITMAN**, president, Send Network; founding pastor, Hope Church, Las Vegas, Nevada; author, *Unburdened*, *The Stressless Life*, and *The Life of a Jesus Follower*

What Jeff calls a "novel" might equally be deemed "the Good Shepherd's prodding of the Western Church," and "a needed glimpse into the fast-approaching future ... or the already-present." With masterful storytelling, Jeff paints a prophetic picture of ministry in a post-Christendom, global world. While the paradigms may be new to many of us, our twenty-first-century culture might just need churches that look like those of Jesus' first-century followers. Thus, my prayer is that this fictional work becomes a force that shapes the non-fictitious church in our time.

—**BEN CONNELLY**, founder, The Equipping Group; servant leadership team, Salt+Light Community, Fort Worth, Texas

For those who have craved a closer alignment of the local church and the kingdom of God, *Once You See* gives us a biblical picture of just what that might look like. Jeff Christopherson crafts a compelling story that helps us see and feel the beauty of Jesus' church and then makes us want to pursue it. I highly recommend.

—**BRIAN BLOYE**, founder and senior pastor, West Ridge Church, Dallas, Georgia; coauthor, *It's Personal: Surviving and Thriving on the Journey of Church Planting*

I suspect most pastors have looked at their church work and wondered, *Is this it? Is this what kingdom-building is all about? It seems there should be more.* Then comes Jeff Christopherson with an answer. And once you've seen it, you will never be the same. And you will never look at ministry in the same way again. This is a perspective-altering, ministry-rearranging, and life-changing book. As one character in the novel says, "He will wreck you for church as usual." What Christianity needs today is more such wrecks. I'm planning to buy a whole box of this book for friends who also want to "see."

—**JOE MCKEEVER**, pastor, cartoonist, author; former director of missions of Southern Baptist churches of metro New Orleans, Louisiana

The work we do at the Church Multiplication Institute is deeply shaped by Jeff's leadership and thinking. *Once You See* has taken his thought-leadership to another level, making his ideas readily available to those who aren't necessarily interested in pastoral theology and academic missiology. Those who want to hand off the mission of God in North America to the next generation need to read Jeff's creative offering with all seriousness.

—**DANIEL YANG**, director, Church Multiplication Institute, Wheaton College Billy Graham Center, Illinois

Once you see … you can't unsee. And once you read Christopherson's book … you can't unknow what you learned in these pages. This book will change the way you think about what we know as "church" in our day. If you let it, it may even change what you do.

—**CONNIE CAVANAUGH**, international speaker, based in Cochrane, Alberta; author, *Following God One Yes at a Time* and *From Faking it to Finding Grace*

In *Once You See,* Christopherson takes us on a journey that ignites a fire for the radical mission of Jesus. In a convergence of seemingly unrelated stories that paint a beautiful portrait of what it looks like for Jesus' church to be on mission, we discover that what was true for the early church two thousand years ago is still true for us today. The seven shifts provide a needed prophetic disruption for how the Western church has come to define success. See what happens when disciples of Jesus seek first the kingdom of God. Read this novel! Once you see, you will not be able to unsee.

—**WILL PLITT**, executive director, Christ Together, Winston-Salem, North Carolina; author, *Gospel Saturation Primer*

Jeff Christopherson is an out-of-the-box leader. Sticking firmly to biblical truth, he gives us courageous but necessary approaches to propel the mission of the church forward while helping us to think with a kingdom mentality. This book will open your eyes and challenge your thinking about the Western church.

—**DR. DHATI LEWIS,** lead pastor, Blueprint Church; founder and president, MyBLVD; author, *Among Wolves: Disciple-Making in the City* and *Advocates: The Narrow Path to Racial Reconciliation*

Once You See is an exciting book, filled with encouragement, exhortation, and challenge. Readers are taken on a fantastic journey. But beware, this powerful story will draw you into a different way of viewing reality. Christopherson knows how to "show" that we may *see* a more excellent way.

—**J. D. PAYNE**, professor, Christian Ministry, Samford University; author, *Apostolic Imagination*

Once You See opens our eyes to what can be. It opens our eyes to how churches can recover their ability to join God in his kingdom. It helps us ask and answer questions like, *What if the church was the church seven days a week? What if the church was the missionary? What if every believer understood how they have been shaped by God for significant service in building his kingdom in their community?* I love this book. I cannot wait to order it by the case to distribute far and wide.

—**DR. DAVID BOWMAN,** executive director, Tarrant Baptist Association, Fort Worth, Texas

Pain, insight, hope, gratitude—are what I experienced reading *Once You See*, very similar to what a person will experience when undergoing surgery; a surgery that is absolutely necessary for the health of Christ's church and the health of Christ's followers. Once you see you won't be able to unsee the transformational potential that is possible in your life.

—**GREG NETTLE**, president, Stadia Church Planting, Cleveland, Ohio

We need prophetic voices; voices that challenge our assumptions, confront our deceptive rhetoric, and expose the twisted ways we pervert the gospel for our own ends. With the skill of a surgeon, Jeff cuts and excises deeply, in order to bring healing and hope. Through the power of story, Jeff describes our problem, prescribes the remedy, and shows us the better way of Jesus. From Luca in the first chapter to the Bedouins of the last chapter, Jeff invites God's people to repentance and renewal.

—**SCOTT HARRIS**, vice president, Church and Global Engagement, Mission Increase, Brentwood, Tennessee

O

N C

E Y O

U S E E

O
N C
E Y O
U S E E

SEVEN TEMPTATIONS OF THE WESTERN CHURCH: **A NOVEL**

JEFF CHRISTOPHERSON

100 MOVEMENTS
PUBLISHING

First published in 2022 by 100 Movements Publishing
www.100Mpublishing.com

ISBN 978-1-955142-26-7 (paperback)
ISBN 978-1-955142-28-1 (hardback)
ISBN 978-1-955142-27-4 (ebook)

For Bible copyright notices, see page 441.

Cover design by Karen Sawrey
Interior illustrations by Revo Creative

100 Movements Publishing
An imprint of Movement Leaders Collective
Cody, Wyoming
www.movementleaderscollective.com
www.catalysechange.org

To those who have seen and followed and received little
of man's praise.
Your King has seen.
And your reward is certain.

Quaerite Prime Regnum Dei

Contents

A Confession xvii
Seven Temptations of the Western Church xxi

1. Luca 1
2. Omar 15
3. Jimmy 26
4. The Shunning 31
5. The Communion 48
6. The Brook 65
7. The Passion 81
8. The Messenger 104
9. The Switch 130
10. The Mission 140
11. The Storm 151
12. The Axe 165
13. The Prophet 179
14. The Hunt 194
15. The Convening 208
16. The Picture 219
17. Regnum Dei 228

18. The Pneumanauts 243
19. The Coup D'état 259
20. The Suit 279
21. The Visitors 300
22. The Pope 311
23. The Partner 325
24. The Kingdom 341
25. The Apprentices 359
26. The Bedouins 380

Epilogue 403
Acknowledgments 411
Discussion Guide 415

A Confession

As I wrote this novel, I was continually reminded of how my affections drift toward my flesh; toward comfort, toward safety, toward me. I wish I could say that the temptations embedded in this story are the dark enticements of others and not of myself—but such a statement would only reveal an eighth seduction in which I voluntarily revel. And my brokenness would only be intensified by a deeper level of self-deception.

To be fair, I struggle with some of the issues highlighted in this tale more than others. A few I can shake off rather readily. But there are others that have a perverse hold on my "Christian" worldview. I tussle and skirmish to find moments of freedom that allow my sight to be lifted above and beyond myself and toward Jesus' beautiful kingdom. And those are intoxicating moments, for in them I get to see reality as it is.

On the journey God has allowed me to travel, I have seen too many extraordinary things to plead ignorance. For several years I have been knee-deep in the mess and the joy of the pastoral and missionary work of the local church. And as many readers of these words know all too well, the intensity of joy and pain of that assignment is difficult to match. But often, amid this very mission, my personal struggles with my flesh are validated and intensified by the expectations of others.

And it appears I am not alone. I lead a denomination of churches, and from that place, I see some of my own struggles being repeated in various contexts among diverse generations and cultures. I also lead two interdenominational collaborative movements, and in doing so, have observed a strange normalcy—wherever we are, and however we are categorized, we all seem to struggle to achieve a kingdom-first orientation. Sadly, it seems that we can almost universally be considered a good church by our peers without owning many of the priorities of our Founder.

But I've seen something else as well. I've experienced incredible power in ministry when my hands were opened wide, and everything was yielded to the mission of Christ. Exhilarating seasons of pragmatic abandonment producing kingdom ripples into eternity. And I've observed other movements speckled across the Western church, and more widely distributed in the global church, that are unexplainable by any human device or sacred system. Obedient disciples are practicing the ways of Jesus and turning the world right-side-up in their wake.

I've seen and cannot unsee.

So, it is because of those fleeting seasons in my life, and because of the global testimony of a remnant who audaciously push against their baser natures in order to live as citizens of a better kingdom, that I offer this story. It is in many ways a simple fable, and as a good fable should be, it is merely an inadequate story with a much greater purpose.

Embedded in the form of a narrative are seven temptations that have often allured me and seem also to be seducing some of my fellow brothers and sisters in Christ. My prayer is that the Spirit of Christ may use the weakness of a simple story for his good purposes in your life and whet your appetite for Jesus' extraordinary mission.

And just in case some of you are reading this before reading my story and are now becoming a bit uneasy, let me offer a kind word of reassurance: the moral of this story will require far less from you and far more from your Sovereign.

On the journey with you,

Jeff Christopherson

Seven Temptations of the Western Church

1. Philosophicalism: "We are a Bible-believing people."
Kingdom Corrective: Essential to a sincere belief in the inerrancy and infallibility of God's Word is an assumption that God calls his disciples to become a Bible-obeying people and not merely intellectual stakeholders of theologically orthodox positions. We understand that true orthodoxy affirms that biblical belief is a *verb*—doctrines that we humbly live and practice—rather than a *noun*—theoretical precepts to which we philosophically subscribe. Therefore, we choose to measure spiritual maturity and doctrinal integrity with the benchmarks found in our everyday obedience to God's Word.

2. Professionalism: "We have a gifted pastoral team."
Kingdom Corrective: The gospel is every disciple's calling—not just a chosen few. Because of this, we seek to multiply Jesus' disciples by developing and deploying the body of Christ into a diverse and infinitely reproducible co-vocational mission-force. Therefore, our vocational leaders see their primary assignment as equippers and multipliers of Jesus' disciple-making insurgency.

3. Presentationalism: "Our worship is inspiring, and our preaching is strong."
Kingdom Corrective: We are the functioning body of Christ in community, not a well-tuned Sunday service. Though we value the weekly gathering of believers for corporate worship and biblical instruction, we also understand that Jesus' purpose for his body cannot be contained in that hour. Therefore, what we most highly prize, publicly celebrate, and consider as our ultimate act of worship is preparing the entire body of Christ as sacrificial servants for Jesus' 24-7 mission and his imminent return.

4. Passivism: "Everybody is welcome."
Kingdom Corrective: We actively search for lost sheep—not hope that lost sheep look for us. Therefore, we happily inconvenience our personal comforts and disrupt our religious preferences for the sake of effectively participating in Jesus' selfless and courageous search and rescue mission.

5. Pragmatism: "We are one of the fastest growing churches."
Kingdom Corrective: The kingdom of God is our only goal, and not the advancement of our individual brand. Because of this, we choose to measure growth in terms of city-wide gospel impact rather than excelling in a competition for an evaporating market share of the evangelically predisposed. Therefore, for the kingdom outcome of gospel proximity, we prefer to selflessly invest in united efforts of gospel collaboration rather than pragmatically contending for our own interests.

6. Partisanism: "We love our country."
Kingdom Corrective: While national patriotism and political perspectives are normal and necessary for healthy and functioning democracies, our highest and exclusive allegiance is to the eternal kingdom of heaven—not a temporal nation, nationality, ethnicity, or political ideology. Therefore, we voluntarily lower all secondary loyalties so that our earthly perspectives might not become a stumbling block to the life and death mission of Jesus' church.

7. Paternalism: "We train pastors around the world."
Kingdom Corrective: We have a leadership that maintains a humble learning posture, holding to a sincere belief that Jesus' church is expressed in a globally diverse mosaic that includes every nation, tribe, people, and language. Therefore, we engage global diversity with a gospel-centered posture that eradicates any hubris of geographical or cultural superiority by seeking to both learn and assist in ways that honor and edify the body of Christ wherever it is found.

Chapter One

Luca

Once you see, you cannot unsee. Once you crane and stretch and peer above the colorless and indistinguishable haze into the heavenlies, that blissful visage always remains. It becomes an indelible and enduring revelation not easily dismissed. For once you see, you cannot unsee.

For one pastor, the blessing of sight became a burden. The burden of that revelation, in the end, appeared to be more curse than gift. And so, although the third cut wasn't at all the deadliest, it was the wound that in the end finished him off. Slumping over the leather-wrapped steering wheel of his Oldsmobile, the Reverend Dr. Josiah Lewis slurred, "St-ell-a." Convulsed. Twitched twice. And then let out one final, thin, breath.

A small puddle gathered beneath the rusted tailpipe as the car idled throughout the night in its designated parking space. And then, as if in a statement of solidarity, it too sputtered, gasped, and then grew quiet, just as yellow-orange light began to filter through the Philadelphia skyline. Man and automobile now both peacefully rested opposite a hand-painted sign that read, *Pastor.* Above them, fastened to muddy red bricks, was a giant billboard that indelicately depicted playful women in scanty swimwear. It announced, *Now Pre-Selling—Liberty Village Lofts.*

The sounds of a city returning to life began to emerge as warm, morning daylight streamed between old, weathered buildings. It was a new day with new prospects and new adventures. But for the people of Mt. Pisgah Baptist Church, this was a day they could have done without. Now, without place or pastor, it was doubtful they would survive.

But there was some good news.

It was unlikely that many would notice.

***

The homegoing service for the late Dr. Josiah Lewis was held the following Tuesday at East Mt. Zion Korean Baptist Church. The coroner's report, which arrived the previous day, found the cause of death to be "natural causes." Pastor Lewis, who had no history of heart disease, had nonetheless expired from a myocardial infarction, a massive heart attack culminating from his final dispiriting years of a broken and disheartening ministry. He was finally at rest.

It was a sparsely attended affair. Maybe not embarrassingly so, but to Luca, the turnout did not seem befitting a man who had faithfully devoted his life to serving the community.

"I'm so glad you can't see this, Papa," Luca mumbled under his breath.

Luca, the only offspring of Josiah and Stella Lewis, stoically planted himself on the front pew, opposite the faux walnut Hammond organ that was about to become very central to this final ritual. Emotionally, he gave nothing away, as he stared vacantly at a large easel placed to the right of the modest coffin. The wooden stand held an elaborately framed portrait of a much earlier version of his father. The photograph captured a memory of his papa that Luca had almost forgotten—a strong, dignified, passionate preacher behind the pulpit of Mt. Pisgah Baptist Church. *They did this*, Luca thought as his disposition darkened. Although this was supposed to be a celebration of his father's life, Luca was not at all in a generous mood.

Seated to his left, and also staring straight ahead, was Chantel, Luca's faithful wife and partner of fourteen years. She was dressed in a simple black dress with a matching wide-brimmed black hat, checking all the boxes for fashion befitting the mourning of family and cleric. Chantel lovingly ran her fingers up and down Luca's right shoulder out of her innate instinct to comfort. She knew the days that lay ahead of them would not be easy.

Flanking Luca on his right was their nine-year-old son, Sanders. If Luca and Chantel projected an image of calm and composure, Sanders conveyed the exact opposite. Leaning against his daddy, face buried in his chest, and almost disappearing under Luca's right arm, he sobbed uncontrollably. He loved his "Pops" and couldn't envision life without him.

Luca squeezed his son securely, in an effort to lovingly reassure him. He could understand Sanders' grief—it was a natural and uncomplicated thing. His grief, as most grief is, was simply love with no place to go. And for Sanders, it was the lonely sting and painful mystery of a first loss.

Luca wished that his own emotions were as uncontaminated and simple. But they were not. There was too much dirty water under the bridge.

Though Luca's stature and expression might convey strength, it was, in fact, a ruse. At least, it was today. Luca didn't feel large and composed at all. He felt small. Very small. Small and abandoned. Orphaned. With both parents now deceased, he was a six-foot-three, two-hundred-and-fifty pound, thirty-eight-year-old orphan with a chip the size of all of Philadelphia sitting squarely on his shoulder.

And this was one orphan who would get even.

As the Reverend Jin Soo Park spoke about heaven and mansions and Jesus being the Truth, Luca involuntarily laughed. He didn't mean to. And he wasn't cheery. It was an instinctive response propelled by frayed emotions. Chantel sympathetically cast a warm smile toward her husband as she patted his left shoulder with extra vigor.

Truth, Luca thought to himself. *Where's the truth here?* Luca's mind was fixated on all the "churchy" lies that led to his papa's death. It was Mt. Pisgah that was responsible for the premature corpse lying embalmed on center stage. And, as he so often had this week, he began to rehearse his long list of grievances against the church where he grew up. Each time he did, the charges escalated in his mind. *They kill't him. They murdered him. They may as well have used a gun.*

Sitting three rows back and dressed in a dark three-piece Giorgenti suit, crisp white collar, and monochromatic silk tie was the murderous gang's ringleader, Marcus E. Robinson. Looking as distinguished and mournful as he could muster, he nodded and gestured to Luca with clasped, praying hands.

Luca pretended not to notice.

Robinson was the wealthy, charismatic, and obviously well-dressed chairman of deacons who led the insurrection against his father's leadership. Year after year, Dr. Lewis cast a single vision that increased with intensity each time it came from his lips. It was a dream of becoming a church that was seen and experienced as good news to the community. A church that dished out good works and good news in equal measure. He remembered his papa saying, "You may not appreciate this image, brothers and sisters, but we need to transform ourselves into spiritual lovechildren of the late Billy Graham and the late Mother Theresa. Our good news clarifies our faith. Our good work verifies it. We can't have one without the other."

It played to mixed reviews.

But when Pastor Lewis' poetic otherworld imagery finally merged with a concrete and executable plan, the nonsense had gone too far. Marcus E. Robinson felt that he had to bring a corrective reality to the naïve musings of their pastor. He was, after all, the chairman of deacons.

One Sunday, after Pastor Lewis preached a stemwinder of a sermon on the sheep and the goats, Marcus E. Robinson had his fill. He snatched the microphone from a lesser deacon who was assigned to pray for the offering and launched his own spiritual counter-offensive.

"Brothers and sisters, becoming the hands and feet of Jesus in the 'hood is all well and good, but let us be practical."

He went on for another ten minutes, proclaiming the virtues of good expository preaching, stirring worship, and deep Bible instruction, and how an attractively appointed "tabernacle" honors the King of Kings. But Robinson wasn't finished. He saved his best stuff for last. He slowed his cadence and lowered his voice as he whispered his big, definitive theological bomb into the highjacked mic. "Now listen up, people, and don't be hoodwinked by a smooth talkin' preacha'. Remember what the good book says: 'Charity begins at home!' Can I get an amen?"

And he did. It seemed like he got all the amens. And, of course, "Charity begins at home" was the only "Scriptural" refrain that gained traction that Sunday. No one even tried to look the phrase up in their own Bible.

So now, all these years later, sitting with crossed legs on the well-worn pew, a smile arrived on Luca's broad face as he recalled the day his father handed out his homemade, hand-stapled treatise entitled *Venal Dogmata*. Like a prophet of old, his father laid down the gauntlet and challenged Marcus E. Robinson and the rest of the insurrection to a theologically brilliant elucidation on becoming the body of Christ in their community.

It was bold and powerful and persuasive. It was one-hundred-proof biblical magnificence, locked and loaded and brilliantly fired straight into the theologically flimsy cream puff of an argument that Robinson had the gall to speak aloud to God's people. Luca chuckled as he stared blankly at the organist while he relived that fateful day. He was so proud of his papa.

But his papa's efforts weren't enough. Not even close.

How could they be, when Marcus E. Robinson had the colossal power of a cultural jingle and the immovable mass of the status quo parked squarely on his side? It was an invincible combination. And at the end of the day, the majority ruled that the body of Christ should continue to be nothing more than a respectable Sunday morning service.

So, the nays got their way, and those whose imaginations were captivated by Dr. Lewis' selfless dream slowly drifted away.

One by one.

And soon Luca and his family joined in the abandoning.

Now, as he listened to the organist mechanically play, "What a Friend We Have in Jesus," emotions of anger gave way to another all too familiar feeling: a deep wash of paralyzing guilt. Luca had deserted his papa. He joined his father's dream—fanned it further—believed it. And then, when they hit a roadblock, he left his papa to the wolves. The loathsome shame Luca felt over this had begun much earlier—almost as soon as he made his quiet exit. It had increased in its suffocating intensity over the years that followed. But now, there was the horrible image of his papa, alone, sitting lifeless for hour upon hour in his old Oldsmobile. And nobody noticed. The guilt was unbearable.

All that Luca had known to do was to shake it off. And fortunately, the emotional shift was made easier by the throng of pretentious churchmen who surrounded him. *Look at Robinson—king of the hill. And all those ungrateful hypocrites who sucked the life out of my papa.* Now, staring at a walnut-colored coffin that contained the body of his father, the body of a pastor whose life was cut short by the pious charlatans that surrounded him, Luca was back and emotionally ready to re-engage the reviewing of charges.

To Luca, the second wound wasn't as much of a singular event as it was a sustained sequence of body blows aimed directly at his papa's already beaten soul. With the church "being on mission" now formally off the table, the good people of Mt. Pisgah had really nothing left to do but find faults. Fortunately for them, this was a pastime in which they excelled. And it seemed Luca's father had more than his fair share. Week by week, he could see his papa age before his very eyes. Year after year he ministered to the congregation of Mt. Pisgah as his sole, small, insular ministry project. But it was never enough. The people of Mt. Pisgah thought of themselves as benevolent for putting up with Dr. Lewis' mediocre efforts—but the truth was, nobody else would serve them for what they paid.

Those were punishing years.

And what little life was left in his father's anemic spirit bled out the day the taxman came. It was a merciless visit. A visit that ham-fistedly knocked over the first domino that eventually forced Mt. Pisgah to sell their church building at a fire-sale rate to the developer of Liberty Village Lofts. With new tax laws in place, Mt. Pisgah Baptist Church did not qualify as a charity under the newly amended tax code—excluding them from the property tax exemption. Now they owed $69,989.08 for the fiscal year. To qualify as a charity, nonprofits must now prove that they were, indeed, charitable. To the city of Philadelphia, that meant they must prove that they existed for the benefit of their community, not their own membership. And that was a litmus test Mt. Pisgah failed in spades.

But it wasn't actually the taxman that Luca found culpable for his father's murder. No, Luca reserved his third charge for someone else, or rather, something else. Luca began to tense up as he tempestuously thought about white evangelicals who, with their insatiable lust for political power, created the conditions for the cultural backlash they were now all experiencing. If it weren't for power-hungry pharisees, like Dr. H. A. Norris and …

Just then, Luca's thoughts were interrupted by Sister Shanice Johnson, who laboriously worked herself into an upright position and then began to lumber toward the platform. She was a sight to see and impossible to miss. In fact, it was difficult to take one's eyes off her. Luca's furrowed brow began to relax.

Papa will love this, he mused.

Shanice was covered throat to thighs with something that resembled abstract splotches on glossy curtain material. Whatever it was, it was much too tight, much too short, and clashed with her neon hat. When she finally made it to the platform stairs, a murmur of disapproval could be heard rumbling throughout the auditorium. The sisters of perpetual suspicion, who stationed their operations on the fifth row, fanned their dour faces and shook their heads in displeasure, "whispering" to the general assembly, "uh-uh, mmm mmm mmm."

But there was much more to Ms. Johnson than fashion sense.

From mentally fomenting his murder charges, Shanice Johnson's entrance instantaneously transformed Luca's brooding mood into a childlike delight. His plan of reprisal was about to roll out.

Sister Shanice cautiously ascended the seven red, well-worn carpeted stairs. Step by painfully slow step. Each red stairstep was to symbolize the seven stations of the cross, and it seemed that Ms. Johnson relished in reenacting the entire pageant as she shuffled upward. Within a minute or two, she gained firm footing atop the platform, carefully grounding herself in front of the remains of the man of honor, and then gave a look that announced to all that a small victory had already been achieved. She then offered a few scripted sympathetic comments as the Hammond organ played wistfully in the background.

She lived for moments like this.

As Shanice set loose her first breathy note of "Take my Hand, Precious Lord," four young men dressed in dark suits simultaneously rose to their feet, as if on cue, and unobtrusively made their way to the front row, each carrying a heavy cardboard box that was stamped, *RightWay Printing.*

Sister Shanice, who appeared completely unfazed by the distraction, continued to hit the husky low notes with skillful precision, one after the next, despite the unusual goings-on. The four young men worked their way down the aisles, distributing the contents of their boxes to all in attendance, one row at a time. And then, as if it had been rehearsed a dozen times before, the young men completed their operation and reconvened in the back foyer by the guest book at the very moment that the Hammond organ faded into silence.

It was impressive by any measure.

After a few announcements and a solemn benediction, the gathered congregation quietly and respectfully made their way out through the front doors of the East Mt. Zion Korean Baptist Church to the wide sidewalk below. There were some tears to be sure. And some laughter. Nothing inappropriate. Many lingered outside the front steps catching up and comparing their opinions on the service. Most seemed quite pleased.

Most, but not all.

Heading through, and almost over, a group of happy mourners while hurrying to his black Lexus was a well-dressed but seething Marcus E. Robinson. With a white-knuckled right hand he clutched the freshly printed and bound copy of the only book the late Reverend Dr. Josiah Lewis had ever authored.

Professionally published posthumously.

Embossed in raised gold lettering set against a matte black cover was his late pastor's familiar yet condemning words, *Venal Dogmata.*

Sitting at his office desk at the Fishtown Y, Luca Lewis played back in his mind the carefully orchestrated grand finale that he had arranged for his papa's homecoming two weeks previously. It all went off even better than he could have imagined. It was nothing short of perfection. But the joy didn't last. Not like he thought. Those strangely warm feelings of gratification and revenge were replaced, within hours, with his more familiar mood of frustration and anger. As Luca looked at the stack of boxes of *Venal Dogmata* that were left undistributed because of the paltry crowd assembled at his papa's homegoing, his mood darkened even more.

He walked over to an opened box and picked up a copy. It was a thing of beauty. The raised gold letters elegantly popped against the matte black cover. The serif typesetting looked so professional. *Papa would have been proud of this*, he mused. Then his thoughts drifted back to the days when it was first penned.

It was before the big vote at Mt. Pisgah Baptist. Back in the days when his father still had a fire in his spirit. A time when Luca and his papa would often dream together of a completely different kind of church from what they had known. One that resembled the church in Acts more than a model inherited from sixteenth-century Europe.

Although his papa was an educated man with an undergraduate degree from Cairn University and two graduate degrees from Westminster Theological Seminary, he did not make a big thing of it. He spoke plainly in a way that most everyone in his community could appreciate and understand.

Well, usually.

Luca remembered like it was yesterday the day his dad had passed around a photocopied and hand-stapled eighty-eight-page booklet to the membership of Mt. Pisgah, three weeks before the big vote. The front cover was of plain white cardstock to add emphasis to the two provocative words that were in all caps and in a large bold font, *Venal Dogmata*.

Dr. Lewis was throwing down the gauntlet, and Luca could not have been prouder of his papa. He was going to make it crystal clear to everyone at Mt. Pisgah Baptist that the choice they would be making was not simply one of ceremonial preference but was in fact one of spiritual direction—one of light or of darkness. We would either exist for ourselves, or we would exist for our King's mission. But there could be no middle ground.

It was, after all, a choice of kingdoms.

Ironically, his selection of the two obscure Latin words—*Venal* and *Dogmata*—was his attempt to be clear, so as not to be misunderstood or mistaken. *Venal* was chosen because it spoke to the concept of being for sale, or open and willing to be used for corruptive purposes. Much like the crooked politicians with their grubby hands held out to the lobbyists who frequent their offices in search of favors, the church was complicit in widespread ecclesiological corruption. The evangelical machine cozied up to power, and yet remained silent about the systemic injustices that were being promoted from that same power. For Dr. Lewis, this was the very definition of venality. And from his perspective, much about the North American version of Jesus' Way had been sold and replaced with a much more convenient Americana version. A version where personal rights and freedoms trumped the ethic of kingdom responsibility. A prostituted version that led modern-day disciples toward personal entitlement rather than toward the selflessness of Christ. It was a venal transaction which would enrich a few and lay waste to many. And the objective—real-time evidence of the spiritual carnage—could be measured by the mission field's sentiments toward the mission force. All trends pointed downward.

Luca could recall his dad preaching, with his left index finger wagging back and forth like a metronome keeping time with his melodic yet dramatic intonations. "And don't give me the tired lame ole song and dance that folk are disinterested in Jesus' church because we're too much on the narrow way—and they're not interested because it's too hard. Don't tell me that we're on the hard road that our neighbors are just too weak to travel. 'Cause does it look to you like we're on a hard road? Church? Does it feel like we are on Jesus' hard, dangerous, faith-filled narrow road? Does it, church? Now I'm talking to you people. 'Cause it looks like to me that we're on Easy Street. We're living large and totally in charge. That we have set it all up for our trivial sensibilities. And I'm saying right now that there's nothing hard or narrow about our way. 'Cept maybe our hard hearts and our narrow minds. Can I get an amen, church? Anybody? It looks like to me that we got things set up just like we like 'em and send to blazes anybody who disrupts our sacred party. We got church to do!"

And then he lowered his voice, clasped his hands together, and gazed heavenward. With teary eyes he stammered, "Forgive us … King Jesus … for preferring our own funky … inbred … spiritually self-centered ways … to the desperation that lost sheep feel while they frantically search for their one … true … loving … Shepherd. Jesus, we are much too much about ourselves. And we are far too little about you. About your mission. Forgive us. And maybe for the first time in a long, long while … please … put us on your narrow road. So we can show others the way."

Memories of moments like that were difficult for Luca to shake. These were powerful and formative moments that had left an indelible mark on his soul.

Dogmata was simply the plural form of dogma. If a dogma was a belief, dogmata was its overarching system. It was the structural scheme that perpetuated a belief. Put together, Luca's father was stating without equivocation that siding with Marcus E. Robinson—the charismatic spokesman for the status quo—was not a decision of spiritual neutrality. There is no neutrality when following Christ—we are either for him or we are against him. We are never undecided. We could continue to pretend to be Jesus' church, and in the comfort of our own sanctuary, amuse ourselves into oblivion, or we could actually become Jesus' church—and selflessly bring good news to a city where it was so desperately wanted.

"Jesus has a mission," Luca could remember his papa pronouncing with the conviction of an Old Testament prophet. "But does he have a church for that mission? Will Mt. Pisgah Baptist Church be a church for King Jesus' mission? It means very little to me whether his mission harmonizes with your inclinations, preferences, or sensibilities! I am past the point of being concerned about such trivialities. I will answer to my King personally for my obedience. And so … will … you."

To Luca's papa, this was not the time to play religious footsie, for the stakes could not be higher. And so, he'd told the congregation in such a way that they might stay told.

But did they?

Liberty Village Lofts seemed to stand as the undeniable answer to that question. As did the stacks of extra copies left undistributed to the mourning parishioners who didn't care enough to show up. In every measurable way that Luca could quantify things, the Lewises had lost.

Luca stood and placed the black book back in the box. *If history is told from the side of the winners, then which spiritual realm is boasting about this story?* he mused.

Provocative models had been pasted on the Liberty Village Lofts billboard that now replaced the old, blackened steel letters that once spelled the name of their church.

Question answered.

Chapter Two

Omar

"Pass the ball … Omar … once in a … while … why don't you?" said a breathless and exasperated football player.

Omar, squatting with his head between his knees, attempting to gather a breath of his own, managed, "Well, we won … didn't we?" Dusty drops of sweat dribbled off his nose and instantly disappeared into the parched gray soil.

And they did win. They almost always did. And Omar Al-Khulani scored the goals.

The University of Aden was Omar's new home, and to say that he was thriving would be an understatement. It was a world away from the chalky, dreary, dusty brown township he had known as home only two short years and a lifetime ago. The city of Aden was spectacularly beautiful. The beguiling dark waters of the Arabian sea curved around the landscape. Date palms and acacias painted sumptuous green swathes across beige homes, trimmed in white, cubed, and stacked—all very foreign, but now, somehow, essential. Life on Yemen's south coast was, to Omar Al-Khulani, a paradise found. And one he hoped he would never leave.

But his greatest affection was for the law. He worshipped it. It consumed him. It was young and developing and growing and very much a living thing. It could one day bring the kind of order that his people yearned for deep in their bones. There were many days that Omar felt as if he was sitting at the feet of grizzled and scarred pioneers who had carved out a new country from war and pain and rock and dust. In fact, that was precisely what he was doing. He understood that it was a great and uncommon privilege to be learning at the revered University of Aden. The Al-Khulani family sacrificed much for Omar to be here. And this burden of responsibility and family honor was something that Omar carried with him every day.

Although Yemen in many ways seemed like a young country, rebuilt from divisions, revolutions, and uninvited reunifications, it was, in fact, an ancient land. An evolving culture that spanned from the bronze age to the digital age, with many interloping occupiers in between. And like most histories, progress was defined by the priorities of the newest regime. But it seemed that Yemen's progress always involved too much blood. And always someone else's blood.

Omar's new mentors had a different vision for their nation. Their ideas allowed room for individual conscience. They spoke words that, until then, Omar thought teetered on blasphemy and were unique to his own impious and corrupted imagination. New realms were opening. Dangerous new worlds. And Omar reveled in them.

For the protection of all concerned, much of what was taught was communicated in subtext. Very few revolutionary ideas were plainly spoken. Professors sent cloaked signals that required the presence of a gifted decoder to notice and then reconstruct. And Dr. Rizwan Raweh, Omar's Comparative Law professor, dished them out liberally.

"Mocha?"

Omar, still quietly reveling in his football victory and sitting squat-legged in the concrete hallway, looked up from his textbook. "Excuse me?"

Dr. Raweh repeated, offering no further embellishments, "Mocha?"

"Yes, absolutely. Now?"

"Unless you'd rather finish your yoga session. How can you sit like that?"

Omar let out a somewhat embarrassed chuckle. "I'd be honored to, sir."

"Off-campus, okay?"

Omar eagerly nodded.

Sitting at an outdoor café overlooking gray piers separating the sea, sapphire from indigo, Dr. Raweh said, "I hear you're quite a football player. How did you become so proficient?"

Omar finished his first sip of coffee—a fairy tale in a white ceramic mug. He smiled with eyes closed, and said, "I never knew. Where has this been all my life?"

"So, you like the coffee. I thought you might. Do you know how much our Mocha sells for in America? Over one hundred US dollars a pound. That's why you've never had it. Americans take it all, just like everything else."

Omar's expression didn't change a bit, as he nursed his treasure as if it were the land's last dewdrop of moisture.

Dispensing with his planned small talk on football, a subject in which he actually had no interest, Dr. Raweh got straight to the point. "Omar, every day I see something that you cannot. I can see faces, reactions, wondering lights in eyes. I can see when dots get connected, and when they do not. I can see the students who dream beyond a diploma to meaning and substance and powerful possibilities. I can see more in a student than can be shown on examinations or case studies. Much more. And I can tell that you, Omar, love the law and can envision its influence. You can see a future that is extraordinarily different from our present. Am I not correct?"

The young law student sat transfixed as his professor inexplicably plummeted deep into his soul and surfaced thoughts, imaginings, and motives that he was sure he kept carefully concealed.

"Well, Dr. Raweh, I'm not sure."

"What are you unsure of, Omar? Your love for the law, or of our nation's need for change?"

"Both, sir. I mean neither," Omar said, without any degree of conviction. "I mean, I'm not sure I see everything as clearly as you think, Dr. Raweh."

"Call me Rizwan," said the professor in a significant breach of protocol. As Omar stammered, Dr. Raweh instructed, "On this matter, discussion is closed."

Omar conceded with a feeble nod.

"So, Omar, how do you see our future?"

Omar started slowly, hesitatingly, as if he were testing the truthfulness of his professor's previously stated convictions. Soon, he was leaning forward, painting vivid pictures of his dreams of an open, free, and just society for all Yemenis. Professor Raweh was fascinated with the depth and scope of vision that this young man possessed.

"Are you a religious man, Omar?"

"Well, yes, sir."

"Sir?"

"I mean, yes."

"Yes, what?"

"Yes … Dr. Rizwan, sir."

And then the professor laughed with delight, "You seemed so much brighter in class!"

"And your mosque?" Rizwan continued to inquire.

"Well, our family mosque is much different than it is in the city.

"Different, good?"

Omar shrugged, "It's fancier here, for sure. But not as friendly. My new imam seems cross most of the time."

Rizwan let out a barrel laugh. "Well, I suppose I'd be cross too if I had you to deal with."

"I suppose, sir," Omar deferred.

Professor Raweh waded in deeper, offering some of his own opinions on Yemen's cultural laws. Ideas that startled Omar. Startled and yet reassured, all at once. Soon the quickest hour of Omar's life had passed as if it were a minute or two. An hour of both intellectual challenge and ethical reassurance. *Maybe I'm not completely mad*, he thought.

"Listen, Omar, we better get back to the books. But before we run, I wanted to invite you to a little discussion group I host in my apartment. A closed symposium of sorts. A few professors, a select few students, a guest speaker every now and then. We talk and scheme and dream of a better society. Interested?"

Omar, completely gobsmacked, instinctively replied without any hesitation, "I would be more than honored, sir."

He handed Omar a carefully folded index card, and said, "Not sir, Omar. Rizwan. Thursdays at 8 p.m. at this address." And then he looked directly into the eyes of his young student and sternly cautioned, "Please speak of this to no one." The professor paused. "Absolutely no one."

***

Omar Al-Khulani found himself dealing with unfamiliar insecurities. Normally he didn't worry about fashion or styles or whether he fit in. He confidently pursued life at full throttle, giving little energy to such trivial matters. But now, standing at the threshold of his professor's apartment, wearing his only blazer (one that he was quite sure was no longer in style), a white shirt with sleeves that were too short, and a green paisley tie, he felt out of his depth.

He took a deep breath and then pushed the buzzer. Almost immediately the door swung open. It was Dr. Raweh. But a very unfamiliar version of him. He was wearing faded blue jeans, an untucked shirt with sleeves rolled up, and sandals.

"*As-salamu alaykum!* Welcome, Omar. We're so glad that you joined us. And it looks like you're going to bring some class to the rest of us reprobates," he said lightheartedly.

"*Wa 'alaykumu s-salam.*" Omar scanned the room. There were three professors, two students, and a face that he didn't recognize. "Thank you, Dr. Raweh," Omar said as he instantly peeled off his blazer, removed his green tie, and unbuttoned and rolled up his ill-fitting sleeves.

Rizwan didn't correct him. Instead, he began to make introductions. "Everyone, this is Omar Al-Khulani. I think most of you know him, but in case you don't, he's Aden's most prodigious football player, or so I hear. And he also has a small interest in the law." The assembly in the crowded apartment chuckled.

Then Dr. Raweh introduced the gathering to Omar. In the room with him were Drs. Mohammed Al-Nono and Nasir Vaz, two prominent law professors, both of whom Omar imagined might likely be in attendance. The two other students were Abdul Al-Hamad, a brash third-year classmate who loved to hear the sound of his own voice, and Yushua Maalouf, Abdul's opposite. He was a thoughtful third-year law student who had always been a bit of a mystery to Omar. Yushua was simultaneously gentle and strong of spirit in a way that was both appealing and convicting. His presence was a welcome surprise.

The person in the room who Omar didn't recognize was Dr. Ali Abdo, a visiting professor from Queen Arwa University in Sanaa, Yemen's capital. He was to give a sixty-minute lecture on theoretical non-binding instruments for the protection of human rights. This was to be followed by another sixty minutes of dialogue. As Dr. Raweh introduced the special guest, his eyes shot over to the group's newest member—and Omar could not hide his delight.

The sixty-minute discourse was nothing short of mesmerizing. Fresh ideas were racing in Omar's mind: concepts and devices for instituting a lasting peace in his nation; elegant designs that had never crossed his spirited imagination. The dialogue that followed was like manna from heaven to his famished soul. Until this moment, he had no idea how hungry he had been for a kinship of heart, mind, and conscience. Omar was giddy and grateful and awestruck all at once.

"Thank you, Ali," Dr. Raweh concluded. "You have given us so much to consider. I think that we all share in the hope that your prescriptions will become a balm for the healing of our land."

Then he stood up, walked over to a mundane framed oil painting of over-ripened fruit, and said, "Let us seal our aspirations together." He then carefully removed the painting from the wall, which revealed a black steel box.

Omar wondered why the professor had a wall safe and what he planned to retrieve from it.

After a couple of failed attempts, Dr. Raweh finally spun the black dial exactly right and the steel door clunked open. He reached in and pulled out a tall, dark, and mysterious bottle. Omar had never actually seen alcohol, but his intuition immediately perceived what might be coming next. His emotions were a jumble of dangerous excitement, anger, disappointment, and admiration. Would the professor drink this? Would everyone?

Dr. Raweh twisted off the cork, gestured to the gathering with the bottle, and said, "And now for our pact."

Omar immediately understood the ethical implications. The fact that alcohol was not only forbidden but illegal made the upcoming pact-sealing all the more binding. To speak publicly of what was discussed also meant confessing to participating in an illegal activity. This was not only a symbolic sealing; it was in fact a very material one. For Omar, this was a moral quandary for which he was not prepared. He, like everyone he knew, was raised with the religious conviction that alcohol was a holy abomination and an assault to their faith. Drinking was to personally participate in Satan's handiwork. Yet, the idea of a pact of solidarity toward a noble goal was in itself intoxicating.

As Dr. Raweh began to pour the reddish-purple liquid into a large, stemmed glass goblet, the group spontaneously fanned out into a circle. Omar, a full step behind, somewhat reluctantly joined the formation, finding his place beside the quiet Yushua. As he stood waiting, he could feel his pulse picking up speed. His face felt flush and hot. Just a minute ago, he was so happy to be included, but now that feeling of inclusion was starting to feel more like an affliction. *Should I leave? Should I run? Is it too late?*

The professor gestured for Omar and Yushua to make room. He then stood shoulder to shoulder between them, holding the glass goblet firmly with both hands. Then, in dramatic fashion, Dr. Raweh hoisted the chalice above his head, and with closed eyes said, "We drink together as a pledge of our fidelity to building a more just country for all our people." And then he slowly took in a sip of the forbidden libation.

"Ameens" murmured in a rumbling chorus of solidarity, as the little band solemnly and defiantly expressed their approval.

"Ameen," said Dr. Raweh.

He passed the cup to his left. "Young brother …"

Omar carefully clasped the glass goblet as if he were holding an armed grenade that required all of his wit and attention. And in many ways, he knew that was exactly what he held. Heavier than he expected. Darker too. But he no longer was in a state of panic. In fact, he was suddenly and mysteriously curious. As he lifted the vessel closer to his lips, he could smell a strange yet familiar scent: spoiled fruit, honey, and baklava all dancing together as a single aroma. More intrigued than ever, Omar raised the abomination to his lips and took a long, slow, steady mouthful. It was different than he imagined. Sweeter. And sponge-like, as if it dabbed moisture off his tongue. And stronger.

It tasted of freedom.

Omar offered no words, as he quietly passed the cup to his left. The group as one said, "Ameen."

One by one, each made the pledge of death, accompanied by the group's agreement, until the process made its way around to the end of the circle.

Now it was Yushua's turn.

As he raised the dangerous elixir in the air, something unexpected happened. The group immediately interrupted with an earnest "Ameen," without Yushua's taking in a single drop of the blood pact. Then he passed the cup back to its owner.

Omar stood completely bewildered. Why was Yushua allowed to escape the contraband? His acute sense of justice would not let this go unchallenged. He would have to find out why. Omar would get answers.

After that, the hour being as late as it was, the secret society exchanged warm farewells. The group quietly departed Dr. Raweh's apartment—all in high spirits.

All except one. The group's newest recruit left feeling guilty, irritated, and befuddled.

A damp mildewy stench hung heavy in the air of Aden's law library. Books, journals, and legal documents were creatively arranged in stacks, on shelves, and piled in bankers' boxes to shoehorn the archives into a cramped cellar. The dankness of the basement was exacerbated by Aden's coastal humidity and together created a pungent aroma that most students tried to avoid. Yushua was one of the few students who regularly logged time there.

Omar, on a quest for justice, strode purposefully to the library the following morning. Sitting alone at a table, encircled by a dozen opened and bookmarked tomes, was Yushua, lost in thought.

"Smell's worse than usual this morning," Omar whispered, interrupting Yushua's trance.

"Huh? Oh, yeah, I guess so."

"It was fascinating to be with you gentlemen last night," Omar whispered. "I didn't know quite what to expect, as you could probably tell by my outfit." Yushua and Omar shared in a muted chuckle. Then Omar stretched his lean torso across the library table and softly asked, "How long have you been coming?"

Yushua straightened up in his chair. "About two years—only a few months after I arrived at Aden."

"Was yesterday pretty typical?"

"Completely. We don't always have a formal symposium, but our time together is always stimulating."

"And the 'sealing,' is that a normal thing?"

"It is," Yushua said, giving away nothing.

Omar would have to try a more direct approach: naked honesty.

And since he was in a state of inner turmoil, perhaps it could be therapeutic.

"It was my first time, Yushua," he whispered. "My first time tasting the devil's drink. I was raised in a strict home where intoxicating drinks were *haram*. I know that foreign infidels drink in our country, but not true sons of Yemen. I don't know if I should return to Dr. Raweh's apartment. I enjoyed the company and loved the camaraderie of thought, but I fear that my soul has been damaged."

Yushua looked with compassion at his new friend. He closed his eyes as he gathered his thoughts, and then said three simple sentences that cut through Omar's tortured spirit like a hot knife through goat cheese: "God knows our hearts, my brother. God gave you your passionate desire for peace and justice. Don't allow a small thing to steal away a great thing."

Omar began to feel a warm wave of peace wash over him.

"Your offense," he continued, "if it is a sin at all, is debatable. And if it is, it is certainly forgivable. Many scholars within Islam take a different position on this than those who make the laws in our country."

"Yes, I know, thank you, brother. Thank you so much," Omar said, feeling several kilos lighter. His feelings of guilt now partially, albeit likely temporarily, assuaged, curiosity rushed to the forefront. And then he came out with it: "So, you've taken the pledge?"

"No, I haven't."

Yushua stopped himself from continuing. He carefully surveyed the library and then leaned forward and quietly whispered, "I have a much more dangerous secret."

Chapter Three

Jimmy

"Well, Jimmy, it looks like we've lost another one. The Hendersons this time," said Tom, the thirty-something executive pastor of LifePointe Chapel. "My niece said she has been seeing them at Cruciform the last few weeks."

"Figures," Jimmy said, without any hint of reaction. "Sometimes I think that we might as well close up shop and send the rest of them over there." Dr. James A. Norris, known only as "Jimmy," except for the copper letters on the forty-five-foot stone monument marking the entrance of their campus, was only partially joking.

"I know, right?" said Tom. "Trust me, this one will leave a mark." As executive pastor, Rev. Tom Butts knew who all the top-tier givers were. And the Hendersons' lost contributions to LifePointe would not go unnoticed.

LifePointe Chapel, located in a northern suburb of Atlanta, had undergone several reinventions since its founding by the beloved Pastor Bruce Goetz in 1978. It originally went by Sandy Creek Baptist Church and was in every way a traditional Baptist church. Pastor Bruce, who never thought of himself as a church planter, guided the ship with solid but unspectacular Bible teaching until retiring in 2000. The 250-person-strong congregation gave Pastor

Bruce Goetz a beautiful calfskin Bible and a warm and sincere send-off. In many ways, he would be missed.

But it was high time for a change.

The deacons of Sandy Creek Baptist Church knew what they needed. They wanted someone who could, as it was called, "Willowfy" their operations. Taking a page from a flourishing church located in the suburbs of Chicago, they "radically" redubbed themselves as Sandy Creek Church. A simple change, to drop the "Baptist," but the repositioning was brilliant. The general mood among the church's leadership was that their former designation of Baptist was nothing but a boat anchor. So, it was good riddance to anything that smacked of sectarianism. Especially if it limited their market appeal.

Then it was off to search for their front man.

After several promising auditions, the church finally settled on Pastor Jon Rogers, and by all observable indications, they found their golden goose. Before Jon discovered his holy calling, he was an actor, and a good one. For six years, he traveled across America with several troupes, working Broadway shows on tour. He was handsome, articulate, and a spellbinding communicator who possessed the rare traits of emotional intelligence and personal charisma. Over the next eight years, Sandy Creek could not make room for their exploding numbers fast enough. Two services. Three. Four. And then five. Finally, they relocated operations to a suburb where they were able to purchase sixty-two pristine acres on the north end of Fulton County. And there, they constructed a model campus that rivaled their Chicago archetype.

Within months, Sandy Creek's numbers swelled astronomically, even finding their name listed as one of the twenty-five largest churches in America. It seemed like they could do no wrong. And Bruce Goetz, now Pastor Emeritus, couldn't have been prouder.

Almost every day he quietly walked through the sprawling system of parking lots and, with grateful tears, prayed for the families that would be attending on the weekend.

But cracks started to surface in Sandy Creek's image in 2008 in the form of ugly rumors. They were first heard in hushed hallway conversations among the staff. Then among the most faithful volunteers. Soon, online bloggers were describing unspeakable things about the deviant sexual activities of Pastor Jon Rogers. Most of the weekend attenders of Sandy Creek chalked it up to sour grapes being spread around by their less successful rivals. But sour grapes couldn't explain why, one Thursday evening, their haggard and unshaven pastor was forced to make a perp walk from a police car to the Fulton County police station through a din of flashes, reporters, and screaming protestors.

This damning scene, when combined with irrefutable facts that the church's elder team were aware of several sexual "improprieties" and covered them up, became the beginning of the end of Sandy Creek's dominance. Like rats jumping off a sinking ship, most of the good people of Sandy Creek were called to worship elsewhere. Within three months of the first headlines, the church's state-of-the-art six-thousand-seat sanctuary looked empty, with less than a thousand scattered throughout.

The next years of ministry at Sandy Creek were painfully difficult. Early on, the church's elders knew that they desperately needed a thorough rebranding to put their past difficulties behind them. They needed a new identity that didn't carry the baggage of their all-too-public scandal. So, "LifePointe Chapel" became their ironic new branding. From there, they went through a series of mostly adequate pastors. Each staying for a couple of years. Each haunted by skeletons of the church's past sins. Each knee-capped by a crippling debt. And each leaving for smaller, simpler, and more hopeful opportunities.

So, it could be understood why expectations weren't high with the calling of Jimmy Norris, at least as far as LifePointe was concerned. But their newest hire didn't share their pessimistic sentiment. Jimmy was a square-jawed, muscular, all-American son of the famed and hard-nosed preacher Dr. Humphrey Alvin Norris.

And Jimmy had something to prove.

Dr. H. A. Norris was an institution in the South, pastoring one of Texas' largest churches for over forty years and authoring numerous albeit unremarkable books. He was not to be trifled with and was considered by many as one of the most respected voices in American evangelicalism. And he had letters. Real letters. His PhD was the genuine article. A proper doctorate. Not a pathetic ThD, or worse yet, a tawdry DMin. There was nothing worse to Pastor Norris than someone coveting standing but who was unwilling to put in the work. Perhaps that's why he despised Democrats with such ferocity. "Most of them are like my indolent brother-in-law: always looking for a windfall without the character to do an honest day's work," he often said. He was tough, plain spoken, and a Republican through and through. And no serious Texas candidate made it to a primary without first kissing the ring.

And so, Dr. Jimmy Norris, DMin, took this lesser station as senior pastor of LifePointe Chapel with the utmost solemnity. This wasn't just a job. It wasn't even a calling. To Jimmy, this was life and death. And unbeknownst to the people of LifePointe, with the lowest salary and fewest benefits that they had offered in twenty years, they had just corralled a workhorse.

Jimmy would give them everything he had.

And so, six years later, through sheer force of will and against all odds, LifePointe mostly stopped hemorrhaging bodies. In fact, on most Sundays, there was even a hint of optimism in the air. Chairs were unfastened and then refastened, spaced further apart to almost fool the eye that the auditorium wasn't inappropriately too large. Mortgages were stretched, renegotiated, and restructured to allow for the smallest bit of financial breathing room. And Jimmy cashed in on his family name to attract a talented stable of staff who, week after week, presented a worship experience that could compete almost anywhere.

Almost anywhere.

"Cruciform again," said Jimmy with virtually no expression. And then, gesturing with both hands in either direction, he said, "Can you imagine what we could do without this sixty-two-acre albatross hanging around our necks?"

"Yep," Tom answered back. "We just can't keep up. It's not a level playing field. Cruciform, The Orchard, New Springs—I know this for a fact—they all get a 40 to 50 percent advantage over us. While we pile dead money into a twenty-year note, those dudes leverage cash into marketing, events, and decent salaries. And most of 'em get paid twice as much as us."

"But who in the world wants a sixty-two-acre albatross?" asked Jimmy. Answering his own question with his next breath, he said, "Cruciform sure as heck doesn't."

Chapter Four

The Shunning

Chantel sat in her favorite chair in the living-room, by the window, laptop open, readers balancing on the bridge of her nose. She had a quality about her that was difficult to catalog. She was attractive, for sure: she regularly exercised and watched what she ate, almost maintaining her college years' proportions. But more than that, there was a glow about her spirit that was entirely striking. It wasn't necessarily a soft or demure charm; being demure was not her thing. She laughed harder, louder, and more often than most, putting friend and stranger alike at ease. But she possessed an inner strength and beauty that shone through whether she entertained or quietly studied in her favorite chair by the window.

Trundling heavy-footed down the stairs, Luca asked, "Preparing for your group?"

"I am. We're going to look at the armor of God," she added, even though Luca hadn't asked. These days Luca rarely showed any interest in Chantel's Bible-study group.

"Ephesians six. So, you're almost through."

"Almost. It's been really good. You should join us tonight." She paused, weighing her husband's reaction. "Tonight might really help you, honey."

"Mrs. Robinson going to be here? Freddy Leonard? Jamal?" Luca asked in a way that obviously implied that he knew the answer.

"Likely."

"Fat chance that I'm coming then. You should know that." And then it broke. "How you could let that phony bunch into our house is beyond me. She was with him the whole time. She sat by and nodded her little black pixie wig while her rich husband tore my papa into pieces. And those other two are no better. When did they ever come to his defense? He was always helpin' them, and the one time he needed somebody ... No ma'am, you keep your armor study and them 'make-believe soldiers' playin' as Christians. Maybe try fittin' some of them hypocrites with that helmet of salvation, 'cause Lord knows, with all their big talk there ain't nothing that I can see."

Chantel quietly closed her laptop, looked into Luca's eyes, and said, "Sweetie, this is not right. You are not right. I don't know what's going on with you right now, but it's killing you. It's killing us. Sanders tiptoes around you because he's half scared he'll set you off. I know you are grieving your papa's passing, but you've got to get this figured out. For all our sakes. Three months have passed, and you're angrier now than when you were at the homegoing." She paused and took a deep breath. "Luca, you've got to forgive them. For your own sake if for nobody else's."

As Luca started to mumble a response, she interrupted, adding one final statement. "And sweetheart, you've got to forgive yourself. Your papa understood."

Luca lifted his gaze from the floor to his wife. His eyes were now cold and lifeless, but Chantel knew well enough that this lack of expression only veiled a seething fury that lurked a half inch beneath the surface. "Forgive myself," he said scoffingly. "Woman, I don't know what you've been reading, but please go sell it somewhere else. I don't have the stomach for it." He turned and walked toward the front door and said, "I'll be working late and should be back by nine. Please have all the good Christians of Mt. Pisgah out the door before then."

Dr. Nasir Vas' lectures on human rights within a Sharia structure were always fascinating to Omar. There were so many exciting possibilities for reform that would be consistent with Islamic law. But on this morning, Omar's mind was entirely somewhere else. He had scheduled an appointment with his imam after class to clear his sullied, guilt-ridden conscience. Omar had concluded that he had indeed sinned, and although his transgression might not have been great, he had stepped out of bounds. For his own soul's sake, there needed to be penance and reparations. And with this decision, his spirit already felt lighter.

"Make sure that your papers are in by the end of the week—it's one third of your grade," announced Dr. Vas as he adjourned his class. Omar carefully arranged his things in his backpack precisely as they should be and then headed toward his mosque.

His backpack didn't quite fit this afternoon, as the straps didn't accommodate the padded shoulders of his blue blazer. But Omar didn't mind the lumpy fit; he wasn't going to take any chances and dressed as nicely and as modestly as he knew how. He had never personally spoken to his new imam, but by the way he carried himself at the mosque, Omar was certain he was a stickler for details.

Small talk and then my confession, or get on with it? Omar weighed the options in his mind. *Just get it over with, straight to the point*, he concluded. *Imam Al-Iryani doesn't seem like a man who enjoys small talk.*

Omar opened the front gate, went through the courtyard, and then heaved open the ancient iron and cypress door of the mosque. It was unusually quiet inside. The sounds of a devout throng saying earnest prayers that vibrated off marble floors and walls were gone, replaced by an eerie silence.

He slipped off his shoes, placed them on the wooden rack, and timidly walked further inside.

"Can I help you, my son?" a voice sounded from behind him.

Omar turned around and saw a large, bulky stranger who must have been charged with mosque security. He nervously cleared his throat and said, "I have an appointment with Imam Al-Iryani."

"Ah, yes. You're the student. Follow me."

As he peered into the great hall, Omar could see the wooden *minbar* where Imam Al-Iryani delivered his stern homilies. Around it stood a wooden cypress balustrade that clearly marked out the separation between the holy clerics and the unwashed sinners. This always bothered Omar. *My home mosque never had this*, he thought.

They made their way to another heavy timber door. Omar's burly escort gingerly knocked and then tentatively pushed it open, gesturing for Omar to walk in. As soon as he stepped in, he heard the heavy door close behind him. He was in another great hall, albeit slightly smaller, and with no *minbar.* He could see the imam sitting with three other men across the room. The white-bearded imam covered in an all-white *thawb* looked like he had been deposited in this room directly from heaven. His three younger, black-bearded companions wore corresponding black robes.

"May I?" inquired Omar.

"Please, please, come," said Imam Iryani, guiding him in with exaggerated gestures. "What is it you wish?" he asked.

So much for small talk, he thought. *Jump in. Demonstrate sincerity and deep regret.*

"Imam, I have sinned a very great sin. I tasted an intoxicant when I knew that I shouldn't have."

"So, you've been drinking the abomination. Did you not know that it was banned?" he asked, as if his question wasn't already answered.

"Yes, yes, I knew. That is why it was a great sin."

"So, it wouldn't have been a sin if you didn't know?" the imam snapped back with a look of spiteful pleasure.

"I guess it would be a sin in either case. But a greater sin for one who knew," Omar said sheepishly.

"Precisely. Your sin is a great sin, young man, and so will be your punishment." He stood up, pointed a crooked finger at Omar, and declared with a voice of authority, "You shall be banned from the assembly of the faithful for no less than forty days. Perhaps this will give you time to reconsider your corrupt ways."

Omar turned to leave but was interrupted in mid-stride. "Stop! Stand still. I am not finished with you," his imam barked.

Omar instantaneously spun around and snapped to attention, flinging his backpack off his overstuffed shoulder.

"Was it that you were drinking alone? Or perhaps you shared company?" he inquired.

"I was not alone," Omar said.

"Tell me then, who were your disgraceful associates?"

Omar's mind began to spin. *This is not how I imagined things would go. What should I do? Why did I come?* Omar cleared his throat and then softly, yet eloquently, said, "Imam Iryani, respectfully, I cannot confess for them. The matter is for their own conscience. Their sin, if it is a sin, is between them and Allah. I can only speak for my own actions."

"*If* it is a sin?" he barked as he instantly stood up and scowled at Omar as if he were speaking to a convicted felon.

"Well, as you know, Imam, there are many within our great religion who do not hold to this belief."

"Dogs and reprobates! Infidels. Swine not worthy to speak the name of the Prophet." Then the imam sat down slowly, leaned back, and clasped his hands against his chest and calmly said, "I will ask one more time, young man. Who were your profane collaborators?"

Omar swallowed, looked his inquisitor squarely in the eyes, and calmly said, "What you ask, Imam, with respect, this is not mine to confess."

"So, I see. Perhaps Allah's true religion is not yours to confess either. Perhaps you'd like to make your own. One that is more accommodating to your sophisticated sensibilities. We will give you time to think about that. You shall be banned from the faithful for no less than one hundred and twenty days. May it be so."

And then he stood up again, stiffly held out both of his arms, and flicked his wrists toward Omar in a final act of humiliation, as if to say that he was no longer interested in beating a stray dog.

The three silent men dressed in black stood up and lifelessly echoed, "May it be so."

***

Thursday came, and Omar found himself sitting in Dr. Raweh's apartment, this time wearing faded blue jeans, tennis shoes, a grass-stained football jersey, and an unhappy disposition.

"What's wrong?" Yushua asked.

Omar shrugged. "I had a tough week, but I don't want to talk about it." And then he sat on a folding chair and drifted into his thoughts.

Although the topic of the evening's discussion on "Islamic legal safeguards for human rights" should have been of particular interest to Omar, his mind was clearly elsewhere. Slouching in a steel folding chair, he blankly stared out a window, lost within himself.

Before long, Rizwan was pulling down the painting, spinning

the black dial, and taking out the dark bottle that was the sole source of Omar's misery. The group reassembled in the same order as they had the week previously, and Dr. Raweh, again, was the first to speak. "We drink together as a pledge of our fidelity to building a more just country for all our people."

And then he paused, looked down, and began to speak more slowly, with a different level of conviction. "And may we be willing to pay freedom's ultimate price for our people. Ameen."

The circle didn't immediately respond. They were taken back by the pledge's unexpected somber addendum. Slowly, and without any synchronicity, the law teachers and would-be lawyers uttered a sober, much more pensive, "Ameen." It wasn't that the group didn't know that there would be a price to pay for their dream; it's just that no one wished to think about of it. And certainly not speak of it.

Dr. Raweh passed the chalice to his left. Again. And all eyes were on Omar.

Omar clutched the hefty glass goblet with both hands and stared into the forbidden drink as if it were a magical cauldron ready to erupt with some kind of prophetic message. He lifted it to his lips and breathed in the strange, but now somewhat familiar, bouquet. And then he lowered his hands, gently cleared his throat, and said, "Two weeks ago, I was certain I had the answers. Sure, I knew I had many things to learn, but I had no doubts about the foundation that things should be built upon. But this is no longer true. I believe in our dream, I really do. Maybe now more than ever. But this dream being realized in our lifetime seems to me to be a fanciful aspiration. Our dream is one that will not come quickly or easily. And it will not come painlessly. But it must come. It must come."

Omar's voice trailed off into a whisper. And then he drank.

Quieter, less self-assured "Ameens" were heard around the circle.

It was a sobering moment. Everyone knew there would be a price to pay and that the men in this circle would likely be the first in line to pay it. But in this moment, this hushed-filled somber moment, it all seemed so worth it.

***

The warm, wet air was like a heavy damp blanket as Omar ran laps on packed gray cinders that surrounded Aden's football field. No scheduled practice, it was just his way to clear his head. He replayed his encounter with his imam over and over in his mind, looking for some hope within his spirit. *This can't be it*, he thought to himself. *There has to be more to my faith than arbitrary rules and capricious punishments. Who made Imam Iryani lord and …*

"Hey Omar," came an interrupting voice approaching him through the steel bleachers. It was Yushua. Omar slowed his gait to a jog, and then with hands on hips, walked toward Yushua.

"Hey Omar, I'd love to finish that conversation with you. The one we had in the library. Up for it?"

"Sure," he said, trying to gather a breath. "Now?"

"Whenever. I can wait for you to finish."

"Finished," he gasped. "So finished. Here?"

"Why not. Seems like we have the place to ourselves."

"Let me grab my water."

The secret society reconvened, at least a small subsection of it, six rows high on the westward facing steel bleachers. Yushua started. "You asked me if I had ever taken the pledge. I imagine you noticed that I hadn't. And I told you I had a more dangerous secret."

"Yes," interjected Omar. "I found that curious."

"The thing is, and all the brothers know this, I am not a follower of Islam. Not any longer. I was for many years—but no more …"

"Are you an atheist?" Omar interrupted once again. "Because I, myself, am almost there."

"No, no. Not at all, Omar. In fact, my faith is deeper and more meaningful than I could have ever imagined possible. It is all-encompassing and has given me great peace and joy and confidence with God. My former religion was like a pale shadow on a gloomy day when compared to the brilliance of what I have found. They are as different as day is to night, brother."

Omar looked curiously, nodding his head as if to hearten his friend to speak openly and clearly about this forbidden world. Looking desperately into his eyes, he said, "Do not hold this secret back from me, brother. Tell me of this light."

And then Yushua leaned forward and whispered, "I follow Isa."

"Isa?"

"Yes. Isa. I follow Isa al-Masih. And you know what happens when the authorities find that out."

Omar was spellbound. He had never met an Isa follower. He assumed they were all in the West. "Yes, I have heard what happens," he said.

"So, you see, the wine pledge is a small thing by comparison. The brothers know that I cannot afford to expose them."

"Makes sense," was all that Omar could cobble together as a response.

"Can I ask you a question, Omar?" Yushua said as politely as possible. Omar nodded. "You mentioned on Thursday that your life's foundation was shaken. How?"

Omar began to unfold for his new friend his crushing encounter with Imam Iryani, not sparing a single humiliating detail. He paused for a second or two, then he looked into the afternoon sky and asked, "If there is no forgiveness for a sin, how can my religion help bring peace to a nation when it can't bring peace to a single earnest heart?" Omar had just expressed aloud something he had not been able to put together in his thoughts before this.

"That is indeed a very good question, my brother," Yushua affirmed. "I do not claim to know everything, but I may have some help for you with this."

Omar was intrigued.

"The Qur'an speaks much about Isa, and in many ways paints a helpful picture of him. The older Jewish Scriptures speak much more of him. In fact, over 350 times, over a period of four thousand years, the Prophets spoke of the coming Isa al-Masih. And the Christian Scriptures, which again predate the Qur'an by six centuries, give eyewitness accounts of him that are verified by numerous contemporaneous historians—many of whom were not at all sympathetic to Isa's disciples." Yushua paused for a minute to let the meaning of his chronology sink in.

"You see, my brother, Isa is at the very center of it all. He's not a side note or a bit player; he is history's center. And this next thing I am going to tell you, this very important thing, is what changed everything for me. So much so that I would be willing to permanently live the death pledge so that I could experience him." Yushua paused again, looking for a nonverbal cue for permission to continue.

To say that Omar was intrigued would be to completely misread him. Hair stood on his neck. Shivers ran down his spine. Leaning forward, he quickly said, "Yes, yes. Please tell me."

"Okay, what I am about to say may sound radical to you. But you're an intelligent man, Omar. Think through this logically."

Omar hesitatingly nodded his head. And then leaned in further.

Yushua looked around the small stadium, ensuring no one could hear him. And then, with a low voice, he said, "Brother, no religion will ever satisfy your hunger. No religion will ever give peace to your heart. No religion will give the forgiveness your sinful heart craves. Not the Jewish one. Not the Muslim one. And for sure not the Christian one. You see, what all religions have in common is that they are some kind of system that is supposed to bring us to God. They ask us to live a certain way, do certain things, perform certain rituals. You have the five pillars. Have you ever done the *hajj?* Have you ever been to Mecca?"

"No, I haven't."

"And you are a Muslim living not so many miles away. How is a poor Muslim on the other side of the globe supposed to find favor?" Yushua asked.

Omar said nothing. He had no answer.

Yushua continued, "The Christian religion has its own set of pillars. Go to church. Read the holy Scriptures. Pray. Give money. Be baptized. All good and necessary things, but like every other religion, they are not things that can fix our big problem."

"So, what's our big problem?" Omar asked.

"The very thing that you crave: forgiveness."

Yushua waited a second or two, then continued, "Why did you visit your imam? You wanted forgiveness. We all want forgiveness. Our hearts are guilt-ridden because of our sins. Many of us try to avoid sin's shame by busying or numbing ourselves, but when we are quiet, and honest, we know that we are broken."

"Yes, I believe this," Omar interjected. "But if no religion can give forgiveness, why do you follow Isa?"

"And now we get to the heart of things," Yushua said. "The Prophets throughout four thousand years spoke of a coming Messiah who was to be a suffering servant and a pure and holy Lamb. A sacrifice once and for all. God becoming flesh. God in the form of a man, sinlessly living among us and then voluntarily giving up his life as the perfect and only possible payment for our guilt. And to prove that Isa was not just another Prophet who died and whose bones can be visited in some religious shrine, God raised him up from the grave. Isa's physical resurrection, seen by over five hundred eyewitnesses, broke the power of sin, guilt, and, ultimately, death."

Omar sat speechless as he heard the message of Isa for the first time. Finally, he managed, "Is this true?"

Yushua answered, "Well, if it wasn't true, if God didn't raise Isa back to life, if Isa hadn't appeared to his disciples, why would they willingly die for a message that they knew to be untrue? Would you die for a lie, Omar?"

"It must be true," said Omar.

"It is true, my brother. I've literally bet my life on it. My life in Yemen would be much easier if I didn't believe. But when something is true, belief is our only natural response. Anything less than belief would be delusional. I must believe. Once you see, Omar, you can never unsee."

"But what about the Crusades? These Christians slaughtered our ancestors," Omar resisted.

"You're right. Man's religion again," Yushua answered, almost interrupting him. "Religions are competitive. They want power. Islam has had a few *jihads* too, if you recall. It's what religions know to do, it seems. But Isa didn't suffer and die to start a new religion. There were already plenty. He came to accomplish, in himself, what no religion could ..."

"Forgiveness," Omar interrupted.

"Yes, my friend. Forgiveness."

Omar managed a small smile, but he wasn't at all happy. Yushua's words made some sense to him, but he still didn't understand how to experience the forgiveness his spirit so desperately craved.

"How?" he asked.

"How what?"

"How can Isa bring forgiveness? How can he when my faith cannot?"

Yushua smiled and said, "Brother, that is the most important question you will ever ask." And from there he explained the good news of Jesus Christ. How God emptied himself from his heavenly position and put on human flesh and was tempted like us in every way, and yet never gave in. How this Godman named Jesus of Nazareth lived a perfect, sinless life as a once-for-all payment for the sins of all humankind. And how this tortured and crucified sinless Son of God became personally guilty, personally condemned for every ugly sin himself, was raised back to life by the power of God. And with Jesus' resurrection came the authority to both cover the guilt of our sin and to conquer the power of sin's hold—forevermore.

"So, Isa became guilty of my sins?" asked Omar.

"Yes, brother. Exactly. Isa paid for your sins on his cross. He became sin for you. He became guilty of your sins so that you could receive his standing of innocence. You see, true forgiveness isn't free, Omar. Not at all. It's an expensive exchange—your guilt for Jesus' perfect life. That is why only he can offer you the forgiveness your heart craves. No religion can do that. Because no one else was perfect—only Isa. And because no one else died for your sins, Omar. Only Isa. And no one else was resurrected from the grave to offer you forgiveness. Only Isa al-Masih. The perfect, spotless Lamb of God who, in his perfect love, gave himself up as the only possible guilt-offering for Omar Al-Khulani's sin. Because Omar desperately needed God's forgiveness."

Tears dropped on Omar's knees as his soul breathed in Yushua's words. For the first time in as long as he could remember, his spirit was hopeful.

"What should I do?"

Yushua clutched Omar's knees as he looked intently into his eyes and said, "Receive the costly gift, brother. Ask God to trade your sins for Isa's sinlessness. He is here with us, Omar. Right here. Receive him and his forgiveness. Receive his Spirit. Let the Spirit of Isa guide your life. And as you follow King Isa al-Masih, he will build his eternal kingdom through your obedience."

***

"Let's list all the things we've tried since we came together as a team to see what worked and what didn't. There's no sense in doubling down on stupid."

Tom Butts was holding court.

It was the annual senior staff retreat of LifePointe Chapel. As had become their custom, they'd rented a five-thousand-square-foot vacation house on Lake Lanier in order to get away, review, and plan for the upcoming year. But over the years, things seemed to have changed. These meetings used to have a life-and-death sense of urgency to them. The team would stay up late, dreaming new ideas, hashing out details, and coordinating calendars. But the last few years had felt as if the team were on autopilot: tweak plans, adjust systems accordingly, schedule.

The strong showing of Cruciform Church in their own backyard had Jimmy spooked. With less staff, almost no facilities, and a fraction of their budget, Cruciform had been scooping the church-going market-share, quarter after quarter. And when Jimmy was uncomfortable, Tom Butts felt the full pressure.

Tom was by the dry erase board, green marker in hand, ready to begin jotting down the list when Jimmy interrupted, "Nope, nope, nope. We are not going to 'past history' our way out of this funk we're in. The ground has fundamentally shifted under us. Can't y'all see it?"

A chorus of "uh-huhs, mmm-hmms, and yeps" followed.

"So, what's changed?" Jimmy asked. "How has our world changed?"

Tom Butts immediately erased his former heading of *What has worked?* on the whiteboard, replacing it with, *How has our world changed?* This was followed by several minutes of awkward silence. Tom, feeling responsible as executive pastor, threw the ball back to Jimmy. "Pastor, how do you see that the ground has shifted?"

Jimmy was waiting for this. Without hesitation he started out, "Well, for one, ever since that pandemic, many people seem less comfortable with large crowds. It seems the 'hip' churches are spinning off congregations to keep them smaller. I don't think we know how to do that."

Heads nodded in a general sense of agreement.

Jimmy continued, "Second, people want to get their hands dirty. They used to want to hire staff to do ministry, but now they want to experience some stuff themselves. But not at church. They want to serve the community. And we don't know how to do that."

Again, heads nodded.

But Jimmy wasn't finished. "And third, and definitely most importantly, people don't trust us. We've lost the moral high ground in our communities for so many reasons. Many folks don't even see us as neutral. We're often seen as the problem to be worked around instead of a force for good."

Heads stopped nodding. Jimmy let that last statement hang in the air without further embellishment while the room grew uncomfortably quiet.

Finally, Chip Bussey, LifePointe's worship pastor, weighed in.

"Jimmy, I know that things have been rough out there for a bit; our own train-wreck is a prime example. But don't you think you've overstated things? I get it that lots of folks ain't excited about church as they once were, but seeing *us* as the problem—I just can't get there."

"Well, Chip, I'd suggest that you do get there. And get there quickly," Jimmy said flatly. "And change the channel, bro. Listen to voices that don't represent you. Constantly hanging out in our own echo chambers will be our own death, I guarantee you that. It might feel good in there. Nice and warm and cozy—comfy for sure, but it'll kill us. I 'spect we've been drinking our own bath water long enough and we gotta get a bigger picture. And maybe that means that some of us should start spending a little more time with regular folks in the community. How else can we see things from their perspective?"

Chip offered no further objections.

"So, what do y'all think?" Jimmy asked again.

After a protracted period of throat clearing, nervous coughs, and spontaneous runs to the restroom, Jimmy broke the silence once again. "Okay, y'all, I get it. You don't know. Know what? I don't either. But you know what else? We better know. It's our stinkin' job to know. So, if we don't know, we better find somebody who does because if we don't turn this ship around, she's going down. Slowly at first, and then, 'poof,' it'll be all gone."

A dazed Tom Butts, still standing by the whiteboard, had not jotted down a word. When Jimmy took his seat, Tom realized that he now had to take Pastor Jimmy's bad-news soliloquy and create something actionable. He managed to close his gaping mouth and then jumped in like a good soldier. "So, Pastor Jimmy has said three important things. We don't know how to reproduce. I guess that's obvious by looking down our family tree."

Ronnie Pratt, their twenty-two-year-old youth intern, interrupted, “Wait, we have a family tree?”

“Sure, we do,” Jimmy said. “It’s just that it’s called a flagpole.”

Nervous chuckles broke out.

Tom continued, “So, we don’t know how to reproduce, and we don’t know how to engage our community with the gospel. Correct?”

No one said a word.

“And the one thing that we do know is that regular folks don’t particularly like us. Did I get things right, Jimmy?”

Jimmy laughed. “I think you nailed it down better than me. You should be the preacher.”

“So, here is where my mind is going,” Tom continued. “I think we ought to hire us a sharp consultant, one who’s been down these twisty roads before. Somebody who can help us figure this booger out. ’Cause what Pastor Jimmy has outlined ain’t small potatoes. These ain’t minor tweaks to our strategic plan that we can figure out on this retreat. Answering your questions, Jimmy, I mean really honest-to-goodness answering them, will call for a fundamental overhaul of LifePointe.”

Jimmy smiled.

He could always count on Tom.

Chapter Five

The Communion

The Gulf of Aden, as far as the Middle East goes, is not a particularly hot place. Rarely does the mercury climb above one hundred degrees Fahrenheit in the height of summer. But, for being a coastal city, it also rarely sees rain. Often, clouds gathering large and ominous over the Arabian Sea seem to over-promise and under-deliver, bringing nothing more than a teasing vapid mist to the city. It's enough moisture to keep lower-lying areas green, but not enough to measure as precipitation. So, when the clouds gathered heavy and low and dark above the city on Sunday, everyone was in good spirits.

Omar, on the other hand, was a dog's breakfast of emotions. He, like most in the city, was giddy. He could smell the life-giving rain coming in, which every dweller of a tropical desert treasured at almost a mystical level. But dwarfing the excitement of the promising weather conditions was a newness and freshness inside Omar's spirit. He had hungered for Allah for as long as he could remember. Ever since he was a small boy, his thoughts would drift to the Almighty. His religious background continually stoked that hunger, compelling his famished soul to somehow merit Allah's presence. But nothing Omar did brought spiritual relief. Nothing brought peace. Nothing satisfied his hungry heart.

Until Isa.

The message of King Isa al-Masih, delivered by his faith-filled classmate, connected all the dots for Omar. And now, for the first time, the aching emptiness of his spirit was filled to his heart's brim by the gift of forgiveness. A simple acknowledgment of his sin, and a simple request for Isa to include him among the forgiven—for his own sins to be covered by Isa's sacrifice on the cross—changed everything. The steel bleachers of Aden became a more holy site to Omar than any attraction a pilgrim could find on their uncertain *hajj* for absolution.

He was forgiven.

As raindrops began to gently speckle the hot pavement and then vanish, Omar's bliss also began to evaporate. It was Sunday, and he had promised Yushua that he would accompany him to a secret community of believers. It wasn't the danger of this association that unsettled his heart; it was its unfamiliarity. His whole life he had heard monstrous stories about the excesses of the Christian infidels. Tales of debauchery and hedonism too vulgar to imagine in any form of religion. But Yushua wasn't like that. Not at all. But what of his friends? He had never met them, and they could be much different. Omar had no good answers.

"Ready, brother?" Omar, wholly lost in his thoughts, hadn't noticed Yushua's arrival.

"Already? Oh yes, okay. Now?"

"Let's go. It'll take us thirty minutes," Yushua said as the rain started to fall harder.

"Maybe twenty minutes, then?" said Omar as he bolted off ahead. "Let's not show up as a couple of drowned rats!"

The two friends were remarkably similar in stature, facial features, and age, and could easily be mistaken for brothers. They kept pace, step for step, loping with purpose toward the east end of Aden. Omar was surprised by Yushua's athletic conditioning.

"You're more than a library cellar dweller, brother—you're in shape!"

"Never had access to a car. These legs have taken me everywhere all of my life." Slowing his gait, he turned and trotted down a deteriorated crumble of a concrete sidewalk. "Here we are," he said as he gestured to an unimpressive brownish-beige five-story building. "The third floor," he said, without a hint of being winded.

"So much for not arriving as drowned rats!"

"The rain is a blessing, brother. And all arriving will be equally blessed, you'll see," Yushua said in a reassuring tone.

They slowed their pace as they climbed the first flight of stairs. Yushua stopped and studied the street below. Everything was quiet. The same thing happened on the second floor. Finally, they arrived on the third floor, walked down a dimly lit yellowish corridor and stopped in front of a door marked 308. Opposite of the door and across the hall was a small wooden table with two vases of silk flowers.

"Watch this," Yushua whispered. "Pink says nobody followed us." And then he reached into the left vase, removed a pink silk rose, and placed it in the vase to the right. Immediately the door unlocked and opened an inch.

"Come on in," Yushua whispered to Omar.

The apartment was larger than Omar expected as he tried to take in everything. *Two bedrooms, maybe three,* he thought. As they rounded the hall entrance, he could see people gathered in the living room. *Nine or ten; seven of them are wet.* Omar was doing the math.

As he entered the large room, a sparsely decorated space with clean but dated furnishings, he was puzzled by the group's reaction. Their eyes beamed of happiness as they welcomed him in with large sincere smiles, but they were almost silent.

"Welcome, brother," the most senior looking man among them whispered. He didn't need many words; his kind eyes spoke volumes.

"Thank you, sir," Omar replied.

"Muhammad. Please call me Muhammad."

Omar nodded deferentially.

Yushua reached into his backpack and pulled out a wet paper bag, half disintegrated, which contained six soggy pitas—they, too, were mostly disintegrated. "Sorry," Yushua said. "I should have put this in plastic. But I was too excited."

Muted laughter erupted. "That's okay, my young brother. We too are happy to see you and are very excited to meet our new brother in Isa, Omar Al-Khulani, I presume?" asked Muhammad.

Muhammad's words caught Omar off guard. *How do they know me? They've never met me before.* But before he could search for an answer, an older woman, probably Muhammad's wife, spoke.

"Omar, my name is Sister Nabila. I am married to Mr. Muhammad. This has been my joy for over forty years. I want you to know, my brother, that we have prayed for you for many months. Yushua told us about you and some of the things you said in class. And he said we must pray for you. That Isa could do wonderful things through you. So, we prayed. And Isa, sweet Isa, heard the prayers." With tears streaming down her cheeks, she walked over to Omar, gently clasped his face with both hands, and said, "We love you, Omar, our brother. I love you, my brother. Welcome to Isa's family."

Omar broke like a dam. He had only spent five minutes with the secret community, but in those five minutes he experienced more love, more joy, more acceptance, and more peace than he had ever known in his lifetime. He sobbed uncontrollably as his new family gathered around him, placing their hands on his head and shoulders. They prayed blessings on him. They asked Isa to prepare him to become a great spreader of the news. They prayed for the Al-Khulani family, that they too would love Isa. They prayed for God's protection. And they prayed for great courage.

Soon, all were crying. And then wiping their eyes they began to quietly laugh. Yushua most of all.

"Kebabs won't eat themselves!" Muhammad announced. "Let's feast together."

Sister Nabila immediately sprang into action and began to direct traffic. Within seconds, the table was covered with various entrees that the community had lovingly prepared. It was a hodgepodge of humble dishes that somehow all melded together to become the most magnificent banquet Omar had ever seen.

Muhammad broke in, "Yushua, since you brought us such wonderful pita mush, could you lead us in our love feast thanksgiving?"

"It would be my honor. Thank you, brother." And then Yushua, Omar's quiet, contemplative classmate, blew Omar's mind.

"Bow with me, brothers and sisters. Our Father, King of Kings, Lord of Hosts. We, your children, gather today to re-pledge our lives to you and your kingdom. We have no allegiance but to you, Isa. We are your sheep, and you are our only Shepherd. We hear your voice. We know your voice. And we follow only you. So, as we eat your food, we take your body, King Isa, into our bodies. As we drink your drink, we take your blood, King Isa, into ourselves. May your food and your drink remind us of your wondrous grace toward us. May your food and your drink strengthen us to serve you with all of our heart, mind, soul, and strength. May we be faithful children to you, Isa. Until our last breath. Faithful until the end. Ameen."

"Ameen," whispered the secretly gathered band.

Omar sensed a depth and intensity of both relationship and

purpose that could only be described as otherworldly. He had always been close with his own blood, but this familial knitting was a different kind of blood. Deeper. Truer. And Omar wanted more.

After sharing an almost mystical meal together, Muhammad stood up and walked across the room toward a green, hammered steel bureau. He unlocked it. Then he pulled the top drawer completely out, reached his arm through the opening, and carefully removed a coverless, tattered volume, bound together with black tape. He held it in his hands with a look of pride and contentment as if he were holding the Crown Jewels. Then he carefully opened it about three quarters of the way to the end of the book, and softly spoke:

"Today, we will obey St. Paul the Apostle's message to Isa's community in Ephesus. The sixth chapter ..."

The term "obey" immediately struck Omar as fascinating. *Not "read," not "learn," but "obey,"* Omar mused. *This must be the Christian Scriptures that tell more of Isa and how to obey him.*

Omar knew he had so much to learn. And he couldn't wait to learn it.

Better yet, he couldn't wait to obey it.

"Twenty-five hundred dollars a day, plus expenses," Tom said. "That's the going rate. He usually charges a grand more. But I convinced 'em that we wasn't as flush as some."

"Shoot, what's he got? State secrets?" Jimmy wasn't at all impressed. "Where's he from?"

"SynerChurch Resources, out of Portland."

"Portland? You're kidding me. Portland? I swear, if he shows up with a hipster beard and skinny jeans, riding a scooter, I'm locking the door."

Tom laughed compliantly.

"So, how many gold-plated days of this dude's precious time are we on the hook for?"

"He's got a two-week minimum. He needs to see our weekend operations. Twice."

Jimmy could do the math in his head, and he wasn't awestruck with Tom's negotiating prowess.

"So, 35K, plus expenses. Around 40K, and he won't lift a finger to change a thing. Just talk. A forty-thousand-dollar talk? I suspect he won't ride up in a scooter. A Rolls, more likely. A skinny-jeaned, bearded hipster, pulling up to our raggedy parking lot in a Rolls …"

"He'll give us a written report," Tom said defensively. "A thorough and comprehensive analysis of his findings with recommendations."

"A forty-thousand-dollar paper? Well, that's a bit better. You shoulda' led with that, brother! But can't we get something cheaper from Kinkos? Staples? Let's ask Marcy ..."

"I thought you wanted this, Jimmy?" Tom said, trying to hide his mounting frustration.

"Yeah, I did, but I had no idea …"

"Look, if you wanna make a bold move, you're gonna need backup. Your say-so ain't enough anymore. You know that the jackals, as you call 'em, they're smelling weakness. Ever since we started bleeding bodies to Cruciform, they've been lookin' for someone to blame. And you know who they're fixin' to take down?"

Jimmy nodded with a sense of resignation. "Suppose so," he said. He leaned back into his leather office chair, and with his eyes looking squarely into Tom's asked, "Tell me this. Will I get something for this? Will he give me something I don't already know? If we're gonna roll the dice with this fella, will I get a silver bullet? You know I need something pretty significant."

The unnerving honesty of Jimmy's question caught Tom by surprise. He was well accustomed to his bravado, but not what his machismo had been masking. In fact, it frightened him a little. He had always been so certain. So convinced. He had known Jimmy for almost twenty years. Worked for him for the best part of that. And he never saw him in a place where he didn't know his next step. Tom was visibly shaken.

Tom took a deep breath, slowed his thoughts down, and then gently spoke to his old friend. "Jimmy, I'm not sure you're gonna get a silver bullet. I don't know. Maybe so. Maybe not. But one thing I know for certain, we can't keep doin' this. When I signed up for ministry, God's call on my life was about something else entirely. Something more important. My heart's not in it anymore, and I 'spect yours ain't either."

Jimmy's chin sank to his chest as he let out a long, slow, hopeless breath. Tom's words were true and frank and stinging. And worst of all, they were spoken in love. Tom was rarely this forthright with his opinions, and it shocked him. But what was more shocking, and more discouraging, was that Tom described his own heartsickness to the letter. *My own superficial ministry interests have leeched out and sucked the life and spirit out of my friends*, thought Jimmy.

"You're so right," said Jimmy softly as he kicked at the carpet. "More than you know. I haven't enjoyed ministry since I can't remember when. It was supposed to be so important, and it just doesn't feel that way. Hasn't for a long time. But what I didn't know is that I've been killing your spirit too. Thought that I was the only one that was disillusioned. What a fraud I've been ..."

Jimmy felt like a failure. He felt like a con artist. He felt like his life and calling had been reduced to becoming a religious huckster, pitching blissful sentiments for the loose change in people's pockets. And what was worse, he wasn't even good at it. Cruciform had come to town and one-upped him on every front.

Tom replied, "Well, we can change, brother. We can. It ain't too late. Who knows, maybe we'll find our ole mojo again."

Jimmy collected himself and then stood up and embraced his old friend. Then, with a twinkle in his eye, he said, "Well, it's do-or-die time, buddy. Looks like we're putting all our chips on Portland and lettin' it ride."

"S'pose so," Tom said, somewhat bewildered in a whiplash of emotions.

"I guess I'll see what kind of silver bullet forty grand will get me. Now off to the jackals—I mean, 'the board.' Gotta pay for the ammo."

Tom managed a weak smile.

Luca stormed out of the house, realizing he had just announced to Chantel that he was going to be working late—an announcement that wasn't at all true. It was the slow season at the Y, and he had trouble finding things to do to fill his shift that ended at 5 p.m. There was no way he could work until 9 p.m. He knew this, but what was killing him was that he knew Chantel knew this as well. His only defense against the truth that his wife spoke was avoidance through a flimsy lie.

I'm not a liar. Why am I lying to the only one telling the truth? he pondered.

He thought about Chantel all that day. Tonight, she would be generously teaching the Scriptures to people who she knew had wounded her family. Deeply wounded her family. And she didn't hold them back. *Just like my papa, Chantel is loving those who intentionally hurt us*, Luca realized. His emotions began to shift from self-pity to disappointment. But this time he was disappointed with himself.

He had lied. He knew it. Chantel knew it. And it couldn't stand. When he returned home, he would make amends. But Luca knew that more was needed. More than apologies. He needed a symbol; something that would visibly express his love to his wife, his rock, who had been putting up with his nonsense while she continued to demonstrate God's grace to the enemy.

Luca knew exactly what to do.

At 5 p.m., Luca drove home from the Y in his father's well-worn Oldsmobile. He'd caused more than a few raised eyebrows when he stubbornly insisted on keeping the car, but despite the sadness attached to it, for Luca, there was a strange comfort in its familiar smell and the soothing memory of his father as he held the wheel. Luca parked a little way from the house and walked up the street to the neighborhood jewelry shop. It was a place Luca did not enter with any sort of regularity; there was seldom extra cash in the Lewis budget for extravagances like jewelry. But today was different. This wasn't a peace offering. And it wasn't an obligation. This was simply Luca's best way to tangibly express his love, appreciation, and admiration to a precious woman who had put up with too much.

He was warmly greeted at Patterson's Jewelry by a woman named Brenda who, by Luca's estimation, appeared to be in her mid-thirties, and fully capable to be his guide within this very unfamiliar arena. Brenda recognized at once Luca's look of awkward uncertainty common to men who came bumbling into her store. She politely asked, "Can I be of help?"

Luca told her that he was looking for a small gold cross on a dainty chain for his wife. To Luca, "dainty" was a veiled euphemism for cheap. It was to be a special gift, a love offering, but not one that would break the bank.

Brenda excitedly exclaimed, "Oh, we have just the ticket, sir." Then, she proceeded to carefully bring out two dark blue velvet trays from the bottom corner shelf. By the dust covering the hinged glass lid, it was obvious that these were not in high demand.

"Now sir, we have both kinds. We have the plain ones, and the ones with the little man on them. Most are in 14K gold, although this row is in 10K. Any one of these catch your eye?"

Luca had to take a step back to gather himself. The innocence of the "little man" description almost knocked the wind out of him. The idea of the cross was as familiar to Brenda as the Antarctic ice shelves would be to a villager in Papua New Guinea. This was deeply troubling. How had he, a pastor's son raised in the streets of Philly, missed something so fundamental? How had he missed the fact that the good news that his church so passionately preached about and so energetically sang about never seemed to walk its way across the street? Why hadn't he noticed before that the gospel was locked selfishly behind stone and cement—a world away from those who needed it the most?

All that Luca could manage was a long, slow, and demoralized sigh.

Once Luca had somewhat regained his composure, he took the opportunity to explain the story of "the little man" to a polite but curious saleswoman. He left Patterson's Jewelry emotionally befuddled. He was excited to have been able to share his faith. And he was eager to go home and make things right with Chantel. Yet he felt a new sadness. A sadness for Brenda and all the other Brendas in Philadelphia to whom he had been so blind.

By 6 p.m., much to Chantel's surprise, Luca arrived home. He asked for her forgiveness. For lying. For being so self-consumed. And he gave her his gift.

By 7 p.m., the stubborn remains of Mt. Pisgah gathered in their Philly rowhouse living room for Bible study. Stirred by his encounter with Brenda, Luca decided he would join them and settled down beside Chantel and Ms. Robinson on the sofa. Freddy Leonard was there. So was Jamaal. Together, with a half-dozen others, they began to conclude their study of Ephesians.

"Let's begin with verse ten." Chantel did her best to lead a buoyant discussion, but it was always a difficult group to inspire. By the time they sludged their way to verse fifteen, the cadre was clearly losing interest. Reflecting on the running shoes necessary to bring the gospel of peace to the community required more gas than the Bible students of Mt. Pisgah had left in them. The exaggerated yawns and frequent glances to wrist watches were the cues to instruct Chantel to hit the brakes and hit them hard. They had had enough Bible for today.

But Luca hadn't. Not even close. With passion and conviction, he told them the story of Brenda at Patterson's Jewelry. He described it all in captivating detail, and in so many ways he was the very visage of his papa. Lowering his voice at the story's conclusion, he leaned forward and pitched it straight over home plate. "This sweet woman had grown up in the shadow of Mt. Pisgah's steeple, and yet had absolutely no clue about the very subject that should have been our mission all along." And just in case some had missed his point, Luca ended with an incisive question. "Where were our running shoes all these years? Where are our running shoes now?"

Ms. Robinson spoke for all when she stood and answered in the sweetest tone, "Well, morning surely does come early ..."

Diesel fumes and desert dust filled the timeworn sixteen-passenger Mitsubishi microbus as it chugged up the unkempt mountain road. The underpowered diesel struggled as it labored to climb eight thousand feet on its afternoon route north from Aden to Dhamar. The six-hour ordeal created tension between the travelers who wanted the windows closed to keep the dust out, and those who wanted them open to flush out the leaking exhaust. The worst possible scenario was the one that ended up carrying the day: a few windows open in the front to allow dust to generously blow in, and windows sealed in the rear to trap it and mingle it in with the noxious gasses.

But Omar wasn't thinking about diesel or dust. His thoughts were consumed with his older sister, Fatimah.

Omar was the third child of four born to Ali and Fatimah Al-Khulani of Bani Badi, a tribal village thirty minutes outside of Dhamar. They were not by any means considered wealthy, but their local standing in all matters was sterling. "Without a name, we have no place. Without a place, we have no name," was the oft-repeated ethical axiom of Omar's father to his family. To Ali Al-Khulani, reputation wasn't just important; it was everything.

The Al-Khulani family were the eighth and ninth generations to breed Arabian horses on their farmstead outside the village. The family bred what they considered to be the archetypal Arabian steeds: Bedouins. Tapered heads, small ears, broad chests with curved backs, and strong legs with oversized joints. They were beautiful and powerful animals, and the villagers of Bani Badi were proud of the Al-Khulanis' pure line.

Omar, as the second born son, and being unusually gifted in academics, was the natural choice to send to law school. A lawyer, dispensing legal advice for their ancient family business in the midst of an evolving country, could be seen as nothing but helpful. Even the extraordinarily pragmatic patriarch of the family could see the wisdom in this. Besides, it was obvious to all that Omar would never be happy as a farmer. He was too much of a dreamer.

Ali, the eldest son, who was a full year younger than Fatimah, was heir apparent for all things Al-Khulani. Like his older sister, the two were namesakes of their parents. But unlike his sister, Ali junior was an exact representation of his father. In stature, appearance, opinion, and temperament, the two Alis were essentially twins—separated by twenty-four years.

Fatimah was in nearly every way the opposite of her mother. She was thin, almost waif-like, with a pale complexion and pronounced cheek bones. She was almost beautiful in appearance, yet at twenty-six she remained single, an exceedingly rare condition in Bani Badi. She was also much more introspective than her drill-sergeant mother. Fatimah senior was a short, thick, quick-tongued czarina who enforced the Al-Khulani domestic code of conduct without compunction. Her namesake, however, was curious about things beyond the surface. Life's whys mattered more to her than its whats and whens.

Omar understood that her appearance, marital status, and philosophical disposition had been impacted by her illness. Ever since Fatimah became a woman, she had been plagued with chronic illness. At fourteen, her father took her to Dhamar to seek medical help for her condition. After months of trips back and forth, doctors from the faculty of Medicine and Health Services at Thamar University finally diagnosed her sickness. The fancy medical term was primary sclerosing cholangitis. The layman's explanation was that Fatimah's bile duct closed shut periodically for reasons unknown, creating numerous related problems. Her liver would become inflamed and enlarged with scar tissue, and her system would become septic, causing far-reaching symptoms that eventually would lead to death. There was no known cure for PSC, and most symptom-alleviating treatments were unavailable in Yemen.

Perhaps it was the awareness that life was precious and short that produced Fatimah's curious outlook. And perhaps it was her physical fragility that gave her overassertive mother the patience for her endless questions. In either case, her mother loved her, accommodated her, and said daily prayers for her.

Her father was a different story.

To Ali Al-Khulani, the eighth-generation horse breeder, weakness wasn't a thing to be mollycoddled. And when he understood there was no chance for his daughter to be "correct," an unconscious switch flipped in his manner toward her. He softened. But it wasn't a softening that emerged from empathy or a father's compassion. It came more from a place of indifference. Like a colt born with an incorrect form, she was Al-Khulani offspring that was unbecoming to the line. So, she was sent to emotionally graze from the lesser pasture, and she would no longer receive his attention. She would be lucky if that were the worst of it, and she knew it.

Her father's reaction wasn't uncommon within the tribal traditions of a patrilineal society—which, of course, was the only tradition she knew. She knew that a woman's value to the clan was tied directly to her reproductive prowess. And Fatimah, showing no encouraging signs of potential fertility, was to her father a domestic liability—not an asset.

And so, Fatimah was resigned to a life on the family periphery. Not loved by her father as a daughter, but instead regarded only by the measure of service she could offer the family. And because of her health, Fatimah knew that the measure would not be great, and would quickly depreciate.

But the Al-Khulani who treasured Fatimah the most was Omar. Omar loved his sister, and Fatimah loved him. Perhaps it was because as children, Fatimah, four years his elder, nurtured him like a young mother. Or perhaps it was their common nature as dreamers that united their spirits. Whatever the reason, there was an unspoken bond between them that was real, and strong, and understood.

As the microbus pulled into the Dhamar station, Omar could see his older brother, Ali, waiting in the parking lot. It had been over a year since Omar had been home.

"Brother, how was your trip?"

"Good. Dusty, but good. These ole buses never seem to give up the ghost. How's Fatima?"

Ali's countenance dimmed as he glanced at his boots. "It's not good, brother. This last attack has been bad. She has nothing left."

"What's she doing? Is she in bed?"

"Yes. She's been in her bed for almost two weeks. But she's getting weaker, not stronger, like she usually does." And then he added, "We think she will die very soon."

The frankness of his brother's words shook Omar. "Can she speak?"

"Yes, yes, she's very much with her mind. She just has no strength. The sickness has not let her go this time."

"Oh," was the only response he could muster.

The two brothers traveled the mountain road to their homestead in silence. The weight of their sister's imminent death hung heavy in the dusty air, and any more conversation seemed to trivialize the moment.

As the old Landcruiser pulled into the yard, the whole family emerged from the various buildings to greet their son and brother. *Almost* the whole family.

After welcoming greetings and embraces, Omar asked, "Can I go see her?"

"She might be sleeping, but she'll be glad to see you," said Omar's mother. "She's in our bedroom because there are no stairs."

Omar left the welcoming party and walked, unaccompanied, into the family home. He walked through the kitchen, through the parlor, toward the door of the bedroom. He quietly knocked as he entered her room.

"Fatimah, are you awake?"

Fatimah lay motionless on the bed. Her pale face, now yellowish orange with jaundice, broke into a wide beaming smile. "Omar, you're here! How I've missed you. Oh, I am so happy to see you, brother!"

Omar, a bit taken aback by the strength of her greeting, responded, "There is no place in God's world that I would rather be, sister. I am so happy to see you."

Omar pulled a wooden chair beside her bed. The two began to talk about Aden, about the homestead, about the troubles of Yemen. They spoke on and on with ease, for almost an hour, as the family collected in the hallway outside the door as if they were witnessing a miracle.

And then Fatimah, seemingly oblivious to her watching audience, broke. "Omar, I am going to die. It will not be long now, and I am afraid. I am so afraid."

Chapter Six

The Brook

The weathered stone stables were a patchwork of additions, all seamlessly melded together to form a single complex that housed forty-six prized breeding mares and their foals. The original section was almost two centuries old with a stone floor and heavy oak beams that stabled a dozen Arabians. Subsequent generations of Al-Khulanis each added native rock and mortar to expand capacity without either one-upping or diminishing what was already built. The stables themselves stood as a testimony to a proud heritage that had endured through many uncertain seasons.

And they were about to see another.

Omar grabbed the heavy cypress door and heaved it open, instantly whiffing a familiar blast of hay and manure. A muted "phew" was all he said as he pushed through. The morning light shining through the large open door illuminated twelve smaller doors, each with brown legs below and a brown head above. Neighs and nickers greeted the once familiar stranger as he rubbed and patted the regal faces he walked by. He stopped at the fourth stall in and asked, "Usma, what should I do? How can I help Fatimah?"

Usma offered nothing.

Omar looked into the mare's dark eyes, *I have to tell my sister of Isa*, he thought. *She needs to know. She needs to see.*

But just how to have this forbidden conversation was another matter entirely. His sickly sister, lying bed-ridden in a house with many ears, seemed to make Omar's task impossible. *Isa, she needs to know. She needs to see you.* Omar's thoughts transformed naturally into a silent desperate prayer.

He finished his rounds of nose rubbing and praying and then spun on his heels, patted Usma's face once again, and said, "Wish me luck."

This time Usma neighed with seeming solidarity as Omar headed for the house.

Arriving in the kitchen, he greeted his youngest sister, Azima, who was barely sixteen and busy grinding chickpeas. He missed his mother's falafels, and secretly hoped his sister's work ended with the grinding. "She's dressed," Azima said.

"Who's dressed?"

"Fatima," as she pointed her elbow toward the parlor. "She hasn't been up in weeks. You must be good medicine for her, brother."

Omar walked into the parlor, and there was Fatimah, bathed and dressed, sitting alertly in their father's rocking chair. "Can we go to our brook?" she asked.

"It's wonderful to see you up. Are you feeling a little better?"

"Maybe a little," she answered. And then she persisted, "Do you think we could visit our brook together?"

"Are you feeling well enough? It's a big climb down."

"With your help, brother," she said with a little smile.

"Okay, then. Let's go to the brook. I'll bring the Landcruiser around."

Fifteen minutes later, Omar was backing the truck into a tight spot between two ledges of rock that would provide the easiest access to the stream. With painstaking gentleness, he helped Fatimah out of the vehicle, and then they carefully picked their way down a well-traveled horse trail.

She had always been slight, but now Omar was astonished at how little she weighed. "You don't like mother's falafels anymore? You need to eat a few dozen a day," he said with a teasing grin.

Fatimah, seemingly ignoring the comment, carefully eased herself down upon a large boulder, wrapped herself in a handwoven woolen shawl, and sighed. "I'm so happy to be here with you. My favorite place, my favorite person, and Allah gave us a glorious morning. I'm so happy."

"Thank you, Father," Omar whispered aloud.

"Father? Why are you thanking our father?" Fatimah questioned. For the last twelve years of her life, her father had been noticeably absent.

"Sister, I wasn't thanking our earthly father. I was thanking our Heavenly Father. I prayed and asked God to give me some time alone with you. I need to tell you some wonderful news." Omar's face was glowing.

"You call Allah your Heavenly Father? That's not right, is it? Allah the mighty. Allah the most holy. But not 'our father'?" she questioned.

"Sister, it is the rightest thing in the world. God doesn't have to be distant. God wants to be close to you, Fatimah. That's why he sent Isa."

Omar spent the next hour sharing with his sister about his story of forgiveness. He told her about the wine. About his confession at the mosque. About his shunning. About Yushua. And about his secret community. But most all, he told her about Isa and his sacrifice.

Fatimah was utterly spellbound. She slowly stretched out her thin yellow arm and pointed to the brook. "Omar, I had a dream," she said, trembling. "Three times, I had a dream. The same dream." Tears flowed down her cheeks and gathered in the hollow by her pronounced collar bone.

"What was it?" Omar asked, giving his sister time to regain her composure.

She stabbed in the air more emphatically as she pointed to the brook. "At that corner, where the water is deep. Where we used to swim as children. There was a glowing man dressed in white who was with me in the water. I asked, 'Who are you?' The man said, 'Isa.' I asked, 'Isa Al-Masih?' He smiled at me and then said, 'Fatimah, when you see him, ask Omar about me.' And then he disappeared. And then I saw you, Omar. In the dreams. You were standing in the brook with me. You told me about Isa Al-Masih. And then you dipped me in the water … and I was cleaned."

Tears were now flowing down Omar's cheeks. Although he had never personally had one, he had heard about the "Isa dreams" many times. Three disciples in the secret community were directed to salvation by an encounter with Isa while they slept—including their elder, Muhammad. Omar's head was spinning with joy, wonder, and holy reverence.

Fatimah continued, "That's why I was so happy when I saw you, brother. I was so afraid I would pass before you told me the good message of Isa Al-Masih."

Brother and sister embraced each other in a joyous celebration of laughter and tears. Together they sat, a world away from cities and problems and divisions. Two farmers' children sitting in the very presence of Isa Al-Masih. And it was wondrous.

After a few minutes, Fatimah said, "Thank you for telling me, brother. What must I do?"

"Believe, sister. Believe." Omar paused. "Believe that Isa loves you. Believe that he died on a cross to forgive you. Believe that he rose from the dead to empower you. Believe that with his forgiveness comes his Holy Spirit to guide you. Believe."

"I do believe," Fatimah said softly.

"Tell Isa right now. Tell him, sister."

"Yes. Isa Al-Masih, I believe you. I do. Forgive me. Please. I believe. Please give me your Spirit. I believe. Thank you, Isa, for showing me how to believe. Ameen."

"Ameen! Ameen, ameen, ameen!" exclaimed Omar in unbridled exuberance.

Fatimah was happy but didn't seem quite as ready to celebrate as her brother. She had a mystified look on her face. The look that one has after a lamb feast: full, grateful, satisfied. But seeing the baklava, crispy and glistening with honey on pistachios, it causes a different hunger.

"But this is not all, is it?" Fatimah asked.

"Yes, you are forgiven by the sacrifice of Isa. Nothing more can be done. Isa did it all for you."

Fatimah didn't seem convinced. "But brother, what about the water?"

"Oh, you mean baptism, sister," Omar said. "Isa told us to be dipped under the water as a sign that our old life, our misdeeds and our selfishness, are crucified and buried with Isa's execution, and our new life is born in him because of his resurrection. It's something all disciples of Isa Al-Masih do to proclaim their allegiance to King Isa."

"Then I want the water," Fatimah said without hesitating. "Can you help me with the Isa water? Like my dream?"

Omar thought back to his own baptism which had been only three months previous. It was the only one he'd seen, and he was the nervous guest of honor. He wasn't sure if he noticed everything. "It was in the bathtub in apartment 308. Muhammad asked Yushua to perform the ceremony. What did Yushua say?" Omar pondered aloud.

"Brother, can I have the Isa water?" Fatimah insisted.

"Of course, Fatimah. We will be just like Philip with the gelded Ethiopian," he replied.

"What is this?"

"Never mind."

With little exertion, Omar hoisted his sister up from the boulder and carefully folded her shawl. Securely holding her left arm, he gingerly escorted her into the brook and then downstream toward the bend. The water grew noticeably cooler as they slowly and deliberately shuffled their way into the deepest part of the bend. The clear, cool mountain water, thigh high to Omar, was almost waist deep on his sister.

"Are you okay, sister?"

Fatimah pursed her thin lips as she exhaled, and then looked at her brother and beamed. Fatimah was so beautiful. Her radiant smile outshone her yellow complexion.

"Are you ready?" Omar asked. "I think so."

Then, shifting perpendicular to her, placing his right hand on the small of her back and shooting his left hand in the air, he closed his eyes as he attempted to recall Yushua's words spoken at his own baptism.

"Like Isa was baptized, and like Isa asked us, I bury you Fatimah in the water, like Isa was buried ..."

Bending his sister backward, and placing his left hand over her nose, he submerged her completely under the brook's cool water. And then, with his right arm he pulled her back out of the water in dramatic fashion.

"... and raised out of the water like Isa was raised from the dead. Ameen." And then he remembered one more thing Yushua had said. "In the name of the Father, his Son Isa, and the Spirit. Ameen."

They both quietly stood in the brook without speaking. Omar was so joyful. So peaceful. His spirit was quiet. He looked at his sister, beautiful Fatimah. She was quiet. Eyes closed. Hands clutched to her chest. Her thin arms were ...

"Fatimah, look at your arms!" he exclaimed. "They're not yellow! Your face is ... it's beautiful!"

She reached around and felt her back, searching for the pain she had known for so many years. Fingers pressing in, feeling for that enlarged, throbbing, sclerotic liver. Hunting for her nemesis. Her own body, always fighting against her. Always pushing painfully out in every direction.

"It's gone!"

***

The front door clicked shut for the final time that evening. Ms. Robinson, who was the first to call for the adjournment, was, as usual, the last to leave. She always had so much to say.

Chantel leaned against the closed door and said, "I have never in my life met a woman who could say less with more words than the high and mighty Ms. Robinson. I need a shower. A long, hot shower."

She had finally seen what Luca had seen. It took her a bit longer, but she got there just the same. She had held out hope that one more Bible study might change the trajectory of their self-focused spiritual lives. But her patience had finally come to an end following the group's response to her husband's story about Brenda at Patterson's

Jewelry. Actually, it was their lack of response that was the proverbial straw that broke the camel's back.

"After you told the story of Brenda, that poor child, who didn't even know who it was on the cross. And it didn't touch them one bit? I have no kind words to say, I'll tell you that right now."

"She wasn't a child. Brenda … I'm sure she was better than thirty," Luca corrected.

"Well, that makes it all the worse." And then she added, "To think that your poor papa put up with them all those years."

"That's what I've been saying, honey—" He stopped himself from continuing, gave his throat a small clearing, and said, "It ain't a church, honey. Not because it doesn't have a building or a preacher. It ain't a church because it doesn't have Jesus. It doesn't have Jesus' purpose. And it ain't been a church for an awfully long time. Papa used to say, 'Jesus has a mission, but does his mission have a church?' As far as Mt. Pisgah Baptist Church, the answer hasn't been in any doubt. We don't have to kill it, honey, 'cause obviously it's already dead. Nobody cares about Brenda? Nobody even fakes a care? So baby, we gotta shake the dust off our feet and start over. We have to become Jesus' church ourselves. Join his mission ourselves. And I've got an idea."

"You mean start a new church?" Chantel asked.

"Kinda. But not like you might be thinking."

Chantel was busy cooking sweet potatoes and scratch biscuits while her instant pot was working over a half-priced pot roast. Mingling together, they filled the Philadelphia rowhouse with a most pleasing memory-making aroma that was sure to enchant their guests. The dining room table was ready, set for six, with three red trivets in the center, each waiting to receive their delicious offerings.

Luca tucked Sanders in bed and returned downstairs to his papa's easy chair, looking over his notes for the evening.

"Everything's almost ready, hun. Mind carving the roast?"

"Love to, unless you want to hide it and serve our guests some of them good fish sticks."

"Luca Josiah Lewis, you'll be eating them good fish sticks if you're not careful," she said with a flirty twinkle.

Luca was in a much better mood these days. Something inside him had started shifting the night Chantel took him on. Forgiving the Robinsons and forgiving himself was a tall order. It wasn't natural, nor was it easy. But Luca knew deep in his heart that it was necessary. He wasn't all the way there yet. At least not always. But his spirit was in a much better place.

He still thought a lot about his father, but in a different way than before. He was not stuck in the painful memories of those last lonely years. The Robinson coup and the ensuing abandonment no longer occupied center stage of his mind. He now thought more about his papa's life, his life's message, and his purpose. He didn't consciously make this shift of thinking, but it happened, nonetheless.

The doorbell rang. It was Kofe and Angelica Wilson. Walking up behind them was Jerome and Choyz Jackson. Both couples were former leaders of Mt. Pisgah, overseeing some of the pastoral work and Bible-study groups. Along with Luca and Chantel, they'd read Rev. Lewis's manifesto and had been excited about the possibilities and his vision for Mt. Pisgah. But following the days of Marcus Robinson's successful coup d'état, the Wilsons and Jacksons had left the church, burnt out with the constant struggle to move the church toward a heart for reaching out to the neighborhood.

"Welcome, friends. It's been way too long."

Everyone apparently agreed, as a round-robin procession of long hugs ensued. After a few moments catching up, Chantel, who, because of a preoccupied husband, had to carve the pot roast herself, invited everyone to the table. Luca, sitting at the head, reached out both thick hands as a gesture of friendship. Together, holding hands, Luca offered a blessing that was warm and heartfelt. His presence, his deep yet melodic voice, his very manner reminded them all how much they missed their beloved pastor.

Chantel's meal, as usual, was a veritable home run. Jerome, whose physical girth indicated that he hadn't often passed up on seconds, made sure that the pot roast evaporated completely. "Don't wanna offend the chef," was his line as he scraped the serving dish clean. Choyz, who was every bit Jerome's equal, looked disappointed as she returned the empty platter to its red trivet.

There was an unspoken sense in the room that this meal was not just a catch up, but that there was a grander purpose for the invitation. Luca, sensing his guests' curiosity, started out with a "well," and then cleared his throat, as was his habit, and launched out. "Friends, we were once on a journey together. You remember? It started out as a beautiful journey before it got its legs kicked out from under it. I don't want to rehash the past, as awful as it was. But I want us to consider the future; a future that we've never quite experienced, but if I remember right, we all desperately wanted to."

He paused for a second, searching for a hint that would tell him there was still a possibility. And he could see in the eyes of his guests that the spark was still there.

Luca reached behind him and grabbed a brown leather notebook off the hutch. He continued, "I want to remind you what my papa, our pastor, said. I've been thinking a ton about this. And I'd like to invite your families to join together with ours to grab that future by the horns. Grab it and run."

He opened the leather notebook, and read, "Three Necessary Shifts for Mt. Pisgah Baptist Church. One, we must be a different kind of church. One that is not centered around a Sunday worship service but is centered around making disciple-makers."

Luca added, "In case y'all hadn't noticed, Mt. Pisgah ain't holding services no more. So that makes things a bit easier."

He continued, "Two, we must have a different kind of church leadership. We must shift from professional leaders designed to produce a worship service to co-vocational leaders deployed to equip disciple-making disciples. Something that's infinitely reproducible."

Again, Luca went off script. "Remember when Pastor would preach on Ephesians 4:11–12? Five functions, five priorities of the body of Christ that together expressed the image of the person of Christ: apostle, prophet, evangelist, shepherd, and teacher."

Angelica broke in with a beaming smile, "It sounds like the old days, the stuff that Pastor used to talk about. Kofe and I were ready to sign up for it all, right there and then."

"But it never happened," Jerome interjected. "Choyz and I kinda understood where people were comin' from. But then it got all personal. It got ugly, and it was painful for us. I'm not sure that I'm right yet."

"I get it," said Luca. "Chantel can tell you that I'm just starting to shake the funk off now. And she's a little funky herself. We all have been disappointed. But who disappointed us? Was it Jesus? Or was it selfish, sinful people?"

"It wasn't Jesus, I'll tell you that right now," Choyz replied. "But that Ms. Robinson. I dunno 'bout her …"

"It wasn't Jesus," Luca said. "That we know for sure."

From there Luca retold the story of Patterson's Jewelry and Brenda, this time receiving a much different response. The potential team commiserated and then began to dream together.

"Which leads us to Pastor's third shift." Luca read from his notes, "A different level of gospel collaboration. We must shift from our church being our goal, to God's kingdom being our goal, and his church becoming his vehicle for his mission. We must give ourselves away, together with other faith communities, so that every man, woman, boy, and girl can see, hear, taste, and smell the good news of Jesus Christ."

Luca dropped his notebook on the floor beside him. He had everyone's attention. "Y'all, we had it all wrong the whole time. We saw it, but we couldn't seem to fix it. Well maybe now it's fixin' time. Maybe now it's movement time. And maybe now it starts with us right here, right now."

It sounds like we're starting some kind of church … are we?" asked Kofe, tentatively.

"I don't know about that," said Luca. "But I sure know I want to live this way. We just need to figure out what roles we'll all play. Jerome and Choyz, you see things from all sides. Remember how you used to run around like sheep dogs making sure that folks were okay? What I'm asking of you is to do that again. But more than that, to equip folks to care for others. Can you see that?"

The whole room nodded in unison.

"Kofe and Angelica. Y'all used to be central headquarters for the neighborhood, remember? You had more strays in your house hearing the gospel than ever entered the holy halls of Mt. Pisgah. Remember how many young people came to faith in your living room? But we couldn't seem to ever get 'em to make the leap to 'real church.' I think we can take care of that problem."

All in the room were smiling and nodding as they recalled those days. Luca was painting the picture brilliantly.

"Your task is to evangelize, yes. But as importantly, it is to equip everybody to share good news."

"And what about you and Chantel? How do you fit into this?" Jerome asked.

"What do you think, Jerome?"

"You and Chantel were always busy scheming how to get the good news sent to all the underdogs," interrupted Angelica. "Brenda's just another example."

"Yeah, I see that," agreed Jerome. "And not just the gospel, but the whole body of Christ. You were figuring out how to bring Christ's community to 'the strays,' as you put it. Instead of getting 'the strays' to straighten up good enough for church."

"Bingo," said Chantel, beaming from ear to ear. "This is so exciting. Now we just gotta figure out how we actually connect with folks and start this thing. Are y'all in or what?"

His navy-blue college T-shirt stuck to his back like a second skin. His neck itched as small particles of hay, dried seeds, and dehydrated horse "dirt" clung to his sweaty banded collar. Stinging beads of perspiration mixed with dust trickled down his forehead and into his deep set eyes. As low man on the totem pole, Omar was unexpectedly spending his summer break at home as the stable mucker. And it was exactly as inglorious as it sounded: shovel up whatever the prized Arabian mares dropped down. And within the enclosed envelope of a stable, the waft of what dropped down quickly eradicated any romantic notions about horse farms.

Omar had taken a leave of absence from his law internship to care for his gravely ill sister. But within days of Omar's arrival home, Fatimah bounced back extraordinarily. Her color had returned. For the first time in years, she had an appetite. Azima, their younger sister, jokingly said of Fatimah, "No falafel anywhere on the farmstead is safe anymore." And she had an energy and strength that made her seem almost "normal."

But there was something else about her—something that was

anything but normal. She was happy. Deeply happy. She carried with her a joy that seemed overwhelming to her usually emotionally dreary family. Among the Al-Khulanis, the source of this newfound happiness was in question. Some assumed that it came with her returning health. Vitality, when one had only known sickly weakness, was bound to bring relief and happiness. Fatimah senior was certain that it was the "family medicine" liberally dosed out in Omar's unexpected arrival that was the miraculous elixir. Omar and Fatimah had always had a special bond, and Omar's unexpected appearance caused the rebound of both health and spirits. Omar and Fatimah's frequent visits to the brook seemed to increase her strength. Eventually, the matriarch's theory found general acceptance. Mother's wisdom became obvious to all.

To all except Omar and Fatimah.

Isa Al-Masih had captured Fatimah's curiosity and interest. She couldn't learn enough about him. Omar had a remnant of a New Testament that contained the complete book of Matthew and the first ten chapters of Mark. It was hand stitched together with a heavy-guage fishing line, and then bound with black tape. He both transported and concealed it within his green canvas backpack under the false-bottom flap that was originally designed to hide cash, but now it transported a far greater treasure. Twice a day, before breakfast and after dinner, the two siblings made their way to the brook to study the sacred pages of Isa. And Fatimah was growing like a weed.

"I would like to have a secret community," she said to Omar. "Can I come to Aden with you to see the community? I would like to meet Isa's people."

"There are actually many secret communities in Aden, and I'm sure that there are some in Dhamar. I am learning about this from Muhammad."

"Many? How many?"

"I don't know exactly, but Muhammad does. It sounds like more than ten. Muhammad meets with the leaders of the others for prayers. I've only been to one other."

"What was it like? Was it the same as yours?"

"Hard to tell. They had a sick man, and I went with Muhammad to bring money, some food, and to pray."

"Pray for his healing? Did it work?"

"Yes, to pray for his healing. He had a large family and got cancer."

"Did it work? Did the man lose the cancer?" she pressed.

"I don't know, sister. But Muhammad says Isa heals as he wills. But we don't always know what Isa wills. So, we ask."

"Like with me?"

"No, Fatimah. That was different. I asked, knowing what Isa wanted."

"How did you know?"

"It was your dream, Fatimah. When you explained your dream to me, I heard the Spirit of Isa Al-Masih say to me, 'Ask me,' so I did."

"I didn't hear you ask."

Omar laughed. "But God did, and that's really all that counts."

***

The Landcruiser's all-terrain tires whirred quietly on the freshly resurfaced pavement, leaving Thamar University Medical Center. Fatimah had confounded the medical scientists as they tested and retested, trying valiantly to rediscover signs of disease and therefore return their patient to her former terminally ill self. But after a full day of poking, prodding, scanning, and injecting, Dr. Fahid

Aziz announced with a most puzzled manner, “There is nothing. I have no explanation. It must be some kind of a miracle.”

Fatimah, beaming from ear to ear, clasped her hands over her chest and said, “It is most definitely a miracle, doctor. God healed me when I was in the brook at our farmstead.”

Dr. Aziz, not knowing what to do with this information, said, “Well praise be to Allah the Merciful, I suppose.”

Fatimah, caught up in the moment, said in a correcting tone, “No, no, doctor. All praise be to Isa Al-Masih, the Healer.”

“Isa?”

“Yes, Dr. Aziz. Isa. Isa Al-Masih. He came to me in my dream.”

And as Fatimah recounted the details of her physical healing and spiritual restoration, a small assembly of doctors, nurses, and medical residents gathered around her and listened intently. All were mesmerized by this unfamiliar message, yet the telling rang true with a strange air of familiarity. Fatimah beamed as she spoke of Isa’s love and forgiveness. She spoke boldly and authoritatively as if she were a messenger from heaven herself.

But Fatimah didn’t know that a heavenly messenger is exactly who she was.

Chapter Seven

The Passion

Omar pulled the Landcruiser into a small underground parking lot, parked, and then the two began to climb the dimly lit concrete stairs to the fifth floor.

"I wish I could have seen his face. You know that all the medical staff are scratching their heads right now. They will not soon forget this day," Omar said. "But you must be more discreet, sister. There are many in our country who hate Isa's disciples."

"I know, Omar. I started to speak and just couldn't stop speaking. I am sorry, brother. I will try to be more careful. But I can't wait to tell the brothers and sisters," Fatimah said as she recaptured her former glow. "Isa might use my story in the hospital. The medical people were moved. Dr. Aziz had tears."

Omar, with both fists high in the air, let out a joyous yelp. "Yes! Thank you, Isa!"

"Shhh," whispered Fatimah. "Now you must be careful. We mustn't expose our community."

For the past six weeks, Omar and Fatimah had been taking full advantage of Fatimah's medical issues. Their frequent medical trips to Dhamar were "coincidentally" scheduled just prior to their secret meetings. Muhammad had made all the necessary arrangements and introductions so that they were welcomed into the Isa community with open arms.

As they walked down the fifth-floor corridor, they glanced over their shoulders for the last time, making doubly sure that they hadn't been followed. The community in Dhamar employed a similar security procedure to what Omar was accustomed to in Aden. A table across from the door had a stack of newspapers. If a brother or sister was followed, they were to pick up a paper and begin to read it. If all was clear, then one would pick up a newspaper and set it right back down.

Omar dropped the newspaper.

The door unlocked and opened a crack. Omar and Fatimah, excited about the moments ahead, walked quietly but confidently through the threshold. They had so much to tell their brothers and sisters. The miracle had now been medically and scientifically documented. It had been objectively certified. And the story of Dr. Aziz was spine tingling.

But something was off. Something felt different. Strange. There were no warm greetings. No smiles. No sounds. All at once, a sense of foreboding replaced the excitement that existed only seconds before.

As Omar rounded the corner to the parlor, he saw three strangers dressed in dark blue uniforms. Each wore a thick mustache, a dark blue beret, and a black nylon belt that carried a series of holsters. The two younger men who flanked the gray-mustached soldier had pistols drawn and pointed at the elder hosts of the secret community.

Holding a brass and silver framed family portrait that once sat prominently in the Al-Khulani parlor, the senior officer asked, "Are you Omar Al-Khulani of the family of Ali Al-Khulani of Bani Badi? Is this you in the picture?"

"Who are you?" Omar demanded. "Why are you here?"

Undeterred, as if he had just heard a tiny mongrel growl, the officer repeated his question. This time more slowly and emphatically, "Are you Ali Al-Khulani's son? Are you Omar Al-Khulani of Bani Badi? Is this you in the family portrait?"

"Yes."

"And is this your sister, Fatimah, with you?" He pointed his stubby cigarette-stained finger at the framed portrait once again. "Is she the one sitting in this picture?"

Omar said nothing.

With both pistols now pointed at Omar, he repeated his question. "Is this your elder sister, Fatimah, little Omar?"

Still, Omar offered nothing.

And then one soldier angrily stomped to Omar and jammed his pistol into the side of his head.

Fatimah could take no more. "Yes. Yes. I am Fatimah, Omar's sister. Fatimah Al-Khulani."

"Very good," the gray mustache said calmly with a menacing smile. "I have but one question for you, my dear Fatimah," he said as he walked toward her. Inches away. Face to face. He reached out and grabbed her tiny waist with both hands. And then with no expression, he quietly asked, "Who is your God, beautiful Fatimah? Allah the Glorious, or Isa Al-Masih?"

But Fatimah no longer looked afraid. A smile broke on her face as her brown eyes lit up and looked directly into the cold eyes of her captor. "Sir," she said, "my God is the One True God. The only God. The God who healed me. The God who loves me. The God who forgave me. I have no God but Isa Al-Masih. Because there is no God but King Isa."

Shaken, either by the manner of Fatimah's response or by the bold words she declared, the commanding officer nervously cleared his throat. And then, taking a step back, his hands releasing her waist and dropping to his side, he asked, "Is this your final word on the subject, beautiful Fatimah? Have you nothing else to say to me but your blasphemy?"

"I do. I do have something else to say." And then with a radiant smile and an otherworldly calmness, Fatimah said, "Please return this message to Bani Badi. Tell my family that I love them. And tell my father that I forgive him for this. But most importantly, tell them all this message: Isa Al-Masih loves them and will forgive them, should they humble themselves and ask."

The senior soldier could no longer look at Fatimah. His head drooped as he slowly shuffled three steps backwards.

There were several seconds of absolute quiet.

And then he nodded.

A deafening percussion rang out in the close quarters of the parlor as Omar saw his sister's head lurch backward and then her body fall lifelessly on the cold tile floor in a sickening thump.

"No! Fatimah!" Omar cried as he threw himself to the floor. "Fatimah ..."

"Get up!" barked one of the soldiers as he grabbed a handful of Omar's hair and pulled him to his feet. "We've got plans for you, little dog."

They zip-tied his hands behind his back. And then the gray-mustached soldier marched him out the door with a gun pushed into the back of Omar's neck. But Omar felt nothing but shock, unsteadiness, and disorientation. *Is this really happening? Did this happen? Is this a dream—a nightmare?* Omar's normally highly tuned senses were now reduced to a foggy swirl of semi-consciousness.

As Omar and his captor made their way down the stairwell to the fourth floor, a muted thwacking rang out from above.

Omar's focus sharpened. He knew what had just happened. Another member of his secret community had been murdered.

"No ..." Omar cried. "Help them, Isa! Help them ..."

And then another.

Omar fell to his knees. He couldn't breathe. "Help us, God," he cried out. "Help us, Isa."

The gray mustache sneered and said, "Here comes your help, little doggy. Listen carefully to your lesson. I want to teach my doggy."

Another shot. Another. Another. Another. Two more. And another.

And another.

And then it was quiet once again.

Blackness. Dark, thick, terrifying blackness. Darkness and the pungent stench of human filth. There was nothing else that Omar's senses could perceive. His jaw throbbed. His nose was clogged, and breathing was difficult. The taste of blood. It burned as it seeped down the back of his throat. Searing pain shot up his arms and shoulders from peeled wrists zip-tied too tightly behind his back. Feet bound together.

As he slowly lifted from his slumberous fog the pain intensified. His head pounded. Breathing hurt. Broken ribs, maybe. The putrid smell combined with the pulsating throbbing of his head began to make him nauseous. The black room was spinning.

"So, Omar, maybe this time?" came the flat voice that sounded only feet away. But he could see nothing through the darkness. And then he felt someone touching his throat. Something was loosened.

And then there was light.

A man stood above him holding a black bag that had been cinched around his neck. He wore a blue uniform with a white patch that was emblazoned with three initials: CSO.

"Central Security Organization," he mumbled to himself, choking, and coughing out more blood.

"So, you've heard of us? Interesting. We try to keep a low profile. How do you know us, Omar?"

"I'm a student ..." he managed.

"Yes, a law student. Very impressive, Omar. Have you heard of our 'extrajudicial detention centers'?"

"Yes ..." Words came with difficulty. "Black sites. Off the ... map. You torture ..."

"So, you're more intelligent than you look, aren't you? But perhaps that's not too high of a compliment right now, is it? So, Omar, are you ready this time?"

Omar had no idea what he was talking about. He scanned the room. It appeared square, about thirteen feet long and wide. Two steel doors with large metal rivets. Ox-blood red painted ceiling. Red ceramic tiles on all four walls. Red painted concrete floor. The floor had a drain in the center. There was a concrete stub partition about three feet high and three feet long that protruded from the wall. It had red tiles on it as well. And two rusty iron rings bolted to the top of the partition with rusted chains running through the rings.

"Well?"

"I do not know what you are asking."

"Well, let's try once again, shall we? Why is it that you are here, Omar? Perhaps that will refresh your memory. Why would important people want you here? Why would your family want you here?"

"Isa?"

"No, no, no, no. Not Isa, Omar. Blasphemy. You have blasphemed Allah." He paused for a few seconds to let that settle in. "Do you know the punishment for blasphemy, young man?"

Omar knew. He had just witnessed multiple counts of the punishment that the CSO doled out to his spiritual community. And to his sister.

"I saw ..."

"Yes, you did, didn't you? Poor Fatimah. I understand that she was very beautiful. Very, very beautiful, I heard. At least she was. Before the unfortunate ... incident. Such a waste. Such an unnecessary waste. Don't you agree, Omar?"

"Yes, I do," Omar said with a mounting sense of anger.

"So, let's stop the unnecessary waste. The unnecessary wasting of your pathetic life, Omar, and of my time. Which, by the way, I value considerably more. Are you ready?"

"Am I ready for what?" he asked, even though he knew the answer.

"To recant your blasphemy and swear allegiance to the true faith, you infantile insect. For some reason your family wants you back, although I can't imagine why. Perhaps to brag of the lawyer in their line. But first you must recant."

"Can I explain?" Omar asked.

"Explain what? Explain how you are the shame and the festering blight to your esteemed family's name?"

"No, sir. No. Explain why the Prophet Muhammad said that Isa Al-Masih was the ultimate messenger of God. It is because Isa, the Eternal, became a man ..."

Omar's head received a thwack and jolted hard to his left. Ringing ears. Head throbbing. Nauseous. Dizzy. Omar lurched and vomited all over himself.

"Still haven't learned, have you, Omar? Your family said that you were smart, but I do not see it. Stupid, I can see. A donkey of a son. A stupid, stubborn donkey. But I can teach a donkey. I'm a patient teacher, Omar, you'll find this out. And maybe, just maybe, your family will have a faithful and penitent son returned to them. Yes? No? You will have some time to consider this, little donkey."

Seemingly pleased with his performance, he curled a smile with half his mouth. And then, several decibels louder, he commanded, "Guards."

Omar, feet bound together, was walked out of the red room to an adjoining cell. The guards unlocked a heavy steel door and shoved him forward. With no stable stance, and with both arms secured behind his back, he plummeted frontward, landing hard on his already beaten face.

And then he passed out once again.

***

As usual, it was deathly quiet in the gym. Apparently, the twenty-five-year-old fitness equipment was no longer the promotional enticement it once was. Tom Butts often said jokingly, "Besides the Upper Prayer Room, it's officially the quietest place on LifePointe's campus."

Jimmy had never thought the joke was funny.

But it was quiet. And in fact, it no longer smelled like a gym. More like a hospital. It seemed that the janitorial staff spent more time cleaning and disinfecting the place than anyone actually using it. Except for one: Dr. Jimmy Norris was its only frequent flier. And you could set your watch by his arrival. Six-thirty every morning, come rain or shine, every day but Sunday. And, the way his tailored shirts fit, it seemed it was entirely worth the effort. His wife, Cindy, was willing to get their three boys off to school without Jimmy's help, if it meant he kept himself in shape.

As Jimmy slowly lowered a thick stack of steel plates after a hard-fought press, Tom breathlessly marched in. "He's early. He asked if he could set up in Staff Conference Room B. He needs video."

"Uuuugh," was all Jimmy could muster as he struggled to breathe. "So, the corporate colonoscopy begins," he said with short breaths. "I'll be there in thirty."

Tom turned around to leave and then stopped at the door, shot Jimmy a wry smile, and said, "And Jimmy, you called it. He's got a big ole nasty beard!"

Twenty-five minutes later, Jimmy walked into Staff Conference Room B, showered, pressed, and looking his general GQ self.

"I'm Jimmy," he said, stretching out a freshly pumped-up right arm, sleeves rolled up two folds. "Welcome to the South."

Jimmy's guest warmly shook his hand. "Pleased to meet you, Dr. Norris. I'm Chad Collins from SynerChurch Resources. It's great to be in Hotlanta again. I'm outta Portland."

"Really," Jimmy replied with a squinting little smile. "You disguise that remarkably well." And then he rolled out a brown leather chair from the center of the board table, sat down, and said, "Well, what do you say that we get this 2,500-dollar day started!"

Tom shot a correcting glance to his boss as if to say, "Jimmy, tone it down."

"Sorry, Tom. My bad. Twenty-five hundred dollars ... plus expenses."

The room laughed uncomfortably.

Jimmy leaned back, gestured across the table, and said, "Chad, the floor is all yours. Start fixin' us."

Chad, knocked a bit off his game, flipped open his laptop and began to stutter through a slide deck about the two-week internal investigation that LifePointe was about to undergo. As he tracked into his well-rehearsed spiel, he gradually began to get his legs under him. He promised that the process would be thorough, engaging, at times excruciating, but in the end, entirely transformational.

All that he asked for was complete honesty.

Tom Butts, the consummate administrator, began to lay out his plan for how LifePointe would engage with SynerChurch's processes and recommendations. They would roll out a five-phase strategy that would begin that day and would enter the fifth and final phase in eighteen months. Tom, standing at the head of the board table, summed up the process: "Today we begin the 'Assessment Phase.' We will ask ourselves, 'How are we doing?' At the end of next …"

"Shouldn't we know what we're trying to do before we answer the question of 'How are we doing?'" Jimmy interrupted. "Seems to me that if we are doing a decent job of something that's insignificant, that's not a winning strategy." Jimmy leaned back, trying to conceal a self-satisfied smirk.

Chad Collins, again thrown off rhythm, attempted to intervene. "Pastor, of course you're right. Implicit in our 'how' is our 'what.' I promise you, Pastor, the 'what' is always first and foremost."

Jimmy nodded with a sense of righteous satisfaction.

"Okay, the second phase," Tom continued. "At the end of next week, we begin the 'Planning Phase.' We determine where we are going. Then, in the days that follow, we will work on our third phase, 'Structuring.' We will figure out who does what and where. Fourth, around three months from now, we start our 'Execution Phase.' We begin to roll out our plan of action. And then finally, SynerChurch will help us with the fifth phase."

"Coaching," Chad interjected. "We will help you to develop a leadership that's fully capable to run the program. Make sense?"

Jimmy watched as his staff's heads nodded. Nothing new or revolutionary was shared, and that made everyone comfortable. Because for most, nothing new or revolutionary was all they ever really wanted.

***

Staff Conference Room B was all set up. Soft drinks, a stainless-steel bucket of ice, tea—both sweet and unsweetened—a basket filled with junior-sized chip bags, and three plastic trays of various sandwiches, no mayo. And cookies: oatmeal raisin, chocolate chip, and for Jimmy, white chocolate macadamia nut. It was standard fare for a LifePointe lunch meeting.

Everyone felt much more at ease. Chad Collins had a charming way about him in disarming the most antagonistic among them. Even Jimmy had good things to say about the past ten days.

"I can't believe you're from Portland, Chad. You genuinely seem like you know what you're doing. Shave, and I'd hire you in a hot second, brother … if only I could afford you," he said with a chuckle.

"Take it," Tom instructed Chad. "Jimmy ain't always so generous in shelling out these big kudos."

Chad laughed, not that he wanted to, but it was necessary. He then stood and liberally thanked the staff team for all their accommodations over the past two weeks. Finally, he was ready to unveil his findings.

Chad punched a key on his laptop and the video wall lit up in forest green, LifePointe's corporate colors. And then a three-dimensional heading, 'What Your People Say,' magically emerged from LifePointe's logo. The team was impressed already.

Chad warned them that this first section would require forbearance. One by one, Chad explained twenty-seven slides showing pie charts, bar graphs, and simple grid tables, all of which painted a picture of their customer's level of contentment with LifePointe Chapel. With painstaking detail, Chad reviewed his quantitative and qualitative processes in an effort to inspire his clients with the authority of his report.

But the news wasn't terrific. After Chad walked them through his complex algorithm, "Somewhat satisfied" was the cumulative score. Scores trended higher on the "likeability of the staff," but "perceived staff competence" dragged the average down. Slide number twenty-eight would only be revealed to Pastor Norris in the private consult that followed.

The next section to be reviewed was, "What the Staff Say." Again, the title magically levitated from the logo. It seemed less impressive this time.

Just seven slides; the seventh, again, reserved for Jimmy. One by one, Chad reviewed his findings. The two main categories to be discussed were "Clarity of Mission" and "Personal Commitment to the Mission." The former averaged a two point one out of a possible five. The latter came to a one point six out of five.

To cushion the emotional blow, Chad offered a carefully worded consolation. "We find that churches that are seeking to reinvent themselves often score lower in these areas. I wouldn't think of this as a problem as much as an opportunity. You could be poised for powerful new breakthroughs."

"Bull-oney," Chip Bussey authoritatively bellowed, launching his belly over the table while somewhat standing and hunching, shaking his finger at the screen. "I know I'm just the worship pastor, but I think we know what our mission is. Our mission is to worship God. It's simple, it ain't complicated, and nothing's changed. And you're saying that we ain't committed to that?"

"I'm saying, Chip, that there isn't a general consensus on exactly what LifePointe's mission is. And the lower score on 'commitment to mission' is simply a corollary to that lack of clarity. Fix one and you have a good chance of fixing the other. Does that make sense?"

Chip shrugged as noncommittally as possible.

"Okay," Chad continued. "The final category we will look at this afternoon is in the area of our personal commitment to the gospel, specifically, a commitment to disciple-making. Again, we have subcategorized this into two major groupings: 'church community' and 'staff.' I have nine slides for us to discuss together."

As he had in the previous sections, Chad outlined SynerChurch's methodologies that were baked into the analysis. Everything was designed to disclose their reality in the clearest way possible, and so, there was a heightened tension in the room. Like a class clown awaiting his parents' return from a parent-teacher interview, no one in Staff Conference Room B was at ease.

"Again, we report this as a score out of a possible five. Five being very active in sharing the gospel, on at least a monthly basis. One being that a person has shared the gospel no more than one time in their life, that they can remember."

Jimmy broke in, "So, I'm taking it that a zero would be zilcho?"

"That's right, never in their lives," Chad said. "So, the 'church community' averaged a score of zero point seven. Again, this is only from the 520 adults over eighteen who had completed the survey. But we have found that the percentage of a church community that takes the time and attention to complete the survey generally carries a higher commitment to spiritual things. On average."

Jimmy coughed. "Well, that explains some things, doesn't it?"

"Likely it does," Chad agreed. "This wouldn't be the lowest score that we've seen, by far. In fact, we've seen lower rates by several churches in this region. All larger churches than yours. But LifePointe would be in the lower thirty-fifth percentile of the churches that we've studied.

"Now to the final reporting, 'the staff's commitment to the gospel.'" And then, as if to prepare the room for bad news, Chad Collins reminded everyone of the rules. "Now let me emphatically reiterate, all of your responses are confidential, and they will remain that way. And from our commitment to confidentiality, I am so grateful for your honest candor. Honesty is critical in this process."

"Uh-oh," Chip Bussey chuckled nervously. "This can't be good."

Chad ripped through the final four slides as quickly as he could. He wasn't enjoying this, either. The trajectory of his graphs and charts were just empirical preparation for the looming wrecking ball that was waiting to be released. The moment no longer felt like a child waiting for a parent-teacher interview but more like a traitor waiting for a firing squad.

"And so, the staff, as defined in this case by the 'pastoral team,' including those four plucky interns, and deducting for the halo effect, is at a rate of zero point nine. Actually, zero point eight five, but we rounded up."

"Halo effect?" Tom asked.

"Well, not to get too deep into the weeds of qualitative research, but there is a tendency, when our reputations or our employment are at risk, to self-report 'illusory superiority.'"

"Meaning?" Tom pressed.

"Meaning, we tend to exaggerate. If we're proficient in one field, and because we perceive another field is important, we tend to overstate our prowess. It's unconscious. Nobody is fibbing. A chemistry professor, because he's a remarkable research scientist, assumes he is an enthralling lecturer—which is often not the case."

Chad paused for comments. None came.

"So, from years of research, we have concluded that a deduction of zero point seven from employment-related self-reporting gets us in the ballpark of reality. But in your case, our research team in Portland decided that might be too high. So, we reduced our deduction to zero point two."

"Because a standard deduction would have wiped us out?" Tom asked.

"Well, it would have been close."

Total silence. No one dared move their eyes from the forest-green colored slide. No one except Chip.

"Well … at least we brought up the church average. That's something," he said in a hollow attempt to lighten the mood.

But nobody laughed.

And then Jimmy slowly stood to his feet. With no hint of a smile, he looked into the eyes of his teammates. "I shared my faith at least two times in the last month. I told you about both of them, Shaun and Michael, and asked you to pray," he said with no inflection. "Chad, you mean to tell me that my pastoral team's evangelism rate is less than one gospel conversation in their lifetime? Less than one?"

"Yes."

"Well, Mr. Chad Collins of Portland, Oregon. You were worth your forty grand just in these last five minutes."

And then Jimmy gathered his things and quietly walked out of Staff Conference Room B.

"Brother. Brother, are you now with us?" said an unfamiliar figure hunching over Omar.

Omar, propped up in a corner, slumping, legs straight out on a concrete floor, began to regain consciousness.

"Who are you?"

"Praise be to Isa! My name is Hussein Nazari from Sanaa. It's so wonderful to hear you speak."

"How long have I been out?"

"Since yesterday afternoon. We did our best to stop the bleeding. We had nothing but pieces of our clothes."

Omar struggled to focus. His pulse thumped painfully within his head. He hurt everywhere.

"There are five of us. With you, we are six."

As he began to introduce his cellmates, Omar's head fell. He passed out again.

The Extrajudicial Detention Center was located outside the village of Rida, safely out of the public eye, tucked away forty-five minutes down a dirt trail southeast of Dhamar. It was a self-contained clay brick compound consisting of five main rooms. There was an office, sleeping quarters for CSO officers, two cells, and an interrogation room.

The cells were roughly the same dimensions as the interrogation room, each about thirteen feet square. There was one small window at the top of the brick wall, too high to see anything, but it allowed evening sunlight to enter and warm the room. In the far corner, opposite the window, there was a gray steel bucket, which served as the common lavatory. And there was a non-functioning grimy white porcelain sink that was fastened to the wall. This was used by the prisoners as a urinal because it had a direct line to the septic tank. And then there was a heavy brown steel door with a hatch at the bottom, and a small window at eye level. The two cells were constructed opposite each other, separated by a narrow corridor.

It was their temporary home.

Thirty minutes later, Omar, obviously concussed, began to regain consciousness once again. He made some grunting sounds, and then struggled to open his swollen eyes.

Hussein, squatting by his side and all smiles, said, "Did you find my company so boring, brother? People usually wait a few minutes before trying to escape me."

"Who are you? Where am I?"

"I am Hussein Nazari from Sanaa. Where we are is a mystery. Prison. Somewhere south of Dhamar, we think."

Memories as distant flashes began to return to Omar. "The red room. Where are my bindings?"

"We untied you. We took cords from the ropes to fasten the

bandages. It's not beautiful, but it should work." And then he gestured to a prisoner leaning against the door. "Rahim is our doctor."

Omar lifted his heavy arms and began to touch his dressings. Cloth on his forehead. On his jaw. His left forearm was wrapped and tied. As was his left knee.

Rahim, now squatting opposite of Hussein, said softly, "You won't be as handsome as you once were, but you'll live." He paused and then added, "At least for a little while."

"I'm so thirsty," Omar croaked, his throat and tongue heavy with dehydration.

"We saved you our water," said Rahim.

Hussein handed Omar a large steel pitcher. "Drink, brother, drink."

And he did drink. Slowly at first. But he didn't stop. He drank until it was gone.

"Thank you, brothers." And then, looking into the faces that surrounded him, with two words he acknowledged the sacrifice that just took place. "Thank you."

"You're most welcome, brother," Hussein replied, speaking for all. "Now, if you're up to it, why don't you tell us about yourself. Maybe start with what we should call you."

Omar managed a chuckle. Everything hurt.

"My name is Omar Al-Khulani from Bani Bali. I am a student at the University of Aden studying the law. And I follow Isa Al-Masih. I have for almost a half a year. And this is my crime."

Dr. Rahim smiled and said, "Well brother Omar, welcome. In here you are among fellow prisoners of Isa. Criminals all. Convicted, without the benefit of a trial. Condemned for blasphemy against Allah. Together we are the most secret of all secret communities in Yemen. But we are also the only ones that wish not to add new disciples to our group. Please, brother, if you're strong enough, tell us your Isa story."

Omar began to recount his spiritual pilgrimage. He told them of the campus political group, his taste of wine, and his attempt at absolution. He told them about Yushua, and Muhammad, and the secret community, and his newfound forgiveness. He started to tell them about his sister, Fatimah, and her sickness. But he couldn't. All he could do was weep.

Hussein scooted beside Omar, carefully wrapped his long arm around him, and comforted him as he wept. And Hussein wept with him.

After several minutes, Omar began to regain his composure.

"I'm so sorry, brothers. They shot my sister, Fatimah, just after Isa healed her. And they shot all the brothers and sisters in our community. And it was my fault. They all died because of me." He began to sob deeply once again. "I do not know why they spared my life. Death would have been less painful than what I feel now."

This time Hussein interrupted him. "Brother, you are not right in this. You may be important, but you are not that important. Neither Fatimah, nor your brothers and sisters, died because of you. They all died because of Isa Al-Masih, and now they live because of him. It's important for you to have this thing straight in your thinking. You are not responsible for them, and you must be thankful you still live. King Isa never makes a mistake."

He waited a minute or two for Omar to regain control, and then said, "Brother Omar, let me tell you our Isa story, which is now your story. Would that be good?"

Omar nodded, wiping the tears from his cheeks.

"Of the six of us, I am the longest serving prisoner. Tomorrow, Friday, will be my fifth week. Our esteemed Dr. Rahim is the second longest serving prisoner. He registered into our membership three days after me. Do you know what this means, Omar?"

Omar shook his head.

"It means that tomorrow, Friday, at sundown, I will join Fatimah and the good people of your secret community. I will also rejoin my wife, Haifa, and our three beautiful children. And I will see Isa. I will see him face to face. So, I will be taken into the red room, and they will try to persuade me against my 'blasphemy.' You have already tasted a little of how they entice faithfulness to Islam. But it will be much worse. They use steam. They rape. And they do things that I will not say. And if they convince me, if I deny Isa Al-Masih, they will return me to my village, they say. Safe and somewhat sound, they tell us, but I think that I will see your Fatimah instead."

"Every Friday at sundown," Rahim agreed. "In the order of our incarceration, they march us ..."

Just then there were three loud bangs on the door. The prisoners, instinctively as one, got up and faced the wall by the window. Omar followed suit. Hussein called out, "We are ready, sir." Then the door opened, something clanked on the floor, and the door closed again.

"My final love feast," Hussein said as he gestured to dinner.

It was a steel bowl of cold, grayish gruel, a loaf, and a steel pitcher of water. The prisoners gathered in a circle around their meal, held hands, and bowed their heads.

Dr. Rahim offered thanks. "Gracious, heavenly Father, we thank you for the food and for the drink you have given us. You have given it to us so our bodies might have the strength they need to be faithful to you, until our last breath."

And then Dr. Rahim picked up the small brown loaf, broke it in half, placed one half back in the gruel and passed the other half to his left. Each prisoner broke off a small piece and held it. And then, in unison, they all offered thanks.

Hussein broke in, "Merciful Father, as we eat the bread, we

remember Isa, the one who was tortured for us for his charge of blasphemy. We take in Isa's life."

Quietly, soberly, the six prisoners ate the body of Christ.

"Ameen."

Dr. Rahim then lifted the steel pitcher of water up to his face. "Brothers, this drink represents the blood of Isa, spilled by his tormentors, for a truth that they didn't want to believe."

Hussein prayed once again. "Father, Abba, we have but one life to give, and we happily surrender it to you. Our torturers are deceived by darkness. They do not understand your love. May our deaths show them the Truth found only in Isa Al-Masih, our Redeemer. We drink now, remembering the One who spilled his blood for our sins, for our forgiveness. We take in Isa's blood."

Dr. Rahim took a slow drink from the pitcher and passed it to his left.

An "ameen" followed each prisoner's drink.

And then something astonishing happened. Something Omar wasn't prepared for. The prisoners escorted Hussein to a spot against the wall where the early evening sun warmed the clay bricks. He sat quietly. And then Dr. Rahim handed him the half loaf that was left in the gruel and said, "Brother, so that you will have the strength to endure to the very end, please eat."

The five silently watched as Hussein ate. The finality of this scene deeply stirred Omar as he watched his new friend, and now his mentor in death, taste his final meal. The serenity of his spirit was shocking. Omar was beginning to understand in a fuller way something about the power of the kingdom of God.

And then Dr. Rahim handed Hussein the steel bowl and the wooden spoon and said, "Brother, eat this for your strength. We know it is not good, but remember, your next meal will be a glorious banquet with Isa Al-Masih in paradise."

The six boldly and loudly shouted "ameen, ameen, ameen," as a statement of unwavering belief.

The next twenty-four hours were unlike any day Omar had ever lived. The five, who had at least seven times longer to live, fasted. Fasted and prayed. The small sustenance that was rationed to the little band was earmarked exclusively for the nourishment and resolve of Hussein Nazari. And that resolve was further fortified by the grieving friends stooping round-shouldered and laying their hands on his head with desperate prayers for boldness, faith, and spiritual power.

But much of that day was about sharing strength in the other direction. Hussein spoke passionately to his friends as a man whose words were now in short supply. He spoke of the coming kingdom they all longed for. A place where Isa's perfect plan reigned supremely over everything and everyone. He spoke of the present kingdom that was being revealed in their cell in the most beautiful and formidable way. Clay bricks and a heavy steel door became the sanctuary of a common allegiance to the most high God.

But most of all, he spoke of their common King. "Brothers," he said. "The kingdom of God is the ultimate reality. It is the truth of the Truth. It is all of God's handiwork working according to God's design. It's what everything looks like when King Isa gets his way."

He paused for a moment to allow his deep words to find a place in their minds. And then he continued, "For the days you have left, brothers—whether they be few or many—live your lives as if the Truth were the truth."

For his final hour, Hussein recited the words of Isa's Sermon on the Mount as if they were his own. The three chapters he had committed to memory as a younger man now became the words of a ministering angel giving guidance and strength to those who would soon follow in his fate. The words powerfully fell from his mouth as if they were spoken by King Isa Al-Masih himself.

"Now when he saw the crowds, he went up on a mountainside and sat down. His disciples came to him, and he began to teach them. He said, 'Blessed are the poor in spirit, for theirs is the kingdom of heaven. Blessed are those who mourn, for they will be comforted. Blessed are the meek, for they will inherit the earth. Blessed are those who hunger and thirst for righteousness, for they will be filled. Blessed are the merciful, for they will be shown mercy. Blessed are the pure in heart, for they will see God. Blessed are the peacemakers, for they will be called children of God. Blessed are those who are persecuted for righteousness, for theirs is the kingdom of heaven. Blessed are you when people insult you, persecute you and falsely say all kinds of evil against you because of me. Rejoice and be glad, because great is your reward in heaven, for in the same way they persecuted the prophets who were before you…'"

Omar was spellbound. He knew these words well as he had read and reread them in his little Bible of fishing line and black tape. For several minutes he forgot that he himself was imprisoned under a death sentence. He forgot that it was a condemned man who was doing the speaking. He could only see Isa. Transfixed, he raised his hands in the air and with a broad smile whispered, "You are my King, Isa. My only King," as if Isa himself were sitting on concrete in their midst.

Hussein paused for a moment, smiled, and said, "Ameen, my young brother. Ameen." And then with closed eyes, he raised his hands as he concluded, "But everyone who hears these words of mine and does not put them into practice is like a foolish man who built his house on sand. The rain came down, the streams rose, and the winds blew and beat against that house, and it fell with a great crash."

"May we do your words, King Isa," said Omar. "May we do your words, King Isa," repeated the six. "May we do your ..."

And then three unnerving booms reverberated from the steel door. The prisoners instinctively sprang up and faced the clay brick wall.

Hussein, with a quiet, gentle voice said, "I am ready, sir."

Chapter Eight

The Messenger

To someone unfamiliar with Philadelphia, Strawberry Mansion might sound like a charming place to put down roots. And it was. Once. Named after a restaurant that famously served strawberries and heavy cream, it was once the center of the city's wealthiest families. And it was Jewish. Very Jewish. At one time, this prosperous enclave had boasted twenty-one vibrant synagogues as Jewish families relocated to put distance between themselves and the problems of crowded South Philly. But like many neighborhoods in Philadelphia, it had changed. The Jewish immigrants who had built this community left for homes in Oxford Circle, Overbrook Park, and West Oak Lane/Mt. Airy. And in doing so, they left behind their history written in brick and stone.

Their once stately park-side mansion homes now sat as eerie monuments to more prosperous days as they posed against greenspace in various states of disrepair. Over the years, several attempts of community gentrification had taken place, but the fad never seemed to stick. Some blamed the persistent crime rates. Others complained that housing values appreciated much too slowly. For whatever the reason, the first wave of artists, bohemians, and sexual nomads was not followed by the usual funky coffee shops, lawyers, bankers, and Whole Foods. Instead, Strawberry Mansion preserved its function as the city's melting pot. Once primarily a community of gritty survivors of the ancestors of the southern slave trade, it was now diversifying, becoming home to new immigrants from around the globe who were searching for a better life.

To Luca Lewis, Strawberry Mansion had always been home sweet home. Without exception, he had lived his entire life in this community. And until his recent promotion as executive director of the Fishtown Y, his work career had taken place wholly within its boundaries. It was ground zero for his personal history because it was here that his papa, the Reverend Dr. Josiah Lewis, had poured out his life's energy.

But for a life's work of a conscientious and competent cleric, there was precious little to show for it. His failed red brick church building stood as testimony to that. And now, the Liberty Village Lofts awaited, to assume the occupied earth of the defunct Mt. Pisgah Baptist Church as another attempt at community gentrification. And even though the jury was out as to its likely success, the question of Luca's papa's success appeared entirely decided. The iron wrecking ball at the construction site awaiting a permit stood as an irrefutable testament to that.

Kofe and Angelica Wilson had also grown up in this neighborhood. Both were raised under the spiritual mantle of Mt. Pisgah and shared in Dr. Lewis' dream of becoming a different kind of church—one that was seen by the community as good news. And both became deeply disillusioned after the Marcus E. Robinson affair, known by those who were hurt the most deeply as "The Insurrection." But they never lost faith. Not completely at least. Their faith in their Savior faltered from time to time but ultimately remained. However, they did lose their affection for church. And this spiritual no-man's-land, as Kofe put it, was an extremely uncomfortable place to live. They often felt an inner compulsion to share how Jesus could help their friends and colleagues in the neighborhood. But without a community to buttress and validate their words, it all sounded a bit hollow.

So, when Luca and Chantel invited them to join them in this new adventure, the pieces started to fall back into place. And for the first time in years, they found themselves becoming spiritually hopeful.

Angelica worked as a beautician at the Queen Bee. Her pink vinyl chair was a counseling couch, a community information kiosk, and an evangelist's pulpit all at once. Because of this, appointments were merely suggested times, as she just couldn't keep herself from entering into the lives of those who came to her Bee. It was a rare occasion when she was on schedule, but few ever complained. Angelica had a way with people.

Kofe had followed Luca's footsteps to the Y, where he ended up replacing him as assistant director in charge of Youth and Family Activities. Luca shaped this position to provide the kind of services and activities that connected with the people in the neighborhood. And so Kofe built upon that foundation with his own personal flair. Where Luca was more of the strategic mastermind, Kofe was the effervescent, warm-hearted friend who disarmed everyone he met. As Pastor Lewis used to say, "If you got a problem with Kofe Wilson then you can be certain that *you* are the problem!"

The Strawberry Mansion Y was part of a pilot project that physically connected the community sports complex to an at-risk middle school. The idea envisioned that student engagement with after-school activities could provide life-changing natural mentorships that would keep kids in school. As Luca began to help sell this idea to private foundations, he didn't mince words: "If you're not in school in our neighborhood, you'll either be in prison or the cemetery." Checks soon followed.

And so, E. Digby Baltzell Middle School, through a consortium of public and private grants, became one of the fortunate guinea pigs of this pilot project. This strategically positioned Kofe not only as director of programming, but as the informal liaison between the Strawberry Y and E. Digby Baltzell Middle School, or "the Dig," as it was known in the community. In this capacity, Kofe had his thumb on the very pulse of Strawberry Mansion.

And this would open the doors to everything.

"So, it's settled. No sense sittin' on a nest egg. We'll give ourselves away to the 'Strawberry Dig' and see what Jesus does." Luca smiled as he rubbed his beefy hands together. "And I don't know about y'all, but I've never been more excited about 'church.'"

The team was starting to come together. Instead of dividing responsibilities for a Sunday service they were building a team that, together, resembled Jesus. Luca, who was perpetually casting vision, opened his papa's well-worn Bible to Ephesians chapter four and read, "And he gave the apostles, the prophets, the evangelists, the shepherds and teachers, to equip the saints for the work of ministry, for building up the body of Christ."

"The purpose of those five equipping functions is to form Christ's body in a community," Luca explained. "The apostle function is a missionary task: Send the gospel to places where it isn't."

"Well, that sure sounds like you, Luca," Jerome interrupted. "And Patterson's Jewelers isn't that far away."

"Ain't that the truth." Luca continued, "The prophet function is speaking God's truth. Measuring everything we teach and everything we do against God's Word and God's mission for us."

"So, who's leading the prophet function for us?" Angelica asked.

"I dunno," said Luca. "I think we gotta pray that one in. I definitely lean this way, as some might have noticed, but we need someone who'll give it full attention."

The group brainstormed for a few minutes, throwing out

possible names. But in the end, there was agreement. No one embodied this passion to a high enough degree. Prayer would be their answer.

"Evangelists equip us to share the good news in ways that feel, taste, smell, look, and sound like good news."

"So, none of us have to become spittin' preachers?" Chantel asked. "Glory be! What a relief," she said with a wink.

"Only Kofe and Angelica," Luca said wryly. "They're our evangelists. We'll pitch a nice ole white canvas tent for them behind the Dig. Let 'em go to town!"

The small band of disciples meeting in the Lewis' townhome laughed with a free and unbridled spirit. There was a freshness and sense of excitement about their new community and its mission. They were genuinely happy to be banded together.

Choyz Jackson chimed in. "So, Jerome and I would be the shepherds. We would gather the sheep and make sure none of them get lost."

"Close," said Luca. "You won't be the shepherds. You will equip the body to shepherd itself. Make sense? You will organize us and train 'shepherdy people' to ensure that needs are being met and nobody falls through the cracks, but there's a whole lot more to it."

"More?" Choyz asked.

"Yes, I think that it's important to keep your goal front and center," Luca continued. "Do you know what the goal of a shepherd is?"

"To feed and protect and care for the sheep?" Jerome replied tentatively, sensing that this was too obvious of an answer.

"Nope. That's a shepherd's means to the goal, but it's never the goal. No shepherd thinks it's his goal to coddle fat ole stanky sheep. The shepherd's goal is to multiply his flock. That's how he makes a living; nurturing an 'un-reproducing' flock is the shepherd's quickest path to the poor house. Everything that a wise shepherd does is designed to reproduce more cute, fluffy little lambs."

Jerome closed his eyes as he voiced aloud his new paradigm, "So we care for the sheep, so that the sheep will make more …"

"Disciples," Choyz interrupted. "Except, our job is to equip shepherds to create environments where disciples are reproduced."

Luca smiled a fatherly smile. He could see that lightbulbs were coming on.

"That leads us to the last of the five: teacher. My papa used to say that the last two, shepherd and teacher, were attached together in the Greek. While that probably is the case, the two words describe different things. They explain different actions, different functions, and different giftings. So, we will treat them that way."

"So, who's our teacher?" Choyz asked.

"Again, just to be rock solid sure that we are all on the same page, we're not looking for a Bible instructor to teach us, are we?" Luca asked in a teaching sort of manner.

"Okay, let me clarify, 'apostle' Lewis," Choyz said, laughing. "Who will equip the emerging teachers among us?"

"Perfect, Choyz, perfect!" Luca exclaimed, clapping his big, thick hands together. "And the answer to your question is simple. I have no earthly idea. Not a clue. But if I were a betting man, I'd lay money that they're somewhere in the Dig lookin' for the gospel."

"Better get my white tent set up," Kofe said with a twinkle in his eye. "Looks like we got us a teacher to find."

"We can do better than that, brother," said Luca. "Many of us been sockin' away our tithes. We didn't know what to do with 'em. Chantel and I have put away a fair bit—10 percent of your pay adds up after a while—and I know many of y'all have been doing the same. Let's put it all together. Let Choyz and Chantel be in charge to keep things honest. And let's meet every legitimate need that we find in the Strawberry Dig."

"In the name of Jesus," Angelica added.

"Amen. Only in the name of Jesus."

Omar reflexively snapped and unsnapped the shiny buttons of his heavy wool tunic. Deep in thought, he stared blankly at the clay brick wall as if it were a window to better days. He thought of his friends, Yushua, Muhammad, and the community in Aden. His friends, now gone, from the community in Dhamar. And his friends, fellow blasphemers for Isa, who once occupied this cell. And he thought of Fatimah.

Although his life had been shorter than he had anticipated, what it lacked in days it more than made up for in wonder. His last six months had been filled with a greater joy than he had ever thought possible. He wouldn't have traded this short time for a thousand more years without Isa. And even knowing what tomorrow would bring, even with all he had experienced in his last days, his heart was peacefully at rest.

The heavy tunic had once belonged to Dr. Rahim, but it had been keeping Omar warm over the last four weeks. Dr. Rahim had brushed it as clean as he could, hung it by the window in the warm evening's sun to freshen it, and then folded it neatly and presented it to Omar on his last day. "May this tunic bring warmth to your body as you have brought warmth to my spirit, young brother," he said. Omar smiled as he remembered that moment.

Although new prisoners were added to the cell across the corridor, Omar was now alone in his. One by one, he had helped strengthen the next sufferer before their upcoming inquisition. One by one, he heard the terrible sounds of a friend's pain-filled cries barely dampened by clay brick walls. And one by one they disappeared. Until only he was left. Alone.

But these past seven days of solitude were not always moments of peace and serenity. There were also moments of great despair. Yesterday's "love feast" went uncelebrated. Omar's attentions were darkened by thoughts of his father's treachery. *What kind of a man would kill his own children?* was a question that often filled his mind in his greatest moments of anguish. And soon a greater doubt would form: *And what kind of a God would allow it?*

For today, though, on this last day, Omar's spirit was completely at peace. Dinner would soon arrive, and Omar was ready to celebrate communion. A common union, but uniquely alone. Alone with Isa. He absentmindedly snapped the tunic buttons open and closed, as his mind drifted to thoughts of paradise. What would heaven be like? Would he see Fatimah? Would she recognize him? How could so many people see Isa all at once? Would he be close like a friend, or distant like a—

A piercing siren shrieked loudly outside the compound. Guards started yelling and scurrying around. Doors were banging, men cursing, and the prisoners across the corridor were slapping the steel door.

"What is happening?" Omar asked aloud as if someone were there to answer.

And then, after a few minutes, the sirens stopped.

Omar pushed his face up to the small opening in the steel door to see if he could see what was happening. There were no sounds at all. Everything was quiet. He could see a face peering through the cell door opposite him, and he asked, "What is it? What happened?"

"We do not know. It seems the guards have abandoned us. Through our window we could see them driving off with great speed," said the voice. "I am Abdul. With me are Emir and Hakim."

"Why are you here, Abdul?" Omar asked.

"We are Hadi political prisoners from the disputed territory. But maybe we are all free?"

"Maybe," said Omar. "I hope so."

Omar and Abdul peered through the small window for hours. They shared their stories with one another. And though Abdul was a devout and faithful Saudi, he didn't seem to look at Omar as an infidel or dog but, more compassionately, as a fellow sufferer. Abdul was replaced by Hakim. Then Emir. But there was no movement outside of their cells. Nothing but the eerie silence of the wind blowing dust and sand against outside walls.

A day slowly passed, and Omar's fear of the red room was replaced with a greater fear of a slow and agonizing death from dehydration. The roof of his mouth and the back of his throat began to burn. He was so thirsty. He wished he had rationed his water, but he had imagined a different ending than this. His tongue searched the seam of the steel gruel bowl in a vain effort to find a droplet of trapped moisture. Nothing. It had now been two days since the last bang on the door. Two days without water. Omar drifted to sleep.

The morning light shone its familiar faded ray across the concrete ceiling. Omar stood with unsteady legs and walked yet again to the door. "Maybe someone will come," he wished aloud. "Isa, send someone."

And then, in the distance, he heard something. Voices. Happy voices. Laughter. *Women's voices? No, no, different. Children's voices*, Omar concluded. He pressed his face against the wire mesh with hopes of an immediate rescue. He stared at the door to the red room. *They must walk through. They must come through.*

More agonizing minutes inched past and still nothing. The voices had not disappeared, but they had become quieter. "Are they leaving? They cannot leave," he said aloud. "Dear Isa, bring them back. Please bring them back!"

Just then the door from the red room swung open with a booming crash. A gang of ten or twelve raggedy adolescents, probably orphans, began to meander into the corridor. Omar from one side and Emir from the other began to plead with their potential rescuers, "Please help us …"

The tallest, who appeared to be the leader, walked up to Emir and asked, "What you give us if we let you out?"

"Anything, everything, little brother!"

"What you have?"

"Nothing with us in prison, but we have money at home," said Emir.

"Nothing? Then I give you this …" and he spit in Emir's eyes. "You like this?"

The little gang giggled enthusiastically.

Omar was unwilling to give up. "Please, little brother, show mercy. We haven't had water in over two days."

"You need water? You should say. I give you water." He walked up to Omar and spit through the window into his face. "There, you have water now!"

The children laughed triumphantly as they left the corridor, through the red room, and out of the prison.

"No!" Omar cried. "Isa, have mercy!"

The children's voices faded into the distance. And hope faded with them.

But then there was a noise. A tiny clicking noise. Omar looked through the window but could see nothing.

More clicking. *It is the lock. Someone, or something, is working the lock,* Omar thought. "Hello?" Omar said. "Is there someone out there?"

Clicking and rattling was the only response.

"Hello? Hello?"

Nothing. And then a clunk.

The door gently pressed open. It was a little girl. A little, disheveled girl, no more than five years old. Her tattered clothes were filthy, but her face and hair were spotless. Bright. And she beamed with the most beautiful smile. So innocent, so beautiful, almost the face of an angel.

"Thank you," Omar said gently. Softly. "Can I help you, little one?"

Holding out the key ring in her little pudgy hand, she said, "Isa sent me, Omar. Isa sends you."

She turned around and skipped out of the corridor and into the red room.

Omar was stunned. The message was more surprising than the unexpected rescue.

"Wait! Come back, child. Please."

He stumbled into the red room, but he couldn't see her. He ran into the office. Nothing. He went into the guard's quarters, but she wasn't there. He limped outside into the compound and looked around. She was gone. She had vanished.

He knelt in the dust, with no thoughts of his thirst, and wept. Overcome by the trauma and emotional turmoil of the last weeks, Omar let go completely. Face in the dirt, he cried dry tears until he was utterly out of strength.

And then, kneeling prostrate in the dirt, he heard something. Faint noises from within the prison. Abdul, Emir, and Hakim were calling out. Omar shakily gathered himself from the dirt and walked into the prison. Clasping the key ring the little girl had given him, he scanned the office. There was a refrigerator. Opening it he saw it was full of plastic water bottles. Grabbing four, he made his way to the cells.

"Omar, brother, what is this? How did you get out?" Abdul asked.

"You didn't see?" Omar asked as he unlocked their prison door and swung it open.

"How did you escape?" Emir repeated.

"The little orphan girl. Did you not see her?"

"No, brother. We heard you say, 'hello, hello,' but we saw no one."

"There was a little girl. You didn't see the little girl? Dirty clothes? Glowing face? You didn't see?"

"No, brother."

"No? She was five years, maybe. She opened the door and gave me keys. You didn't see this?"

"We heard you speak, and we saw your door swing open. That is all," said Emir.

"Did she say anything? Did she say where she was from? Or where we are, perhaps?" Abdul asked.

"Yes, she did say one thing. She said, 'Isa sent me, Omar. Isa sends you.'"

Omar's three dehydrated fellow prisoners were bewildered. "'Isa sent me, Omar. Isa sends you'?" Abdul repeated.

"Yes. And then she gave me the keys."

"Where is she?" Emir asked.

"She walked back into the red room and then vanished. I checked every room and the compound. She disappeared."

"To paradise?" asked Emir.

"I don't know, brothers. I don't know where she is. But I do know who sent her to us."

"Isa," said Emir.

Omar handed out the bottles of water. "Yes, Isa Al-Masih sent her to us. And brothers, you must always remember who it was that saved you. It was Isa Al-Masih. And I think he has work for you."

***

"Have you opened it yet?" Jimmy asked. "Be honest, Tommy. Take a little peek?"

"No, sir. I don't think that this message was intended for my eyes first," Tom answered. "Besides, I didn't have to stare down the jackals to pay for it."

"Jackals, ha! Or jackasses. Don't remind me. Board PTSD isn't that easy to shake off."

Jimmy and Tom had booked the day to review the recommendations of Chad Collins and the SynerChurch Group. They wanted solitude away from prying eyes and endless problem-solving, so they booked two junior suites and a small conference room at the Marriott by the airport, a full hour away from LifePointe. Their plan was to thoroughly review Chad's research and then begin to draw up some preliminary action responses in light of his investigation.

"Here it is, signed, sealed, and now, delivered." Tom flopped the thick manilla envelope on the table.

"The forty-thousand-dollar gold-plated keys to the kingdom. They better open something worth having," he said dryly. Jimmy carefully pulled the quarter ream of reports from the envelope. "You'd think those liberals from the left coast would send a digital copy. Save a stinkin' forest."

"They did, but they were sending a hard copy anyway," answered Tom.

"Hope it's worth the sequoia." Jimmy started fanning through the pages. "Well, let's see what Mr. Forty K Collins has to say …"

The report itself was divided into four main sections. First, ministry engagement. Are LifePointe's strategies to reach the community appropriate and/or effective? Second, staffing and leadership. Is LifePointe's staffing/leadership strategically appropriate and/or competent? Third, connectivity. Are the people of LifePointe relationally connected with leadership and with one another? Fourth, finances. Is LifePointe in a healthy financial position in weekly giving and cash reserves? Each section included data from the corresponding slides that Chad had previously reviewed with the staff. It also included the undisclosed slides that Chad discussed with Jimmy the following day. Finally, the SynerChurch Group made a series of recommendations as possible remedies to shore up areas of weakness.

"Here goes, Tommy. Buckle up; this won't be pretty."

Jimmy's lips were moving as he read through the first section on ministry engagement. Tom, as usual, was hovering by the whiteboard, marker in hand, ready to draft a table, a list, or a flow chart. Whatever the intelligence required.

He pulled off his readers and began to gesture with them toward Tom. "So, it looks like 91 percent of our Sunday attendance has either been attending a church for twenty years or more or is a kid of someone who has attended for twenty years or more. Seven percent have attended ten to twenty years. That means ..."

"We suck," Tom interrupted. "We totally suck."

"It sure sounds like we do. I knew we were aging, and I knew we weren't reaching many. But I had no idea it was this bad. Ninety-eight percent. Sheesh."

Jimmy put his readers back on. "Let me scan the next section."

Tom formatted Jimmy's highlights on the whiteboard while Jimmy flipped through more pages of the report.

"Okay, Tom, ready for this? The most liked staff member, and the one that's perceived as most competent is—can you guess who?"

"I'm hoping it's you, Jimmy."

"Nope. Not even close. I'm in the middle of the pack on both counts. Ready for this? It's Chip Bussey. Numero uno on both."

Tom's marker arm drooped lifelessly down, leaving a small green stripe on the knee of his dockers. "Chip? That dude? Chip

Bussey? If he couldn't sing, he'd be working somebody's drive-thru. Is he even saved? Chip Bus ... Are you sure? The same guy that collects porcelain cats? That Chip Bussey?"

"Apparently, the hard work of quoting the chorus of your next song in a sultry, breathy voice really connects with our target demographic," Jimmy said without smiling. "Who knew?"

"So, where am I in this meaningful ranking?"

"Trust me, my friend, you don't want to know the answer to that."

"Well, if it's on the opposite end of Chip Bussey, maybe that ain't all that bad. Good grief. Well, I'm depressed now."

As Jimmy returned to thumbing through the thick stack of paper, Tom walked up to the whiteboard, uncapped his marker, and stared blankly, hoping that the lovely, glistening sheen might spark a helpful categorization. But nothing came.

"You see, this is what I don't get." Jimmy pulled off his readers once again. "How can it be that our staff has no clarity on our mission? We drafted the stinkin' statement together. We hit it almost every staff meeting. Every year I preach an entire sermon on our vision. It's written in gaudy stainless-steel three-dimensional letters in our main entrance. Why's it not sinking in?"

Tom took a deep breath. Exhaled slowly. And then gently said, "I think I have an idea on that, Jimmy. What's our mission statement?"

"'Helping our friends and neighbors find their way back to God.' It hasn't changed since we came."

"Do you believe in this mission?"

"What? Yes, of course I do. I came up with it."

"How much do you believe it?"

"Like on a scale from one to five? Five. Five. Five!" Jimmy wasn't amused with Tom's line of questioning.

"Five. Okay. Stay with me, Jimmy," Tom said slowly, in an attempt to lower Jimmy's blood pressure. "So, without any reservation, you believe that our church's assignment is to help our congregation to be able to guide their friends and neighbors to Jesus, right?"

"Okay . . ." Jimmy said with a sense that he could see where Tom was heading.

"So, what have we changed? What substantial things have we changed about LifePointe to make that mission possible?" Tom recapped the green marker and turned to face the whiteboard to give his friend a moment with his thoughts.

Jimmy took a long pause as he stared at the whiteboard. Holding his head with his elbows planted on his knees, he said, "We really haven't changed anything. We've tweaked, but nothing has substantially changed. Things are pretty much the same as they were before we came. We're just better at it now."

"And that's why Chip is the hero and you're not: we've tweaked everything in Chip's favor. It's a big feel-good show. Chippy gets up there and does his big razzle dazzle and has 'em eating out of the palm of his hand."

"He is a showman, that's for sure," Jimmy agreed.

"And then you get up there and preach an uncomfortable sermon on our mission. And who really wants that? Everything's set up for Chip."

"And nothing that we do is set up for our mission."

"Almost nothing," Tom agreed. "Other than a sermon every now and then. Nothing structurally is in place to advance our mission. In fact, our structure opposes our mission."

"You're right, Tom. Even though our worship service is pretty 'seeker friendly,' it's a rare day when a seeker shows up."

Tom, now tapping his marker against his khakis, said, "And why would they? Church is for church people. Librarians don't tailgate at NASCAR. Ultimate Fighting fans don't sip with their pinkies up at wine tastings."

"That's not a thing," Jimmy said dryly.

"Maybe not, but you get my point."

"Everything we do is for us," interrupted Jimmy. "Our Bible-study groups are for church people. Our ministry groups are for church people. Our concerts are for church people. Our children's events are for the kids of church people. Even our softball teams are in the church league. It's all for us."

"That's why 'mission clarity' is an issue. We have the right mission, brother. It's just that everything else we do buries that mission."

"I need a cigarette," Jimmy said in a humorous attempt to hide his distress. "I may need more than a cigarette."

Tom placed his green marker on the whiteboard's aluminum ledge. "Let's knock it off for tonight and get back at it in the morning. Don't know 'bout you, but I've got a big ole hankering for some chicken fried steak."

"It does seem like a good time for grease and gravy, doesn't it? Maybe we'll get blessed with a massive coronary."

"C'mon, Jimmy, it ain't that bad."

The next morning, Jimmy and Tom reconvened in the Marriott's small boardroom. Fresh ice water in pitchers and hotel branded pads and pens were once again carefully placed by every chair as if they were expecting a dozen guests. And more pastries were laid out on two large platters, carefully displayed atop white cloths against the red mahogany credenza.

"Maybe I should have worked out," Jimmy said as he grabbed a powdered-sugar bear claw. "I eat like a porker when I'm depressed."

Tom started out. "Last night I cracked open the file Chad sent. Read through it all. Read it a couple of times. It was very eye-opening."

"So, you saw how highly the good folks at LifePointe value you. I'm sorry, brother," Jimmy said in a sincere attempt to console.

"Naw, that stung a bit at first, but I got to thinking. They don't know me. I just represent everything that makes 'em uncomfortable. When do they see me? Budget time. Fundraising campaigns. Whenever we appeal for personal sacrifice. I'm the face that interrupts their cozy nap. I wouldn't like me either if I were them. We set everything up for their benefit, and a couple times a year I show up to tell them that there's a price to pay."

"Hmm, that makes sense in a twisted sort of way," Jimmy said as he licked the powdered sugar off his fingers. "So, we got to turn up the heat. All of us turn up the heat. Even Chippy. Especially Chippy."

Tom continued in the only way he could: logically. He began to lay out a case that came to him throughout his sleepless night. "Remember our staff's evangelism numbers?"

"Ah, can't forget that bit of amazing news," Jimmy said as he got up and walked over to the pastries and picked out a chocolate glazed.

"So, how's a team ..." Tom paused to gather his swirling thoughts into a coherent idea. "How is a team who shares their faith less than once per lifetime, on average, supposed to turn up the missionary heat? How would that be possible? There's something fundamentally missing, Jimmy. How is Chip Bussey supposed to be part of our answer?"

"I see that, but I can't fire them. The Chip Busseys are holding all the ... 'chips.'" Even Jimmy didn't like his pun. "You're at the bottom of the popularity pile, and I'm not much better off. If I make a move to correct this, there will be one heck of an explosion within LifePointe."

"You're right. An explosion that neither of us would survive." And then Tom walked over to his whiteboard and wrote a single word: "Missions." "Chad's recommendation is that we move our people to the margins. Let them feel the pain of lostness. Let them taste it. The reason that we have the mission statement, 'Helping our friends and neighbors find their way back to God,' needs to somehow find its way inside their souls."

"Inside our team's souls," Jimmy repeated.

Tom looked at Jimmy who was finishing off his chocolate glazed and said, "I can't see any value in restructuring toward our mission. Not at this point. Not yet. We have to disciple the team first. We first must have a team that believes in the mission. They gotta believe it before they can lead it. And believing is gonna take some time."

Jimmy, with a look of defeat written all over his face, slowly rose to his feet, rubbed his fingers on a white cloth napkin, and said, "I gotta hit the gym."

"I don't rightly know what to say. Ya caught me a wee bit flat-footed," said the Irishman. "It's not every day I hear a proposition such as this. There must be some kind of a catch? What's your angle on this? You must have an angle."

"No catch," Kofe said to his boss. "I'm just a part of a group. Luca's a part of it, too. We all have jobs. God has provided for all our needs, and we want to help. We save each month and put it in a pot together. We want to make sure that nobody in the Strawberry Dig goes without."

"How large is the following?"

"We've just started. So far, we're around a dozen."

"Twelve's all? So, how much is your kitty? Am I askin' too much?"

Kofe had long ago learned to interpret his boss's colorful expressions. "No, no, it's okay. Over forty thousand, but some of us have been saving for a while."

"Wud ya get outta th' garden, Kofe! Ya must have some mobsters among ya? Or someone's a poor-mouthing."

"Just regular folks. Everyone's living on a little less so they can give more. It's been a long habit for most of us."

"Well, I'll be. That's beautiful, that's what that is, Kofe." And then he said, "Perhaps you've heard the news about Santiago Parra at the Dig? Might be that you lads could chip in there?"

Campbell MacKay was in some ways a bit of an oddity in Strawberry Mansion. As a fire-red-haired Irish immigrant, he tended to stand out in almost every way possible. He and his wife, Riona, moved into the neighborhood when Riona landed a teaching post at the Dig. English Lit. To the kids of the Dig, most of whom had never been out of Philly, her Irish lilt quoting Shakespeare's sonnets was spellbinding. She was an attraction all in herself.

Within weeks, Campbell was offered a position as assistant director, opposite Luca. His responsibility was to drive up both the membership and the Y's level of community engagement. This was a responsibility that Campbell considered a calling, and he worked harder than anyone. Within months of Luca's move to lead the Fishtown Y, the Strawberry Y's executive director position became vacant, and Campbell MacKay got the nod.

Kofe brought Campbell MacKay's news to their group. Sophia—Santiago and Maggy Parra's only child—was born with a heart valve defect that was going to require a delicate surgery with no guarantee of success. To make things worse, the kind of health insurance that was available to an inner-city schoolteacher and an assistant manager in a clothing retail store meant that their baby daughter's care would be second-rate at best. According to Riona, Santiago and Maggy were beside themselves.

"Sure, I know Santiago," said Luca. "He teaches Language Arts. He's a wonderful teacher from what I can tell; the kids flock around him like little birds."

"Luca, do you want to see what they need?" Choyz asked. "Perhaps go with some armloads of groceries and see where we go from there?"

"I would be delighted to, and I'll bring Campbell with me. I've got a feeling …" Luca said with a smile.

"Jerome and I will bring groceries over here tomorrow afternoon," Choyz said. "A couple and an infant, right?"

"Right," said Kofe. "A little baby girl, six months old."

"You can deliver them tomorrow evening."

"Well, yes ma'am, Miss Choyz, thank you," said Luca. "And remember, go overboard. Way overboard!"

"Is there any other way?" said Choyz, as she poured herself another cup of tea.

***

Together, Luca and Campbell struggled with eight overstuffed brown paper bags of groceries as they wrestled their way up three flights of stairs and through three fire doors to reach the Parras' apartment door.

Luca's large fist knocked as cheerfully as it knew how.

A young Latino man who appeared to be in his late twenties cautiously answered the door. He viewed the food cache around the stranger's feet and with a quizzical look asked, "Can I help you?"

"Santiago Parra?" asked Luca.

"Yes …" was the unsure reply. "Police?"

"Noooo, not quite," Luca laughed, beaming widely. "Santiago, I am Luca Lewis, and this is Campbell MacKay. We live in the neighborhood, too. We heard about your baby daughter Sophia's upcoming surgery and just wanted to know how we could help."

A female voice called out from within the apartment, "Who is it?"

Santiago was flummoxed. "Neighbors, honey." He gestured toward the brown paper bags, "Are these groceries for us?"

"They surely are," said Luca. "Can we help you bring them inside?"

They carefully loaded six bags onto the small, faux marble kitchen counter. The last two bags were deposited in the sink.

"Thank you so very much," Santiago stammered. "Coffee? Is it too late?"

"That would be wonderful. Okay with you, Campbell?"

"Fine, yes fine. A cup would be lovely."

The sparsely furnished apartment revealed all you needed to know about a teacher's salary at the Dig. Everything was clean, well maintained, and carefully arranged. But most of the furnishings were twenty years older than the couple who owned them. Too new to be considered retro and too old to be wanted. But just the right vintage to be both useful and free.

Santiago, as politely as he could, finally worked out a question. "So, how did you know about Sophia?"

Luca jumped in and pointed a thumb to his left. "Campbell told us. You work with his wife, I believe. Riona MacKay?"

"Oh yes. Riona. Yes. We teach together in the English department. Although most of us can't always understand …" Santiago glanced at Campbell and then stopped himself. "So, you work at the Y, Mr. MacKay?"

"Campbell," he corrected. "Aye. As does Mr. Lewis." And then he corrected himself, "I mean Luca. He's now at Fishtown."

"So, this is a gift from the Y?" Santiago asked.

Luca leaned back and waited patiently for Campbell to answer that question.

"Umm, no, not that exactly. Not the Y. Tis a gift from … How would you lay out things, Luca?"

Luca leaned forward and with the slightest smile said, "Jesus. Santiago, this is a gift from Jesus."

Campbell stared uncomfortably at his shoes.

"Jesus? Jesus is delivering free groceries now?"

"Yes. He's been delivering groceries for centuries. He thinks you like steaks. T-bones, maybe?"

"Wha?" Campbell choked on a swallow of black coffee.

Santiago, appearing unphased, rolled with Luca's silliness. "Well, we Chilenos do love our beef. But seriously."

"Santiago, I am a part of a small community of Jesus followers. We try to obey the things that Jesus asks us to do," Luca explained.

"In the Bible?"

"Yes. And when Campbell told us about little Sophia, we knew we had to try to help. We wanted to."

"Wow," said Santiago. "I don't really know what to say. Why don't you both come in and I'll fix us a drink." And he ushered them into the living room where Maggy was sitting in an old painted rocking chair, carefully cradling Sophia in a hand-knitted blanket.

Santiago made formal introductions. "Maggy, this is Luca Lewis and Campbell MacKay."

Maggy, a small, slender young woman with long jet-black hair tied back in a ponytail, had tears streaming down her cheeks as she struggled to form words. "I was listening," she said. "I heard what you told Santiago … we are so afraid. Thank you for your kindness." And then she broke down into sobs, her tears falling onto Sophia.

"Maggy, you are most welcome," replied Luca. "We really want to help Sophia and there are a few ways we would like to do that, if you're agreeable. First, we'd like to take groceries off your family expense worries for the next few months. We'll take care of that. Is that okay?"

Blank looks of shock came back to Luca.

"I'll take that as a yes. Second, I assume the surgery will be at the General?"

"That's correct," Maggy answered.

"Wonderful. We know some people there. Is it okay if we try to make some arrangements on your behalf? Keep costs down and make sure Sophia gets the best possible care?"

Again, no answer came.

"Can I take that as a 'yes'?" Luca pressed.

"Yes, yes … yes!" Santiago exclaimed. Tears were now spilling out of his eyes.

"Great. We'll get a start on that tomorrow." Luca paused for a second, lowered his voice, and said, "But we have one more gift we would like to leave you with. I think you'll find it's our best one." Luca paused for another second or two. "We would like to pray for you and for Sophia's healing. Would that be all right?"

Maggy, now a puddle, answered with no hesitation, "Oh, yes. Please. We need help."

"Our group that meets will be praying for you and Sophia every day, so please know that we are here for you. If you like, I could pray for you now, while we're here?"

Maggy looked over at Santiago and smiled. "Yes," she said. "I think we would like that very much."

Luca stood and gestured for everyone to stand. Santiago and

Maggy walked toward Luca. Luca covered Santiago's shoulder with his left hand. Santiago wrapped his left arm around his wife.

"Campbell, would you join us?" Luca asked gently.

Campbell timidly stood up and moved toward the group. Luca grabbed his shoulder and Campbell in turn nervously put his right hand on Maggy's shoulder.

"Let's pray together," said Luca.

And then Luca prayed. He prayed as if Jesus were standing in the room with them. He prayed for healing, for protection, for grace. He prayed for Sophia's future, that she would grow strong and healthy. That she would grow to become an advocate for righteousness and truth. He prayed for their family, that it would be unshakable, built upon the rock of Jesus Christ. And he prayed for Campbell, that God would continue to use his life to be a blessing in the neighborhood.

When Luca said "Amen," everyone in the little circle felt as if they had been in heaven.

"Thank you, Luca. Thank you, Campbell," said Santiago.

"Yes, thank you. I feel so peaceful now," said Maggy. "I feel like Jesus has taken away my burden."

"Told you that we was saving the best for last." Luca looked at Campbell. "I guess we better leave these fine people alone. It's getting late."

The three-minute drive back to Campbell's house was quiet. Very quiet. As Luca slowly stopped his car at the curb in front of the MacKay townhome, Campbell opened the car door, and then closed it again.

"Luca," he said. "What was that? I mean, what happened there?"

"What do you mean?"

"I mean, you really believe that Jesus stuff, don't you?"

"I do."

Staring out the windshield Campbell said, "Where I come from, we bout over it, even to the death. Religion is everywhere. It's thick and mean and it's dirty. But I've never met anyone who believed it. Not really. Not like that. I always thought it was a crock of … well, you know. But this was beautiful, Luca. Christ wasn't an ole plaster statue in that apartment. I could touch him. Felt like I could, at least."

Luca smiled.

And then Campbell turned toward him and said, "Can you teach a cabbage like me how to believe like that?"

Chapter Nine

The Switch

The truck geared down as it prepared to make its late-night delivery of Vimto soft drinks to the markets and grocery stores of Aden. Its air brakes swooshed as it stopped, diesel still purring, awaiting its next instructions. This was the first of many deliveries for the evening.

"Thanks so much for the ride, sir," said Omar. "I cannot thank you enough."

"You be careful, young man. You should see a doctor."

"Thank you," Omar repeated, and then waved to the driver as he limped his way down the dark street, disappearing into the darkness.

The sea air smelled like freedom, and Omar was so glad to be home. And this *was* home. After the events of this summer, an exclamation point was indelibly etched behind that fact. It had only been a few months since he had left, but in so many ways it felt like a lifetime. The stars shining above Aden's tranquil harbor looked like streetlights reflecting upon themselves. Heavenly lights of hope. Omar was home.

Slowly he trundled down the dark streets, putting the least amount of weight possible on his left leg. The laceration on his knee had mostly healed, but something was obviously damaged internally. He couldn't recall exactly how he sustained the injury—the events of his abduction and interrogation were a blur to him. He could only recollect waking up to Hussein's warm smile and then noticing pieces of his cellmates' clothes fastened to his injuries.

Hobbling downhill was difficult, but sea-level was where he had to be. He had to find Yushua. Muhammad's apartment was much closer, but he wasn't going to put the secret community at greater risk. It had to be Yushua. So, he made as direct of a path as he could while still avoiding lighted streets. Slowly, methodically, and painfully, Omar pushed himself toward the campus.

He knew he couldn't go straight to Yushua's apartment because his roommate was already a bit suspicious about his extracurricular activities. He had to somehow locate Yushua when he was alone. And he knew just where that would be.

As the sun finally rose, Omar was concealed between two rusty-gray dumpsters. He positioned himself so that he had a direct line of sight to the basement stairs that led to the university's mildewy library, Yushua's home away from home. Already this morning, Omar had counted seven students who descended into the dank rooms—more than he had imagined. Each time a student rounded the bend in the sidewalk, Omar's heart raced. Seven times he was disappointed.

And then he saw it: a familiar red and white backpack. He stood up and took a few steps into the open. "Yushua, Yushua," he whispered as loudly as possible. Nothing. He needed more. "Yushua!" he called.

Yushua slowed his gait. He looked in every direction but couldn't get a fix on where the voice came from. "Yushua!" Omar called again, waving his arms. Yushua turned in his direction, squinted, and then stopped with his mouth gaping open as if he had just seen a ghost. Without another second of hesitation, he broke for the dumpsters.

"Omar, we thought you ..." Yushua started. "Muhammad received word from Dhamar that ..." Yushua couldn't find words to say what he thought had happened.

"Yes, brother, it's true. My father led the CSO to the secret community. They killed everyone, including Fatimah." Omar's countenance changed as he shared the news.

"You, brother ... you look ... bad. What happened to you?"

"I'll tell you all about it. But first, can you hide me? I was thinking the small room beside the football equipment room. I know where they keep the key."

"Okay, brother. Stay here, I'll bring some clean clothes and a hat. We'll go after that."

"Please, brother, bring some food. Anything. All I've had in the past three days is a Vimto."

"Yes, brother, I'll be right back."

In less than an hour, Omar was safely concealed in a windowless closet. Surrounded by old mops, worn-out practice footballs, cleaning products, and his friend Yushua, Omar sat on a pile of castoff uniforms, shoveling down a stack of *malawah* bread and cold braised chicken.

"They'll be looking for me," said Omar. "They'll be hunting me, I'm sure. I escaped from prison and set free three other prisoners. My Houthis captors left to fight an Al-Qaeda uprising, and God opened the door ..."

From there, Omar recounted the events of his summer away. Yushua flipped over a mop pail and crouched to listen. He was mesmerized as he listened to his friend's account of Fatimah's dream and the miracle at the brook of Bani Badi. He heard of the Dhamar secret community and of the massacre of Fatimah and the brothers and sisters. Of Omar's abduction and torture, and his five faith-filled cellmates. And of the little girl that no one saw. The one that said, "Isa sent me, Omar. Isa sends you."

"Brother … I am so sorry and so sad. But I am also so inspired and humbled. Isa is with you, Omar. He has plans for you—I always knew that. But I know it more now. We must get you to safety."

"Thank you. Have you any ideas?"

"Dr. Raweh. We can trust him—you know that. He knows so many important people; I'm sure he'll know what to do."

"Yes. I'll hide here while you see him. I need to sleep. I haven't slept for many days."

Omar arranged a sleeping pallet by restacking the old uniforms in a line. He had never been so tired, and almost instantly fell fast asleep.

The escaped convict didn't hear the scratching, grinding sound of the door unlocking. But he did hear, "Omar, psst, Omar …"

He looked up to see Yushua and Dr. Raweh hunching over his makeshift bed.

"We didn't know if we'd ever wake you, little brother," said Dr. Raweh. "You must be exhausted. You look …"

"Huuuuuph," Omar sat up, stretched, and rubbed his face. He had just been lurched out of a deep sleep and had yet to get his bearings. "Dr. Raweh …"

"Yes, I am so happy to see you. We all thought that you—well, it is so good to see you, my friend."

"It's good to see you, too. I've thought of you often. Prayed for you as I was in prison. Thank you for seeing me."

"It's all arranged, Omar. I know a UN official who can get you into the Al-Mishqafa Refugee Camp. That will keep you safely hidden from the CSO for now. From there, if Allah wills, you'll be taken to another country where you are not so hunted. But Omar, those camps are not to be trusted. They have ears. Do not ever use your real name. Ever. Invent a new identity and stick to it. After today, Omar Al-Khulani can be no more."

The plan was for Yushua to drive Dr. Raweh's car from Aden through rebel-controlled territory to Sanaa. And if this eight- or nine-hour journey weren't perilous enough, it required that they pass through the very heart of Dhamar. When, and if, they made it to Sanaa, they were to use a public telephone and call a UN official named Francis Murphy at the Mishqafa Refugee Camp. He would meet them in Sanaa, and then would smuggle Omar out of the city to the camp.

Dr. Raweh passed on the instructions that he had received. "There will be two checkpoints on your trip. One thirty minutes north of Dhamar. The other as you enter Sanaa. You are traveling to do research at Sanaa University. I have arranged for Yushua to meet a colleague of mine after the transfer."

He handed Yushua a slip of paper with a name and telephone number. "Just in case the checkpoint wants to validate the story. They usually only ask for the driver's credentials, but sometimes they ask for passengers as well. Make sure that Yushua is driving. The rest is up to …"

"Isa Al-Masih," said Omar, with a resolute sense of conviction.

"Okay, little brother. Isa."

Dr. Raweh's pearl white Skoda Octavia was the nicest vehicle either student had ever driven. Omar, disguised as much as he could without looking disguised, was wearing Yushua's gray hoodie, his ball cap, and his favorite pair of tortoiseshell sunglasses. Omar's hip-hop attempt at whiskers, stragglier than ever after his incarceration, were now shaven clean. He had stealthily showered in his former football team's locker room and felt more refreshed and secure than he had in weeks.

"My go-bag is in the trunk. It's yours now." Like most Isa followers he knew, Yushua had a backpack prepacked and ready for flight. At a moment's notice, Yushua had a small amount of cash, a few clothes, identification documents, and a few other incidentals ready for a quick evacuation.

"I cannot thank you enough, my brother. I wish that somehow I could repay you."

"Being a part of your story is payment enough. Now I get to join the angels in aiding your escape. Who gets to do that? One day, this will be a tale for my children and grandchildren."

Yushua listened as his friend elaborated in spine-tingling detail the events of his summer. As Omar recounted his story aloud, the faith inside him seemed to enlarge and embolden. The fear and dread he had experienced the past days began to morph into a quiet, peaceful joy. And Yushua was spellbound as he witnessed firsthand the amazing transformation of his former unbelieving classmate.

There were no welcome signs as they entered the city, but Omar knew exactly where they were. He slumped down in the passenger seat as the white Skoda diesel chugged into Dhamar. Yushua drove the car cautiously, carefully, desperately trying not to draw any attention to themselves. *Don't stand out, don't stand out*, Yushua rehearsed in his mind as both of his fists tightly clamped the leather-wrapped steering wheel.

And they didn't. Soon, and without incident, the buildings of Dhamar became further and further apart, until the city was completely behind them.

"Thank you, Isa!" Yushua exclaimed.

The thirty-minute drive to the first checkpoint took hours, or so it seemed. They saw in the distance armed uniforms waiting ahead, and they slowed down and coasted to a stop. Five PSO officers manned the gate, each appearing more ominous looking than the next. The Political Security Organization was both powerful and unaccountable, as it was the only security force that reported through channels directly to the president. The highway division of the PSO had as its main objective the stymieing of movement of their many political rivals vying for power.

"Where you from?" came the voice of a heavily bearded officer.

"Aden, sir."

"Aden, the city of rebels," he said in a lifeless manner.

"Yes, there are many political radicals in that region, but we are not. We are students heading to Sanaa University to research," Yushua answered.

"Somehow, no one is a rebel at my checkpoint. It is interesting how that works. How long?"

"Just a day. Two at the most."

"That's a long trip for one day," the officer said with a suspicious tone.

"Yes, it is, sir. But the legal archives are not online. We have to dig through the dust ourselves," Yushua said in the most disarming manner he could muster.

"Trunk."

"Yes, sir, I'll pop it."

The officer walked to the back of the car, rooted through the professor's things. And then slammed the trunk closed.

"Go."

Yushua pulled away as nonchalantly as he could muster. Now on to the next one.

Omar could see that Yushua was inordinately shaken from the

encounter. “Are you alright, brother?” he asked. “That wasn’t so bad, was it?”

“What if he looked in my backpack ... I mean, your backpack. I have cash. That would be suspicious for a day trip. And there’s something else.”

“What something else?”

“There are pieces of a New Testament that I stitched into the lining.”

“Let’s stop and hide the cash. I won’t need it in the camp anyway. We’ll take our chances with the special lining,” said Omar.

After a brief stop to rearrange three elastic-banded stacks of rials from the go-bag to beneath the spare tire, the journey resumed. Both travelers were quieter now. For Yushua, his thoughts were focused on the next checkpoint and all that might go wrong. Omar’s thoughts were on the uncertainty of the new life that lay before him, and the grief that the only life he’d known was programmed to vaporize within hours.

“There it is,” said Yushua, breaking the silence.

He downshifted, gradually slowing as he approached the second checkpoint. But something out of the ordinary was happening. Blue and red lights were flashing as five or six officers surrounded a transport truck. Yushua creeped closer, unsure what his response in this situation should be. The PSO officers, with their automatic rifles pointing at the truck, were shouting commands and obscenities to whoever was in the truck’s cab. There was no response.

Even though the gate was lifted, Yushua stopped at the empty booth and waited for permission to proceed. But nobody seemed to be aware of their presence. The tension on the other side of the booth was escalating. The PSO, now clearly out of control, began to fire rounds into the air.

“Yushua, go. Go, go!” Omar commanded. “Go, but go slowly.”

Yushua stepped on the gas and eased forward, slowly, and steadily increasing speed. Omar stared into the side mirror, eyes fixed on the booth to see if they would be followed. But there was no one coming. Slowly the booth faded from sight.

There were no shrieks of celebration. No shouts of joy. Just long, deep exhales. They had made it through.

"More angels. More beautiful angels," said Yushua. "Isa's kingdom is everywhere!"

"Thank you, Isa," breathed Omar.

As instructed, they found a public telephone, and Omar punched in the number for the Mishqafa Refugee Camp.

"Hello, is Francis Murphy there? … Thanks."

And then there was a long pause. Too long. Omar wondered if he should hang up and try again, and then …

"Hello, this is Murphy, who is it?"

"Umm, hello Mr. Murphy. This is, um, this is, ummmm …"

"Is this the gentleman from Aden calling?"

"Yes! Yes! This is he. We are here in Sanaa. We made it!"

"Wonderful. I'll meet you at the Déjà Vu Café in the old town district. In one hour. Will that work?"

"Déjà Vu Café? Yes. Yes. I'll be there. I'm wearing a gray hoodie. Blue cap. Green canvas backpack. Sunglasses."

"Perfect. I'll be the red-headed guy that looks like he doesn't belong in the country."

"Okay, I'll find you, I'm sure. Thank you, Mr. Murphy."

Dr. Raweh has come through, Omar thought as he returned the receiver with a look of boundless relief. The plan was working.

Omar and Yushua mapped out their routes, which both happened to be in the old town district of Sanaa. Yushua would head to Sanaa University to complete his cover story. He would do a few minutes of random research in the law archives, and then would meet with Dr. Raweh's contact. Omar would go to the Déjà Vu Café and wait to spot Mr. Francis Murphy of the UN. Since both locations were within walking distance, Yushua found a parking lot somewhere between them. As instructed by Dr. Raweh, for Mr. Murphy's security, this is where they would say goodbye.

"I introduced you to Isa, and to many troubles, my brother," Yushua said as he pulled his go-bag out of the trunk.

"Indeed, you have, my friend. But the troubles cannot compare to the gift of Isa that you brought to me. I would not change a thing, Yushua. Not a single thing." As the words fell from his mouth, his mind immediately snapped to Fatimah's gruesome murder, and he instantly regretted the careless way that he spoke. Of course, he would have changed that day. He would have erased it completely if he could. But now was not the time to correct his expression of appreciation. He did not regret following Jesus. He only wished Fatimah was with him—oh, how he missed her.

Yushua unbuckled the leather straps of the canvas bag, reached into an inside pocket, and pulled out a handful of his identification documents. Then he opened the car's glove compartment and carefully placed them inside the maintenance manual, shut the lid, and then shut and locked the car door.

"I have one more gift for you, Omar. Not quite as good as the gift of Isa. But it's the second-best gift I could give you."

Yushua handed his friend a small black book with gold inlaid letters and a golden eagle embossed on the cover. It was a passport from the Republic of Yemen.

Omar opened it and saw a photograph of a young man who looked remarkably like himself. And to the right of the picture was Omar's new identity.

Yushua Maalouf.

Chapter Ten

The Mission

"Can I bring you anything, sir?" said the middle-aged flight attendant in a royal blue pants suit. "We'll be landing shortly."

"No, I'm good. Thanks so much though. Tom?"

"Yes ma'am, I'd love another Diet Coke. Plenty of ice, please. And do you have any more of those chocolate things? They was really good."

"Right away, sir."

Jimmy Norris and Tom Butts were on a scouting expedition. They had started thirty-six hours earlier in Atlanta and were now on their third and final leg. Aboard a Yemeni A-350 out of Abu Dhabi, they were finally about to touch down in Sanaa. Their mission was to formalize an international mission partnership.

Chad Collins' recommendation of getting the people of LifePointe involved in missions had taken on a formal structure that they called their Acts 1:8 Strategy. This strategy meant they would have four targets of involvement: Jerusalem, which meant for them, Fulton County. Judea, which they considered anywhere in Georgia. Samaria, their thoughts on this would be somewhere in the liberal northeast. And some distant godforsaken place that would become their remotest region, also known as "the ends of the earth."

The first three places in the strategy didn't really capture Jimmy's interest in a significant way. He knew they had to engage the church in reaching their local neighbors, but it seemed like an uphill battle, and one that lacked the glamor or excitement-factor worthy of a new church strategy. But the idea of going global, going to some hard place, set his imagination reeling.

"If we go international first, let our people experience how bad things are, they'll be grateful for America, grateful for what we have at LifePointe, and want to roll up their sleeves to 'mission' at home. Before we lose the homeland altogether."

Jimmy knew how things worked.

"We'll start internationally and eventually work our way back to our own backyard."

Chad Collins had connected Jimmy with a Christian global relief organization that specialized in ministering to Jimmy's target of "the most miserable places on earth." In Jimmy's mind, a good chunk of the world fit in this category, but he had his sights set on the Mt. Everest of wretchedness. Although not scientific, he had a shortlist in his mind: Somalia, Pakistan, Venezuela, Nigeria, and Mexico. However, he ruled out the latter, knowing it would be impossible to get his people enthused about helping a country that was on the news every day because of an invasion of their illegals. But the mission field that his heart was set on was the crumbling nation of Venezuela. He was sure his people would line up to get a first-hand look at the damage that Marxist socialism brings to a country.

Jimmy knew how things worked.

But after several consultations with Chad's contact, Jimmy had a complete change of heart. Although Venezuela was indeed in dire straits as a nation, there was already a large Christian presence, both indigenous and imported. LifePointe's efforts would be just another blip on a busy missionary radar and being just another blip didn't interest him in the least. On the other hand, Chad's contact had told Jimmy about vast refugee camps numbering in the tens of thousands in the country of Yemen. Seas of humanity, the poorest of the global poor, with almost no missionary attention. Here, LifePointe could leave a mark. Exotic enough to attract the globe-trotting crowd, painful enough to reel in the bleeding-heart crowd. It couldn't miss.

"I sure hope this Francis Murphy fella is as good as they sold him," said Jimmy as he reorganized his backpack for landing. "We've invested a lot in other people's say-so."

***

Omar Al-Khulani's new identity of "Yushua Maalouf" was now legally certified. When he arrived at the Mishqafa Refugee Camp, he had a three-week probationary period where his status as a refugee was investigated. In Yushua's case, this was merely a formality, since Francis Murphy had first-hand knowledge of his situation. Nevertheless, Yushua was processed, registered, and held in a segregated area while he awaited his file's completion.

After being legally validated as an international refugee, Yushua was given his refugee effects. This included his first two-week supply of food rations and ration cards for the upcoming months. His rationed daily diet worked out to be nine ounces of maize, seven ounces of milled flour, three tablespoons of lentils, one tablespoon of vegetable oil, and one teaspoon of salt. Everything that was necessary for human survival and nothing more.

Along with his foodstuffs, Yushua was given a bar of soap, a jerry can to transport water, a steel cooking set, a sleeping mat, and a white tarpaulin to build a shelter. Francis Murphy personally escorted Yushua to a section of the camp that was as far away as possible from a militant Islamic gang that tried to police the camp's twelve thousand desperate souls.

"You should be safe here, my friend. But just remember, when people are despairing, radical beliefs become intensified. There are people within these walls that would lose no sleep in ridding the world of you, if they discover what you believe. So be very careful whom you trust," warned Murphy. "But that said, let's continue our conversations. I find them fascinating."

For the last month, two afternoons a week, Yushua and Francis had met in the administration building for "cultural exchanges." In Francis' office, with the door closed, they discipled one another in a mutually beneficial interchange of doctrine and experience. Francis, who had the benefit of a larger theological perspective, helped Yushua understand the grander narrative of how sixty-six books of the Bible told one central gospel story. Yushua, whose Bible knowledge was limited, had been witness to tremendous spiritual power through a yielded obedience to Isa. Without the customary obstacles of status or hierarchy, one brother formed the other—and both were reveling in their new spiritual discoveries.

Francis was from Canada. St. John's, Newfoundland was his home and the land of his ancestors. The day they met in the Déjà Vu Café, Francis was wearing a T-shirt that had Newfoundland's coat of arms emblazoned across it. Yushua, whose native language was Yemeni-Arabic, and who later had learned Farsi and English, could not make heads nor tails of the words below the crest: *Quaerite Prime Regnum Dei*.

"What is this *Quaerite Prime Regnum Dei?* What does this mean? Is this English?" he asked.

"No, not English. Latin. It means, 'Seek first the kingdom of God.' It's the long-forgotten motto of my home province."

"This is from Isa's message on the mountain," Yushua said. "This is what they believe in Canada?"

"No, I'm afraid not. Maybe at one time, but that was long ago. I wear this shirt to remind myself about where we came from, and where we need to return."

"*Regnum Dei.* The kingdom of God. Hussein Nazari, my teacher in the prison, told us many things about this. This beautiful kingdom is shown when Isa's will is obeyed by his people. Do you know about this kingdom?" Yushua asked.

"I am learning. Eighty-six times Jesus spoke of the kingdom in the Gospels, and then the book of Acts starts, ends, and is filled with the apostles declaring the kingdom. And yes, your teacher was right; it's what everything looks like when Jesus gets his way. It's the miracle that is left when I get my will out of God's way."

From the very first meeting, Yushua was taken with Francis. He knew so much of the Holy Scriptures. He knew more than the real Yushua. More than Muhammad, more than anyone in the Dhamar community, more than Hussein. More than anyone he had ever known. And Yushua was determined to learn everything that Francis knew.

"Oh, Yushua, before I run, there are some visitors coming this Wednesday from the United States. Why don't you join us? Who knows what doors may open."

"I would very much like that. Thank you."

Then Francis raised his fist in the air and quietly said, "*Regnum Dei.*"

"*Regnum Dei*," Yushua returned.

***

"Can you take us here? Can you bring us here? Bring us to this place?" Tom Butts was pointing to a printed document that said "Mishqafa Refugee Camp" in English, and some Arabic script below. He was counting on the fact that the squiggles somehow contained the name and address of their destination.

"Yes, boss," he replied.

Jimmy and Tom hopped into the back seat of an old white and yellow Opal that was virtually a collection of small dents. As Jimmy fumbled to find his seat belt, he said, "If this ole girl makes it there and back, we'll have our first miracle."

"How far is it to the Mishqafa Refugee Camp? How long will it take?" Tom asked.

"Yes, boss."

"Thank you," Tom replied politely. Tom knew that "yes, boss" would now be Jimmy's official verbal hashtag for the remainder of the journey. And probably for longer than that.

Forty minutes later, the camp's chain-link-fenced enclosure started to become visible. At least the beginning of it. It went on for as far as their eyes could see. And the ground inside the wire appeared to be covered with snow. White plastic tarps arranged as makeshift tents were lined up row after row after row. Thousands of them.

"This is unbelievable," Jimmy said. His eyes were wide as he gazed at the mass of humanity caged behind the fence. "How bad does it have to be for this to be better?"

Tom sat silently and took everything in. "Oh, my Lord. Oh, my dear Lord," was all he could say.

The taxi driver stopped the car at the entrance gate, jumped out, and spoke at length to a UN guard. Finally, the guard went to his booth and made a phone call. Several minutes passed, then he came back out and waved in the taxi as he opened the gate.

"What are we getting ourselves into, Tom? I had no idea. Can we do this? We can't do this ..." Jimmy appeared to be in a state of shock as the taxi drove through a section of tarps to the main admin building.

"Hang on, Jimmy. Let's see what happens here with Murphy," said Tom as the cab came to a stop in front of a more permanent looking temporary building.

"Yes, boss," the cab driver said with a big smile.

"Thank you. You wait here, please. Wait here," Tom said as he gestured with waving hands.

"Yes, boss."

"Atlanta? LifePointe Chapel?" asked Francis Murphy as he walked out to greet his guests.

"Yes. I'm Dr. Jimmy Norris. This is Rev. Tom Butts."

"Well welcome, gentlemen. I'm Francis Murphy. Just plain Francis. I never quite finished my PhD. Ended up bailing on my dissertation when the whole Syrian thing blew up. What's yours in, Dr. Jimmy?"

"Well, it's not quite a ... It's a DMin."

"Ah. Not familiar with that. Why don't you boys come inside? Does a cup of American coffee suit you? Or as close as I can come up with?"

"You can do that? That would be awesome. Haven't had a decent cup in a few days," said Jimmy.

"It's no problem. We just take regular good coffee and water it down, 'Americano style.'"

Francis guided his guests to a small boardroom of sorts. It had four plastic folding tables arranged together as one large rectangular table. Surrounding it were twelve blue plastic stacking chairs haphazardly arranged. Two walls were covered floor to ceiling with boxes. One wall was a bulletin board.

While Francis was organizing the coffee, Jimmy took a seat at the far end of the table. Tom sat in the middle and flipped open his laptop to capture whatever intelligence was gained. Jimmy started, "So, what can you tell us about this place, Francis? Anything special we should know?"

"Well, I don't imagine there's anything too special here. There are three main camps in the country. Each over ten thousand. We're part of a camp network that cares for over 2.6 million displaced souls around the world. Fifty-four percent of them are children. Everyone comes thinking it's a temporary measure. Just enough time to stay safe while things blow over. A month or two at most. But sadly, twelve years is the average stay. This is the newest camp in country. And it's full. More than full."

There was a lot more that Francis could say; he'd done the song and dance for curious visitors countless times. But every minute he spent entertaining meant something important wasn't getting done, so he got straight to the point.

"Here's your coffee, gentlemen. Hope it's to your liking. Now let me ask you a question, if I could be so forward. You've traveled a long way. Halfway across the planet. You've come to one of the world's most forgotten places. And now you're sitting among the most forgotten people within that most forgotten place. We've a handful of workers struggling to care for the needs of a hopeless city of people who are crammed into this tent compound. And now you have my full attention. How can I help you?"

Jimmy was caught off guard by the directness of Francis' question. He was counting on hearing a pitch for his church's help. But two things happened that he didn't expect. First, he never planned on being emotionally overwhelmed by the scope of the problem. What difference could a handful of volunteers from LifePointe make in a human calamity that was this immense? Any heroic half-formed plan that he had brought with him had now totally evaporated. And second, he didn't account for Francis Murphy. He expected him to grovel like a man who was begging for a meager handout. Instead, he asked, "How can I help you?"

As Jimmy attempted to string words together to appear as a coherent thought, there was a quiet knock at the door.

"Yes?" said Francis.

A young woman in her early twenties leaned in and said, "Mr. Maalouf is here. He said you wanted to meet with him."

"Yes, yes, send him right in." And then Francis lowered his voice. "You might find this quite interesting. Perhaps it's the reason you've come."

***

Philadelphia Freedom was the name. It had to be. The appellation was a crafty double-entendre that beckoned back to another era while at the same time spoke of a yearning for a future that was deep within his spirit. One part past, one part future. It was all very clever.

At least Luca thought so.

The historical part was taken from the title of an old Elton John song. Luca didn't quite remember all of it but recalled his mother singing it around the house when he was a child. The only part that stuck in his mind were a few words and a semblance of a tune that he'd always managed to mangle in a most cheerful manner: Something about shining a light and loving Philadelphia freedom.

It was particularly remarkable that, as frequently as Luca would break out in the ditty, it was never actually performed in the same way twice. "You could be canonized as a saint," Santiago would tease him, "because it's a documentable miracle that our 'theme song' has an infinitude of lyrics and melodies—all written and performed by you!"

But to Luca Lewis, the melody and its history were largely insignificant details. It was the future that grabbed ahold of his imagination and wouldn't let go. The visionary future that the new name spoke of had two intentions as well. One was for a shared dream that was first cast by his late father and was captured in the hearts of Luca's small cadre. The other was a deep yearning for the city of Philadelphia itself. Luca had a vision for a Jesus movement that would start in "the city of brotherly love" and from there "shine its light" across the entire globe.

Luca was finished with thinking small.

The newest recruits to the budding movement were Campbell and Riona MacKay, and Santiago and Maggy Parra. And they were all in. A dramatic and eternal shift took place in Campbell's and the Parras' hearts on that first day of the grocery delivery and the honest and earnest prayer that followed. Soon Riona was swept up in this new spiritual community and found authentic purpose and peace through heartfelt repentance. Sophia's surgery had gone well, and she was making an incredible recovery. And now, for the first time since they could remember, they had something that their hearts had ached for their entire life: community.

Luca was quick to deploy. "MacKays, I don't want y'all to change your personalities one bit. You've always been hospitable. You're always looking for ways to help folks. Keep doing what you're wired to do. Just bring Jesus into it all." Within days, the MacKays were linked up with Kofe and Angelica Wilson and neither couple held anything back.

"And my Chileno friends. You've chosen the hard place. Teachers try their best to leave the Dig, not come to it. Maggy, you've said it's a 'calling' for your family. And it has been a calling. God's called you to Strawberry Mansion to teach. But I 'spect it's teaching more than just Language Arts in the school. I'm gonna train you to be *our* teachers in the biblical sense of equipping. Together, we'll teach obedience to Jesus." Luca stopped for a moment, looked at the infant in Maggy's arms, and said, "And I wouldn't be surprised if our precious Sophia teaches us all a whole lot more."

Chapter Eleven

The Storm

The scenes on the news and from the window didn't look like a picture of Philadelphia. Miami or New Orleans, maybe. But not Philadelphia. A natural disaster of this magnitude happens less than once in a lifetime in the Northeast. But it was happening nonetheless. And Luca was ready.

The Fishtown Y and the Strawberry Mansion Y were two of only a few handfuls of spaces in Philadelphia with power, a shelter strategy, and the ability to provide meals to the thousands who would go without. While most community services were waiting for some kind of coordinated government response to eventually descend, Philadelphia Freedom had already rolled up their sleeves.

The ice storm of the century had left a blanket of ice three-and-a-half inches thick across the city; a white blanket that stripped the stoutest trees of their magnificent branches and brought them down through roofs, onto cars, and through almost every power line in the city. The city was paralyzed.

"There's no time to wait for FEMA to get their stuff together. We have to open our Ys," said Luca. "If we don't, I don't know what's gonna happen to the people. People can't survive long in this city's winter with no heat."

Even though the majority of homes were heated with natural gas, the furnaces that transformed that gas into circulated heat were all electric. As a result, most homes in Philadelphia were about to become uninhabitable.

The building designers of both Ys had the foresight to install backup generators for just such an occasion. They weren't powerful enough to carry the full electrical load of all the Y's operations, but hopefully they would hold up for Luca's survival plan.

The friends of Philadelphia Freedom gathered in Luca's townhouse for an impromptu emergency meeting. They had already decided what they were going to do. They would open both Ys as virtual homes for those in the neighborhoods with no place to go. But now they had to work out the how.

"Choyz, what we got left?" Luca asked.

"37,000 dollars, give or take."

"Thirty-seven. Hmm. I've got room for 17,000 dollars on my Visa," said Luca.

"I've got about that, too," Campbell offered.

"We've got room for three or four thousand," said Santiago.

This continued for a few minutes. When they added up their spontaneous offering, between banked tithes that Choyz and Chantel managed, personal savings, and credit availability, the little group came up with $141,500 on the spot. What one would expect to be a series of excruciating financial decisions became a natural impulse, as the small cadre of disciples weighed the potential catastrophic cost to their community of inaction.

"Well, that'll get us started," Luca said. "Now let's divvy up responsibilities."

Santiago took charge. Together the group brainstormed a list of all the essential services that would be required. Then, in broad strokes, they broke each one down into basic tasks that had to be accomplished. Santiago's logical mind amazed the group. Within an hour they had divided the work into six major functions: shelter, meals, registration and public awareness, facility operations, finance, and security. From there they subcategorized the list into thirty-three essential operations.

"You sure you're an English teacher?" Luca asked. "From watching this, I would have guessed you was a colonel in the Army Corps of Engineers."

And then Luca shifted into director's mode. He assigned a team leader to each of the major functions. "Now remember, you have to do all this, times two. Meaning, you recruit two directors under you. One for Fishtown and one for Strawberry. You lead 'em both. Got it?"

Heads nodded. This was a bigger leadership challenge than any had had before. But none failed to realize that this, for many, would be a life-or-death operation.

"Chantel, you got feeding. Campbell, you got facilities. Kofe, you got registration and public awareness. Jerome, you got security. Santiago, you got housing. And Choyz, you got the finances for all this. The rest of us will take care of logistics. When Santiago has secured a thousand cots, or Chantel finds us a thousand cases of Campbell's soup, we're gonna figure out how they get there. Questions?"

"Yes," said Santiago. "It is now 9 a.m. When do we want to be fully operational?"

"Great question, brother. Fully operational by 9 a.m. tomorrow. But open and somewhat operational? Noon today. We have no choice. People need to get warm. Anything else?"

Choyz raised her hand as if she were in school, "How do we do the budget on this?"

"Another great question. For now, everyone calls Choyz for her okay on any spend. Sister, you got 141K to try to balance between everything. It won't be enough, but it'll get things rolling. Team, do not spend a dime without Choyz' say so. She's Daddy Warbucks, and what she says, goes. Good?"

Heads nodded in a sense of eager anticipation. Philadelphia Freedom had just been born and was already about to be set loose.

By noon, both locations had the lights on and six large coffee urns gurgling, emanating the most welcome aroma. An assembly line of neighbors were building stacks of sandwiches and cooking large stock pots of homemade soups in the Y's kitchen. Kofe and Angelica had a team of teenagers covering A-frame signs with poster boards that read, "Warm food, hot coffee, warm beds. At the Y. All welcome."

As people came in and registered, many asked if they could help, and Angelica assigned them to a team. Trucks with chains on tires started to arrive with cots, blankets, and numerous supplies—and the neighborhood unloaded and set up everything. By 7 p.m., four hundred army cots were set up inside the gyms, mezzanines, and classrooms of each Y.

Soon, the local media came to report on the story. Two Ys out of fifteen in the Philadelphia area had opened their doors to the community. No response on any level of local government had mobilized as quickly or effectively as these two Ys.

One reporter tried to interview Choyz Wilson as she was manning the phones coordinating payments. He noticed a multicolored stack of credit cards on the plastic table that was ops central. He asked, "Whose cards are those?"

"People from our group, Philadelphia Freedom. We took an offering this morning to get the ball rolling."

"Can I ask how much you collected?"

"Yes, I guess so. We gathered 141,500 dollars."

"Holy cow," gasped the reporter. "How many people in your group?"

"Ten."

"Ten people did this? How is that possible?"

"You'll have to ask Luca Lewis about that. All I know is that something had to be done; we couldn't let our neighbors freeze. The radio says it could be weeks before the lines are repaired, and you know that Strawberry Mansion will likely be the last neighborhood in Philly to be brought back. Nobody can go weeks without power. And we knew Jesus wouldn't want our folks to go without heat."

"And that stack of credit cards. Those are yours?"

"No, not just mine. They're everyone's. Luca had three."

After that, the Fishtown and Strawberry Mansion Ys became the operational centers for many of Philadelphia's media outlets as they reported on the ice storm. Regular reports originating from the Ys documented the sacrificial effort and warmth of community that was being fostered. And Luca Lewis, in his deferential way, shared his kingdom motivation.

"We just believe that Jesus loves people and that we cannot claim to love him without loving those who he loves. And when this crazy ice storm came, we knew we were called to be Jesus' hands and feet and pocketbook. But what has been most amazing is how our community has come together. We arranged for security, but we haven't needed it. Hundreds of people jammed together for day after day, and—listen, can you hear that?"

Emanating from the gym and out into the corridor where Luca was being interviewed was an impromptu ensemble of young voices, singing in harmony.

***

Mrs. Bobbie Landry was surprised to see a student move into her basement studio apartment with only one cardboard box of belongings. The small basement apartment in her Roswell, Georgia home had been subsidizing her income since her husband passed almost ten years previously. Looking after "my boys," as she called them, brought her a sense of purpose. And she treated them well.

Part of the rental agreement is that her boys were required to take care of all outdoor chores. And in this, Mrs. Landry could be a stickler. She used to pay "the Mexicans" to do it, but she became increasingly uneasy with all of that. The ways she heard them described by the politicians on the news cemented her opinion on "illegals," which was now her new designation for those who looked like they were born south of the border. Instead, she deducted from the monthly rental fee the rate she once paid her former landscapers. As far as Mrs. Landry was concerned, this was a win-win for her.

But she wasn't feeling exactly like a winner right now. This new boy with the single box of belongings appeared to be some kind of immigrant. And not the good kind. She knew that she was going to house a refugee, but somehow, in the realm of the theoretical, it seemed better. But now she had laid her own eyes on him in the cold light of day, she was unnerved. He didn't look at all like a regular foreigner from a "normal country." No, he looked like trouble. He was disfigured with scars across his face. His long, crooked nose was bent. And he walked with a most unpleasant limp. Mrs. Landry was beginning to regret letting that smooth-talking minister, Tom Butts, talk her into this.

"Take them down the stairs, dear, to the room on the left. There're fresh sheets on the bed, but you'll be taking care of that from here on in."

"Thank you, Mrs. Landry. I am very honored to stay in your fine home," said Yushua. "It's very good to be safe in America."

"Well, I wouldn't know about all that, but make sure you keep your room clean. I don't want any roaches coming upstairs from … well, you know."

"Roaches? What is this, Mrs. Landry?"

"Never mind. Just keep my house clean."

"That I will, Mrs. Landry. I'll be your tidiest guest."

Yushua Maalouf's move from a Yemeni refugee camp to a basement apartment in Roswell, Georgia, happened in near record time. Between his adept mastery of refugee law and his powerful connections within the State Department, Francis Murphy knew how to get things done. With his proficiency, coupled with a motivated sponsoring partner like Tom Butts and LifePointe Chapel, the job couldn't have been easier. LifePointe promised a two-year contract employing Yushua as a church custodian, as well as committed to securing affordable housing for him. That's where Mrs. Landry's "generosity" came in.

Yushua carefully arranged the contents of his box within his new, one-room apartment. Mrs. Landry's offering was seen as austere and out-of-date by many of her previous lodgers, but to this prisoner-turned-refugee, it was a palatial sanctuary.

As Yushua was pressing the three shirts that were given to him by Francis, a muffled screeching sound came from outside his basement door. It was an exasperated Mrs. Landry leaning down over the stairs, hunching red-faced and shouting.

"Yes, Mrs. Landry? Can I help you?"

"Finally. What took you so long? I'm not going to become your private secretary, so you'll need to get your own telephone."

"Yes, Mrs. Right away. I will try."

"Like I've said three times, Pastor Tom will be by to pick you up in an hour."

"Thank you, Mrs. Landry. I'm so sorry, Mrs. Landry."

In precisely an hour, Tom Butts pulled into the driveway in an old navy and faux woodgrain Dodge minivan. Yushua, who was waiting on the front steps, stood up as quickly as he could and hobbled over to him.

"Hello, Pastor Tom. It is so wonderful to see you again."

"You got in all right? Planned on meeting you at the airport, but something came up with my kids. Sorry about that. You found my Uber, it looks like?"

"Yes, a man with a red coat helped me. The airport is so big."

"Biggest in the world. Or busiest. One or the other. Anyway, isn't Mrs. Landry a peach?"

Yushua, having no idea what Tom meant, nodded noncommittedly.

"Yeah, she's been housing students for years. Seems to work out well." And then with a smirk he said, "Just a word of warning: keep her tea roses blooming. If you kill 'em, you won't be staying there long."

Tom signaled and then turned off the road onto a private street. Manicured shrubs and carefully arranged flower gardens surrounded a large, rectangular concrete monument. "LifePointe Chapel" was written with twenty-four-inch patinaed copper letters. Below it, with eighteen-inch letters that were much less weathered was written, *Dr. James Norris, Sr. Pastor.*

Yushua was gobsmacked as the minivan drove by parking lot after parking lot that covered the sixty-two-acre campus on its way to the staff lot. As they turned a corner around a small forest, he got his first glimpse of a series of tall brick buildings. Standing proudly facing the interstate below was a church campus that dwarfed his university in Aden.

"This is a church? All this? One church?"

"Pretty impressive, I guess. Over ten thousand people used to come here. Now we're less than two. It takes almost everything we got to keep this thing going. But now we got some cheap labor, so that should help," Tom said with another smirk.

Tom pulled into a parking spot marked "Executive Pastor," turned off the minivan, reached into the backseat, and grabbed a blue file folder. "I had my assistant prepare this. There are employment forms, a Fulton County bus schedule, an application form to Truist Bank—that's who we deal with. There's also an application form to the Georgia Tech Law Department—international student forms. You'll want to get on that one ASAP."

Tom then handed Yushua a small white box. "Here's a phone. It's one of Jimmy's old ones, but we hooked it up to the church account. It'll give you six months until you get some credit here in the States. Now let's go inside. I'll show you around."

Yushua was already overwhelmed. As they walked from one hallway to the next, he couldn't help but contrast what he was seeing to Muhammad's humble apartment. *These are both churches? These Isa communities are the same thing?* Yushua wondered to himself. *Maybe, in time, Yemen's Isa communities will look like this.* He smiled ruefully to himself as he wondered what Fatimah would have thought of this American church.

"We're almost to the staff building. We got a little surprise for you."

Tom rounded a corner to another hallway marked "Executive Offices" that was blocked by a glass wall and double glass doors. He punched in a security code, and they entered.

"Morning, Janice," Tom said to a blonde middle-aged lady at the front desk.

"They're already there. Most of 'em anyway," she said. "And you must be the Joshua we've heard so much about, bless your heart. Welcome to LifePointe."

"Thank you, Miss ..." Yushua hesitated.

"Janice Bellows. Mrs. Janice Bellows. Janice, this is Yushua."

"Oh my gosh, I'm so sorry. 'Yoo-shoo-waa,'" she said in an exaggerated manner with big red pursed lips. "It might take me a while, but I'll get there. I'm usually pretty good with funny names."

"Thank you, Mrs. Bellows."

Tom turned and led Yushua further into the staff complex. They passed office door after office door, each complete with a name plate that described a ministry function. *So many Isa community jobs I've never heard of before*, he thought to himself.

"What is a 'Boomer Director,' Pastor Tom?"

"Mostly it's the guy in charge of taking the old people on trips," he answered. "It sounds like fun, but it's really a major pain in the you know what. It's a pretty high maintenance crowd."

Even though Tom used simple English words that Yushua easily understood, he still had no idea what Tom just said. *How is taking old people on trips a function of an Isa community?* he wondered. Yushua knew that he had so much to learn.

"Okay, here we are." Tom led Yushua into Staff Conference Room A. There were nine people sitting around a large boardroom table with an enticing cake and about a dozen empty chairs. "LifePointe team, this is Yushua. Yushua, this is ..."

Janice interrupted, "So sorry, Pastor Tom, I should have mentioned this earlier. As you know, Jimmy's annual staff golf tournament is this afternoon, and he wanted to take the guys out for an early round. 'Get the rust off,' he said. He'll try to stop by to say hi on Monday."

Tom, seemingly unphased, continued introductions. There were four ladies who served as assistants, two men who worked IT, and three custodial staff. "Yushua, you'll be working closely with Juan Rodrigues; he's in charge of everything at LifePointe. We wouldn't survive a day without him. And then there's, uh, Julio, and then, uh ... Gey ..."

"Guillermo Lopez," Juan came to the rescue.

"Yes, Guillermo. He works the outside. He does a fantastic job. You might wanna bend his ear for a little intel for Mrs. Landry's tea roses," Tom said with a wink.

Yushua smiled unconvincingly.

"Welcome, Yushua," Juan said. "It'll be an honor to work with you, my friend."

"Well, let's dig into that cake," interrupted Tom. We don't want to offend Janice."

"Kroger, actually," Janice said as she watched from the doorway. "I just love their butter cake. It's even better the next day. There are paper plates and napkins on the credenza so y'all can just help yourselves."

"So, tell us why you came to America," said Ethan, who was a rather round IT intern, doubling this afternoon as LifePointe's in-house journalist.

The church leadership was in the midst of launching their first ever Christmas missions campaign, and no effort would be spared. The proceeds of the operation would go to hire a missions pastor, who would be responsible for mobilizing the people of LifePointe in hands-on experiences. The inspiration was taken directly from Chad Collins' recommendations, with only the slightest of modifications. When the senior team was brainstorming for inspirational stories they could leverage, Tom Butts immediately thought of Yushua.

"You're not going to hear a more powerful testimony than Yushua Maalouf's story," said Tom.

"Ya mean our janitor, Mr. Limpy?" asked Chip Bussey, in the most dubious tone he could muster.

Chuckles and snorts reverberated around Staff Conference Room B. Even Jimmy had to cover his mouth to conceal his tickle.

But not Tom. Not at all. His blood was boiling. He had heard the comments before, but he always kept his tongue. But he could no longer. "Listen, Chip. Listen everyone. Our 'janitor' limps because he was kidnapped and imprisoned for Jesus. He was tortured for weeks and still would not deny Jesus. He watched his sister and his church family be executed. Shot in the head. Yes, they were all shot in the head in front of him. And he still remained faithful. It kinda makes singin' in church look like pretty much nothing, doesn't it, Chip? Huh? I think his faith just about trumps everyone else's in this room. What do you think, Chip? Think that you could go toe to toe with 'Mr. Limpy'? I don't think so. Y'all should be ashamed of yourselves."

And then Tom stormed out of Staff Conference Room B.

Apparently, a different tone was struck following Tom's prophetic tongue lashing. Though Tom was no longer in attendance, somehow Yushua had gone from being the butt of a cruel joke to becoming the centerpiece around which the missions campaign would be built. The theme would be called "Our Global Church," and would highlight how LifePointe was called to teach the world to make disciples of Christ. And they would go to hard places. The hardest. And they would leave the Venezuelas of the world to churches of lesser grit. If LifePointe was going to do missions, they would go the whole hog.

So, Jimmy gave clear instructions to Chip: "Go buy him a whole new wardrobe. The whole nine yards. And burn his old stuff. I mean literally, burn it. I'm gonna check. And make sure he gets a decent haircut. And by everything that's holy, do something with those whiskers. He's about to represent LifePointe, so he'd better start looking like LifePointe. We're only gonna get one shot at this."

The video package was to include five three-minute stories. They would produce it all in-house, to the high standards that their people demanded. They would start running the videos five weeks before Christmas, culminating with the big ask. And to reinforce the message, a weekly Community Group discussion guide would be produced that would match the themes of the videos. The whole thing was brilliant.

First, there would be a story on why Yushua came to America. It was to strike a patriotic chord without being overbearing. Second, there would be a video on why Yushua rejected Islam. This was to help LifePointers see and viscerally feel the truth of their faith. Third, a video on how LifePointe could help reach Yemen with the gospel. This would prepare the congregation for upcoming mission trips. Fourth, a video on Yushua's story of the underground church. Give people a sense of gratitude for all the blessings they have at LifePointe. And everything would set the table for the final week. The fifth and final story would be Yushua telling people why they should give sacrificially to missions.

If they did this right, they should be able to underwrite their missions pastor's salary, plus some program budget to keep things moving forward. And they would do things right. They were now doing missions in a way that was natural to them.

"Why I wanted to come to America?" Yushua asked.

"Yes, in your own words. Just talk; we can edit so everything comes out just right," Ethan said as encouragingly as he could.

And Yushua had a lot he could say. He had been a refugee in Atlanta for almost a year and his life had changed entirely. He had re-started law school, this time at Georgia Tech. His TOEFL and his LSAT scores were so high that he was admitted in the first round of applications. He enjoyed his custodial work under the supervision of Juan Rodrigues. And even Mrs. Bobbie Landry had warmed up to him. Likely it was because her tea roses had never looked better. So much had changed for Yushua.

But the one thing that changed the most also troubled Yushua the most.

Isa seemed an ocean away.

Chapter Twelve

The Axe

It was a beautiful, sunny winter Friday afternoon in North Fulton County. Local golf courses and tennis courts were humming with activity as professionals with flexible schedules took advantage of stunning weather. LifePointe's campus, as usual for a Friday, was almost completely empty with most of the salaried employees taking off for unscheduled urgent appointments off site. There was a handful of administrative staff remaining, the custodians, and the ever-faithful Tom Butts.

But Yushua's countenance didn't match the sunny weather that was outside. He walked into the maintenance break room this Friday afternoon looking completely bewildered.

"I think I've been fired," he said to Juan Rodrigues. "Tom said there were budget cuts, and that my position had to be eliminated … But I think I was fired."

Juan looked completely shocked. "What? I hadn't heard anything about this. Why do you think you've been fired? You've been doing good work."

Yushua didn't look up. "I do not know for sure. Tom's eyes weren't telling me what his lips were telling me. He did not believe the words he was saying. Besides, we all know that LifePointe celebrated its best year financially since Pastor Jimmy arrived."

Juan looked even more confused. "So, why do you think you were fired then?"

"It must be because I told the truth. And you cannot do that in this place. Truth is forbidden. You are only allowed to agree with the lie," Yushua said, rubbing his furrowed forehead. "Sometimes this place reminds me more of our mosque in Aden than a true Jesus community."

"What lie must we agree with? What are you talking about?" Juan asked, more mystified than ever.

Yushua, inspecting the crack in the concrete floor between his feet, slowly shook his head. "I've said enough."

Juan, now with an increased measure of concern, raised his voice. "What did you say? Was it something about our maintenance team?"

Yushua sat down on a plastic chair beside a wire shelf that held LifePointe's cleaning products. "No, brother. Nothing like that," he said in a reassuring tone. "After the Christmas videos I was invited to speak to many of the church's Community Groups. They wanted to hear more of my story about the mosque and Muhammad and Fatimah and the prison. I told my story many times. Maybe more than seven."

Juan looked confused, "And they're firing you for this?"

"I think so. Well, not really that. But I think for what happened at Pastor Chip's house."

"What happened there?"

"The group that meets at his house asked me to come and speak. But after that, Pastor Chip said that Pastor Jimmy didn't want me to speak anymore. And they removed the videos from the website."

"What did you do there, Yushua? What happened?"

"I told my story, and everyone clapped at the end. It was just like the other times. And then one man, an older gentleman, asked a bad question."

"A bad question?"

"Yes. A dangerous question."

"What did he ask?"

"He asked, 'Why don't we see God do things like you experienced in Yemen here at LifePointe?' And I didn't know what to say. How do you answer a question like that and not get in trouble?"

"What did you say?" asked Juan.

"I said nothing at first, I just tried to escape. I said, 'You must see them, maybe it's just that you don't remember them right now. If it's a Jesus community, you must see God things.'"

Juan, leaning forward, slowly nodded his head as if to say, "That makes sense."

"Yes, and Pastor Chip agreed with me. He said, 'Remember, God moves in mysterious ways. Sometimes we just can't see what he does.'"

"And this will get you fired?" Juan asked, more concerned than ever.

"Well, there was more. Things didn't exactly end there." Yushua paused as he stared into the distance. "Most of the people disagreed with Pastor Chip. They didn't like the words, 'God works in mysterious ways.' There were many people talking all at once …"

Yushua stood up and nervously paced in a small circle around the breakroom table. "The older gentleman was very irritated. Vexed. He said, 'I've never seen anything at LifePointe that I couldn't explain in a business plan. Nothing different than my years at Verizon. I've heard stories like yours from missionaries before. Many times. My grandson planted a church in Seattle and then in Vancouver and he has many God stories. They're amazing. But not here. Never here. I've been a part of this church for over twenty years, and I can't think of a single one. Nothing like your sister's dream and her healing in the brook. Nothing like your escape from prison. Nothing even close. Maybe a good parking spot on a rainy

Sunday morning, but that's about it. Where is God at LifePointe? Why doesn't he ever move here?'"

"That is bad," Juan agreed. "But it was the old man who spoke, not you, Yushua."

"Yes. And I remained quiet. Until ..."

"Until what?"

"Until Pastor Chip's wife, Mrs. Lisa, asked me, 'Yushua, do you have an opinion on this? Why have you had so many God stories and we here have had so few?'"

I didn't know what to do. I didn't know the right thing to say. I mean, I knew what to say, but didn't want to say it. Do you know what I mean?"

Juan nodded unconvincingly. "So, what did you say?" he asked.

"I said, and perhaps this is where I went too far, but I said, 'Maybe we don't need God stories at LifePointe? Maybe, like the man said, we can just roll out smart corporate strategies and grow 5 percent year over year. But does any of that really require God? Maybe God stories are only for those who need God.'"

"You said that?" Juan asked. "What did they do?"

"Yes. And maybe I should have stopped there. But I didn't."

"You said more?"

"Yes, a little. I felt led by Jesus to retell them his story of the wealthy young master, but LifePointe style. I said, 'What if we knew for certain, for 100 percent certain, that Jesus was asking us to sell our beautiful church property, give the money to one hundred different ministries, and then relocate services to the high school. And what if we knew that this decision would shrink our LifePointe's congregation by one-half our size. But what if we also knew, for certain, that the kingdom would advance one hundred times the size of LifePointe because of that selfless decision. If we knew that, would we lead the charge to follow Jesus in this way? Because if our answer is "no," or even "maybe," I shouldn't expect to see any God stories in our future.'"

"*Híjole*! And for this you were chopped?"

"I don't know. Probably. Pastor Chip was very cross with me that evening. When he drove me to my apartment that night, he told me I should have minded my own business and stuck to cleaning the toilets."

Juan was counting on his fingers and looked slightly puzzled. "The Christmas videos were over two months ago, so why now?"

Yushua looked up, smiled at his companion, and said, "This is a mystery to me as well, brother. I must believe that Jesus has a new assignment for me."

Luca sat at his desk at the Fishtown Y and stared at the wooden-framed photograph of his father, the late Dr. Josiah Lewis, his dear, sweet papa. "I'm a lot like you, Papa … I have your dream now too," he said out loud to the smiling man looking back at him. The season of harvest that followed the great Philadelphia ice storm had put the beginnings of his movement into motion. And he owed so much of it to his father.

He picked up a pen and began to doodle as he thought. How could he express what was becoming more and more clear in his own mind and heart? How could he convey it in a way that others could understand and be motivated by? He needed a compelling vision to guide the movement. A statement of countercultural values that would shape the kingdom culture his papa had yearned for.

He needed a manifesto.

With bold block letters he wrote at the top of the page, *THE VENAL DOGMATA MANIFESTO.*

He knew his idea wasn't just a reaction to what he didn't like. He had long grown beyond his frustration with the Sunday-morning-centeredness of Mt. Pisgah. Instead, his vision for Philadelphia Freedom was coming out of a newfound recognition of the spiritual disorders that lurked everywhere he looked.

He thought about his shopping trip to Patterson's Jewelry and all the other Brendas around the city who live their lives unaware of any good news that could unburden their anxious souls. As he leaned back at his desk and once again recollected that fateful encounter, he realized that this was the seminal event that had shifted his soul.

And it would stay shifted.

DISORDER #1: THE SPIRITUAL LIMITATIONS OF THE PEOPLE IN OUR COMMUNITY, he wrote in big block letters. He was convinced that most people in his community had no axe to grind when it came to the gospel. The ice storm proved that. People were simply totally unaware of the true Christian message. *How many more Brendas are out there?* he contemplated. *Neighbors who have not rejected the good news of Jesus—they simply think that we have a different gospel? One that has more to do with a cultural, economic, and political worldview than anything else.* Luca was fully convinced that it wasn't Brenda's responsibility to seek out the church. It was the church's responsibility to go and find the Brendas.

But will the church? Do they even want to? he wondered. *Do we really care in the first place?* He knew the true answer, which led him to the next disorder:

DISORDER #2: MALAISE IN THE CHURCH, he slowly wrote.

Sure, most churches could work up some emotion and manufacture some passion within the walls of the building during the appointed worship hour—but then what? Why did it almost never translate into gospel action? Why did it all seem so put on?

He put down his pen and leaned back in his old chair. He knew why. He had seen it all his life—in fact, he had had a front row seat to the source of the problem. There was little to no action beyond the Sunday spectacular because the gospel wasn't really anybody's responsibility except the pastor's. They paid him for that. Plumbers don't ask the pastor to snake toilets, mechanics don't ask pastors to change crank shafts, and pastors should take care of the religion business and let plumbers plumb and mechanics twist wrenches. Certainly, nobody would state it quite so crassly, but he knew that was the general sentiment. No one saw the gospel as their job. It was hired out. Contracted. And that was a problem.

THE BIG IDEA. He wrote those three words with deliberate strokes and a determined expression on his face. Luca's big idea was that the gospel would be everyone's mission. All Joes and with far fewer pros. Plumbers, mechanics, schoolteachers, and accountants all had a mission: they had a gospel responsibility. In fact, they had two vocations, both holy callings: one which put bread on the table and gave them missional opportunities in the everyday rhythms of life, the other to equip the body of Christ toward the mission of Christ. Conjoined together, they made it possible to serve their community in the name, power, and authority of Jesus Christ; co-vocations that seamlessly synced together as a singular kingdom-centered parish that was infinitely reproducible.

Luca could already imagine the kingdom punch. In fact, he was watching it play out in front of him. And the thought of it made him smile.

However, thoughts of Mt. Pisgah Baptist Church reminded him that there was an additional limitation to any future movement, one he would need to be vigilant to safeguard if Philadelphia Freedom was ever to become a movement.

DISORDER #3: THE CIRCULAR LOGIC OF HOW CHURCHES OPERATE, he added to his list.

If the gospel was going to hit the streets instead of lingering stagnantly in safe sanctuaries, then churches would have to organize leadership around that gospel mission and not simply around Sunday services. There would always be a shepherding function to care for the needs of those in distress—but that would be only one of several roles required for a missionary advance.

He scribbled a random design around the edges of the paper while he thought about what needed to happen. To Luca, internal preoccupations had long proven ineffective for external advance. If God were to unleash the potential of Philadelphia Freedom, it would be by reconciling the local body of Christ with the Person of Christ. Through multiplying a diverse leadership team structure, they together would resemble the person and ministry of Jesus Christ. Just as Jesus was all at once a missionary, truth teller, evangelist, good shepherd, and teacher, so too his body on earth should embody and prioritize all these functions. At least if Luca had his way. And Ephesians 4:1–16 would become their movement's constitution.

Luca leaned back again and recalled his papa's growing frustration with Mt. Pisgah in the days leading up to the big vote. One sermon in particular was as vivid in Luca's memory as the day it was preached. He remembered his papa walking to the pulpit to preach from this text, and he introduced it by saying, "Today, I am going to show you from God's Holy Word how too many local churches have become, in our day, impotent, frivolous, irrelevant religious institutions instead of being the most powerful influence for good in the world—the influence that it was designed from all eternity to wield."

From there, Dr. Josiah Lewis traced back through the past decades of church history how things had become undone. He started by expounding on God's eternal intentions for his church. He preached, "Apostolic leaders are our missionaries. They think mission. They plant churches that think mission. The prophets among us keep things honest. They filter everything through questions like, Is this in line with God's Word? and, Is this in line with what God has asked of us? The evangelists create an engaging culture with the outside world. They recruit the new kingdom troops. The shepherds care for the needs of the flock. And the teachers equip the body to obey the Head. You see, God's plan is designed for movement!"

Luca remembered that the congregation seemed to be in agreement with his papa to this point of the message, with hearty "amens" and "preach" and "say so's" generously and frequently offered.

But then his father began to meddle.

"But what has happened? Why do we not see this apostolic-missionary impulse present in the very church today that claims to bear Jesus' name? Why don't we see it in our church? I'll tell you why!" he said with the conviction and authority of a man who had just come down from a holy mountain. "It is not because we are theologically confused by differences between offices and functions. No sir! And it's not because we do not understand that the body of Christ is supposed to function with the same priorities as the Person of Christ. No sir! And no ma'am! It is only because we have become a very selfish people."

From this point of the message onward, the "amens" and "uh-huhs" were no longer a thing. The room was still and quiet. But Luca's papa did not relent. "Missionaries think mission," he shouted. "But the ninety and nine safe sheep in the fancy air-conditioned sheep pen cry, 'meee, meee.' And they do not stop. They never stop. They go on endlessly crying to have their precious needs met. They can only think of themselves, and their minds are on themselves all the time. So, the apostolic leaders grow tired, frustrated, exasperated, and weary with the unwillingness of the self-absorbed church to join Christ in his redemptive mission. And so, they leave.

"Now the church no longer has a compelling mission or a gospel-obeying people. So, the prophets have nothing to do. And they leave.

"And with the prophets gone, the evangelists have nobody in the house to keep them honest, so they'll do anything to get a sale. 'Raise your hand if you want to go to heaven!' Can I get a witness?"

But no witness was to be found. Only more silence.

Luca remembered his papa, dramatically slowing his cadence, hunching over and whispering into the microphone. "And this leaves the shepherds and the teachers—God bless 'em—to care for, and attempt to disciple, a largely un-re-gen-er-ate congregation that doesn't care a lick about the mission of Jesus Christ."

And then Dr. Lewis grew quiet. With both elbows firmly planted on the mahogany pulpit, clasping his hands together and with closed eyes, he said softly, "Beloved, this history that I have just described is the very history of our very own Mt. Pisgah Baptist Church."

The room was in shock. The only sound in the hushed sanctuary that Luca could recall was the twirling blades of the ceiling fans above them.

"Seventy-six years previously, we started as an inner-city rescue mission under the courageous and apostolic leadership of the Reverend Isaiah Townsend. But look what we have become today. Now, we have to have a vote on whether or not we will be a selfish, self-centered, and self-consumed people. How can this be the church of Jesus Christ?"

Memories like this do not easily fade away. For Luca, this one moment cemented his resolve and prepared his spirit for a new life that lay in front of him.

And it could be a big life.

Luca thumbed through the tattered pages of his well-worn Bible and pored over the Ephesians text once again. As he read, deep emotions rose to the surface. His spirit was whirling with feelings of both excitement and aggravation. Excited about what could be. What was becoming. What was going to be. And aggravation by what had been. Because it didn't have to be. If only Mt. Pisgah had had the courage and conviction to represent the mission of Christ instead of the conveniences of their precious status quo.

If only.

But then his frustration gave way to a profound, singular feeling of excitement. A broad smile grew across Luca's face that turned his eyes into narrow, deep slits. "We're doing this, Papa," he said with a quiet conviction. "We are doing this. Right in your backyard. Just like you said."

Then Luca leaned back in his chair once again and read out loud from Ephesians four to the familiar, loving, and sympathetic face that was always smiling back at him:

"I therefore, a prisoner for the Lord, urge you to walk in a manner worthy of the calling to which you have been called, with all humility and gentleness, with patience, bearing with one another in love, eager to maintain the unity of the Spirit in the bond of peace. There is one body and one Spirit—just as you were called to the one hope that belongs to your call—one Lord, one faith, one baptism, one God and Father of all, who is over all and through all and in all. But grace was given to each one of us according to the measure of Christ's gift ... And he gave the apostles, the prophets, the evangelists, the shepherds and teachers, to equip the saints for the work of ministry, for building up the body of Christ, until we all attain to the unity of the faith and of the knowledge of the Son of God, to mature manhood, to the measure of the stature of the fullness of Christ, so that we may no longer be children, tossed to and fro by the waves and carried about by every wind of doctrine, by human cunning, by craftiness in deceitful schemes. Rather, speaking the truth in love, we are to grow up in every way into him who is the head, into Christ, from whom the whole body, joined and held together by every joint with which it is equipped, when each part is working properly, makes the body grow so that it builds itself up in love."

It was all so obvious to Luca. He knew what he must do next. He had to flesh out role descriptions, responsibilities, and the characteristics of the people who would fill them. He would describe it as "a diverse co-vocational leadership team unleashed for kingdom revelation outside the safety of church walls." The thought gave him goosebumps already.

But first he had to finish this list. The final disorder, as he saw it.

DISORDER #4: THE PROBLEM OF CORPORATE GRAVITATIONAL PULL. Looking at the words he had just written brought to his mind the decision-making process that Mt. Pisgah Baptist's leadership had always used. Every decision was made based on a single criterion: Would this be good for the church? It had seemed obvious to Luca that to the board of Mt. Pisgah Baptist Church, the preservation of the church would always be the option that protected them from exercising faith. His church's motto might just as well have been ripped off Bowman's Construction's billboard that was now ironically erected on the new site of Liberty Village Lofts, which broadcasted in bold letters, *Safety First!*

To Luca, playing it safe was the very antithesis of following Christ. The $141,500 passing of the hat had proved that forever. And God had proved faithful in all the provision that had poured in to pay back their generosity through crowdfunding and donations, following the ice storm. Yet safety was the singular impulse that guided Mt. Pisgah. Even though Jesus spoke of the spiritual death mingled in the activity of "saving ourselves," looking back, Luca's churchmanship had not discipled him to become a follower of Jesus. To follow Jesus, you have to go somewhere. Luca could see through the smokescreen of the flowery spiritual language that had rechristened darkness to the more palatable terms of "corporate stewardship" and "sustainability"—and he was no longer fooled by the sacred sleight of hand. Though the spiritual obfuscation may have bamboozled many, Luca was no longer among them. His papa had shown him many times over that "the shell game was always rigged in favor of the house. And it's seldom God's house."

He chuckled to himself as he remembered the day he had cheekily said to his papa after an exhausting covenant membership meeting, "Say what you want, Pops, but darkness is what darkness does."

His father, always the teacher, replied with a wink and yet a slightly corrective tone, "I think you mean, 'A rose by any other name would smell as sweet.'"

To which Luca blurted, "Or, more fittingly, Pops, 'A pile of purse-poodle poo plopped in a Chestnut Street Gucci bag—still stinketh to high heaven!'"

They had both bent over in cathartic laughter and howled until tears ran down their faces. "Sh-Shakesp-Shakespeare had never been quite so eloquent, son," Luca's papa managed to stammer, desperately trying to regain composure.

There had been some good memories.

But now, looking ahead to the challenges to come, the gravitational pull toward corporate security was almost impossible to overcome in the Sunday-centric version of "church" he had known. It had been linked too deeply for too long to our fallen selves. So, Philadelphia Freedom would have to de-link itself from the problem by rejecting the self-saving cry for *addition*, and instead, lean into the self-sacrificial call of *multiplication*.

Luca was craving some strong coffee. The last thing he added to his well-doodled page was the phrase that he knew would lock all of this down. Permanently. It would in fact change everything: *Philadelphia Freedom is a growing group of friends who give themselves away to reveal the beautiful kingdom of God.*

Luca Lewis was now living and leading his papa's kingdom dream.

Chapter Thirteen

The Prophet

"Should I bring a tie, hon?" Luca asked.

"I would. It's easy to leave it in the closet. Hard to fix once you're there and don't have it."

"Right. Makes sense. Call me an Uber? I'll be ready in ten."

"Got it. Give me a sec."

"Thanks. Blue tie or red?"

"Not red, definitely not red … Okay, it's a silver Honda Accord. It'll be here in twelve minutes."

"Thanks, sweetie."

Luca Lewis wasn't by any means a world traveler. He much preferred staying close to the comforts of the world that he knew. But this day he was off to speak at a national meeting of Y directors. Normally, he avoided this gathering, not for any fault of the meeting itself; the few times that he had attended, he found it helpful. His reluctance was only because it wasn't held in Philly. Chantel, who would have preferred to see a bit more of the world, would often tease him, saying he was the original homeboy.

When he'd said goodbye to Sanders that morning, he'd promised to pick him up a souvenir. He seemed particularly keen on getting a keychain, so Luca was hopeful he'd be able to find something at the airport if he didn't get a chance for shopping. It might be the most expensive keychain he'd ever bought, but it would be worth it for that nine-year-old's smile.

"Bye, hon. I'll be back on Friday."

"Love you, baby. Kill it like usual. I'm so proud of you."

"Thanks. Give Sanders a squeeze from me, and I'll try to call to say goodnight."

Luca bounced his overnighter down the steps and tossed it into the open trunk. Then he shut the back door that was open and waiting for him and sat in the front passenger seat.

"You mind? I hate feeling like I'm being chauffeured. This way I can make a new friend."

"No problem at all. Airport, sir? Which terminal?"

"Whatever Delta is. I'm sorry, I should have looked that up."

"D, I believe. No problem. We will see the signs to make sure. But I think I remember 'D for Delta.'"

The Uber driver appeared to Luca to be in his mid-twenties. Likely from Iran or Iraq. But unlike most of the immigrants that he dealt with at the Y, the driver's English was impeccable, as was the Honda. Even though it was one of the oldest rideshare cars he'd been in, there wasn't a wrapper, smudge, or speck to be seen.

"Nice car. You sure keep it nice. These Hondas are great."

"Thank you, sir. It's not mine. I rent it from someone."

"I see. How long have you been with Uber?"

"A very short time. Two months. Three, I guess now … So, where are you flying to?"

"Atlanta. I'm speaking at a conference there."

"Congratulations. That is very nice. What will you speak on?"

"Thank you. I lead the Y over in Fishtown, and a dear friend of mine leads the Y in Strawberry Mansion. When the big ice storm paralyzed the city, we teamed up with a church and became one big ole rescue mission. I lead the church, too. So, we kind of teamed up with ourselves. It's complicated."

"So, you're speaking about the church or the partnership? Or both?"

"Both, I guess. Even though the 'C' in YMCA stands for 'Christian,' most directors are pretty hesitant to get involved with religion. And I get that. A lot of bad has been done in the name of 'C,' especially in recent years. What I hope to show is that when folks serve the community in the name of the real 'C,' Jesus Christ—not the religion that's named after him—a lot of good can happen. That's what happened here in Philly."

Luca paused for a second to gauge the interest of his companion. "Does that make any sense to you?"

The Uber driver said nothing. With his hands firmly planted at ten and two o'clock on the steering wheel, he stared vacantly through the windshield giving no visible cues that he had heard anything Luca had said.

Luca, now a bit uncomfortable, tried something that he regretted he hadn't thought of earlier. "I'm Luca, by the way. Luca Lewis."

"Yes, I see that. Thank you … Something that you said has bothered me. I've only been in America a short time. Less than two years. Can I ask you a question about Christianity?"

"By all means," Luca responded. "But just so you know, I'm not its official spokesman."

Once again, the driver had no reaction.

"My question is this: Why does Christianity in America …" he paused to restart. "Why do churches …"

"Go ahead, my friend. You won't offend me, I promise. Ask your question."

"Okay. See my face? What do you see?"

"Do you mean those scars?"

"Yes, the scars. These are scars for Jesus. Where I came from, churches—'secret communities' we called them—suffered in order to live like Jesus. The words of Jesus shaped how we thought, how we lived, and even how we felt. I watched friends die because they believed that Jesus' words were truer than the threats of Jesus' enemies." His voice became husky. "I watched my sister die for the same reason."

Another pause from the driver. And then a heavy sigh.

"My question for you is this: Why do Christ followers not believe Jesus' words? Why do his communities in this country think that their organization is Jesus' kingdom? Even when their organization behaves in ways that are exactly opposite to his kingdom? And why do they try so hard to 'save themselves' from ever having to walk by faith? From ever having to put Jesus' words to the test? And then, how can these organizations, who are full of people who don't really know each other, ever become Jesus' transformed body?"

Now it was Luca's turn to let out a heavy sigh.

"Brother, what's taken you less than two years to see has taken me my entire lifetime. I don't have any answers for you. But I know that you're asking the right questions. I think you've just taken my own pesky questions to a deeper place."

The driver pulled over by the domestic Delta gates. "Here we are, terminal D. Thank you, Luca Lewis. You have encouraged my soul today. May Jesus use you powerfully in Atlanta. May your audience never forget what the true 'C' really means."

Luca was reeling. He had been given truth that had been nailed to the deepest part of his soul, and it hurt. The question, "Why don't Christ followers believe Jesus' words?" stuck to his heart like glue.

"Why don't I believe?" Luca said, not realizing that he had said it out loud. "Thank you, brother. Thank you so much."

Luca grabbed his bag from the trunk and disappeared into the crowd.

It was the calm before the storm. Luca had arrived in Atlanta a day early to prepare his speeches and to decompress. Working a full-time job leading the Y, plus the demands of keeping up with Philadelphia Freedom, left Luca with precious few minutes to himself. Friends and acquaintances from across the country would be descending on the Marriott later in the day, turning the hotel lobby into a giant, exhausting meet n' greet. Luca was grateful for the quiet.

"Let's see, I'll have a grande Americano with an extra shot. Leave some room please." Luca was proud that he pulled off the order like a pro.

With coffee and notebook in hand, he made his way to a quiet corner with two vacant wingbacks. He pulled over a side table and set up his office for the morning.

He had no sooner sat down when he heard, "Seat taken?" A clean-shaven man in his early forties sporting a white Nike golf shirt gestured toward the empty chair.

"By all means," Luca said, gesturing to the other wingback.

"Thanks. Mind if I leave my stuff and grab a coffee? Need anything else?"

"No, I'm good, thank you."

Luca glanced at the pile he left on the chair. *An Atlanta Journal-Constitution* draped over a couple of books and a black leather Bible. A silver laptop was at the bottom.

A Bible. That's something you don't see every day in the streets of Philly, Luca thought to himself. *I'm not in Kansas anymore.*

In a few minutes, the stranger returned. "Thanks. Coffee's just what I needed. Think I'm still waking up this morning."

"Not a problem whatsoever." He pointed to the pile that was being moved on the floor. "Your stack really did the job … I couldn't help but notice that you brought the good book. Are you a Christ follower?"

"Yes sir, I am. I pastor a church north of the city. I come to this hotel a couple times a year to meet with some staff—get out of the fray and hopefully get some fresh perspective. I'm Jimmy. And you are …?"

"Luca. Luca Lewis, out of Philly. Came for a conference that starts tomorrow."

The two strangers set their coffees on Luca's makeshift office table and then shook hands.

"Pleased to meet you, Luca."

"Likewise."

"So, what brings you from Philly?"

"Did you hear about our big ice storm last year?"

"Well, yeah. It was on the news nonstop. Looked terrible."

"It really was terrible. I lead a Y in Philly, and I also lead a church. Well, sort of a church. It doesn't look much like most churches, I suppose. Anyway, when the ice storm hit, we knew our neighbors could freeze to death if we didn't do something. So, the people in our group ponied up all the cash we could spare, and we opened two Ys in the area to house and care for people who had no place to go. It was the most amazing thing. For three weeks we tended to our community, and God showed up like nothing I've ever seen before. We saw rival gang members reconcile with one another. Big, tough, tattooed gangsters all huggin' and cryin'. We saw drug dealers flush their products down the commode. I didn't tell the city about that one. For one fella, Fizzy was his name, that was a whole lot of flushes. We watched estranged husbands and wives repent and then reunite."

"Wow, that's beautiful, brother," said a mesmerized Jimmy, holding his untasted coffee.

"It was unbelievably beautiful. And we saw dozens and dozens of folks in the neighborhood repent and follow Jesus. In the last year, we've started six new missional communities that are already bursting at the seams. We're having a hard time keeping up with things."

"Holy cow. Praise God, that sounds amazing," Jimmy said. "So, you're here for a Christian conference to share that story?"

"Oh no, not at all. I'm here to speak at our national Y gathering. I will be speaking about leveraging our assets through community partnerships for the benefit of our neighborhoods. The example I'll use is what happened with the Philly ice storm."

Jimmy spoke slowly as he thought it out. "So, the Y's properties become assets for the neighborhood's welfare instead of for the organization's benefit?"

"Exactly. It shouldn't be much of a shift for most directors, but it can be for some."

"Hmm. Maybe our churches could learn a thing or two from the Y," Jimmy said, as if the words that were formed and emerging from his mouth came as a surprise to him.

"I believe you're right, Jimmy. My father was a pastor of a Baptist church in the city. Philly that is. For the life of him, he couldn't get the congregation to see its real mission. They could only see Sunday services as their reason to be. He literally died trying to make the shift."

"My daddy was a pastor, too. He's still alive, though. H. A. Norris. He left quite a shadow for us kids to follow."

"Oh, wow," Luca said, somewhat startled. "Yes, I've definitely heard of your father. I guess who in America hasn't? That would be some shadow. One that I wouldn't fit under for a number of reasons, I'm guessing."

"I get it. He always had political opinions, but, just between us, I think those last years of his ministry he got totally carried away. He just wouldn't listen to anyone. It's too bad, too. He's gonna forever be remembered by those days. Not by his forty years of ministry before that."

"Well, legacies are what they are, I guess. S'pose what really matters is our faithfulness to Jesus while we're breathing the air on this side of heaven. Bizarrely, I was most profoundly reminded of that yesterday by my Uber driver, of all people."

"So that sounds like a story I'd like to hear!" exclaimed Jimmy, eyebrows raised. "Oh man, I just realized the time. My boys have been waiting on me for a few minutes now. I'm not worried—they'll live. I'd really like to continue this conversation, though. Would love to hear more about what you've been doing with your 'sort of' church in Philly. Do you have anything written that I can see?"

Luca flipped through his notebook and pulled out a draft of his value statement and handed it to Jimmy.

"*The Venal Dogmata Manifesto.* Latin?"

"Sorta. I could explain if I had more time, but I think that it'll explain itself."

"How long you here?"

"Fly out Friday morning. Really have nothing urgent happening on Thursday."

"Thursday night for a good ole Southern dinner? 6 p.m.? My treat?"

"You bet. Would be great to chat more."

"Great. Give me your number, and I'll shoot you an address."

"I'll look forward to it. It was a pleasure to meet you, Jimmy Norris."

"For me too, Luca. I can see that I've got a bunch to learn from you already."

***

The fourteen-minute ride from Luca's hotel to the original Mary Mac's Tea Room took almost thirty minutes. *You'd think they'd account for a little rain and traffic,* Luca thought to himself.

Luca jumped out and made a dash to the front door. He hated being late.

"Luca Lewis looking for a Jimmy Norris. He's probably been waitin' on me."

"Yes, he's expecting you. Right this way." A young, attractive woman, dressed in all black, escorted Luca through two different dining rooms to a waiting Jimmy Norris who was holding a tall iced tea.

"So sorry, Jimmy. My Uber got caught in this traffic. Took thirty minutes."

"Ah, I should have picked you up. Didn't think about you not having a car. Sorry, bro. And it's absolutely no problem. Had three of the best sweet teas you'll find in Georgia."

"Well, I got to get me one of them then. So, this place is good?"

"It's terrific. Nothing healthy here. Everything's just delicious. If you feel guilty and need a vegetable, their broccoli soufflé is incredible. They hide it. You don't even know you're eating broccoli."

"Well, we won't tell my wife about this then," Luca said with a wink.

"How hungry are you, Luca?"

"Well, let's just say that the mushy pasta salad that we were served for lunch didn't go over too well."

"Nasty. Anything that you don't care for?"

"Apparently, soggy pasta salad. Other than that, I'm pretty low maintenance," said Luca, laughing.

"Shoot, then there's nothing here for you," Jimmy laughed. "How 'bout I order us a full slab of ribs and some of their bone-in chicken breasts with the cornbread stuffing? And try a couple of their smoked pork chops. Sound okay?"

"Sounds like you're profiling me," Luca said with a half-smile.

"No, no, no. I order this every time I come, I promise. It's incredible. I've never had better."

"Okay. All right. I got ya. Well, that's three meals where I come from. But don't want to offend my host. And so, we just skip the greens altogether?" asked Luca.

"And the gravy. So, there's that. Sounds healthier already, doesn't it? Besides, the cornbread stuffing has to be some kinda vegetable …"

The two laughed so hard that the tables around them stopped and smiled in their direction. From there, the two began to carry on like old friends.

"Luca, I read and reread those pages you gave me a half dozen times. Wow. I mean, that was powerful. I think you're really hittin' on something that I've felt but haven't been able to express. Not like that. Those four disorders were insightful. Number three kicked my butt."

"You mean the insanity that our churches are structured for the sole benefit of the ninety-nine safe sheep? And that we expect them to have some level of missionary IQ to reach out to the lost one?"

"Yes. Exactly. And when you think about it, the numbers, in reality, are almost exactly flipped. When we remember the people outside the walls of the church as well, we're looking at a handful being safely in the pen of our churches, and ninety some percent wandering around with no spiritual direction. And then the sheep pens of the churches compete against one another for market share of the few saved ones. We're bleeding people to another church 'cause they're the newest flavor of the day. But who is going after the lost sheep?"

"It's sinful," countered Luca. "My papa used to go on and on preachin' to us that we're trying to build a sixteenth-century-based church, which was built upon the cultural assumptions of Christendom, and we just cannot expect that to thrive in a twenty-first century world. Not gonna happen. Not in the secular world we're livin' in. Nor can we ever expect to see results like the Christians of the first-century church saw when we've got the twenty-first-century church's low level of sacrifice. It's a nonstarter from the get-go."

"I'd never thought of that," Jimmy said slowly. "So do you think the culture of today is actually closer to the Apostle Paul's than it is to Martin Luther's or Calvin's?"

"My father thought so. Much closer. But you're the trained seminarian, Jimmy, not me. I think we've limited our theology to answering the questions that were being asked in the sixteenth century—with all the cultural assumptions of Christendom, where society was based around the Christian faith. How do we expect people in our churches to feel equipped for the questions of today? Questions that aren't from a culturally Christian worldview? Questions that come from communities with zero religious memory?"

Jimmy, who was leaning forward with both elbows on the beige tablecloth, asked, "What do you mean by 'zero religious memory'?" as if he were already agreeing with something he didn't fully understand.

"I'm talking about being in a society where people don't start from a place of Christian beliefs. So that means we need to ask different questions when it comes to issues like human sexuality. Or, what it means to be consistently pro-life beyond the abortion argument. Or how do we hold a view that is above our political ideology of the separation of church and state. How do faithful Christ-followers engage the political process? What is the biblical medicine for social transformation?" Luca paused for a minute. "Because, and no disrespect to your father, what we just came through—this marriage of politics and church—has been a train wreck. And we won't quickly recover from that mess."

"I get it. I do. I think. We've trained our preachers to teach about things that are important, but we've not updated our approach ..." Jimmy was uncomfortable with how that came out and corrected himself midstream. "... I don't mean 'change' when I say 'update.' I guess I mean that we have to include applications that the reformers hadn't considered."

"And some things they should have considered. I'm talkin' like I would have done better," Luca said with a chuckle. "But using worldly power to convince people of your own theological truth? That's a point where I think the reformers went wrong. Their followers ended up massacring one another to prove they were on the side of the Almighty. How messed up is that? It's the exact opposite of what we see in Scripture's example for us. And some folks point to those days as if it was the high point of our spiritual history—but I don't think so. More like it was some of the beginning fixes of one of our lowest points in history."

"And I see folks like my dad repeatin' it," Jimmy said softly. "Mixing politics with religion, and confusing, or even conflating man's power with spiritual authority."

"Both sides of the aisle are guilty of it," said Luca. "This ain't a one-sided sin. My papa used to get so frustrated by preachers in our community who used politics to grow their influence—but all the while leaving the gospel way on the sidelines." He chuckled, "He used to say, 'Know what you get when religion and politics go to bed together? You get one nasty looking offspring who looks nothing like Jesus.'"

Jimmy and Luca both laughed loudly, causing diners around them to look their way and smile once again.

Jimmy quieted himself and said, "So, religion and politics aside, what is the question that folks are asking these days?"

"I'm no philosopher, brother, but I'm thinking that it's less about what is 'truth' these days, and more about which truth 'works.' Seems like a post-Christian world ain't much different from a pre-Christian world. In either case, when there is no religious memory left in your community, you're pretty much startin' at ground zero. You gotta prove, through how you actually live your life, that the gospel is true—that it has power to put things right. Just by tellin' folks that Jesus is the 'Truth' without livin' a life that shows the power of that truth gets us nowhere."

"Maybe worse than nowhere," said Jimmy. "Might drive things a long way backwards."

"Maybe just a bit," Luca agreed. "I think you get what I'm sayin'. Most everything that we do is set up to answer questions folks were asking five hundred years ago: 'How is one belief within Christendom superior to another?' Folks that I know ain't splittin' those hairs today. They're essentially asking first-century questions about an unknown God. And an evangelical political action committee ain't gonna get 'em an answer. It's just gonna get them farther from the Answer."

Jimmy savored Luca's insights like a little kid tasting chocolate for the first time. He was leaning in and mentally reconstructing his world in ways he had never thought possible. Great chunks of his Christian worldview that never seemed to properly fit were finding a natural home in the way Luca explained the kingdom of God.

And he knew that he needed more.

"Bottom line, Jimmy: the church didn't start in the sixteenth century. It just reached back to earlier days and made some mid-course corrections. It had gotten way off course, and it made some adjustments. But within the confines of Christendom, it couldn't seem to adjust its way back to the first century. But now we have a new chance, brother. The smothering blanket of Christendom, of cultural Christianity, has been ripped away. Why can't the church reinvent itself back to Jesus' kingdom purpose? Why can't the 'Sermon on the Mount' become a literal way of living for Jesus' people …?"

"… Instead of just being explained away," said Jimmy.

"Instead of being explained away," Luca agreed.

"I've got to admit, I've always had a hard time with Jesus' teaching on the kingdom. I found that most times I make all the applications on 'how to get into the eternal kingdom,' not 'how we live in the world as kingdom citizens.' I dance around a whole lot of things. Seems it's pretty hard to grab attention, grow churches, and win elections while being 'poor in spirit.'"

"Yep. What we do to lure them actually starts them down the opposite path to kingdom."

"Do you think it's a total rebuild, Luca?"

Luca paused as he reorganized his silverware. "I think things are gonna get a whole lot smaller and poorer before things get better and purer. I'm afraid that many folks will ride the old idea all the way down to the bottom 'til they can't afford not to change. I saw this with my father's church. Long before the whole thing petered out, he worked tirelessly to course correct. He taught, he preached, he wrote a book, he developed a plan, and he brought the whole thing to a vote. But the good folks of Mt. Pisgah weren't interested in changing course. They actually voted 'no' to the Great Commission. And even when they lost everything, they still couldn't see a mission beyond themselves."

"I can see that. I can see that happening to LifePointe … That is what's happening to LifePointe. When we finally wrap the thing around a tree, that's when we'll start pumping the brakes."

Luca laughed. "But from what I've seen, most aren't going fast enough to do much damage. It'll be a slow, plodding, gradual ending for most. When the horse they've been riding has finally been declared dead, then a few will dismount and search for a new way. But most, I'm afraid, will just keep sittin' in the saddle, unrepentant, crying for a revival."

"Other people's revival," said Jimmy.

"Yep. It's always those other folks who gotta change."

Chapter Fourteen

The Hunt

"So, you're the teacher. Teach me, 'cause for the life of me, I can't figure it out," said an exasperated Luca as he handed his phone to Santiago.

"It's gotta be in the app," said Santiago. "Somewhere it should be there."

Santiago swiped and pressed and swiped some more, but there were no signs of victory emerging on his face.

"Maybe you used a different rideshare service? Lyft maybe?"

"No, I know for sure it was Uber. We even talked about the …"

"Wait a minute. Got something," Santiago interrupted. "Here's a place where you can edit your rating of the driver. It says, 'Your trip with Yushua.' Does that make sense?"

"Yes, he was definitely of Middle Eastern descent. 'Yushua' does sound right. Now how can I find him? Is there any contact info? A last name?"

"Nope. No links either. Maybe call corporate, but privacy laws will likely keep them from disclosing any personal information. I'm not sure what else you can do."

Luca's furrowed brow was on full display, as he thought through possible options. "Where could the largest concentration of Ubers be seen?"

"I'd guess the airport would have the most," Santiago offered.

"My guess, too. Since we already know that he works that route, it makes the most sense. So, it looks like I've got some old-fashioned detective work in my future."

"I hope you know what you're doing—seems like a bit of a long-shot to me, even if you do end up finding him."

"I know it sounds like a wild-goose chase. If I were you, I'd be totally skeptical too. I would. But you had to be there, brother. There was something about this fella. A quality I've never seen before. He had nothing to prove, yet he was holdin' the cards. I can't explain it. But everything inside me says I need to get to know him."

"Well, pack a lunch. Airport food is usually bad."

"And always expensive," said Luca.

Luca did pack a lunch. And a thermos of coffee. And a folding camp chair. And a book. And as an important afterthought, two dozen donuts. He was going to bring Sanders with him, but Chantel convinced him that an airport roadway was no place for a young boy to spend his Saturday. And of course, she was right.

He arrived early to catch the cars that were dropping off passengers for the busy morning flights. By 6 a.m., after a friendly chat and donut breakfast with the drop-off zone security guards, he was stationed off the South Commercial Road at pickup Zone 7, where all rideshare fares funneled.

"This is perfect," Luca said aloud. "No silver Honda is gonna get by me."

Soon, cars started to arrive at a regular clip. And it appeared to Luca that most of them were silver. He would pop up and down from his camp chair and walk up and down the sidewalk to get a better look. He soon realized that the camp chair was an unnecessary extra effort, and so, it became the "shopping cart" for his stuff.

As the hours slowly passed by, Luca began to have the unsettling thought that he might be looking for the wrong car altogether.

He mentioned that he rented the silver Honda from a friend. What if he had since purchased a car? Or rented a different car? Luca realized that he'd have to step up his game and look at the faces of all the rideshare drivers who arrived at PHL. Any one of them could be Yushua.

"Lord, show him to me. Please show me Yushua," was the prayer Luca breathed almost constantly as he looked through windshields. Every driver who parked and stepped out of his car, Luca would accost, "Do you know an Uber driver named Yushua? He has scars on his face …" But blank stares, hunched shoulders, and the occasional "no, sorry," was all he ever got in return.

By 10 p.m., the traffic had slowed to a trickle and Luca was completely out of energy. As he bailed his car out of short-term parking for a small fortune, he reminded himself that he knew that this wouldn't be easy. This would take time. But everything inside him sensed that it would be worth all the effort. Maybe Monday.

There were some advantages to being in charge, one of which was that Luca had ultimate say over scheduling. And so, on Sunday afternoon he made some quick adjustments and freed up Monday for a second day of stalking. Though his body was tired, his enthusiasm was undaunted. He was not one to be easily discouraged.

He arrived early once again, set up his station, and went to work, this time with more comfortable shoes. "All drivers get a windshield look, silver Hondas get a side window look," became his operating credo. And he stuck to it. He moved his sizable frame up and down the concrete sidewalk hour after hour peering into windshields and side windows. But to no avail. There were many drivers dropping off and picking up at PHL, but never the one he was searching for.

He eventually began to notice that there were a handful of drivers who were frequent arrivers to zone seven. He pieced together from numerous brief discussions that the majority of drivers wouldn't nab the airport runs. Instead, they preferred shorter and more frequent trips within the city to net a bigger payday. It was only a few drivers, who preferred a less manic approach to the business, who scooped up the longer hauls. This new intel caused Luca additional concern. *Maybe Yushua avoids this place?* And this new knowledge began to dampen his spirits.

By 10 p.m., Luca was done, in every sense of the word. Thirty-two hours in two days of running up and down zone seven, staring into windshields, had netted absolutely nothing. He was not one inch closer to finding Yushua than if he'd stayed home and watched football. On Sunday he had entertained thoughts of switching shifts with Campbell and returning on Tuesday, but those thoughts evaporated by mid-afternoon. This was indisputably a fool's errand. And Santiago had been right all along. He checked his car out of long-term parking for a slightly smaller fortune, and with a heavy heart, headed home.

Tom Butts had no use for a golf course. Although most of the senior team at LifePointe could be convinced to take an afternoon away from the office for eighteen holes, Tom wasn't one of them. "I can find better uses for four hours and a hundred bucks than chasing a little ball around," was his standard line. But Jimmy could get him out on one of those virtual golf chains that were popping up in the suburbs. If for no other reason, Tom would come for the buffet. So, for Tom's sake, Jimmy arranged for this staff retreat to accommodate his friend's athletic sensibilities. He would need Tom in his corner.

After a couple hours of "bonding," which consisted of Tom's

general humiliation, coupled with heroic displays of Jimmy's prowess, the team was ready for business. Schedules had been cleared, and they had reserved one of the golf center's meeting rooms for the full afternoon. Everyone sensed that this wasn't going to be a normal meeting; Jimmy had something on his mind.

"I want to start out by apologizing to y'all," Jimmy said after clearing his throat. "I think I've been a bit neurotic. Emotionally, spiritually, and mentally I've been all over the map. I'm not gonna Sigmund Freud myself in front of y'all, but I know I've been a bit of a mess."

Jimmy paused for a response, but none came from the wide-eyed underlings staring back at him.

"I've been sending contradictory signals to you, which I know has to be confusing. One week it's one thing; next week it's the opposite."

"Whatcha mean, Jimmy?" asked Tom on behalf of the bewildered room.

"I mean, I think that I've been having a bit of a spiritual crisis. I only know of one kind of church—and that's this thing that we've been doing together. Puttin' on the big show. Preach in a way that is biblically accurate and hopefully a little entertaining. Watching people come and go. Try to keep more coming than those that are goin'. Because that's how ya win. Keep people at a distance—protecting yourself from getting too emotionally involved with anyone. This is all that I know. This is church."

Tom, once again, was the lone voice to break the silence. "I get it, Jimmy. We talked a bit about this after Chad Collins. I remember what was on my heart when I left the corporate world—and this wasn't it."

"No sir, you're right. And that's my problem, Tom. I only know one thing, and I'm more and more convinced that it isn't the thing that church was supposed to be. It should be simpler. More honest. More meaningful."

"So, you're sayin' that we ain't a church, Jimmy? We ain't a legit church? Is that what you're sayin'?" Chip Bussey blurted out in an angry tone. "'Cause if you're say'n that, I believe you're way out of line."

"No, I'm not saying that, Chippy. So, take a pill, brother. I know that we're a church. But I just don't think that we're all that great of a church. Sure, we can out-preach, out-sing, out-smile, out-program, and out-hustle most churches in our area, but is that what a church is supposed to do? Is that it?"

"If we're not that great, it's your fault, Jimmy. You're our leader," Chip snapped back.

"No arguments there, Chip. I've just been doing what I know. Just like you have been. We've all been doing what we know. But maybe we don't know everything. Is that a possibility, Chip?"

Chip had nothing to say.

Jimmy continued. "I had a conversation with a pastor from Philadelphia. And in one evening, that man made me think harder and deeper about the nature of Jesus' church than I ever had in my life. I'm sure that I don't agree with everything he said, but I think that he's way closer to the right idea than we are. Way closer."

And then Jimmy snapped open his three-ring binder and pulled out some sheets of paper.

"Tom, pass these around if you would. Three sheets each."

Chip was the first to speak. "*The Venal Dogmata Manifesto*? What the blazes is that?"

"Forget the title, Chip. That's not important. Read the four disorders."

"Something from that Philadelphia fella? There even any

churches in Philadelphia? Certainly, no good churches—liberal social justice …"

"Yes, Chip," Jimmy interrupted. "Just read through it. We'll discuss this in a bit."

After Jimmy finally convinced Chip to read, he walked over to the whiteboard and turned it around so nobody could see. And then, without any help from Tom, began to write summary answers to Luca's four disorders.

Passivism: We need to meet people where they live—not require them to search for us in the church building. Therefore, we will be willing to disrupt our sacred preferences for the sake of Jesus' lost sheep.

Professionalism: The gospel is everyone's vocation—not just a chosen few. Therefore, we model and celebrate a diverse co-vocational mission-force.

Presentationalism: We are the body of Christ in the community—not just a Sunday service. Therefore, we equip the entire church for 24/7 works of ministry.

Pragmatism: The kingdom of God is our only goal—not the advancement of our individual brand. Therefore, we seek a united effort of city-wide gospel collaboration, rather than competing with other churches.

About twenty minutes later, Jimmy could see that everyone had finished reading.

"So, I know you didn't have any context, but what did ya think?"

"Seemed complicated to me," Chip said. "I wasn't sure what he was getting' at."

Jimmy didn't respond. He looked at the others, hoping desperately for some sign of intelligent life. Other than Chip's exaggerated yawns, the room was dead quiet. Papers flipping, small nervous coughs, nothing else.

"Okay, let me boil this down a bit for y'all," Jimmy said as he spun around the whiteboard. See these four ideas? I think they answer those four disorders listed on your papers—in broad strokes."

And then Jimmy passionately began to expound on each idea, often finding himself using the very phrasing Luca used at Mary Mac's Tea Room. For forty minutes he held court—and everyone's attention. He was vulnerable, compassionate, and compelling. And Tom Butts couldn't have been prouder.

"Jimmy," Tom broke in as Jimmy was winding down. "Disorder number two. I've often thought about that one. If I woulda' stayed in the corporate world—and hooked up with a few other leaders—we coulda' done church right in the middle of our office complex. Co-vocationally …"

"Which brings us to that third disorder, Tom, doesn't it? Co-vocationally, you team up and form the body of Christ smack dab in the middle of lostness. And it's not Sunday worship service jobs that define our priorities …"

"Because it's not a Sunday service that we're building. It's Jesus' community, seven days a week. A community that lives connected lives with lost and searching sheep," Tom finished.

"Excuse me, Jimmy. I don't want to interrupt this fancy hippie talk, but you're startin' to sound more like our ole janitor than a preacher. Ole what's his name. The Arab with a gimpy leg?"

"Yushua Maalouf," Tom answered with his arms tightly crossed, showing no hint of good humor.

"Yeah, that dude. Didn't we just can him for saying more or less the same stuff? I mean, he stirred up a hornet's nest in our community group. A mess I'm still trying to fix."

"We did," Jimmy sighed. "We did."

"And it was sinful, and immoral, and blackhearted," blurted Tom. "We were wrong. And I cannot get his scarred face out of my mind. He knew that I was lying. He's smarter than me. Smarter than most of us, I'm sure. He knew there were no budget cuts. He just accepted it, and then disappeared."

Jimmy looked sympathetically at Tom as he could see him glaring down into his coffee cup. He'd known it was unfair to ask Tom to be the one to have the conversation with Yushua. He had known that letting Yushua go wasn't the right thing to do either, but with Chip Bussey and his community group in disarray and several members of the board asking awkward questions over what Yushua had said, it had seemed like the easiest way out.

"Where did he go to, Tom, do you know?" asked Jimmy. "Maybe we can make it up to him."

"No idea. Juan Rodrigues said that he told him that 'Jesus must have another assignment for him.' He may be somewhere in Atlanta. I don't know. He may be back in Yemen. I just couldn't bear to face him. God saved Yushua's life, and then sent him to us, Jimmy, and we turned our backs on him. How do we get past that?"

"I don't know," Jimmy said. "I don't know."

***

"Uumphff," is all Tom Butts heard echoing in the empty fitness center as he hastily made a path through the cardio section straight to the weights. There he saw Jimmy on his back, legs spread on either side of a black vinyl bench, grunting as he pushed a large stack of cast steel weights skyward.

"Jimmy, can I interrupt you? It's important, I think."

Jimmy dropped his arms to the floor, let out a loud, long exhale, and slowly sat up. "Hey Tommy, what's up?"

"Nothing good, I'm afraid," he said with eyes fixed squarely on Jimmy. "You know how I can see everyone's calendar? Our way of makin' sure our people are working …"

"Yeah, somebody not busy?"

"Somebody's *too* busy, I'm afraid. Chip. He's got a 10 a.m, 'brunch' meeting with three of our board members, including the chair. And it's held off campus."

Jimmy offered no response for a protracted pause. Then he swung his leg over the bench, stood up straight, and with almost no expression said, "So he wants to join the pack. The jackals need an inside man, and they found one of their own among us. Where they meeting?"

"Mamacitas."

"Mamacitas. Interesting. What you suppose Mr. Bussey is up to?"

"I think he's reporting on your 'hippie talk,' as he called it. You showed some vulnerability, and he's gonna use it as a club against you."

"'Weakness' is another word. He's chummin' the waters." He paused for a few more seconds and then mischievously said, "Feel like some *huevos rancheros*, Tom?"

Tom patted his sizable midsection, "Spontaneous Monday brunches will never be turned down, my friend."

"Great, let's have a 'scheduled' off-campus meeting in a quiet corner at nine-thirty. Wait for the jackals to show." He took a couple steps toward the door and said, "And wear a hat."

"I'll put it on our calendars for cover," Tom said. "Meet me at my car at nine-fifteen. They won't notice a blue minivan."

Nine-thirty quickly came, and their trap was set. Jimmy and Tom were disguised with ball caps and strategically concealed in the far corner booth, away from the windows. They placed their orders as soon as they arrived in order to make a well-timed exit. Jimmy, being more recognizable, had his back to the door. Tom, head down, faced the heavy Mexican-themed doors, carefully sneaking glances as patrons unknowingly entered the hunting grounds.

Tom tensed up. “They’re here.”

“Bobby Berringer?”

“Yes. Jackson and Munroe, too.”

“Bussey with ’em?”

“Yep. He’s leading the way. Oh, perfect …”

“What? What’s perfect?”

“They took the big round party booth. Plenty of room for a couple extra friends,” said Tom with a wink.

“Kay, let’s let ’em get settled. Let ’em order and get drinks. It’ll be easier to invite ourselves in before they have their meals.”

Jimmy and Tom remained almost silent for the next few minutes, as nervous tension began to arise. Now, their only conversation was Tom’s reconnaissance reports on the table movements.

“Okay, Jimmy, we should be good. They’ve ordered.”

Jimmy and Tom casually regathered their props of books, notebooks, and a large three-ringed binder, put on their coats, and casually headed to the door.

“Bobby Berringer, hey buddy what’s up? Oh wow, Phil and Greg, too. And Chip … What in the world? Well, hey, can we join you fellas?”

The party table looked wholly uncomfortable, as eyes darted to one another.

Tom and Jimmy set their pile of “work” on the floor and took off their coats and hung them on hooks.

“Great to see you, fellas,” Tom said cheerfully. And then he gestured toward the booth. “May we?”

“Of course,” Bobby Berringer, the chairman of the board, said with an unconvincing tone.

The four scooted awkwardly to the center as Tom and Jimmy sat at the two ends, blocking any possibility of escape.

Jimmy leaned forward and said, “Singing lessons?” as he raised an eyebrow.

"'S'cuse me?" responded Chip.

"Well, I'm just trying to imagine why the chairman of the board, the vice-chair, and the secretary-treasurer are all meeting together with my worship guy? Singing lessons seemed like the most likely explanation. Or at least the most palatable one."

"Of course not, Jimmy. Can't good friends get together? Why do ya got to be so that way?" said a red-faced Chip.

"What way is that, Chip?"

"You know. So, distrustful."

"Distrustful. Maybe you're right. I probably am too distrustful. I gotta work on that. By the way, Chip, what are Phil's kids' names again? You know, your good friend? He has three."

Jimmy waited in silence, never taking his eyes off Chip Bussey.

"Well, that was a tough one, Chip. Let's try something easier. What is Greg's wife's name? Your buddy Greg?"

More silence.

"Okay Pastor Jimmy, you made your point," said Bobby Berringer. "We are here for serious church business."

"So, the officers of the board have gathered for serious church business, and they invite middle management? Didn't we miss something here? A step or two perhaps?"

"Hey, hey, hey Jimmy," Chip spouted. "I'm not middle management. I'm in charge of ..."

"... Mutinies. I get it, Chip," Jimmy interrupted. "Now, why don't you just try to stay quiet while the grown-ups talk."

Everyone at the table unexpectedly coughed a laugh. Everyone but Chip.

"So, Bobby, what's the important secret church business that I wasn't supposed to know about?"

Bobby Berringer took a couple of stabs at clearing his throat and then said, "Well Jimmy, we've been hearing some concerning rumors ..."

"So, you're here with …" Jimmy pointed to Chip but seemed unable to voice his name, "… him—to hear rumors? Well, I guess if it's rumors you want, there's no better guy to come to than him."

"Now listen, Jimmy, we are concerned with the direction that you're taking our church. It doesn't seem like you have your eye on the ball anymore," said Bobby in a stern but somewhat amicable tone.

"Really," said Jimmy. "Let's see. Are we down in attendance or up, Bobby? Up, right? Six percent. How about giving, Bobby? Down or up? Up again, right? Eight percent. How about baptisms? What do you think, Bobby—down or up? 'Up you say?' Boy, you're right, Bobby. Five percent. Are my figures right, Tom?"

"Seven percent on baptisms, Jimmy," corrected Tom.

"Sorry, Bobby. Looks like we're up a couple more points just sitting here. So, what is it about our direction that concerns you so much? 'Cause you know that almost every church in our region is down in all three of those areas. You knew that, didn't you?"

"It's some intangibles that we find troubling," Bobby countered.

"For instance …?"

"For instance, some of the staff expressed concern about your last meeting."

"'Some,' that would be Mr. Singy Pants here, and …?"

"That doesn't matter, Jimmy."

"Figured. Well, I'll leave the 'intangibles' for you fellas to work out. Sounds important. And Chippy here sounds like he'll be quite the expert for you. Tom, guess we should get going. We've interrupted this godly church meeting long enough."

Tom and Jimmy put on their coats, gathered their things, and headed for the door. Then suddenly, abruptly, Jimmy stopped and twirled around to face Chip Bussey.

"Chip, what was it that you were in charge of at LifePointe again?"

"Uhh … worship …"

"Ahhh, right. Worship. That's it. Ironic, don't you think, Chip? A bit? Anyway, go ahead and take the rest of the month off. With pay of course. I sure don't want to stress you. I understand that all those intangibles can be a killer."

Chapter Fifteen

The Convening

"Yeah, I'll be there in forty-five. Good with you still?" asked Campbell MacKay.

"You bet. Looking forward to it. And who knows, maybe we'll discover something," said Luca. "'Sides, can't keep operating out of here. Gonna get our hands slapped sooner or later."

"True. The wee little boss-man from New York is chock full of reservations. And when he's holding the cards, that's never a dandy thing."

"Don't I know it. Napoleon was struttin' around here last week, pokin' his nose into everything. They loved our ice storm effort for the story. Made bank on it. And hated it for what the story tells of 'business as usual.' To sustain this for the long-term, we'll need some separation for sure."

"Agreed. So, have a couple of your famous pour-overs ready. I'll see you soon."

Campbell MacKay had organized three site visits of abandoned warehouses through a celebrated commercial realtor in their neighborhood. Two visits in Fishtown and one in Strawberry Mansion. María Cardoza-López, the city-center's maven of all things warehouse, had made all the necessary arrangements.

"Here you go. One perfect pour-over, ruined just the way you like it," said Luca when Campbell arrived.

"Ah, thank you, mate. 'Tis a thing of beauty. If the Almighty didn't want us to have heavy cream, he wouldn't have made jerseys so beautiful … Oh, María rang up, she's already at the site."

When they arrived at the three-story red-brick warehouse in Fishtown, the "Queen of Commercial," as María tagged herself, was leaning against her gleaming white Mercedes, speaking theatrically on her leopard-print phone. Luca and Campbell nodded as they walked past her and began to survey the building's exterior. All the windows on the first floor had been boarded up and decorated by several layers of graffiti that documented the rival gang history of the street. Second-floor windows were a hodgepodge of undamaged and broken windows. The third floor appeared intact. Weeds, waist high, grew in abundance where a busy parking lot once existed. And garbage littered the back lot like a landfill.

"This will be no trifling task," said Campbell. "And we have yet to step inside."

"Think she's saving the best for last? Or would this be the best?"

"Well, this one is the steepest. It's a pretty penny. If that means 'best,' then we could be in for a long afternoon."

"Oh," said Luca as he pulled his vibrating phone out of his front pocket. The call display read, 'Fishtown Y.'

"Hello? Hi Tiana … Yes … What? ... Who? ... Say that again please, Tiana … Holy cow … Yes. Yes. Yes. I'll be right there."

Luca, somewhat stunned, returned his phone to his pocket as María Cardoza-López came trotting to the back lot.

"So, what do you handsome gentlemen think of this place? Tons of potential, don't you think? Been trying to get my hands on this for years—finally, they're selling. Italians, you know. Anyway, it should go in a hurry. Ready to go inside and start dreaming? You're going to be amazed."

Luca, still reeling from his office call, was much too distracted to respond.

"What was that?" Campbell asked.

"Italians?" replied María. "Well, not all Italians, but Giuseppe Bonetti can be a real …"

"… No, no, sorry. I was talking to Luca. What's up?" Campbell looked quizzically at Luca.

"Gotta head back to the office. I'll walk, brother. Only three blocks. So sorry, Campbell. Ma'am." And then Luca, with long hurried strides, made his way to the Y.

As he pushed the heavy glass door open, he felt the cold air conditioning on his sweaty, shaven head. He was far from being in fighting shape. He made a beeline to Janice at the information kiosk and then bent over, hands on thighs, as he struggled for a breath.

"She's in the community room, Mr. Lewis."

"… Tiana?"

"Yes. She told me to get you as soon as you arrived."

"… Thanks."

Luca, still breathing much too heavily for the short trip, stopped at the door to the community room in an attempt to regain his composure. He took several slow, deep breaths, and then walked in.

"Luca, thanks for coming so quickly," said Tiana Phillips, his intern assistant. "But like I said, it wasn't really an emergency. He's in the lounge drinking coffee. Kinda strange if you ask me."

"Okay. Good. Did he say anything?"

"Not much. Said he knew you from Atlanta? Does that make sense?"

"No. Not really. Maybe."

As Luca entered the staff lounge, he could see the back of a man with a red ball cap sitting on the black leather sofa. He walked toward him, extending his right hand and warmly said, "Hello, I'm Luca Lewis, how can I help you?"

The guest rose quickly and shook Luca's hand. "Yes, Mr. Lewis. I remember you. My name is Yushua Maalouf. I took you to the airport several months ago in my Uber car. Do you remember this?"

"Do I remember?" exclaimed Luca with a beaming face. He dropped his guest's hand and wrapped his big arms around Yushua's slight frame. "I remember, Yushua. Boy, do I remember."

"So, it's pronounced, 'Mae-loof.' Did I get that right?" asked Luca.

"Yes, exactly." And then he pursed his lips and teasingly said, "And yours is pronounced 'Loo-wis.' Correct? These American names are a real mouthful."

Even though they had just formally met ninety minutes previously, Yushua had gladly accepted Luca's spontaneous invitation for dinner. The two of them sat like old friends in the living room while Chantel scurried around the kitchen preparing a meal. She worked quickly but with no sense of panic. To the Lewis household, unexpected guests were not an uncommon occurrence.

"Can I give you a hand, sweetie?"

"Everything's under control. As long as you gentlemen don't mind another edition of 'cream of bottom shelf' for dinner?" she said laughing. "Luca's always bringing home friends. I've learned to roll with it."

"It's an honor to be in your home, Mrs. Lewis. This is actually the first time I've been in an American person's home for a meal. You have such a beautiful home."

"'Chantel' please, Yushua. 'Mrs. Lewis' passed years ago. And thank you. Our townhouse is truly a gift from God, and we want to use it to be a blessing to others. So, how long have you been in the US?"

"About two and a half years. But only a short time in Philadelphia. I'm originally from the Republic of Yemen. Have you heard of it?"

"Of course, Yushua. We're so glad you're here with us. And I'm sorry it took so long for you to find American friends."

"It's a blessing to be here, Mrs. Lew…" and then he corrected himself. "Chantel. I'm a student, so a real meal is truly a treat."

"Whatcha studying?" asked Luca.

"Law. Second year."

"U of P?"

"No, Temple University. Beasley School of Law."

"Very impressive," said Luca as he stroked both of his cheeks with his left hand. "That's a super hard program to get in. How did you manage it?"

"I guess I did pretty well on my LSATs. And my grades from Georgia Tech were good."

"Georgia Tech. Is that where you transferred in from?"

"Yes. And before that I was at Aden University. That's in my country."

"Interesting. So, how long were you in Atlanta?"

"I was there for two years. A little more. The weather there was much better than here. But so far, I think I like the city of Philadelphia better."

"You do? Why's that?"

"I guess people seem more …"

"… more accepting?" Luca interjected.

"Maybe. There are more families living here that are from

my region. Maybe people are more accustomed to my kind in Philadelphia."

"Is that why you left Atlanta?"

"No. Not really. Well kind of … It's a long story …"

Yushua was ready to change the subject. His brief Atlanta season wasn't at all the high point he had hoped for. In fact, it was the opposite. Sorrow and disappointment were the emotions that welled up when he thought of it. Sorrow and disappointment, tinged with varying degrees of anger. And these were not dissimilar to the feelings that surfaced within Yushua when he thought of his family in Bani Badi. Excruciating emotions of betrayal that he preferred to not unearth.

"Can I ask you a question?" Yushua asked. "How did your big speech go at the Y convention? Did they understand your ice storm idea?"

"It was fine. I'm not sure that I moved the needle much, but who knows."

"I'm sure that many were inspired."

"Soup's on!" announced Chantel.

Luca stood up and gestured to the kitchen. "She ain't servin' soup. I guarantee you that."

After dinner, Luca stood up to clear the table. Yushua followed suit.

"No, no, Yushua. Sit, sit, sit. Please. I want to get to know the man who sent my man 'round the bend."

"Pardon me, Mrs. Lew—Chantel?"

"I need to know what you're about, young man. One trip to the airport, and my husband about lost his ever-lovin' mind. Did you know he made camp at the airport in a lawn chair for thirty-two hours looking for your Uber car? A silver Honda Accord, right?"

"Yes Mrs.—Chantel. But I don't understand?"

"Well, that makes two of us, doesn't it, Yushua? But whatever happened in your silver Honda made quite the impression. He came back from Atlanta possessed with the idea of finding you."

"Your husband made quite an impression on me as well … Chantel. I thought often about what he told me of how your church served the community during that terrible ice storm. I hadn't seen that level of courageous kingdom selflessness since I left the underground churches of Yemen. Every time I prayed, I sensed the Spirit of Jesus nudging me to find your husband. Since I knew that he worked at a local Y, the search was not too difficult."

Luca, who was standing at the kitchen door, drying a cast iron frying pan, playfully broke in, "Well brother, you could have saved these ole bones a whole lot of pain if you looked a bit sooner."

"Okay, so, what did you tell him that stuck under his saddle like that?" Chantel pressed.

"Honestly, I do not know. I only remember hearing the story of …"

"Honey," Luca broke in once again. "Like I mentioned before, he just painted a picture of Mt. Pisgah even though he'd never seen it. And he described what was on my heart for Philadelphia Freedom even though I never spoke of it. It's like …"

"… I've lived both experiences."

"Yes," Luca said softly as he set the frying pan on the table and sat back down. "I understand, or at least can imagine, where you'd seen a kingdomy church. The underground church in Yemen, yes?"

"Yes."

"But where did you experience Mt. Pisgah?"

"If by Mt. Pisgah you mean a church that is absorbed with itself, that was the church I was a part of in Atlanta."

"Why didn't you leave?" Chantel asked.

"It's complicated. First, I didn't know that people left Jesus communities. In Yemen, the only ones who left their faith community were either fleeing from our persecutors or graduated."

"Graduated?" asked Chantel with a confused look.

"That's what we called it. Promoted. Promoted to heaven. Many of my brothers and sisters were killed for Jesus."

Luca looked mystified. The idea of absolute and unreserved commitment to a community of believers had never crossed his mind. Not really. Church had always been something you opted into. Almost everything about church was based on personal preference, in his experience. It's the way it was. He had watched families come and go from Mt. Pisgah for the most frivolous reasons—normally it had something to do with his father's performance. Yet Yushua's understanding of a spiritual community seemed to Luca as tremendously genuine, yet somehow naïve.

"So, you stayed in that selfish church because you didn't know you could leave it?" Chantel asked.

"Not really. It's more complicated than that. This church sponsored me while I was in a refugee camp. They gave me a job as a custodian in their church. They helped me find an apartment. I was very grateful."

"So, why did you leave?" asked Luca.

"I didn't leave. Not really. I was fired. They said it was 'downsizing' for budget reasons, but that wasn't true. I was fired." Yushua paused and stared at his feet. "And if they didn't even want me to clean their toilets, how could I ever be a meaningful part of the community?"

"I see, brother. Can I ask ..." Luca softly pressed further. "Why did they send ya packing?"

Luca and Chantel, with elbows on the kitchen table, leaned forward as Yushua related the story of the previous year's Christmas missions' emphasis. He told them about the video productions, his community group appearances, the Chip Bussey affair, and his last meeting with Tom Butts.

"Gee-whiz, Yushua, that musta left a mark. I woulda went, too. You had to," said Luca. "The ungodly things that go on in the name of Jesus …"

"… Make me so very angry," Chantel finished Luca's sentence with thin, tight lips. She took a deep breath and then let out a long, slow exhale. "I am so glad to have met you, Yushua. I now understand my husband's manic obsession. I do hope that we see each other again."

"Thank you so much Mrs.— Chantel. I hope so as well."

"So where in Atlanta did you live?" asked Luca.

"Roswell. It's north of the city."

"Is that where your church was?"

"No, it was a bit further north."

"I see. Pretty, I bet. I'm not too familiar with the geography down there. I got a friend who pastors a church in that area somewhere. I know there's a million churches down there. It's called LifePointe Chapel. Jimmy Norris is the pastor's name. Ever heard of it?"

***

"Why's Chip not here? We had a meeting scheduled this afternoon. Margy said he's taken the rest of the month off? What's up with him?" asked Leonard Elkins, LifePointe's senior youth pastor.

"Go ahead with your meetings. Randy's fillin' in," answered Tom, in such a way that sounded like he actually answered Leonard's question. But clearly, he hadn't.

"So, Chip's gone then?" pressed Leonard.

As an administrator, Tom Butts was top drawer, but quick on his feet he was not. As he began to fumble for words to try to explain the unexplainable, Jimmy walked in.

"Hey, team. Good morning. It was a great day yesterday, wasn't it? What a Sunday! Love them baptisms. Seven. What a day! All right. First off, if you hadn't already heard, Chip's taking the rest of the month off. Randy's pickin' up the slack. Thanks a ton, Randy, I'm gonna owe you big time. What's going on? Chip and I are sorting through a few things. Nothin' to worry about. Mom and Dad are gonna get it figured out. So don't go startin' a bunch of rumors—that's a sure way to get on my bad side. Just hang tight and everything's gonna be okay. In the meantime, Randy's on point for Sundays. Everybody okay with that?"

Heads nodded.

"Spectacular. All right, Tom, why don't you lead us through our stats."

As Tom stood and Jimmy sat, a text illuminated on Jimmy's phone. It was from Luca Lewis.

Jimmy, pretending to listen to Tom's quarter over quarter report, thumbed the notification to read what Luca had sent.

Jimmy. Discovered my P. The one to fill the 'prophet' function. We need to talk. Call me ASAP. Luca.

"Excuse me, Tom. Have an emergency phone call to make. Everything's all right but take over for me. Thanks, everyone. Again, amazing day yesterday." And then Jimmy slipped out of Staff Conference Room A to his study.

"Hello?"

"Hey Luca, Jimmy here."

"That was quick."

"Hey, when the eminent bishop of Philly says call ASAP, I ain't fooling around. What's up?"

"Remember I told you about my Uber driver? The one who dropped me off at the airport just before we first met?"

"Yes."

"Well, when I got back, I went on an all-out search. I spent thirty-two hours runnin' down Ubers at the Philly airport like a crazy person. Came up with nothing but blisters. Nothing. Then guess who waltzed into my office at work this afternoon?"

"Your Uber driver?"

"My Uber driver. Guess what else, Jimmy?"

"What?"

"My Uber driver's name is Yushua Maalouf."

The sound of breathing was the only response Luca heard.

"Jimmy?"

"Yeah, Luca, about that. I'm sorry. I feel so bad about that. We were so wrong. I was trying to fix something and …" Jimmy thought about his next words and decided against them. "Nope. No excuse. I've been feeling so bad about this one. Is he angry?"

"I think that he may be a little angry. Nothing inappropriate. He's starting over in law school again. Temple University."

Jimmy's usual bravado was gone. His voice was shaky. "Oh, I'm so sorry."

"'Spect it's not me who you should be apologizing to."

"Yes, you're right. I feel so bad, Luca. Like I kicked a puppy."

"Want Yushua's number?"

"No, not really."

"Pardon me?"

"This ain't a phone call, Luca."

"What do ya mean?"

"This is personal. A phone call can't fix this. Think I can fly down next week?"

Chapter Sixteen

The Picture

Luca pored over the diagram. It made so much sense. It made sense the very first time his father drew it out for him on a napkin. And when he first saw it, formal and printed in his father's handmade book, it seemed irrefutable. And when his papa distributed it to the congregation of Mt. Pisgah before the big vote, he knew everyone else would get it too. They had to. *Once you've seen, how can you unsee?* thought Luca.

But apparently it was possible. Easy in fact. Especially if the convicting truth that is revealed threatens the comfortable myth that is preferred. Luca found out firsthand that when it comes down to conviction versus comfort, the odds usually run toward easy street. *It's a whole lot easier believing the unbelievable than squaring things up with reality*, thought Luca.

The diagram was two circles with five equal points running to a center axis. Spider-graphs, his papa called them. At each point where the line intersected with the outer circumference stood a letter. Five letters were equally distributed around the circle's perimeters: A P E S T. And then, starting from the center axis and running to the outer perimeter, was a series of ten calibrated markings. Ten "ticks" from the center point to the "A," from the center to the "P," and so forth.

But that was all the two circles had in common. From there they told two vastly different stories. Luca was about to share his papa's thesis with his newly completed team. For most, this would be a review, but it had been years since his team would have seen this, back when his father shared it with them. But for Yushua, it just might be brand new.

Luca closed his papa's book and began to prepare his living room for what felt like the most important meeting of his life. It had all gone horribly wrong for his papa when he had shared the manifesto with Mt. Pisgah, and despite Luca knowing this team were likely to have a whole different type of response, he couldn't help feeling nervous. Six kitchen chairs filled in the spaces between the two upholstered chairs and the sofa. Four folding chairs that were stored in the basement were sandwiched in the entryway and in front of the staircase. A medium-sized whiteboard permanently mounted to an aluminum easel prominently stood in front of the fireplace. He was ready.

The last to arrive, as usual, were Jerome and Choyz. As natural-born "shepherds," they seemed to have the most difficult time extricating themselves from one conversation to get to another. Luca had learned not to wait for their arrival before beginning a meeting, but today was different.

"Sorry we're so late. We had to run by Walmart to get some diapers for a single mom in our neighborhood. She's the sweetest thing, but is so …"

"We're glad you're here. Looks like we saved the sofa for …"

"What can we say? We're givers," Santiago interrupted Luca.

"Okay, givers, let me introduce the one I told y'all about: Yushua Maalouf. We're so honored to have you here today, brother."

"Thank you so much. But it is my honor. I've been very much looking forward to being here with you."

"As I mentioned to you before, we have not filled the 'P' role for our team. We agreed that I would do double duty until it was clear that God has shown us who he has picked. We will decide this together, but I really believe it's quite likely that God has brought Yushua to us to lead the prophet function of Philadelphia Freedom. But time will tell. Why don't each of you introduce yourself to Yushua. Share a bit about yourselves and how you fit on the team."

Luca smiled with a fatherly pride as he watched the unpretentious introductions that followed. There was no posturing. No turfism. No hubris. Just servant-hearted disciples, genuinely desiring to be a part of a movement that obeys Jesus.

When the introductions had made their way around the living room, Luca stood up and walked to his whiteboard and drew his father's two identical spider-graphs. Under the first one he wrote, *The Person of Christ*. Under the second he wrote, *The Body of Christ*.

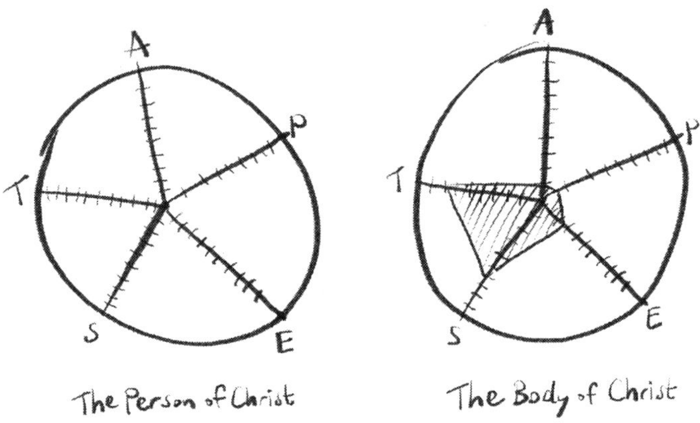

"Let's talk about the 'Person of Christ.' Let's go through the functions of Ephesians 4:11–12, one by one, and see what we can learn about Jesus."

Luca circled the "A." "Was Jesus apostolic? Was Jesus missionary?"

"Yes," Santiago quickly answered.

"How do we know that, Santiago?"

"John 20:21," Santiago answered. "'As the Father has sent me, I am sending you.' He was sent, and he was sending."

"Bingo," said Luca. "The sent and sending Jesus is the very picture of the apostolic. Perfect."

Then Luca circled the "P." "Was the 'Person of Christ' prophetic? Did Jesus speak God's truth even when it wasn't religiously or culturally received?"

Santiago's hand flinched on his thigh, struggling with his desire to answer and his sensitivity not to dominate.

"I believe so," Choyz said hesitantly. "In Jesus' Sermon on the Mount, a number of times Jesus said, 'You have heard that it was said … but I say unto you …' Seems to me that Jesus was reorienting his disciples back to the true meaning of God's Word, and away from the confusing manmade mess that the religious leaders concocted."

"Someone give my sista one of them Oreos!" smiled Luca. "Choyz, you nailed it. Jesus' prophetic correction taught the children of this world about the 'upside-right' nature of the kingdom of God."

"But you meant to say 'upside-down,' didn't you?" asked Choyz.

"No ma'am, I sure did not. The world is 'upside-down' when Jesus' ways are ignored. Obeying him turns everything 'upside-right.'"

"I see. That makes sense, I guess."

"So, Yushua," Campbell MacKay started, "will it be difficult for you to straighten us up when you're all knackered from school and work? Can you do it on half a tank?"

Yushua looked helplessly at Luca for some assistance.

"Allow me to translate," said Luca. "He's asking if you'll have the moxie, the chutzpa, the wherewithal to get up in our grills when you see that we're wrong. Lots on your plate already with work and law school ..."

Santiago interrupted. "Think we may need a UN interpreter here—don't think your clarification clarified much, Luca. As the only other non-native English speaker, let me try. Yushua, after a long day of work and school, will you still have the emotional stamina to correct your brothers and sisters when you see us in error?"

"I don't know," Yushua said as he stared at the whiteboard. "But I wouldn't think that it would be the prophet's job to straighten people out. Godly correction should come from one another should it not? Perhaps it's the prophet's role to help inspire all of us toward a culture of pursuing God's truth?"

"You're hired," Campbell said with a chuckle. "He's correcting us already."

Luca was pleased with how Yushua handled Campbell's unprompted pop test; pleased with both the content of his answer and the manner in which he served it up.

He smiled as he thought to himself: *Wisdom and humility? Check.*

Luca walked back to the board and circled the "E." "All right, was the 'Person of Christ' an evangelist?"

"Well that one's easy," said Campbell without a second's hesitation. "Jesus was in himself the good news. His presence was good news personified wherever he strolled. And his death and resurrection were the grandest bit of news in the history of this rock. So, I'd say, 'Yes.' I think so."

"So that would be a 'yes' then Campbell, correct?"

"Aye. Definitely."

"Okay." Luca drew a circle around the "S." "Was he a Shepherd?"

"'I am the good shepherd …'" said Jerome.

"Yes. Where's that from?" asked Luca.

After several seconds of silence, Santiago could take it no more. "John 10 is where Jesus taught his disciples about the difference between the 'good shepherd' and the 'hired hand.' Jesus sacrifices his life for his sheep. The hired hands run away."

Luca was amazed at how Santiago was so quickly grasping the Scriptures. In just a few months, he already had a better handle on God's Word than so many at Mt. Pisgah who sat through a lifetime of his father's expository sermons.

"That is so right on, my brother. The 'Person of Christ' was a good shepherd."

Finally, Luca drew a circle around the only remaining letter. "Was the 'Person of Christ' a teacher?"

Chantel, who like Luca had been enjoying soaking up all of what God had been assembling, raised her hand.

"In Mark 10, we read about the rich young ruler who called Jesus 'good teacher.' Seems to me that he wasn't only a 'teacher,' but he was a 'wonderful teacher.' That's one of the reasons the multitudes kept coming to hear him speak."

Luca walked over to his bride and offered a high five. Chantel smiled.

"All right, y'all. You did good. This circle represents the fullness of Christ. When Jesus walked on this earth, he was all at once apostle and prophet and evangelist and shepherd and teacher. He, in himself, was complete. And Ephesians 4:11 says that he gave those same gifts to the church. For what reason? Anyone?"

Santiago stood up and read verses twelve and thirteen.

"To equip the saints for the work of ministry, for building up the body of Christ, until we all attain to the unity of the faith and of the knowledge of the Son of God, to mature manhood, to the measure of the stature of the fullness of Christ …"

He stuck his finger in the passage, closed his Bible, and said, "He gave those gifts to equip God's people to live and look and sound and serve just like Jesus."

"All right, all right. So how we doing? How is his body living and looking and ministering? Let's take a look."

Luca walked up to the second diagram that was labeled, *The Body of Christ.*

"Think about Mt. Pisgah. Or LifePointe, Yushua. Or the average 'evangelical church' in North America. And let's go in the same order. From one to ten, one being terrible, ten being 'off the charts.' 'A,' apostle. How much of a priority is it for the average church to send its best away to multiply itself in another place? How urgent is the calling for the average church to sacrifice itself so that people who will never attend their church can hear the gospel? One to ten."

A smattering of numbers was called out ranging from zero to two.

"So, we'll say, 'one.'" Then Luca drew a black dot on the first calibration for "A."

"Okay. Prophetic. How seriously does the average church challenge itself to conform to a kingdom culture, and resist a culturally American version of religion? How much of the 'Sermon on the Mount' characterizes the culture of our churches? If you stripped away all the religious talk, how different would a church person look from their lost neighbors? One to ten."

After a brief deliberation, "two" became the consensus. Luca drew a black dot on the second increment.

"Okay, now we're talking evangelism. I want to be clear on this one. We're talking about urgency. A willingness to inconvenience ourselves for the sake of those who are far from God. We're not talking about preaching weekly evangelistic sermons to Christians. We're talking about regularly seeing death to life conversions. How common is this? One to ten."

Again, the numbers called out ranged from zero to three.

"All right, let's be generous. Let's say three." Then he drew another black dot on the third tick.

"Stay with me, team. 'S,' shepherding. How important is it to the average church to care for its flock?"

Choyz had something to say. "I think that some churches are much better at this. Mt. Pisgah had deacons, study groups, and socials. Pastor Josiah was always lookin' in on people. I think that we do this one better."

"All right, Choyz, I tend to agree. One to ten. How much of a priority is it to see that everyone is tended to?"

Once again, after a brief discussion, Luca walked to the whiteboard and drew a black circle on the sixth mark.

"Finally, we get to Santiago's 'T.' How important is it for the average church to faithfully teach God's Word? Let's skip the 'equipping people to teach God's Word' command and just go with straight up 'biblical teaching.' One to ten."

With the lesser understanding of teaching, seven was the consensus.

Luca walked over to the first circle that was labeled, *The Person of Christ*. "Now remember, Jesus filled up this circle completely in himself." Then he took a red marker and redrew the entire circle.

He took a step over to the second circle that was labeled, *The Body of Christ*. He took the same red marker and connected the dots on the spider-graph. A little wedge appeared inside the circle.

"The left circle represents Jesus in fullness and power. The right circle's little red wedge represents Jesus' church. Is there any wonder why the church is losing ground?"

Yushua raised his hand.

"Yes, brother? By the way, you don't have to raise your hand here."

“These pictures are very good. They show us what we already know. To gain ground we must find Je …” Yushua stopped himself mid-sentence. “I’m saying this wrong. To gain ground, we must give up our church. We must …”

“Give ourselves away?” said Luca.

“Yes, we must give ourselves away. To Jesus.”

Chapter Seventeen

Regnum Dei

"I'll take Papa's car to work so you can run Sanders," said Luca as he thumped down the stairs.

"You're comin' home late this evening, honey?"

"I 'spect. Ten, I imagine. Ten-thirty, tops. Too old to go much later."

"All right. I'll be praying for you, sweetie."

"Love you." And then Luca jumped into his dad's Oldsmobile and headed to Fishtown. It would likely be an uneventful workday, but the evening was a different story. Luca would be heading to PHL at 6 p.m. to pick up Pastor Jimmy Norris and his executive pastor for a reconciliation meeting with Yushua.

Recalling the amazing Southern experience Jimmy arranged at Mary Mac's Tea Room in Atlanta, Luca wanted his guests to experience classic Northeastern fare. He made dinner reservations for 7 p.m. at Fishtown's own Talula's Garden.

The day went by quickly enough, and Luca soon found himself waiting in the Oldsmobile at the airport's designated cell phone parking lot. He shot a quick text to Yushua to confirm that he was ready for the evening.

As he waited for a reply from Yushua, a text notification lit up his phone.

We're here. No checked luggage. Meet you in front in 5. Jimmy.

Luca replied, *Be there in 3. Big brown Oldsmobile.*

He pulled the old Oldsmobile in front of domestic arrivals, parked, and began to scan for a well-dressed, well-built, clean-cut white man in his early forties.

"Bingo," Luca said out loud. Jimmy came hustling out of the automatic doors in a tailored dress shirt and slim fitting jeans, pulling a small carry-on. Beside him in an untucked plaid shirt and dockers was his heavy-set traveling companion. Luca flashed his headlights on and off and waved his arm through the driver's side window. Jimmy signaled back.

"Thanks for getting us, Luca. Sorry that we're a few minutes late. This is Tom Butts."

"Pleased to meet you, Tom. I'm Luca Lewis."

"Heard a lot about you," Tom said as he made several attempts at trying to close the back door.

"Sorry, Tom. Old car. Was my late papa's."

As they merged onto the freeway, Jimmy began to clap his hands. "What are the chances? I mean, of all the people in America, God hooks you up with Yushua Ma …"

"Maalouf," Tom helped.

"Seriously," Luca agreed. "I remember my papa leading our church through a Henry Blackaby study years ago: Experiencing God. And there ain't no such things as coincidences for Christians. God is showing us something. And this something must be pretty special."

"No coincidences," Jimmy repeated. "I'm excited and nervous and embarrassed."

"Exactly," said Tom.

They arrived at Talula's Garden ten minutes before their 7 p.m. reservation and were cordially escorted to a corner banquette. It was obvious to Luca that tensions were high among his dinner guests. But he felt no compulsion to ease them; they needed to feel the full weight of their duplicity. After the usual discussion of the inferiority of iced tea outside the South, they decided on a large bottle of San Pellegrino while they waited. And while they waited, Luca's generally optimistic spirit faltered. Something felt a few degrees off.

Yushua, as was his custom, arrived precisely at seven and was escorted by the crisply dressed hostess to their table.

"Good to see you again, buddy," Tom offered.

"Yes, great to see you, friend," repeated Jimmy. "What a small world, isn't it?"

Yushua sat down beside Luca on the vacant wooden chair that directly faced Jimmy. "We are friends, Pastor Jimmy? This would be new information to me."

"Come on Yushua, are we gonna start that way?" Jimmy snapped back while continuing to smile.

"What way would that be? Truthful? Should we pretend that we were friends? That we are friends? If so, I might skip the remaining festivities. I don't do pretense very well."

Tom Butts' round face was quivering. His eyes were moist. With a shaky voice he said, "You're right, brother. We've not treated you as a friend. I lied to you. I have asked for God's forgiveness, and I came here to ask for yours. I am so sorry, Yushua. I am sorry for treating you as an inconvenience to be disposed of. I am sorry for not standing with you as you spoke truth to our people …" Tom's words, now hardly understandable, came out punctuated by sniffs and snotty snorts. "I'm so sorry … for … for being a coward."

Yushua was taken aback by the sincerity of Tom's manner. Tom had always been a straight-ahead, no-nonsense business administrator. He had never seen this emotional side of Tom Butts, and it impacted him.

Yushua quietly cleared his throat and said, "Brother, I have been a coward many times in my life. I forgive you. Thank you for coming to see me—this means so much."

Tom dabbed at his eyes with a napkin and mumbling "Thank you" and "Sorry for getting all emotional," as he glanced up at Yushua.

"Well, it was the least we could do, Yushua," said Jimmy. "But we're delighted to see that you landed on your feet here in Philadelphia. And with Luca Lewis. Wow. I couldn't believe it when Luca called me. God's ways are amazing, aren't they?"

Eyeing Jimmy, Luca asked, "So, this was your decision, Tom? It was your decision to cut Yushua off at the knees?"

"Well, it wasn't really my decision. But I went along with it. And I shouldn't have."

"Whose decision was it then, Tom, if it wasn't yours?"

"Well, it was … guess it was ultimately Jimmy's." Tom glanced sideways at Jimmy, looking decidedly uncomfortable.

"So, Jimmy," said Luca. "Anything else to say to Yushua 'sides you're glad he landed on his feet?"

"Well, that's exactly why we're here, Luca. To fix things. Like Tom said, we didn't do right by Yushua."

"Who didn't do right?" Luca pressed.

"C'mon, Luca. Why are you pickin' at this? We flew all the way here to fix this. It doesn't help LifePointe one way or the other whether we did this or not. We're here 'cause we want to be."

Yushua once again gently cleared his throat. "Jimmy, remember when we first met. At the refugee camp?"

"Of course."

"Do you remember Francis Murphy from Newfoundland?"

"Yes, I do. He was quite the character. Luca, you woulda' loved him."

"Do you remember our code word? He taught it to you."

"Um, no, not really. Something strange. Latin?"

"*Regnum Dei,*" Tom interjected.

"Yes, Tom. *Regnum Dei.*" Then Yushua knocked his chest twice and pointed to the ceiling. "Francis Murphy, a high-ranking UN diplomat, and Yushua Maalouf, a nobody with a borrowed name and borrowed clothes, became brothers. He didn't ever treat me as anything but an equal. Do you know why, Pastor Jimmy?"

Jimmy shrugged his shoulders to suggest he didn't know.

"Because in God's kingdom, there is only one King. It wasn't a UN diplomat. Nor a refugee from Bani Badi. Only Jesus. The *Regnum Dei* demanded character and conduct that was consistent with our kingdom confession."

"That's socialism, not kingdom," Jimmy retorted. "Yes, we're all brothers and sisters, but we aren't all the same. Some of us have studied and invested and grown and paid a price. Some of us have large spiritual responsibilities. Others have smaller assignments … looking after themselves. Diplomats and refugees are not the same. He may have made you feel that way, but I'm sorry, it ain't so. He goes down and it affects everyone. You go down, and it doesn't. Sorry, but we don't need more socialism …"

Luca appeared to have a difficult time containing himself. "Look at your brother, Jimmy. Look at him. You think he ain't paid a price? You think you've paid a higher price? You think—"

"It's okay, Luca," said Yushua as he squeezed his big forearm to calm him. "I think that Pastor Jimmy may have missed my point. Let me try again. I agree with you; there is no doubt that we all have different stations in life. You have a high one at LifePointe. I was a lowly nobody, a janitor. Your work affected a thousand people. My work affected almost no one. Okay. We've established the religious org chart. Now let's talk kingdom. Would that be okay?"

Jimmy shrugged once again.

"Do you remember how Jesus started out his Sermon on the Mount?"

No sound came from the other side of the table.

Luca broke the silence. "Well, I do. 'Blessed are the poor in spirit, for theirs is the kingdom of heaven.'"

"Yes, isn't that beautiful, Jimmy? Jesus, the Creator, came not to be served, but to become a servant. He was 'poor in spirit' even though he was Almighty God. Jesus, God in human flesh, walked on water and washed filthy feet. So yes, Jimmy, your station is high. Mine was low. But *Regnum Dei* requires the humility of Christ to be the spiritual marker of his people, despite their human stations. That's what Francis Murphy was doing. We reveal his kingdom when we revel in our nothingness. And we advance the darkness of man-made religion when we leverage it for man's praise."

Jimmy Norris and Tom Butts looked deferentially across the table at the scarred face of the young refugee facing them. In every human way they were his superiors. But they didn't feel that way right now. They felt more like elementary schoolboys in a doctoral seminar. They understood all the words that Yushua said, yet somehow they knew that they didn't fully comprehend the ideas behind them.

"I need a beer," Jimmy said. "I don't drink, but I'm sure I need one. Probably more than one."

The moment lightened with Jimmy's unexpected insertion of humor. Then looking into Yushua's eyes, he said, "Brother, you're right. You are. I've spent a lifetime building a house of cards. I've got to protect everything and protect myself to keep it all standing. But none of it is real. Not really. I know it. Tom knows it. We've talked some about it but don't really know what to do. It all looks good. Fools most people. But this *Regnum Dei* stuff has been the furthest thing from my mind. *Regnum* Me is more like it. And to make my kingdom work, I had to sacrifice you, Yushua. I had to sacrifice truth. I had to sacrifice the Truth."

Jimmy thought for a moment more, as he stared at the cloth napkin on his lap. Then he looked at Yushua and said, "To make my kingdom work, I had to kill his."

***

The first time Yushua flew into Atlanta, he had to work out his own way to Roswell. Everyone was too busy to bother with the needs of a confused and disoriented refugee. This time Yushua arrived to a very different welcome. Both Jimmy and Tom waited at the foot of the escalators between the north and south terminals of ATL to greet and chauffeur him northward. And the dramatic change did not go unnoticed by Yushua.

About an hour later Tom's minivan pulled into the familiar complex of brick and stone. "I forgot how big this place is. You just don't see this in Philadelphia." But Yushua's emotions were much different in this sighting than they were at his first. Two and a half years previously, it was aspirational. A point of arrival. It was something for his people in Yemen to achieve. Now it stood more as a cautionary notice, a warning sign before a treacherous cliff. It represented a set of venal priorities that should be avoided at all costs. Yet peculiarly, the more Yushua looked at it, the more appealing it became. "This is certainly an impressive campus," Yushua commented.

"We have thirty minutes. Anything you need?" asked Tom.

"One of your ice teas?"

"Unsweetened, right?"

"Please."

Jimmy escorted Yushua to Staff Conference Room B.

"A few things have changed. Like it?"

Yushua took stock of the room he had cleaned dozens of times. A new boardroom table that was fitted with every possible electronic connection. New large screen monitors, seamlessly built into the walls. New executive chairs. The back wall was entirely white cabinets with a matching white built-in refrigerator. And the carpet had been replaced with bleached hardwood.

"We're giving this treatment to all our meeting rooms. Minimalism, they call it."

"It looks very nice," said Yushua politely.

"All right, have a seat." Jimmy gestured to the center of the boardroom table. "I don't fully understand all this 'APEST' business that Luca goes on about, but some of it's starting to sink in. So, give it to us with both barrels."

Yushua descended into a luxurious leather chair that supported muscles and bones that he didn't know he had. It took him aback for a second. "You mean, speak honestly about what I noticed about LifePointe, correct? This is what you want?"

"Absolutely. I'm even bringing Chip Bussey out of exile for this."

"Pardon me?"

"Never mind. It's a long story. Just be honest. Hold nothing back. Of anyone on God's green earth, you are probably the one who has the best perspective on our church. I'll reintroduce you and then hand it over to you. Take as long as you need."

Like clockwork, all twenty executive chairs were filled by one o'clock. Jimmy had prearranged for all senior staff to be in attendance, plus the three officers of the board. Already this was a highly unusual meeting by virtue of its composition, but the strangeness was about to enter a new level due to the surprise keynote speaker Jimmy had slated: Limpy, the janitor.

"All right gang, thanks for being on time." Jimmy paused for everyone to settle into their seats.

"Gerry, Phil, Greg, thanks for representing the board. Chip, good to see you back. You had a much-needed rest, I trust. And who's this stranger? Welcome back Yu-sh-ua! It's great to have you with the LifePointe family once again." And then Jimmy paused.

"Thank you, Pastor Jimmy. It's an honor to be here," said Yushua.

Jimmy took a long, slow drink of Dr. Pepper and then cleared his throat. "I imagine that many of you are wondering what this is about. Well, let me tell you. Some of you had noticed, as I had confessed a few weeks back, that I've been a bit off. Chip called me a 'hippie' if I recall correctly—and maybe he wasn't too far off in some ways. For a long time, there has been a restlessness in my spirit about what we're doing here … for years, actually … before Chad Collins and the SynerChurch report … probably, if I'm honest, even before I came to LifePointe. I often go through seasons where I desperately crave something simpler. Something more authentic. But eventually I push it all down, put my head down, numb my heart, and push forward. 'The show must go on and all that.' But I can't do that anymore. I can't …"

Jimmy's usually velvet voice struggled as tears started to form in his eyes.

"This ain't some form of emotional breakdown, I promise. It's affecting my emotions, yes, but it's much deeper. Maybe some of you know what I'm talkin' about?"

He paused again to take in any nonverbal feedback. Tom Butts was nodding. So was Yushua. But that was about all. Most everyone else wore completely blank expressions, stunned once again by the newfound transparency of their pastor. But not all the nonverbal was neutral. Chip Bussey's and Bobby Berringer's body language spoke convincingly in an entirely different direction.

Jimmy continued, "There have been several times in my ministry when I have regretted my decisions. Usually, they were wrong decisions made from incomplete information. But only a few times can I say that I deliberately went against my conscience. But I did that this spring. I did that when we fired Yushua."

Jimmy had to stop again to steady his emotions. He glanced at Yushua who was smiling strength back to him.

"Let me begin by correcting the record. There were no budget cuts. That was a ruse. A lie. Nor had Yushua failed in his custodian duties. Juan said that he was our hardest working staff member. Nor was he divisive. I've heard that one, too. All of those excuses and rumors are simply bald-faced lies. Here is what Yushua is guilty of: speaking spiritual reality into a church that is drunk on self-adulation. He's guilty of speaking truth to a church that simply won't stand for it."

Then Jimmy pieced together the events that took place at Chip Bussey's community group. As he laid out his case, he attempted to make it as difficult as possible to come to the conclusion that "more of the same" should be LifePointe's future. And he could see in some of his colleagues' faces that he was finding agreement. And now was the moment to bring out the big guns.

"Most of you will remember me telling of a Philadelphia pastor who was used by God in an amazing way during their big ice storm a couple of years' back. Well, I've developed a friendship with him. His name is Luca Lewis. We speak together every Wednesday afternoon. And I've learned more from him these last few months than I think I learned in seminary. In fact, I'm seeing that I must unlearn a whole bunch of things I thought I knew. Unlearn and repent if I am ever able to truly relearn."

Jimmy pressed a button, and an illuminated glass sheet descended from the ceiling. He uncapped a thick marker and wrote *APEST* in glowing fluorescent yellow letters.

"This is how Luca divides up the work of his church. It comes from Ephesians four. Apostle, prophet, evangelist, shepherd, teacher. We won't get into all that now but suffice it to say that he was short of a 'P.' Luca needed a truth teller in his leadership structure to equip others to make sure that things stay on track."

Greg Jackson, the board's lawyer asked, "So this was his staff structure? Instead of minister of this and that ... this is how he organized his pastoral staff?"

"Kinda," said Jimmy. "His staff, including himself, are all co-vocational, meaning they have two common callings. They're called to share the gospel in their everyday work world, and they're called to be servant leaders that equip their members for ministry. Nobody's paid, and everybody's included."

"A small church?" Greg asked.

"It was when they started ... just a dozen or so. But they're already over four hundred, and they're really just gettin' started. Four hundred spread out across thirty-some 'missional communities.' Most all of 'em engaged in ministry."

Jimmy could see the gears moving in Greg's mind.

"So, as I said, Luca was short a lead 'P.' They didn't know who it was. You can't go to a church HR website to find that profile. So, they did something strange. Strange for us, at least. They prayed. Prayed for more than a year. Then Luca was asked to speak here in Atlanta for his work. That's where we met—at the airport Marriott. Luca leads a Y in Philly and was asked to speak at their national conference. So, he catches an Uber to the airport. And his Uber driver blows his socks off. He spoke to the heart of things like Luca had never seen. It took him a few days, but eventually it sank in—'maybe that Uber driver is my 'P'?' Luca thought to himself. So, he goes on an all-out search. He told me that he was doin' it. Spent two whole days at the airport in Philly flaggin' down Ubers. Nothing. Then guess who waltzes into his Y?"

"The Uber driver?" asked Greg Jackson.

"Yes, sir. The very same Uber driver. And let me introduce him to you. LifePointe, meet Luca's 'P.' Mr. Yushua Maalouf."

There was a holy hush in Staff Conference Room B at that moment. For some in the room, Yushua's testimony in the Christmas mission videos already gave him a mystical spiritual authority. And now this. Even Chip Bussey was leaning forward in anticipation.

"Thank you, Pastor Jimmy," started Yushua. "It's good to be back with you, and under such incredible circumstances. Truly, only followers of Jesus get to walk on the water with him. And we've all just got to experience a bit of that now, haven't we?"

Yushua reached into his carry-on, pulled out a white plastic grocery bag, and carefully placed it on the table in front of him. "When I was in prison in Yemen, I shared a cell with six Jesus followers. All were sentenced to death because they would not compromise their allegiance to King Jesus. One of my brothers, Hussein was his name, on his last day, preached Jesus' Sermon on the Mount from memory. For Hussein, and the other five brothers, the promise of Jesus' kingdom was more real than the threats of their persecutors. One by one, their lives were extinguished. As were the lives of my sister, Fatimah, and the Jesus followers of our underground church in Dhamar. But that was not their end."

Tears streamed down Yushua's scarred cheeks as he relived those joyous and pain-filled memories. Chip Bussey handed him a bottle of water, and Yushua took a long, slow drink.

"That was only the beginning. Their obedience to Isa—to King Jesus—threw pebbles into eternity … the kingdom ripples that go on forever. Their executions were not the end of their impact. Their obedience is impacting people right now. Maybe it's impacting some of you."

"That is true, Yushua," Greg Jackson agreed. "When my family watched your video and heard your story, Jan and I felt compelled to send a rather large donation to a missions ministry that operates in the majority Muslim world. And now Jan is researching how we might adopt a child from that war-torn part of the world. 'Eternal ripples.' Never thought of it that way."

"Yes, Greg. Our obedience or our disobedience serves to reveal and advance the spiritual realm that inspired our choice. Consequential ripples in either direction. But my story was to be different from theirs. God, in his sovereignty, saved me from the prison and put me in the one refugee camp that was run by a crazy, courageous, faithful Jesus follower. Francis Murphy was his name. He taught me much more about Jesus' kingdom. He helped me understand the big story of the Scriptures. And he arranged to bring me to you. But before I left the camp, he gave me this …"

Yushua reached into the white plastic grocery bag and pulled out a carefully folded, yet almost threadbare, T-shirt. He gently unfolded it, as if he were unearthing a prized ancient relic, and then held it to his chest. "This was Mr. Murphy's. This printing is the coat of arms of his home province in Canada. The words say *Quaerite Prime Regnum Dei*, which means, 'seek first the kingdom of God.' This primacy, this first order of allegiance, marked all the Jesus followers that I knew. Jesus' kingdom was life and death for everyone."

As he stopped for another swallow of water, his countenance changed. His peaceful, otherworldly appearance was replaced with a look of sadness.

"Until I came here. Here I found a different way …"

Tom Butts broke in. "I think that we should all apologize to Yushua for how we treated him …"

"No, no, brother Tom. That's not what I am saying. Perhaps how I was treated is a symptom of what is wrong. The problem is much deeper than the unjust firing of a lowly janitor. The janitor is okay. God's sovereign plan accounted for the darkness of your deception, and he gave me a new assignment. Deception is the issue. And not your feeble attempt to deceive me, but your self-deception."

"What do you mean?" Greg asked.

"I've thought and prayed about this. I think at the heart of things is that you are deceived as to who owns this church. You think that you own it. So, you misuse words like 'stewardship.' You make them owners' words. You want to be good stewards of what you own. It leads you to ask questions like, 'How much can we give away and still be safe?' Your church has become your business. And you make business decisions as owners. But this is not Jesus' church. This is your church. You are the sole proprietors."

The quiet hush was back in Staff Conference Room B, but this time it was dead quiet. Yushua quietly refolded his T-shirt and carefully placed it back in the grocery bag. And then he sat down. No one moved.

Jimmy slowly rose to his feet, cleared his throat, and quietly said, "Last week, when Tom and I were in Philly with Yushua and Luca, I realized something for the very first time. Something so simple yet so completely devastating. To build my kingdom, I had to kill his. Yushua's right. We own this church. Jesus doesn't. It's ours. And I don't know about y'all, but I don't like what we've bought."

Jimmy's flushed-red face quivered as he spoke. Something deep was shifting in his spirit.

"Beginning now, starting today. This moment. Right now. I'm taking my grimy hands off it."

He looked to the ceiling with his arms stretched outward and whispered, “Jesus, if you want it, I want to give it back to you. If you still want me ...”

And then he broke down and began to sob. Deeply. Tom Butts got up and knelt beside him, and with his arm draped over Jimmy’s back, wept with him.

And Yushua prayed.

Chapter Eighteen

The Pneumanauts

In most church leadership settings, Kofe and Angelica Wilson and Campbell and Riona MacKay would be having a big problem. The Wilsons, who were more seasoned in their faith and who were part of Luca's original cohort from the beginning, were appearing to take a back seat to the MacKays. But what may not have been obvious to a casual onlooker, the Wilsons noted and accommodated: Campbell and Riona had greater leadership abilities and larger community platforms than them. What also wasn't obvious at a quick glance was the depth of Kofe and Angelica's emotional and spiritual maturity to make space for others and choose to support them.

From the onset, almost immediately after the ice storm efforts, the Wilsons made a strategic tactical decision. And this decision would change the very nature of their efforts for days to come. 'Equipping equippers,' for most leaders, becomes a top-down trickle-down organizational structure. But the Wilsons had a different picture in mind. They saw themselves at the very back of the parade. The ones with the shovels and buckets cleaning up what the show horses left behind. And for them, that meant serving the MacKays.

But this wasn't purely a decision motivated by their generous and altruistic spirits. Kofe and Angelica had been witnesses to something revolutionary. Something heart-shifting. And again, once you see, you cannot unsee. And when one's heart is right, you really don't want to.

It was during the frantic efforts of the ice storm relief that the Wilsons saw the vast kingdom potential pent up in these newly minted Irish disciples. While Kofe and Angelica were stressed and somewhat operationally paralyzed, they watched the MacKays gently swoop in and intuitively help them sort out processes and priorities. The Wilsons initially chalked it up to Campbell's administrative acumen.

And then Riona's instincts led her to make a staffing suggestion that was far from the norm; an idea which the Wilsons objected to at first but later capitulated. The MacKays wanted to mobilize unchurched volunteers from the community at large to help serve needs. But the Wilsons could see little strategic value to this ministry approach. "How would the community know that our church is doing this in the name of Christ?" was their basic counterpoint. Jerome and Choyz sided with their thinking. It made perfect sense.

But two things happened that changed their thinking. First, the scope of the need soon outstripped the human resources available in their little fellowship of believers. Had they persisted in restricting the labor force to those with church credentials, it would have exhausted their workforce, and the ministry would have sputtered to a stop before it got off the ground.

But secondly, and more significantly, the Wilsons learned something profound about the natural process of disciple-making from the MacKays. While the physical ministry of service was reluctantly shared with the general community, so was the spiritual miracle of evangelism. Serving shoulder-to-shoulder with friends and neighbors, Campbell and Riona spoke naturally of the new hope that they found in Jesus. Deep and honest questions were asked and thoughtfully answered. Perspectives changed. Repentance, in its truest form, became a commonplace response to the witness. And in the aftermath of the ice storm, almost 70 percent of the people who joined new missional communities were those who had served and volunteered. "Belonging precedes believing, and behaving follows believing," became the cultural axiom that guided their missionary efforts after that event.

In the weeks that followed, Kofe and Angelica spent every spare moment they could scrape together to prepare the MacKays' spiritual foundation for the leadership mantle that awaited them. And the spiritually parched Campbell and Riona gratefully slurped down everything that was served up. Stories, testimonies, warnings, biblical insights, failings—nothing was held back. It was all life and death. The Wilsons knew that their proteges had remarkable leadership capacity—gifts that could help push the movement forward much faster than they themselves could. But they also feared that if their gifts were not contained in a depth of spiritual character, a disastrous train wreck loomed in their future. So, every opportunity for correction and encouragement was taken.

Part of the Wilsons' prep course strategy was to invite the MacKays to Philadelphia Freedom's Sunday evening leadership meetings. There they could observe how passionate and spiritually mature leaders make difficult decisions while deferring to one another in a generous spirit of interdependence. And after Campbell's first visit, he was blown away.

"Nowhere on this big blue rock have I seen a sight such as that," Campbell later said to the Wilsons. "Big Luca listened. He listened to Santiago. He turned about and walked in an entirely different direction because of the words of a wee piker."

"We're all learning," said Kofe. "Luca's setting the pace for all of us. The body of Christ isn't any one of us."

Aromas of freshly roasted coffee mingled with linseed-oiled wood permeated the senses of the group, as they chose seats and settled into the leather couches surrounding a large marble coffee table. The basement room was lit by spotlights, spattering rays across the room, and despite there being fewer snacks provided than were usually on offer in the conference rooms at Lifepoint, their host, Greg, had ensured a selection of fresh pastries from his local deli were neatly placed on platters with napkins.

Jimmy had begun with a vision to gather an exclusive and clandestine coalition of his most trusted leadership. He called them the "Pneumanauts." These would be leaders who were willing to consider the possible radical moves that it might take to turn the good ship around. People willing to chart a new course. To move out into uncharted waters so LifePointe might resemble something that mattered. The group's designation was a smashing together of two Greek words into something totally new: "*pneuma*" meant breath or wind but was often translated in the New Testament as "Spirit." The suffix "naut" simply added the energetic denotation of voyager, traveler, or sailor. Together this cadre became a fellowship of Spirit-sailors who earnestly desired to hear from Jesus so that they might chart a new course and become a church for his mission.

In order to find leaders for this new group, Jimmy and Tom devised a screening tool that would serve as an assessment process of sorts. A series of questions that would naturally eliminate any distracting voices and at the same time identify the personalities who could be helpful. To Jimmy, it was essential to have a team of co-conspirators that could be trusted, so that was the question of the highest order. Could their character be counted on? They were about to workshop any number of half-conceived ideas, and the emotional maturity of their collaborators needed to be without question. Secondarily, but also significant, was the rest of the list. Could they influence others? Were they satisfied with the status quo, or were they hungry for something different? Could they be both creative and strategic? And then finally, were they likable?

Jimmy and Tom filtered names through their screening process and came up with four names. As bad as that sounded, it was actually much worse: there were only two names if they didn't count themselves. Greg Jackson, corporate attorney and the board's secretary, and Julia Mumsford, a former Olympic gymnast turned LifePointe's children's director. They both ticked all the boxes and were the intuitive and immediate picks of both Tom and Jimmy. Many subsequent hours were spent combing through LifePointe's rolls in search of additional recruits. But for one reason or another, either Jimmy or Tom vetoed all prospects.

Twitching a fluorescent pink Post-it note that was stuck to his index finger, Jimmy said, "Might as well pastor a house church. Two thousand well-dressed churchmen, and this is all we got. Two stinkin' names."

"Well, we gotta start somewhere," answered the ever-peacemaking Tom. "'Sides, we can always add more once we've got the basics nailed down."

For three successive Tuesday mornings, the group had gathered in a somewhat surreptitious manner, cloistered away in Greg's oak-paneled basement lounge, as they openly discussed their perceptions, their disappointments, and their most daring dreams. The meetings were skillfully designed to organically lay out the emotional and theological groundwork for Jimmy's seismic shifts that he and Tom had been quietly dreaming about for weeks.

But today's edition of the loyal order of Pneumanauts was going to be different in two significant ways. First, Jimmy was going to show his hand. He had consolidated their conversations into three simple yet groundbreaking constructs. To Jimmy, they were elegant encapsulations of three big ideas that were both easy to understand and memorable. And best of all, every Pneumanaut thought they were their ideas. Second, they were going to develop an actionable plan to gather new recruits to their numbers. Jimmy had learned long ago that gaining acceptance of big ideas required the appearance of momentum, and crafting momentum over these kinds of selfless notions would require every ounce of leadership ability that he had.

But he was sure he was up to the test.

After a brief session of wordsmithing Jimmy's outline, changing the word "new" to the word "different," Greg summarized his thoughts. "Now this makes sense. It isn't a *new* kind of church that we're dreaming of; it's an *old* kind of church. It is as new as the book of Acts. But to us here in the buckle of the Bible Belt, it is certainly 'a different kind of church' to what folks are accustomed to."

So, to keep things parallel, Tom grabbed a red dry-erase marker and substituted "different: for "new" in the second and third ideas as well.

"So y'all are happy with it now?" asked Jimmy. "Think we got it right?"

"It is delicious," said Julia. "It is perfect. So exciting to think that we're going to actually do this. I can't wait to start overhauling our whole children's department around this!"

Jimmy, with both hands signaling in the air, said, "Sssslllllooooowww, slow, s – l – o – w down, my sister. We gotta lot of work to do first. Worst thing we can do is shoot this bullet before we're ready. You know how things work around here."

And Julia Mumsford did know. That's why she was so excited: because things were about to change.

Once again, the food service tables of Staff Conference Room B were loaded with all the staff's favorites, plus a few tactical extras. The presence of Heath Bar one-bite brownies, Blue Bell Ice Cream Cups, and Cuzzin Izzy's jalapeño poppers all suggested that this was to be no ordinary meeting. Even Chip's special mallomars were added to the snacking extravaganza. For this important meeting, Jimmy wanted everyone lubed up in their best possible mood.

This was step number one of a six-step process that had developed around this very table one week earlier. Jimmy and the Pneumanauts had surprised even themselves with the shrewdness of their plan. It was to be a well-organized, well-executed ground game that would systematically gather the strategic influencers of LifePointe until their momentum was inevitable.

And it all started now.

By 9:01, the senior team was seated with plastic plates overloaded with goodies, ready for the morning's agenda. The customary level of tension that accompanied most weekly staff meetings seemed to have dissipated, replaced instead with the good-natured banter of an intramural softball team.

Jimmy stood at his usual station at the middle of the board table. He cleared his throat and launched out, "Thanks, team, for getting down to business on time. That's important. Shows respect for each other. No special prima donnas here. And I really appreciate that."

"Had I known about the jalapeño poppers, I'd have camped out here last night," Chip chirped in. "So, when did you start pickin' up Christian food, Jimmy? Thought you was some kind of health nut."

Jimmy managed a laugh that easily passed for the genuine thing.

"So, this morning I want to, as clearly as possible, articulate where I want our church to start headin'. A vision for our future. A roadmap. A roadmap with three main markers. This won't take me too long, but I want to reserve our whole morning for questions, discussion, and pushback. Sound all right?"

Swollen cheeks stuffed with assorted sweets and hors d'oeuvres nodded in unison.

"Terrific. This will be simple and straightforward, but I believe it's something that could be a game changer for us. Again, I stole a lot of the inspiration for this from my Philadelphia friend, Luca Lewis. But I've been ruminating on this for a while, and I think that I have made it my own. Our own. Something that fits us. Something that will set us free to be the thing many of us always have wanted. And the thing that Jesus set up in the first place. You ready?"

There was less chewing and less nodding this time. Mostly blank stares.

Chip Bussey, with a mouth full of mallomars, offered an unintelligible mumble and then immediately redeployed his complete attention back to working on his mound of nibbles.

"All right then," Jimmy continued. He stood up, cleared his throat, unfolded several pages of handwritten notes that were tucked into his brown leather folio, and then launched out. "Three shifts we gotta make …"

For twenty-two minutes, Jimmy eloquently and passionately painted a vivid picture of the future LifePointe Chapel as he saw it. He outlined three priorities that were much more than new tools or new programs; they were three paradigm-shifting values that would fundamentally change almost everything that LifePointe stood for.

"And so," Jimmy's cadence slowed as he paused momentarily to look deeply into every pair of eyes. "I'm wondering, how many of you think this is a future worth pursuing? You gotta know that this ain't no silver bullet that'll return us to our glory days. I can promise you that right now. No, this would be a slow, methodical, and sometimes pain-filled journey to a more Jesusy future. And at the end of the journey, we won't be LifePointe circa 2012. No sir, not at all. But we just might become something that we can be proud of. Something that our kids might want. Something that we would want for our kids. Something that our community would see and be astonished. Astonished 'cause it looks so different from what they were expectin'. And maybe, just maybe, we might build something that we could each point to when we meet our Maker and say, 'King Jesus, I hope that your bride in North Atlanta looks and acts and thinks more like you than it ever had before. I hope that she pleases you.'"

Jimmy sensed the wind of the Spirit propelling him forward as he prophetically spoke kingdom life into his comrades in arms. There was a stillness in the room that was uncharacteristic of a LifePointe staff meeting. No one was looking around. No nervous throats were being cleared. The air was thick with the presence of God.

Tom Butts leaned back into his chair and closed his eyes. The tears that had been forming in his eyes immediately began to stream down his puffy cheeks. "Thank you, Jimmy. Thank you," was all that he managed to get out.

Julia Mumsford, as if on cue, rose from her office chair, grounded herself with her knuckles digging into the boardroom table, and said, "This, Pastor Jimmy. This. This …" Tears began to spot the table as she stammered for words. "This … I would die for. This I would do … for free. Who wouldn't? This is what I always thought ministry was."

She swiped her face with her LifePointe sweatshirt sleeve and then quietly sat down.

"Thank you, Julia," Jimmy said. "I agree with you, sister. I'd do this for free …"

Chip Bussey skidded his empty plastic plate away with his right hand, hoisted himself up, and said, "What are y'all talking about? Do what for free? Do your jobs for free? You plannin' on firing everybody, Jimmy? Some of us got families to feed. Some of us don't have famous preachers for daddies. Some of us need our jobs."

"Hold on there, buddy," said Jimmy as calmly as he knew how. "Nobody's gett'n fired. It was just a figure of speech. When you love something enough, you find a way to do it even if you aren't being paid for it. That's all Julia was sayin'."

Chip was obviously unconvinced with Jimmy's warm reassurances. With crossed arms and a flat voice, he said, "Well it seems to me that you've got it all figured out, don't you Pastor Jimmy? Change everything. Everything's rotten. It's all bad. Blow it all up. You got yourself a better way. Jimmy knows best. You're the great Dr. James Norris. Second best preacher this church has ever had. Who are we to stand in your way? It's just our lives you're talkin' about."

And with that, Chip Bussey rose from his chair and stormed out of Staff Conference Room B.

The mood in the room changed entirely.

Jimmy looked anxiously at Tom for any sort of nonverbal guidance.

Tom shrugged, grimaced, and then gobbled down two jalapeño

poppers. The rest of the staff began to tidy their plates and gather their things as if the whole room were waiting for permission to leave. No one would be quite as crass as Chip, but his general sentiment summed up the fears of many. Their uncomfortable squirms, nervous throat clearing, and eyes glued straight on the boardroom table were all clear body language indicating that most desperately wanted to leave.

It was then that Jimmy realized without a doubt that the Pneumanauts' overhaul plan was a big, fat, miserable fail.

"We need three floors. Or at least three distinctly separate sections," Yushua said. "That way this can become both reproducible and immediately sustainable."

"Yes. As much as I hate to, I got to agree with Yushua," said Campbell MacKay with a twinkle in his eye. "We surely got to give it a lash. The manky way it's been done in the past won't do now."

"Uh, thank you, I think," said Yushua. "For those of you who do not speak English as eloquently as our esteemed Mr. MacKay, he said, and I will loosely translate, 'As usual, the distinguished Yushua Maalouf is entirely correct.'"

The circle of friends gathered in Luca and Chantel's townhouse erupted in a chorus of heartfelt laughter. Luca said, as he held his left side with his right arm, "You may not have the spiritual gift of interpretation, my brother, but you sure have the gift of embellishment."

Much had happened with Philadelphia Freedom in the busy months that followed the big ice storm. The group went from a small and incomplete leadership gathering to something that was beginning to feel like the edges of a movement. Campbell and

Riona's instinct to integrate community volunteers seamlessly into their ministry leadership led dozens of Philadelphians to move from being religiously antagonistic to becoming spiritually curious. From there, many of their friends and neighbors repented of their sins and became disciples of Jesus. Soon, their numbers began to multiply as friends, co-workers, and family became spiritually inquisitive after personally witnessing the radical transformation of their loved ones. They began to ask impossible questions to which the gospel of Jesus was the only answer. And then one missional community became two. And two soon became three. Three became five. Five became eight. Eight became eleven. Eleven became nineteen. And nineteen was now over thirty.

And the little band of leaders of Philadelphia Freedom were feeling the full weight.

Luca leaned back, pulled a brown plastic lever with his right hand, and fully reclined his papa's leather chair. "Y'all figure this one out yourselves. Yushua's thinking makes sense to me. But I don't know if we need to get too caught up in all the philosophical niceties right now—we just need space to train leaders. Our townhouse ain't fittin' the bill no more."

"Agreed," said Santiago. "Our apartment has become Grand Central Station as well. Sophia loves it, but bedtime is getting much too late."

Campbell stood up and said, "Well then, I'll ring up María Cardoza-López and see if that beauty in Fishtown is still up for snatching. But right now, I'm knackered. Everyone good with that?"

Everyone stood and nodded in agreement as the group moved as one toward the Lewises' front door.

"Yushua, make sure that you can be there," Luca called out. "We really need your eyes on the place. You more than the rest of us. You'll see it ain't much. So, you'll have to use that sanctified imagination of yours."

"Wouldn't miss it for the world."

***

María Cardoza-López was once again leaning against her lustrous white Mercedes, working a deal through her pink leopard-print smartphone. Her lively gesturing and confident smile, red lipstick generously applied, revealed a personality that was anything but understated.

"Good morning, Ms. López," said Yushua softly as he walked by as if to announce his presence.

"Be with you in a sec, honey," she loudly whispered while covering the bottom of her phone, flashing her lengthy pink acrylic nails.

Ten minutes later María came rushing over to the back parking lot as fast as her heels would allow, calling out excitedly, "So lucky! Can't believe that this property is still available. Such a gem. We're so lucky!"

Campbell looked toward Yushua and said, "Yes, looks like the winter is helping with the weeds. Only thigh-high now. Guess we're lucky."

Yushua asked, "How long has this warehouse been up for sale, Ms. López?"

"Not long, a couple of months."

"Well, Luca and I visited this 'gem' over a year back," Campbell said, correcting the record. "Not sure how long it was up before then."

"Exactly," María agreed, seemingly unaware of the contradiction. "Beauties like these never last long."

Yushua had planned on giving María a summary explanation

of his vision for the three floors of the Fishtown warehouse, but this initial exchange had tempered his expectations of her interest. "Can we walk through the building?"

"Well, that's why we're here, isn't it? Of course, we can … Josh …"

"Yushua."

"Yushua. Of course, Yushua. You ready?"

She unlocked a pair of black iron security bars that protected the front entrance, and then, without any struggle, opened the old, riveted steel doors. Streams of dusty light beamed like theater spotlights from the south-facing windows onto the brick red concrete floor below. The exposed wooden-plank ceiling stood fifteen feet above them, adding to the dramatic feel of the room. Greenish gray iron staircases flanked both sides of the factory floor, leading to an obviously brighter second level.

"What was she?" Campbell asked María.

"Many things," she replied as she pulled out her fact sheet from a glossy folder and began to refamiliarize herself with the details. "Built in 1885 as a furniture factory and remained as such for more than one hundred years. Hyman Meerbaum Furnishings. Really quality pieces. Ever since the nineties, this place has been one thing or another. Vacant for a few years then somebody would try something. A cabinet shop. Welding. A couple of other things. Giuseppe Bonetti bought it about ten years ago on spec. He was hoping to turn it into three floors of retail, but this section of Fishtown never really gentrified. So, he's finally a seller, and that's good for us. And at 1.2 mil, it's a steal."

"Think he'll go lower?" Campbell asked.

"Pretty sure. I know what he paid. If he could double his money, he may go for it."

"Meaning?"

"If we came in with an offer of eight, we could likely get it for eight seven five or nine. He'd talk like we were bandits, but he'd be fine."

"Maybe we shouldn't get ahead of ourselves," Yushua interjected. "Might we take a look around?"

"Of course. Follow me, boys."

María Cardoza-López made a beeline for the south staircase as if her three-inch pumps were tennis shoes. Yushua and Campbell shifted into a new gear, attempting to keep up. Ascending into the second floor they were immediately struck by the light. Most of the glass on this floor was intact. And with fewer boarded windows, light filled the space, illuminating heavy wooden beams, wooden floors, and painted brick walls. Tall ceilings again, about twelve feet, from which heavy green industrial light fixtures descended. A single iron staircase on the north side of the building led to the third and final floor.

"Whatcha boys think? She's a beauty, isn't she?"

"What might the dimensions be?" Campbell asked.

"The listing says that the building is 9,450 square feet. That's 3,150 on each floor. The building is 70 feet by 45. And the property is .73 of an acre, so it's a really good size. Lots of parking."

"Well, that's a lot more than I was envisioning we would need," said Yushua.

"Not me!" interrupted Campbell. "Can you imagine your plan rolled out in here? Deadly, Yushua. Deadly. Let's crack on to the third."

Campbell led the way up the staircase to the third floor where they found almost a carbon copy of the second.

"Ceiling is impressive," commented Yushua. "Ten feet you think?"

"Aye. I'd say ten is just about right. But must be eighteen at the center beam. That's a picture, isn't it?" Campbell said with no attempt to cover his excitement. "And would you take a gander at that wall."

Campbell pointed to the west-facing wall made of antique glass blocks from floor to ceiling, all in seemingly perfect condition.

"Can you imagine what could happen in a place like this?" Campbell asked, twirling around like an awkward ballerina. "I can see this place as a veritable trainer packed with new recruits. Tell me that this isn't lightin' you up, my brother. You're not that thick, are ya?"

"No, no, I see the possibilities. A lot of work and a lot of money and—"

"And a lot of movement. A whole lot of movement. Three floors just like ya ordered, lad. And it couldn't be more on the nose."

María Cardoza-López, smelling the scent of a weakness, moved in for the kill. "So, should we write up an offer? Nail this baby down before someone else scoops us? Hate to lose these gorgeous windows."

Chapter Nineteen

The Coup D'état

The soft "ding" from Jimmy's smartphone turned out to be a starter pistol's shot announcing a prearranged battle that he knew nothing about. The arrival of a new email was hardly an uncommon thing for a busy senior pastor, but this one would be considerably different from the rest of the barrage that usually flooded his inbox. It was brief. Very brief. Only one paragraph long. And it had a legal tone to its formality and vocabulary. But what it lacked in length, it more than made up for in punch. And its punch would wreak havoc on everything on Jimmy's calendar for the next two weeks.

And probably much longer.

"Jimmy, check your email," was Tom Butt's morning greeting as he entered into Jimmy's office like a semi-truck running out of fuel.

Jimmy, who skipped his morning workout routine, was dressed, pressed, and ready to go at 6.15 a.m. "Saw it land in the middle of the night. After reading it there was no more sleepin'."

"What do ya think they're after, Jimmy?"

"Ain't it obvious? They're after my scalp. And you know that it's Chipper behind all of this."

"If it was just Chip Bussey, I wouldn't worry, Jimmy. But the letter was signed by Bobby Berringer. He's the chairman, and he carries a lot of sway with folks. Being an attorney, people listen to him."

"I know it. Said I couldn't sleep."

Jimmy spun his chair around and stared into his laptop. "So, in two weeks they're going to shoot me at sundown. All nice and legal. Take me out in a business meeting, as if I have no say so. Fire me, the guy who brought this church back to life. Fire me like some kind of janitor ..." He immediately regretted his choice of words but pressed on. "I don't think so. No sir. If they want a fight, I'll give 'em one they won't soon forget. And I wouldn't bet against me. 'Cause I generally do not lose."

He spun his chair back around toward Tom and asked, "How many folks you 'spect will come to this meeting?"

"Well, you know it's usually only a handful. We did away with quorum requirements years ago. Normally, it's only about twenty or twenty-five. Mostly those who've got nothing better to do. But this is different, Jimmy. They'll come crawling out from under every rock to see this. Folks always love a good lynching. I'd expect hundreds."

Just then, Jimmy's phone rang. The call display had an unknown number originating from Philadelphia, PA. He stood up and pressed the red button on the screen.

"Hello?"

"Hello, Pastor Jimmy. This is Yushua Maalouf. Sorry to be calling so early."

"Yushua, how nice to hear from you, buddy. You all right?" Jimmy motioned for Tom to take a seat.

"Yes, I'm doing well, thank you. But how about you?"

"Why do you ask?"

"I'm asking because I cannot pray without seeing you. The Holy Spirit won't let me pray about anything else. Just you. Is there anything I can do for you, Pastor Jimmy?"

Jimmy sat back down on his chair, exhaled, and then slowly explained the morning's devastating news. The telling was therapeutic, and Jimmy seemed to relax by the minute. Yushua carefully listened, offering no interruption or comment until Jimmy was finished laying out the whole picture.

"So, Pastor Jimmy, what do you think Jesus wants you to do?"

"Save the church of course. We've got a plan and a vision, and Satan's trying to stop it. And I ain't gonna let that happen."

A few long seconds of silence elapsed, and then Yushua finally spoke. "So, Pastor Jimmy, how will you save the church?"

"Well, they started the war, and I intend on finishing it. I'll beat them at their own game."

"But respectfully, Pastor Jimmy, you didn't answer my question. How will you save the church?"

Jimmy, growing a little exasperated by Yushua's inability to understand the obvious, turned up the volume and said, "By surviving Chip Bussey's mutiny, Yushua. Surviving so that I can lead out in our new vision. You know, the one you helped form."

"So, this will save the church? Hmm …"

Yushua paused for a second and then asked another question. "How many do they need to fire you?"

"At LifePointe, it's a super-majority. Sixty-six percent. Simple majority won't get the job done."

"So, let's say you rally your troops, and they only get 50 percent, and you survive. Will the church be saved then?"

"I'm not following ..."

"Can I be frank, Pastor Jimmy?"

"Please."

Yushua paused for a second or two and then started slowly. "Okay, I think that, at its core, your thinking is flawed, Pastor Jimmy. If you fight fire with fire, I believe you can win this battle, but you will never win the war. It's impossible. You will most definitely lose the war. Because, ultimately, this will never be a war of politics. It is a war of kingdoms. And that's what so many in this country get wrong. You think that the will of God is determined by the majority, but that is almost never the case. Look at Scripture. Every time the majority decided something, they voted against God. The majority will almost always vote for comfort and self-interest. Rarely for faith."

Jimmy slowed his pace and said, "So then, brother, I'm supposed to roll over and let Chip Bussey and his gang run over me? I'm supposed to surrender this church to its very worst people? Seems like I got a responsibility to protect God's flock."

"Yes and no, Pastor Jimmy. How can you reveal the kingdom of God by lowering yourself to the ways of your opponents? Is it possible?"

Yushua let his penetrating question hang in the air for several seconds before he asked another. "So let me ask you one more time, Pastor Jimmy: what does Jesus want you to do?"

Jimmy's shoulders sagged as he let out a long, slow breath. With almost no expression in his voice, he asked, "So, Yushua, what do you think Jesus wants me to do?"

"Well, I cannot say for certain on the particulars, but it might involve several principles. Three immediately come to mind. First, pray. Pray a lot. Enlist others to pray with you. I'll get our Philly people praying. Pray like you've never prayed before. Pray like everything depended on it. And then Pastor Jimmy, be righteous. Don't lower yourself to their mudslinging ways. And don't go and try to gather a gang to defend you. Only more darkness comes from that. Remember, Jesus didn't enlist his disciples to fight for him. He rebuked Peter for that. He just asked them to pray. And Jesus didn't even defend himself."

"So, passivism is what you're prescribing?"

"No sir, Pastor Jimmy. Not even close. I'm saying fight a war of kingdoms with the weapons of Jesus' kingdom. They're expecting you to come out swinging. They're prepared for it. But instead, be kind. Be gentle. Be loving toward your enemies. Pray for Chip Bussey. Pray for him until you feel God's love and compassion for him. Because after all, he's not really your enemy. He's your enemy's tool. So, separate yourself from earthly personalities and fight this battle where it belongs. Fight in the heavenlies, and let everyone see Jesus' kingdom in how you lead. And when people see you, let your countenance remind them of Jesus. This is what Hussein taught me. This is what all my brothers in the prison taught me. It's all the same. The enemy will use a self-righteous imam, or a hardened torturer, or even a silk-tongued pastor to advance his destructive agenda. His ways are always the same. But our response is the difference."

Yushua waited for a response, but there was only silence. Seconds passed before Jimmy even attempted to form a sentence. Finally, he sat down in his chair, closed his eyes, and said, "Okay ... I know you're right, brother. I mean, I've preached this stuff, but I guess I've never really seen it lived out. And there's more?"

"One more thing, Pastor Jimmy. Speak the truth. Don't worry about defending yourself. God will do that. And history will do that too, I think. But for right now, just speak the truth that God has given you over these past months. But speak it in love."

Yushua paused for a second or two, and then concluded his counsel with one final thought. "And then let's see what Jesus wants to do with his church."

"And then, if I should lose the vote," interrupted Jimmy, "at least I can sleep at night knowing that I may have lost darkness' game, but I played by God's rules."

"Exactly, Pastor Jimmy. Exactly. And when you play by God's rules, God rules. His kingdom is revealed. Not everyone has eyes to see it, but some will. There will be some. There's always a remnant. Flesh's power is demonstrated in the strength of majorities. But the kingdom of God is revealed in the weakness of remnants. And it seems it has always been this way."

"So, I guess sometimes losing isn't losing?"

"And quite often winning isn't winning. Sometimes in the kingdom of God, true gain only comes from loss."

Tom had been sitting in the guest chair facing Jimmy's desk and had watched a miraculous transformation take place before his very eyes. In fifteen minutes, he saw his pastor and friend go from being an insecure street brawler to having the quiet confidence of a monk. And with this spiritual metamorphosis came a feeling in Tom's spirit that he had not felt in months: hope.

Jimmy pocketed his phone and let out a long, deep sigh.

"Sounds like quite the call. And the timing … " said Tom.

"No doubt. That Yushua's quite the guy. Never met anybody like him."

"So, your strategy has changed?"

"I guess so, Tommy boy. Let's gather the Pneumanauts and see if we can learn how to pray in two weeks." He took a couple of steps toward the door and then turned to Tom and said, "Maybe this is something we should have tried earlier."

Parking Lot A of LifePointe Chapel, which was considered by most church members to be premium parking, was unusually busy for a Wednesday evening. Twenty years ago, cars filled this lot on a Wednesday night for a "prayer meeting," which was mainly just the handing out of a printed sheet of all varieties of ailments, followed by an unremarkable Bible study. The flock's appetite for "prayer" slowly waned, so the night became reserved for scheduling and hosting various church events. Wednesday was also a night reserved for LifePointe's quarterly business meetings when a couple dozen of those who considered themselves the most faithful came to ensure that the ship was on the proper course.

But this Wednesday night was different. It was an "Extraordinary Business Meeting of LifePointe Church," called by the chairman of LifePointe's board, Bobby Berringer. According to the church bylaws, any unscheduled congregational vote required two weeks' posted notice, which Bobby fulfilled to the day when he issued his carefully worded email to the congregation. Bobby was no rookie, and he wasn't going to allow a constitutional technicality to unravel God's work that needed to be done. Everything had to be legally precise because nothing less than the future of their beloved church was at stake.

Jimmy had spent a lot of time praying, reading, and fishing during those two weeks and, taking Tom's advice, hadn't stood behind his pulpit once. "Let 'em get a chance to miss you, Jimmy," Tom said. "And when they do see you—let 'em see Jesus."

But "seeing Jesus" aside, if Bobby Berringer had calculated correctly, Jimmy's hiatus would last longer than two weeks.

Much longer.

The balcony was roped off with heavy blue nylon cords, as were the left and right seating wings on the main level. This left four sections of pews, front and center to the stage, available to seat those who would come to participate in the church's democratic process. Parishioners started to trickle in uncharacteristically early. Normally an on-time arrival to a LifePointe event meant folks arriving a few minutes after things got started so they could avoid uncomfortable and unnecessary small talk. But on this day, there were about fifty in the pews ten minutes before the scheduled start of seven o'clock. Congregants were scattered across the designated area of the auditorium, maintaining a distance from one another. There was no buzz, no talking, no coffee, no mood music. Just dead quiet, interspersed with the odd cough or nervous throat clearing.

By seven o'clock, about 150 had trickled in and found their seats. One minute later, Bobby Berringer, dressed in a seersucker suit and a red bow tie, stood up from the front row where he had been waiting, and walked toward a black music stand that was positioned on the main level in front of the stage.

"Thank you, LifePointe family, for showing up in such strong numbers this evening. It is so encouraging to see the people of God so entirely dedicated to pursuing his will for his church. In that spirit, I would like to call this extraordinary business session of LifePointe Chapel to order. And I think that the only fitting thing to do for a meeting of this magnitude is to start before our Heavenly Father in prayer."

Bobby, somewhat theatrically, failed to bow his head as was standard protocol for a LifePointe prayer. Instead, with hands clasped tightly by his chest, he faced the heavens and uttered a most humble and eloquent petition. His carefully scripted supplication was a respectful appeal to the Almighty to grant the good people of LifePointe the wisdom and courage necessary to do the difficult things that must be done. And to do it all in a Christian spirit of unity and love.

The soft "amens" of agreement that rippled throughout the

auditorium was all the feedback that he needed to move straight ahead. After unclasping his fingers, Bobby firmly gripped the music stand, and with a slow and gentle cadence, began to introduce the business at hand. "Tonight, our business agenda has only one item. This will give us plenty of time to prayerfully and thoughtfully come to a fitting decision on the motion that is before us."

Bobby flipped open his well-worn brown leather folio and cleared his throat. He was ready for business. "Before I read the formal motion, which was included in the correspondence that you received two weeks ago, allow me to explain the process that has led us to this point."

The auditorium was as quiet as the usually low-attended, quarterly business meetings at Lifepointe, despite the 275 souls that had now found their seats. No one moved.

"Our board began to receive some disturbing reports from the staff about the behavior of our beloved pastor, Dr. James Norris. Now before you jump to any conclusions, allow me to clarify. There was nothing overtly inappropriate of a sexual nature reported. Nor was there any financial malfeasance that anyone has discovered so far. Although, to be completely transparent, we have not had time to thoroughly investigate the books. But what was most troubling to our board were the reports of theological and ecclesiological experimentation that our pastor has been entertaining. He has publicly shared some very disquieting ideas to our staff that have caused a great deal of discomfort and unneeded stress. Notions that might border on heresy, so I'm told, although I am no expert on these matters."

Bobby Berringer, as an accomplished trial lawyer, was in full courtroom mode. All eyes were on him, and he knew it. He dramatically paused while he strategically shuffled a few papers to allow the gravity of the charges to sink in the hearts and minds of his jury. Everyone in the auditorium was anxiously waiting for his next words.

"And so, our board began to investigate the claims that were being made against Dr. Norris. And I would characterize our findings as troubling. So concerning, in fact, that his continued leadership will very likely negatively affect the future of our church. Or even the future existence of our church. In fact, if Dr. Norris is allowed to continue to lead LifePointe, our board is uncertain whether we will have many days ahead of us at all."

Bobby nodded to the control booth and a slide appeared on the screen behind him that displayed the wording of the motion in question. With black letters above the text was the title, *A MOTION OF NON-CONFIDENCE.*

"Now again, let me be clear. This was not a unanimous recommendation from our board. But it almost was. And it far surpassed our necessity of a two-thirds majority. And so, for this motion to be accepted and binding, it too, according to our bylaws, will require a two-thirds majority of this esteemed body. Is this understood?"

A generally positive murmur from the pews signaled to the chairman that the congregation was following his lead.

"Now, for the record, allow me to read aloud the motion that is on the floor."

Bobby once again cleared his throat and then slowly and carefully enunciated every syllable. "Due to a lack of confidence in the leadership of our senior pastor, we, the board of elders of LifePointe Chapel, recommend to the people of LifePointe Chapel that Pastor James Norris be immediately removed from his responsibilities of leadership, for cause."

Bobby looked up from his notes, pocketed his reading glasses, and said, "Now this is a motion from our board, and therefore does not require a seconder. So, this brings us to a time of discussion.

And before we get too deeply in the weeds of this, our board thought it might be best if you heard firsthand some of the troubling things our pastor has been entertaining."

Bobby paused yet again and stared at the ceiling as if he were expecting a message from heaven. One arm across his chest and the other propping up his chin, he said with a soft voice, "Now as you know, Pastor Chip Bussey is LifePointe's longest tenured and most respected staff member. He is someone deeply familiar with theological issues and has a historical perspective that is necessary when considering doctrinal aberrations. He can speak to the biblical issues in a way that we, as laymen, simply cannot. We are not trained as pastors. So, Pastor Bussey, the board invites you to take the platform. Please share with the good people of LifePointe the concerns that are most troubling to you and your fellow pastoral colleagues."

Bobby Berringer knew how to prepare a witness, and nothing was left to chance. For this momentous evening, Chip Bussey was gussied up to the nines. He wore a blue oxford that was tucked in, a red tie that struggled to make it three fourths the way to his belt, and his best navy blazer with brass buttons. Polished penny loafers, crisply ironed dockers, and a fresh haircut completed the package that was carefully created to say, "You can trust me."

Chip Bussey moseyed up to the music stand and with both thumbs hoisted up his britches from his belt loops, trying his best to hide a smile. Then, with his right hand, removed a set of index cards from his breast pocket and began to read, "Good evening. This is a very grave matter that we are discussing, and none of us take this lightly. But we have a problem. A big problem. We have a charismatic, gifted pastor who secretly plans to turn LifePointe into some kind of religious experiment. And I for one do not approve. Neither do many of my colleagues on our staff…"

Then Chip tucked his cue cards back in his breast pocket and said, "Shoot, I don't need these. I'm gonna speak from my heart to y'all. You know me. It's ole Chipper. Been part of y'all for twenty-seven years. That's most my life. That's all of some of yours. So, when I say, 'Jimmy's gotta go,' you know it's serious. 'Cause I've never said anything like that b'fore. Not in all my years. But ya see, Jimmy's gotta go. He does. He's all mixed up in the head. He's talkin' crazy talk about everybody going without pay. Volunteerin' out our jobs. He doesn't think that gatherin' and worshipin' our Lord is the most important thing. He's been under the spell of some Philadelphia witchdoctor who has him all turned in knots. And some of us think he's having a mental breakdown. Comes to staff meetings cryin' for no reason. Then he's mad. I love him, I really do. He's a wonderful preacher, nobody denies that. But he's a ticking time bomb for LifePointe. He's liable to blow it all up if Philadelphia tells him to."

And then Chip paused. He looked at Jimmy, who was seated three rows back with his wife, Cindy, and their three boys and said, "Jimmy, we love you. We do. Nobody but you could have turned this ole church around like ya did. But I'm scared that you'se gonna kill the thing you helped save. So, for all that's holy, please Jimmy, move on. You're done here. We don't need you no more. Like the good book says, 'When God closes a door, he opens a window.' God's openin' a window for you somewhere else. You just need to skedaddle and find it."

All eyes were now on Jimmy as Chip swaggered back to his pew. But few were prepared for what they were about to see. Jimmy was glowing. Not a sarcastic wince. Not an "I told you so" sneer of smugness following Chip's misattributed and mangled window and door reference. No, this was something else entirely. It was a tranquil, warm, and genuine expression of peace; something stirring from deep within.

"Questions? Questions? Do you have any questions?" Bobby Berringer asked in an attempt to shift momentum back to where it needed to be. "This is your opportunity to ask the board, or Pastor Bussey, or Jimmy for that matter, any question germane to the matter at hand. We have three microphones prepared, one on each aisle. Speak one at a time, and the chair will recognize you in the order that you arrived."

Painful seconds passed with no movement toward a microphone.

Finally, after many awkward seconds, a middle-aged man in a blue polo shirt and brown corduroy pants walked up to the mic.

"Yes sir, at the center mic. Go ahead, sir."

"Thank you, sir. I'm Gerald Wigginton, kinda new here. Been coming a couple of years. But I'm kinda confused. Why is it that you want to fire Dr. Norris? I think I must have missed something in the presentation."

As Bobby drew a thoughtful breath to address the question, all eyes were suddenly on Chip Bussey as he clumsily lurched his way to the left aisle microphone.

"I'd like to answer the man. Don't know how he missed it, but I'll give it another go. Gotta listen folks, gotta listen. This stuff is important. Okay, it's 'cause he's unfit. Sometimes it's scary the way he is. Sure, in the pulpit he's all *Cool Hand Luke*. But, the rest of the week, he goes from *Psycho* to *Driving Miss Daisy*. I mean we're really in *One Flew Over the Cuckoo's Nest* territory round here. That's why. And he's our main preacher. Idn't that enough?"

Gerald returned to his seat even more confused than before he asked his question. Bobby Berringer, reading the temperature of the courtroom and seeing that he was quickly losing his jury, knew something had to be done. It had to be quick, dramatic, and powerful. And then he made a split-second decision that was nothing short of genius.

"Now, if it's okay with the congregation, we would like our board members to share how they came to the decision as to why our beloved pastor should find a better fit for his unique skill set. Lord knows that there are many places that could use his rare abilities in turning around a dying church. And so, Phil—Phil Jackson—as our vice chair, why don't you be the first to share your prayerful, well-thought-out rationale?"

Phil Jackson had the look of a man who had just been caught with another man's wife. His jaw dropped and his eyes were wide with disbelief.

Phil coughed, wheezed, cleared his throat, and then stammered, "Be glad ... to. Thank you, Bobby, for this opportunity …"

Phil Jackson, who ran a string of auto dealerships in Roswell, Dunwoody, Johns Creek, and Cumming, was not unfamiliar with thinking on his feet and therefore was the perfect choice to start the damage control from Chip Bussey's awful showing. Phil instinctively knew how to deal both with people's spoken objections and their unspoken fears, all the while staying completely likable in the process. And Bobby knew that Phil was their only hope to get the train back on its track.

Phil, just like Chip, was wearing a navy blazer, khakis, and loafers. But unlike Chip, his ensemble actually looked nice. He stood tall, and projecting both sincerity and empathy began to systematically eviscerate their pastor with his kind words. When he was finished, Jimmy Norris was simply a one-trick pony who could only turn around a dying church and had no leadership chops to lead a real one. A one-trick pony with the strong possibility of an undiagnosed mental illness.

Six more board members came to the front, one at time, and each essentially reworded Phil Jackson's testimony. But each also added a little something extra that drove yet another nail in the coffin of Pastor Jimmy's future.

Bobby Berringer could not hide his expression of relief as he once again stood to draw the meeting to its inevitable conclusion. With a muted smile he said, "Now, as the chair, I am to remain neutral in these proceedings. But do not think for a minute that I have no opinion. Because I have a strong one. And it is an opinion that has been informed by a thorough investigation. But for fairness of the process, I will not share it. Are we ready to vote on the question?"

Thelma Kay Boggs, a widow in her early eighties who had been a fixture at LifePointe since the early days of Sandy Creek, slowly stood and spoke some words that nobody understood.

"Mrs. Boggs," Bobby politely interrupted. "Would you mind stepping to the microphone?"

Thelma immediately turned to her left, stepped around three other seniors, and walked to the center mic carrying a menacing look. "Are we going to take a vote on Brother Jimmy without hearing his side of things? We are going to just run him out of town, after all he has done for us, without giving him any opportunity to speak? This isn't right. This isn't Christian. And I for one will not let this stand!" Pointing her wrinkled index finger at the chairman, she said, "Will you please invite Pastor Jimmy to come up to defend himself?"

With that, Thelma turned around and sat back down, this time on the front row, right in front of Bobby. There was a smattering of clapping that broke out around the auditorium that either indicated agreement with her demand, or admiration for her pluckiness to take on Bobby Berringer. In either case, it had an effect on the chairman.

"Well, Mrs. Boggs," Bobby answered, "we certainly did give Pastor Jimmy an opportunity to defend himself. He could have spoken up at any time. That's why we were having a discussion. But he chose to sit with his family and say nothing. But allow me to ask for you, Mrs. Boggs. Jimmy, do you have anything you wish to say?"

The house spotlights weren't turned on, but they were not needed at this moment. All eyes were on Jimmy. He stood straight and said, "I guess there's something I'd like to say. You wouldn't mind, Bobby?"

"By all means, Pastor Jimmy, the floor is yours."

"Thank you."

Jimmy calmly picked his way around legs and feet and handbags, and then walked to center stage. But there was something unexpectedly serene about him. He didn't look like a man who had just undergone forty-five minutes of ugly character assassination. There was nothing angry or vengeful about him. He was composed and calm.

He stood quietly for a second or two, looking at the assembly, and then said, "Well, this has been quite an evening, hasn't it? I've never seen one quite like it. And to be honest with y'all, I'm not really sure what to say. There seems to be some fear about change. That's understandable. Change can be unsettling for some folks. Do I believe that things need to change at LifePointe? Yes, I do. I think that you've heard some of that in my preaching. Have I been of two minds on this matter? Yes, I have. Sometimes, to be honest, I just want easy street. I just want to keep people happy and run with the status quo. But other times, deep in my spirit, I know that things aren't right. I know, down in my bones, that Jesus wants our church to become his church. He wants our mission to be his mission. And, church, for that to happen, easy street and the status quo cannot be accommodated. So, yes, while I don't quite see it the way you've heard it said here tonight, I do know I have been sending some mixed signals to my staff. And I have apologized to them for it. Change is hard for me as well."

Jimmy sighed and looked down as tears began to form in his eyes. "Church, do you know what I've done since I got the same letter from Bobby that y'all got? Something unnatural to me. You see, my own nature is to fight and defend myself. I've always been a bit of a fighter. But God spoke to me through a wise counselor the morning that the letter landed. And he reminded me that this battle, a battle that has been brought to our doorstep, is not of human origin. It is a spiritual battle of light and darkness. So, for these past two weeks, I've prayed. That's about all I've done. Prayed. I've prayed by myself. I've prayed with my precious family. I've prayed with some trusted friends. And I've had some spiritual giants from across the country prayin' for us. And you know what? I've never, ever had a greater sense of God's peace as I have had during this storm."

Jeb McCarter, who was stationed three seniors away from Thelma, lifted his hand and then shuffled to the center aisle microphone. "Pastor Jimmy, can I say something?"

"Absolutely, brother Jeb."

"I am sorry." Tears spilled out of his old gray eyes and ran down his weathered face. With a trembling voice he stammered, "We are not … doing right by you. This isn't right. And I am so sorry."

"Thank you, Jeb. But I am okay. Really am. But it's so kind of you to say so. Thank you, Jeb. It means a lot."

Bobby Berringer, eager to put to an end this open display of affection, stepped back to the microphone and gestured for Jimmy to take his seat.

"All right, are we ready for the question? Ready to vote?"

An arm rose up from the back of the auditorium.

"Yes, sir. You in the back. Come to the microphone and state your name for the record."

A large African American man in his mid-forties stood up and made his way to the center aisle microphone.

"Mr. Chairman, I am not a member of this church, but I do have a question. I know that I cannot vote, but I was wondering if it would be permissible for me to ask a question? Would that be possible?"

Bobby Berringer visibly looked put off, and curtly said, "I'm sorry sir, but ..."

"Let him speak!" came a shout from somewhere in the back of the auditorium.

"Let him speak! Let him speak!" soon emanated from all corners.

"Oh, all right. This is highly irregular, but I'll allow it. Okay, what is it?"

"Thank you, Mr. Chairman. But my question isn't actually for you. It's for Pastor Jimmy."

The veins on Bobby's neck bulged as he tried to conceal his ire. "Fine, but state your name for the record."

"Of course, sir. Thank you. My name is ... Well, I guess that y'all refer to me as 'the witchdoctor.' But my given name is Luca Lewis. I'm from Philadelphia, Pennsylvania. Sitting at the back over there is your old janitor, Yushua Maalouf. I trust that you might remember him."

A collective gasp pulsated throughout the worship center as every neck craned to get a better look at this Philadelphia preacher who was reported to have caused their church so much trouble. He was tall and husky, and unimpressively dressed in a plaid shirt, department store blue jeans, and comfortable shoes. But even after just a few short words, it was obvious that there was an inner strength to this stranger, unlike the chairman who was supposedly in charge. A gentle potency that was both rare and magnetic.

Turning to his left, Luca faced the Norris family, offered a reassuring smile, and then said, "Brother Jimmy, before democracy has its way and these fine people tell us what God's will is, can you answer one question for me? In your two weeks of praying with your family and trusted friends, what did Jesus say to you?"

***

It was their third location, and things had grown much faster than any had anticipated. They started out in a carriage house, then moved to a small warehouse that originally stored cotton for the Quaker Lace Company. But with the national success of his innovative "split cane" seating, Hyman Meerbaum was forced to borrow $18,500 from The Pennsylvania Company Bank to build a three-story furniture factory to keep up with demand. And in 1885, the Meerbaum Furniture Company moved into the building that would become its home for the next one hundred years. With a Fishtown address on East Norris Street, the new, state-of-the-art factory now had easy access to send and receive freight from both the Pennsylvania Railroad and the East Delaware River. And the company thrived.

"Sure, it's a hot mess. But it has amazing bones," said Choyz Jackson in her usual effervescent manner. "And we can do a lot of good from there. 'Sides, we've got over 25 percent to put down."

Choyz was working her magic with Bob Renfrew who was the loans officer for their local PNC bank. Philadelphia Freedom had a signed agreement to purchase the old furniture factory on East Norris Street, subject to financing. María Cardoza-López had shown why she earned the nickname the "Queen of Commercial," as she completely outfoxed Giuseppe Bonetti in the hard-nosed battle of value negotiations. By her third volley, Bonetti was almost begging to discount the price by 35 percent. Eight hundred thousand dollars flat was where the bleeding had finally stopped. Well, almost where it stopped. Bonetti was also on the hook to clear and resurface the parking lots.

"Where did you come up with the two hundred?" asked Renfrew. "That's a lot of cash."

"We passed the hat. I think we will have double that. We're going to need it for the renos."

"Impressive. Didn't know churches could raise that kind of cash these days. Hats off to you, Choyz. And it's a really impressive plan. Whose idea was those three floors?"

"One of our leaders. Yushua Maalouf. He's got a great big brain."

"Well, I'm really interested in that second floor. Think that I could help. Both personally and through the bank as well. It's genius."

"I'll be sure to pass that on, Bob. That's really encouraging to hear."

Choyz Jackson hung up the phone, calmly stood, and then arching her back and throwing both arms in the air, let out a celebratory squeal that could be heard in Allentown.

Chapter Twenty

The Suit

The weathered outline of the letters spelling *Dr. James Norris* were still visible on LifePointe's concrete entrance sign three years after they were pried off. During those three years, the church had employed and unemployed two and a half people for the coveted role of senior pastor. The "half" was Chip Bussey. He finessed the board into letting him try on the job with an interim status. If it was apparent that he was the right fit, the pastor search committee would disband, and Chip would assume his rightful mantle. But unfortunately for Chip, it became apparent to most of the congregation by week one that he wasn't up to the task. His seventy-six-minute initial sermon, devoid of central point or passage, was also his swan song. Ronnie Pratt, LifePointe's intrepid youth pastor, picked things up at week two until a competent interim could be located. Within the year, the church had located and called a pastor that fit to a T the hiring profile that the committee had designed.

Dr. Shaun Bohlen, professor of theology at the Westminster-Covenant Theological Seminary, had impeccable credentials. Though he had not pastored a church before, he was theologically and ecclesiologically conservative, and an above-average communicator. He, according to LifePointe's Board of Elders, was the right medicine to heal the deep wounds inflicted by the theological nonsense of their previous pastor. He was perfect. And although he was initially apprehensive, they wined him and dined him, and dined him some more, until he became almost giddy about the opportunity.

But what no one thought to inquire about was the breadth of their new pastor's theological interests. Or the breadth of any interests for that matter. Dr. Shaun Bohlen had precious few, and he wore this narrowness of thought as a badge of honor. In fact, he unapologetically equated his theological opinion to the very gospel itself. Literally. His opinions on the incarnation defined for all the very limits of the gospel. And so, observing this reductionist's scope, Bobby Berringer vividly described his preaching as, "About as wide-ranging as a nun's wardrobe." Dr. Bohlen's annual preaching calendar was exactly one sermon that was packaged in fifty-two remarkably similar ways.

And somewhere in the second trimester of teaching on "Christians, churches, and teachings that don't measure up," attendance noticeably began to thin. But Dr. Bohlen wasn't actually troubled by this. To him it was simply real-time evidence of his major thesis: infidels leave. That's what they do. None of his elect had succumbed to the drift. The chosen had persevered.

But, unfortunately for Dr. Bohlen, revenue had also drifted. And his status of being LifePointe's "chosen" lasted only fifty-one weeks. One week short of the full preaching calendar.

No one could imagine enduring another punishing round.

Ironically, his custom polished copper letters for the entrance sign elected to arrive in week fifty-two. So, they were individually sold off at the youth mission trip fundraiser as wall decor.

The pastor search committee tweaked its candidate profile

algorithm a few degrees, now favoring "practical" and "winsome," and hoping for better results. And within three months, they found their match.

Rev. William Jones, who had only earned a Master of Divinity degree, was down-to-earth, endearing, and had a proven track record. Billy, as he preferred to be called, had grown a county-seat church in Indiana from 800 to 1,100 in six years. He was folksy in a charming way and was a veritable evangelistic powerhouse. LifePointe's board could almost smell the chlorine from all the weekly baptisms that were in store.

However, what nobody accounted for, was that those who had drifted away were the people who would have most resonated with Billy's approach to ministry. Those who persevered had no time for "Indiana Jones" unsophisticated preaching, nor Billy's incessant evangelistic appeals. Soon, they, too, left in droves.

Seven months later, Billy Jones had had his fill of LifePointe's dysfunction and found a more satisfying place to serve in Springfield, Illinois.

His copper letters were never ordered.

A green and white taxicab stopped at 2100 East Norris Street and a young couple with a rambunctious toddler hopped out. A harried man in his twenties with a West African accent valiantly juggled paying the cab driver with one hand while holding back a two-year-old who was pulling like a miniature Clydesdale. The woman, who appeared to be a few years younger, had Middle Eastern features, was professionally dressed in a blue business suit, and was carrying a diaper bag and a small leather briefcase.

"Have a good day, Mamadou," the woman said with a hint of a

British accent as she slung the diaper bag over the man's free shoulder. "I'll swing by at five."

"Okay, my love. Make good monies today, Farah. Princess and I will miss you much."

"Love you."

Farah took the right-hand stairwell upstairs to the second floor and walked past three businesses until she got to a door marked "GroundWorx." She unlocked it and let herself in.

Mamadou walked Princess down the main floor until he reached a brightly painted multicolored facade that resembled a theme park. On the sign overhead was written, *A New Story Childcare.* They walked into a vestibule that was a miniature version of Noah's Ark, and Mamadou placed the diaper bag on a small wooden shelf that hung under a porthole-shaped mirror that displayed Princess' name.

"You be good girl for Papa with school, yes?"

Princess smiled, stomped her purple rubber boots three or four times, and then disappeared into the outstretched arms of a smiling worker in a blue apron.

"Bye-bye, Princess."

There was no reply.

Mamadou turned to his right, picked up his pace, and marched deeper into the main floor. Above the last door on the right were the letters *EMSL.* Mamadou swung the door open and hustled inside.

"Sorry for late. No taxi stop for us."

Santiago Parra led a team of volunteers to staff a unique version of a community service that taught newcomers to Philadelphia how to master the English language. His program was called, "English for Multilingual Speakers," because for most immigrants, English was in no way their second language. Mamadou, for example, spoke French, Arabic, Yoruba, and enough English to survive the streets of Philly. But what was exceptional about Santiago's approach is that his teaching staff was comprised entirely from volunteers from the Dig. Both students and teachers alike rolled up their sleeves and helped their new neighbors gain the tools that they needed to flourish in their newly adopted country.

"Not to worry, Mamadou. We are glad you are here, brother," replied Santiago. "Trevon is prepped, ready, and excited to go, aren't you, Trevon?"

"You bet, Mr. Parra. Come on, Mamadou. Let's do this." Then the high school junior winked and said, "And then maybe you can teach me some French. I hear that really helps with the ladies."

They both laughed.

The Philadelphia Freedom Center had been in full operating mode for eighteen months and almost immediately had become the living room for its community. It originated in the fertile imagination of Yushua Maalouf but would have never come into existence without Luca's bold leadership, Campbell's connections, and every member of the leadership team playing their part. And the teamwork was inspired.

Yushua had a vision. In his mind, the three floors would synergistically work together as one perfect and powerful system that would pack a potent kingdom wallop. The first floor would meet the felt needs of the community, engage the community itself in meeting those needs, and then become Jesus' petri dish for natural disciple-making opportunities. It was brilliant in its simplicity, and Luca wondered why churches hadn't always been doing something like this.

The second floor was devoted to what Yushua called "Social Entrepreneurism." To Yushua, this meant starting and franchising sustainable businesses with the goal of employing the difficult to employ. This meant that members of the community who had limited English skills, or who had little educational background, or who suffered with physical disabilities, or even who had been marginalized because of a prison record, could find employment and see a clear pathway for a meaningful career. And, as an added bonus, Jerome and Choyz Jackson developed a sliding scale of fees that funded operations. An increasing percentage of business profits were reinvested into the Philadelphia Freedom Center to pay for the ongoing ministries of the first floor. And business leaders of the city flocked to be a part of this vision, including Bob Renfrew of the PNC Bank.

The third and final floor, known as Fatimah's Floor, was dedicated to equipping. Philadelphia Freedom had no plans to provide space to house Sunday services. To Yushua, the notion of a Sunday-service-driven church was the primary reason that the North American church was in such rapid decline. And Luca, from his own personal and painful experience with Mt. Pisgah, agreed wholeheartedly. With Philadelphia Freedom, the experience of worship became smaller, more local, more reproducible, less produced, and much more obedient. And the third floor was all about preparing leaders to build and multiply that reality: Philadelphia first, and then the world.

Yushua had been able to articulate this beautiful vision and God surrounded him with a crew that could pull it off. And what a team it was.

Chantel had a vision for aesthetics. Though she was never formally trained, she had an innate ability to put random things together in a way that made sense and was truly lovely. And for a community that was used to leftovers and hand-me-downs, the Freedom Center would feel very different. Brilliant. Clean. Pretty. Substantial. These were the code words that Chantel repeated to every subcontractor who entered their doors. And the results were stunning. Hundreds from the Fishtown community, rich and poor alike, walked into Meerbaum's old factory with a personal sense of ownership and pride.

Campbell had a vision for a workforce. What he had stumbled into during the big ice storm became the very centerpiece of his strategy. "Belonging precedes believing" was their new credo, and so he carefully fostered a culture where all could contribute. "Nothing makes ya feel more like kin than gettin' tossed the ole dish rag," was Campbell's colorful way of explaining things. As a result, ministry volunteers were not in short supply. Neither were new believers.

Santiago had a vision for training that workforce, and it was a vision that was shaped in no small part by Luca Lewis. Since the earliest days of his faith, he cut his teeth on Luca's ideas that ministry gifts are intended to equip God's people to do the work of ministry. He had never learned the far more common, yet far less biblical, approach of using ministry gifts as an end to themselves. So, when belonging moved into believing, new believers began an equipping journey that kept their feet firmly planted in the unselfish posture of service to others. And this is where the third floor, Fatimah's Floor, came to life.

And Choyz had a vision for funding the enterprise. There was much more to Choyz Jackson than an ability with numbers and bank managers. She took Yushua's seed of an idea and turned it into a full-blown strategy for ministry sustainability. Where most mercy ministries are forced to beg for outside assistance to keep things afloat, the Philadelphia Freedom Center, because of the genius of the second floor, sustained itself with a surplus. What's more, because of their "teach them to fish" philosophy, corporate sponsors tripped over themselves to be associated with the Center. So much so that most of the renovations that transformed

Meerbaum's Furniture into the Freedom Center came courtesy of generous donations from the private sector. And Choyz oversaw the whole thing.

And then there was Luca. He was the one with the natural skills to mélange it all together like a chef de cuisine skillfully preparing a perfect entree for the royal family.

But for Luca, this spread was reserved for someone of a higher station.

It was all for his King.

And it was delicious.

***

"Pass the ball. Please pass the stinkin' ball. Please! Yeesh. They're gettin' clobbered, and they keep the runnin' game on. Come on!" Jimmy said to the TV with as much passion as if he were actually in charge of the team.

"Who'd they pass to? They're all over us like flies on stink," said Tom Butts. "'Sides, we've been dropping everything in the air."

"I don't know why you guys get so amped up about a silly college game. It's not like anybody on your team is going to be playing football in two years anyway," said Duane, an African American man in his mid-thirties.

Duane Harris was obviously an import to Atlanta. He was one of those Northerners who immigrated to Georgia from New York City because of the booming tech sector, and who never really quite got the South. He was a mechanical engineer, a Columbia grad who specialized in robotics. But robotics had little to do with his work at APS Systems. Six years previously, APS was a small software spinoff from the behemoth Ingram-Lund.

APS saw a future in last mile delivery tech, and they went all in.

As the delivery economy expanded, few were investing in a technology that could scale for the small to medium sized retailer. So, APS began to build a platform with a user-friendly interface that could easily connect local businesses with local customers.

Growth was steady but unspectacular. And Ingram-Lund needed wins for its unpredictable stockholders, so they dumped it at a fire-sale price. Duane Harris, along with three other colleagues, leveraged everything they owned and outbid all comers to become the sole shareholders of a somewhat speculative idea.

But no one saw the pandemic coming.

With a rising cultural call to "shop local," coupled with an increasing appetite for online shopping and contactless delivery, APS suddenly found themselves within the very sweet spot of the emerging goldmine. A lot had happened in six years. It went from being a small Atlanta-based company of a dozen or so employees to becoming one of the country's fastest growing IT companies. It all came courtesy of a global pandemic. And Duane Harris was ready.

This was Duane's first time as a guest in Jimmy's house. Three years ago, Jimmy and his family moved from their sprawling Milton suburban home into a modest condo in Midtown Atlanta. The excuse, or talking point, as Jimmy called it, was that the daily grueling bumper battle was much more than he had an appetite for. But in reality, he needed to put some distance between himself and the painful reminders of LifePointe.

Tom Butts, a software engineer by training, was given a senior level position within weeks after he voluntarily resigned from LifePointe. APS was always hiring.

A few weeks later, Tom saw an opening that could fit Jimmy's skillset entirely. It took a bit of work to convince a team of religiously reluctant engineers to hire a preacher to lead their sales training division, but out of respect to Tom, they agreed to give him a look.

And the rest was history. Jimmy wowed them in his interview. He wowed them on how quickly he grasped his role. He wowed them on how well he fit in. And then he wowed them on how smoothly his sales division operated as it gobbled up market share.

"You New Yorkers are all the same," replied Jimmy, half laughing. "You can't appreciate a thing of beauty unless there's a big price tag attached to it."

"Jimmy, I don't know if we should call these Dawgs a thing of beauty this year," corrected Tom as he got up to refresh his nachos. "But at least the pain is almost over."

In actuality, the pain was very minor. There were no true Bulldogs fans gathered in Jimmy's condo. Two Texans and a New Yorker had other teams that had a place in their hearts. This game, at least for Jimmy and Tom, was an excuse to go deeper in a friendship with Duane, a friendship they hoped would someday include Christ.

"When's them wings comin'?" asked Tom, patting his extra-large plaid shirt. "I'm starved."

"There's still a half an ounce of nachos you haven't hoovered," Jimmy said laughing.

Just then the doorbell rang. Tom, who was already up to clean up the nacho residue, volunteered, "I'll get it. Hope they sent blue cheese."

Tom, smiling large, opened the door to see a man dressed in a gray suit. Stiff, flat, and somewhat nervously, he said, "Are you Dr. James Norris?"

"No, sir. But I'll fetch him. Jimmy, it ain't wings."

"Hello?"

"Are you Dr. James Norris?" he repeated as flatly as he had earlier.

"Yes, sir."

Then he reached into a small satchel and pulled out a manilla envelope. With a rigid arm, he handed it to Jimmy, and then mechanically said, "Dr. James Norris, you have been served." And then turned around and walked away.

Jimmy closed the door.

"What was that?" Tom asked.

"Some process server, I guess."

"What's it about?" Duane asked.

"I dunno."

"You get a lot of these, Jimmy?" Duane pressed.

"No. First time."

He jabbed his finger in a small opening of the envelope and tore it open. Inside, there was a blue legal folder that contained a cover letter and three pages of legal verbiage. The cover letter was from Bell, McKnight, Arthur and Associates of Roswell, GA. In capital letters across the top was written, *NOTIFICATION OF LAWSUIT.*

Jimmy scanned through the cover letter.

"It's LifePointe. LifePointe is suing me."

"What's LifePointe?" Duane asked.

"It's the church where Jimmy and I served before coming to APS," answered Tom.

"They're suing me for violating terms of employment."

"What?" said Tom.

"Just what I said. I guess I signed a non-compete when I came on. I don't remember that. But anyway, says I can't lead a church anywhere within one hundred miles of LifePointe."

"You lead a church?" asked Duane, raising an eyebrow.

"No."

"Maybe our missional community?" asked Tom.

"Surely not."

"What's that?" asked Duane.

Tom, not wanting to get too deep in the weeds, simply said, "Sort of a Bible study."

"A Bible study? How much are they suing you for?" asked Duane.

"One hundred and fifty-five thousand. My last full year's wages."

"One hundred and fifty K for holding a stupid Bible study? I knew that religion was a nasty business, but this is beyond the pale," said Duane in an angry tone. "What are you going to do?"

Jimmy sat back down on the sofa, closed his eyes, let out a long, slow breath, and then said, "The only thing I know to do. I'm gonna pray. I wonder if you fellas would pray with me?"

"Absolutely, Jimmy, you know that," said Tom.

"Uhh, I'm not sure I'm much help here," said Duane nervously.

"You're help to me just being here, Duane. Thank you. Let's pray together. You don't have to say anything, Duane."

"Well … okay. All right …"

Tom pulled an oak kitchen chair in front of the sofa where Duane and Jimmy were seated, plopped himself down, and then extended both of his fleshy arms. Jimmy smiled warmly and then grasped his old friend's hand. Duane paused for a second or two, and then in quiet reservation, with palms up, offered both of his hands.

Hand-in-hand, three senior executives of APS humbled themselves before the Almighty and prayed. Tom started. He asked for grace, and patience, and for a gentle and forgiving spirit. He asked for protection for his friend. He asked for softened hearts at LifePointe. And he asked for peace.

And then Jimmy prayed. And he didn't ask for anything.

Instead, he thanked God for his goodness, for his kindness, and for his grace. He thanked him for his Son, Jesus, who forgave him of much greater sins than this. He thanked God for his gift of peace and courage and boldness, that he would, by faith, receive. He thanked him for his calling to the good news of Jesus. And then he thanked him, by name, for the thirteen new Christ followers who gathered each week in his condo. He thanked him for his long and encouraging friendship with Tom, and for his new friendship with Duane. And finally, he thanked God for the gift of his Holy Spirit who had flooded his broken heart with joy and peace.

"Amen, amen," Tom whispered softly.

Tom and Jimmy opened their moist eyes only to see Duane, whose trembling head was still bowed, spilling silent tears on his jeans.

Faltering and stammering, between sniffs and snivels, he finally managed to utter, "God, if you're really … God … really there … really … real … then I want that. I want that. I want what these guys have …"

***

Being the youngest of three children born to an Iranian petrochemical businessman, Farah Akintola had plenty of advantages. She was born and raised in a happy home in Mashhad, galaxies away from the pain and intolerance that existed on the other side of the white concrete wall that surrounded their estate. At seventeen, she ventured ten hours west for an education at Tehran University where she, following in her father's footsteps, majored in business. And she thrived. Graduating a full year early, and with her family's blessing, she journeyed further west, enrolling in the MBA program of the prestigious London Business School in Regent's Park.

But within a few months of her arrival, she began to hear disconcerting news coming from her homeland. The economic sanctions imposed by the US and their global allies, coupled with the rising spirit of extreme Shiism, led to a series of military takeovers of businesses that were deemed essential for the survival of Iran.

And then what Farah most feared finally happened. On one warm September morning, everything in her life was taken away. Their family business was gone. Their family home was gone. And her family was gone, eliminated by a drone-guided missile while all were sleeping peacefully in the safety of their home.

And now, orphaned and alone, every lifeline she once knew was also gone.

Farah earned her first paycheck as a front desk agent at a Marriott on Regent's Park. But it wasn't enough to keep the rent up for her apartment, so she was forced to move. After a quick succession of descending moves, she found herself in a tawdry apartment in Southwark, on London's southside, a neighborhood filled with immigrants as desperate as she was.

But this was also where she would find the love of her life.

Mamadou Akintola, like many Nigerians, was a hard worker and a dreamer. He wasn't afraid of hustling, and almost nothing could discourage him. He scraped and scratched and clawed his way to the UK by sheer will, and he hoped that he would never leave. From where he started, South London was heaven on earth.

He had no specific skills and no educational background worth mentioning, for he hadn't been blessed with an abundance of opportunities. But he could outwork anyone and had a smile that could charm a pleasant glance out of the stodgiest socialite. And he used it often.

They met quite by accident. Farah was brewing coffee at the Old Spice Roastery, which also was on Mamadou's delivery route. The effortless way he unloaded pallets of seventy-kilogram sacks of raw coffee beans caught Farah's attention. She couldn't budge one—she had tried. He was handsome, strong, and had a smile that made her knees weak. She was smitten.

A few flirtatious glances later and Mamadou had her phone number. A few phone calls later and Mamadou had a date. A few dates later, Mamadou and Farah were officially a couple. They soon moved in together and dreamed of starting a family.

Soon Farah was pregnant. To make their union official, they went to the register office, filed the paperwork, paid the fees, and endured the world's most unromantic ceremony. But they were in love. And they were happy. As happy as an heiress-no-longer could be in South London. Farah had experienced more—and wanted more. Soon, she convinced her new husband that the US held better prospects. So, under her new name, Farah Akintola, she began to apply to MBA programs in America.

With the distinction of having been accepted to the London School of Business, every prestigious MBA program to which she applied wanted her; the acceptance letters poured in. But unfortunately, since she hadn't yet completed a single course in London, no scholarships were offered. And without a scholarship, tuition would be impossible for the penniless heiress. But then Philadelphia came to the rescue. Drexel University's LeBow College of Business looked at the big picture and considered her high academic achievements at Tehran University as both valid and noteworthy. They offered her a full ride.

Princess was born in the Mercy Catholic Medical Center, six weeks after the Akintolas arrived in Fishtown, and she immediately became the apple of her papa's eye. Mamadou split his time between doting on his bride and baby daughter and working a construction job at an old furniture factory on East Norris.

His life was full.

***

"Can they arrive before October?" asked Farah. "We're opening two new locations, and we need to be up and going for the Christmas rush."

Farah was trying to get two commercial coffee roasters delivered from Carson City, Nevada, to two new franchises that were scheduled to be opened in Strawberry Mansion and Fairmount Park. "GroundWorx," which started as an ethereal notion in her "Business and Social Responsibility" course at Drexel, soon became an all-consuming passion.

And two years later, after proof of concept was confirmed, it was about to become a reality in three Philly neighborhoods.

Farah Akintola approached a local Fishtown attorney, a Mr. Yushua Maalouf, about an idea she had that might fit well with the new Freedom Center that was being built in her own backyard. Her idea was taking the business model she had observed while working for the Old Spice Roastery in London, simplifying it, focusing it, and scaling it by developing a socially conscious, turn-key franchising model.

"Simplifying" would be evident through the menu. Only three categories would be on offer: fresh coffee beans roasted on site, the best tasting coffee served in the city, and three simple food items.

"Focusing" would also be evident through the menu. It would be an entirely glocal experience. Their ethically sourced coffee would celebrate its global origins. The three simple menu items would be derived from the local tastes of its neighborhood. Global and local: glocal.

But the true brilliance of Farah's idea was in how she envisioned scaling it. Front and center in her mind was the image of her husband, Mamadou, a hard-working immigrant with limited English and no connections or opportunities. Mamadou became the profile for all future franchise owners and employees. She would set up GroundWorx as a nonprofit, with all earnings being reinvested back into the community, while employing an overlooked and disregarded workforce.

Yushua loved the idea. It was perfectly in sync with his vision for the second floor. In fact, it couldn't have been better if he'd thought of it himself. So, he went to work and processed all legal work for Farah pro bono. He then connected her with Chantel Lewis for design. The second-floor office of GroundWorx would take care of the administrative needs for franchising.

But the proof of concept would be on the first floor, with premium street access.

And it would be rent free.

Cease and desist. Cease and desist. The legal words rolled around in Jimmy's mind like a steel-toed work boot in a clothes dryer. What could LifePointe be thinking? What were they so afraid of?

He thought of the faces that would gather in his living room later tonight. None of them would have gone to church before meeting the Norrises and the Butts. Not one. In fact, what LifePointe did to lure prospective churchgoers would have sent most of them running in the opposite direction. These people had no interest in production excellence as a spiritual value. And most would see the fine, state-of-the-art bobbles that LifePointe surrounded themselves with as an immoral outlay of cash. The fourteen formerly lost sheep who would gather in his condo would never have been found by LifePointe. Never. Not in a million years. They were geographically and culturally from two different worlds. So why a lawsuit? Why? Weren't they supposed to at least pretend as if they were on the same team?

And Jimmy didn't have $155,000. He had downsized his lifestyle on his move out of Milton, so he didn't have the debt he once had. But who has that kind of cash lying around? He could likely get it, but it would mean liquidating almost all his assets. Starting over. And he had three boys heading to college soon. Why would LifePointe want him to pay such a steep penalty for sharing the gospel? "Cease and desist. Cease and desist," he said aloud.

And the more he said it, the angrier he got.

He replayed in his mind the troubling moments when the lawsuit landed on his front door. Jesus' peace seemed to immediately cover his spirit like a soothing lotion over a piercing burn. He didn't have to work for peace. Peace came to him. And that heavenly gift of peace directly led to Duane's repentance. But where was that peace now?

He slipped his phone out of his jeans to check his email. Several days ago, he had scanned the lawsuit documents and sent them over to Yushua for advice. But he hadn't received a reply. Not a word. Maybe now?

"Still no reply," Jimmy muttered.

And Jimmy got angrier.

With a grim face he thumbed through his phone, punched a button, and then held it to his ear.

"Jimmy, I've been meaning to call you. So behind here. Saw your email ..."

"Well shoot. I wished you woulda' called, brother. I'm dying here. You didn't think that this was important?"

"So sorry, Jimmy. I really am. So, LifePointe is at it again. Bobby Berringer?"

"Likely."

"Have you advertised? Social media maybe?"

"Advertised what? All I have is fourteen people meeting in our condo on a Tuesday. No, I haven't advertised."

"So, how have they heard?"

"Well, this isn't communist China, Yushua. We're not hiding under the beds. Not intentionally trying to keep this a secret. Maybe Tom said something. He still speaks to a few of those folks. I don't know."

"Okay, all right. Let's keep calm."

"Sorry, brother. I am just so ticked off. I really can't believe this."

"I understand. The demon is deep there. It assaults any sense of kingdom justice. I would be angry too, Jimmy."

"Really?" Jimmy said in a surprised tone.

"Certainly. You're not angry for a selfish reason. I think you worked through that on your exit from there. You're angry because fellow believers are trying to stop the gospel. They would prefer your fourteen friends live in hell for an eternity over the slightest chance that you might show them up. That is righteous anger, brother."

Jimmy paused, sighed, and then let out a slow breath.

"So, what should I do?"

"Nothing. Nothing different, that is. Keep doing what you're doing, and don't change a thing. Except maybe instruct Tom to cease and desist his reports."

"What if they come after me?"

"Do you have 150K?"

"No."

"They're bluffing. They want to punish you for resigning."

"But they were fixin' to fire me," Jimmy interrupted.

"Yes, they were. But the way you resigned … and what you said. They won't soon forgive you for that. They looked so bad."

"All I said is that I didn't want to divide the body of …"

"You took the high road, Jimmy," Yushua interrupted. "They were already many miles down on the low road. On the low road and running downhill as fast as they could. The whole room could see the difference. Your manner and actions said that in God's kingdom, it is better to suffer an injustice than to participate in it. Light and darkness were on full display. Word would have traveled about that."

"So don't worry about it?"

"Don't."

"And if they do come after me?"

"If they do, just remember, there are two justice systems: one in Georgia and one in heaven. As a lawyer, I can't see a winnable case for them in Georgia. And as a disciple, you know which side our righteous Judge in heaven will choose. I believe that he shares your righteous anger. Inspired it in fact. I see two 'not guiltys' in your future."

Yushua's words were once again timely, instructive, and lifegiving. He wondered how he could have been so blind to have missed this treasure. His former janitor knew more about what it meant to be a disciple of Christ than any pastor or professor or Christian leader he had ever met. How many other kingdom giants had he overlooked because of their lack of pedigree? Why was this upside-down kingdom so opposite to "church" as he had always known it?

Yushua interrupted the silence and asked, "Jimmy, have you a minute or two to discuss something else?"

"Uh, sure. What's up?"

"Luca and I have been doing a bit of scheming together. You've heard about our center but haven't seen it yet, right?"

"Right. Sounds amazing, though."

"It's really humbling to see what God is doing. Our Fatimah Floor is now booked solid, seven days a week equipping disciples. Shoe-horned in. Seriously. We can't keep up."

"Holy cow. I had no idea. That's incredible, Yushua."

"It's unbelievable. Luca shows up most evenings with a big old goofy grin like a proud father. He saw it all in his mind's eye, and now it's here. And Santiago has things running like clockwork. God is really setting something special up. And it's just starting. We are already seeing a third generation of disciples equipping others. Third generation, Jimmy. In four-and-a-half years. Only God does this stuff.

Yushua hesitated for a second or two to measure his response. But none came.

"Anyway, Luca and I were wondering if you might want to come for a bit of a visit. Spend some time with us. A week or so if you can spare it. You and Tom. And bring your families. They'll be key. Maybe bring a few of your new disciples, too. We can host you, Philadelphia style. Because I promise, Northern hospitality is actually a thing. Everything we do revolves around kingdom hospitality."

"So, come to learn?"

"Yes, Jimmy. Learn. Soak it in. Because this is much different than the LifePointe we both experienced. I'd love for you to catch it."

"Sounds like fun. Think I could do this?"

"Yes, I do, brother," said Yushua without any hesitation. "And we'd like to give you everything we have."

Chapter Twenty-One

The Visitors

The room smelled of coffee. Good coffee. Good coffee and Turkish honey. The sweet aroma that mingled with coffee and filled the room was wafting from the unique local pastries that were freshly made-to-order by GroundWorx. They were from the local menu, which was designed around the large Jordanian community that lived in and around Fishtown. Perfect triangles of baklava glistening with honey and topped with toasted pistachios were symmetrically arranged on white ceramic platters like soldiers on Bastille Day.

It was Wednesday, the day that Santiago loved the most. Six evenings a week, Fatimah's Floor buzzed with laughter, testimonies, training, heartfelt prayer, and worship, as different gatherings took place for regional groups, ministry-leads, and teams. But Wednesdays were special. It was the day reserved for the gathering of leaders from Strawberry Mansion, Brewerytown, and North Central—his own region. And so, for Santiago, Wednesdays became more personal, more urgent, and much more rewarding than any other day. These were the men and women he served with. This was his platoon. And the victories and losses that they lived together knitted them like family.

Fatimah's Floor was arranged exactly as it was for every other day. There were four "squad rooms," along each side wall, eight in total, each partitioned with tempered glass. Each squad room had a large round white table with ten black chairs and an eight-foot whiteboard that was mounted on the outside painted brick wall.

The gathering room was the length of the whole floor and was made up of three main sections. At the front, a small platform with two microphones stood silhouetted against the impressive glass block wall. It was from here Santiago orchestrated a growing team of teachers that poured into the leaders of the Philadelphia Freedom movement across all the different regions.

The center section was devoted to seating. Eleven rows, each with twelve black plastic chairs lined up with precision, waiting for their missionaries to assemble. Part of the equipping curriculum for the training team was the discipline of arriving early and praying for the lives that would soon be occupying these chairs.

Emerging out of the stairwell, at the back of the room, was a small open lobby that accommodated three black bar-height coffee counters. Though most evening meetings were scheduled for a 7 p.m. start, coffee and desserts were to be ready to go by 6.15 p.m., for the praying equippers. And the room was almost always full and abuzz by six forty-five. Genuine fellowship was a value that was both spoken and lived.

Santiago, as was his habit, arrived at six. After work, he would run home for a quick dinner with Maggy and Sophia—and, more often than not, another family who had joined them for food from their missional community—and then he'd take the bus to Fishtown. He had the whole process down cold. If everything ran on time, it was a thirty-one-minute commute, door to door.

Coffee smells especially good tonight, Santiago thought. *Yemeni beans?* he wondered. Both he and Campbell were hooked on Yemeni coffee after Yushua introduced them to his personal stash of the exotic elixir. *This will help,* he thought.

Judging by the response he had seen from Monday's and Tuesday's gathering, tonight might not be easy. Luca and the leadership team felt it was God's timing to start introducing a larger global vision to the movement leaders. They sensed they were already late and waiting even longer wouldn't fix things. But Santiago, Yushua, and Luca were all surprised at the pushback they received when they announced plans to multiply and send teams to Belfast, Toronto, possibly Atlanta, and a city yet to be determined somewhere in the Middle East. They had worked on building a kingdom culture that happily sacrificed to bring the gospel to a neighboring community—so pushback was an unhappy surprise. Their movement had hopscotched from one neighborhood to the next until it had a staging place in almost every corner of the city. *Sending disciples is our bread and butter, so why the pushback now?* Santiago mused.

Familiar heavy footsteps trundled to the third-floor landing. Luca was usually the second to arrive.

"Hey, brother," he said winded, grabbing the threshold.

"Hey, Luca. Worked on a different approach for today."

"Ya did? What's that?"

"Instead of soft-selling, I thought it might be wise to throw it straight over the heart of the plate. Say we're looking for marines, which we really are. Tell 'em about our training camp. Just put it out there."

"Well, things can't go worse than yesterday, I suppose. Shocked me."

"Didn't shock me, Luca. I get the feeling. It's tough making deep friendships in the battle, only to see them move out to a new place. It hurts every time. And the hurt piles up. And I think that the idea of moving friends across the ocean was just the proverbial straw that broke some backs."

"Shepherds, right?"

"Mostly. Some teachers, too. Campbell had a little uprising on Monday with his evangelists."

Luca rubbed his furrowed brow.

"You see Luca, here's my take. The folks that say, 'When you give God your best, he gives you better back' tells me only one thing."

"What's that?"

"Tells me that they've never done it before. Because, when we give God our best ..." Santiago said, holding his hand high above his head, "... he gives us this back..." he said, lowering his hand to his thigh. "And we have to spend years building them up."

"You're not lying, brother."

"And by the time they become our 'best,' they've become so relationally linked into folks' lives that the sacrifice is excruciating."

"Yep, I can see it, brother. That's a good word. That's a real good word," said Luca. "So, we just gotta own it. Say we see it and thank them for it. Tell 'em it comes with the kingdom territory."

"I think so," agreed Santiago.

Luca stroked his cheek and then said, "And remind them about all the big payoffs we've seen coming from their sacrifices."

As Santiago reached for a fist bump, voices could be heard echoing up the stairwell. Soon, a steady stream of happy troops began to arrive. The coffee was good. The baklava evaporated.

And the missionaries of Strawberry Mansion, Brewerytown, and North Central began to dream about the world.

***

"Princess, you must eat your fish," said an exasperated Farah as she watched her toddler sweep broccoli off her highchair onto the restaurant's tile floor.

"Those eyes. She must be one of the most beautiful children I've ever seen," said Duane Harris.

Farah laughed, somewhat self-consciously. "She has her father's eyes. And his smile. But unfortunately, she has my temperament."

"No, no. Princess is beauty like her mother," corrected Mamadou, smiling from ear to ear.

Duane Harris was a part of the Atlanta team that came to Fishtown for a week-long exploratory visit. When Yushua learned of Duane's coming, he scheduled a series of mentoring meetings between the experienced and successful entrepreneur, and Farah, who was in the early stages of rolling out a franchising plan for GroundWorx.

"Yushua told Jimmy and me about some of your ideas. Got to say Farah, I'm really impressed."

"Thank you. We are excited. Who is Jimmy again?" asked Farah.

"He's my pastor. We have a small church in Atlanta."

"I see. So, you are a Christian?"

"I am. Pretty new at it. How 'bout you?"

Farah looked at Mamadou, paused, and without answering his question she asked, "What were you before being a Christian?"

"I guess an atheist. Or an agnostic. Never had a religious background and never gave it much thought. Thought it was all a bunch of crap. Excuse my language."

"So, why did you change? That seems like a big leap."

"Honestly, because I watched two real Christians. I watched them every day at work. I watched how they handled themselves on good days and on bad days. And there was something about both of them that inspired me. Tom and Jimmy are their names. You'll meet them this week."

"What was it?" asked Farah. "What was so different about them?"

"It's a bunch of stuff. They were secure. They weren't struggling to get noticed or fighting for their rights. They genuinely looked out for what was the best for my company, and what was the best for my employees. Both were that way. They naturally played second fiddle and didn't make a big thing of it."

"So, that is why you changed religions?"

"Well, not really changing. Didn't have one. But that was probably how I first noticed that my soul was not right."

"And shifting to Christianity changed that?"

"Sorta. Well, not really. It wasn't so much Christianity that did. But I witnessed Jimmy in a terrible circumstance and saw how he reacted. Former colleagues of his brutally double-crossed him. I was there when he found the news out. And I was expecting a normal response. Anger. Vengeance. Self-pity. That's how I would have reacted. But there was none of that."

"What did he do?"

"His first instinct was to pray. He praised God for his peace, comfort, and for the courage that he would receive by faith. And his friend Tom prayed for those who were persecuting Jimmy. It wasn't a thing from this world—it was something else. And looking at them, I saw myself for the first time. They were like two mirrors that revealed how ugly and petty and self-absorbed I really was. I didn't want their religion. I wanted their God. I wanted their lives. That's when they told me about Jesus and his forgiveness."

"So, the Christian religion is different from Jesus?"

"From my perspective, Farah, which is admittedly very limited, there seems to be very little in common between the two. At least in how things play out around here. One pressures us from the outside to act differently. But Jesus restores us from the inside so we can become different. I wanted nothing to do with religion 'cause all I saw was folks telling other folks to be more like them, to think more like them, and to vote more like them. The more I saw, the more I was repelled. I wanted nothing to do with their religion. But Jimmy and Tom lived a different way."

Mamadou, who with his left hand was pacifying Princess with a plastic keyring, was transfixed by Duane's words. He fled his native Nigeria because of the pain and oppression religion had caused his family. Freedom to him meant freedom from religion and all its painful trimmings. But his newfound freedom had not quieted his soul's hunger. Even with a beautiful family and the safety of his new homeland in Philadelphia, his life was lacking meaning. He could see something different in Yushua and Santiago and numerous others who were a part of the Freedom Center. They were at rest. And he was not.

Mamadou broke his silence. "How long for praying with Johnny until peace?"

"Jimmy," corrected Farah.

Duane smiled. "Immediately, my friend. Jesus' peace came immediately."

***

"Eight hundred K. Nearly that much again for renos. Our people completely paid off the building note in twelve months. The renos were mostly paid for by businesses in the community. And not a donation plaque advertising the donors to be seen anywhere," Luca said with the look of a proud father.

He was personally giving Tom and Jimmy a guided tour through the whole complex of the Freedom Center. He wanted to make sure they understood the interdependent purpose of the three floors. They needed to see beyond the obvious to understand Yushua's master disciple-making plan. But casting vision wasn't easy, for every third or fourth sentence he was interrupted by a volunteer wanting to hug him, or shake his hand, or just say "hi." And he didn't seem to mind at all.

The center was small by LifePointe's standards. It could easily fit into any one of the four buildings on their campus. Small, but a thousand times more Jesusy. Every square inch was thoughtfully put into action to serve its community. And pound for pound, Jimmy was seeing more kingdom impact in this repurposed furniture factory than in any church building he had seen in his life.

"Think about reach, gentlemen. Every day we have over 160 people volunteering in the ministries on the first floor. Those 160 are serving the needs of well over 1,500 people each day. Seventy-seven of our volunteers have become Christ followers in the last calendar year. And this year we can directly track over 430 new believers whom we first met through ministries on this floor who are now in missional communities."

Jimmy and Tom were mesmerized. There was a cacophony of sounds reverberating against the high ceiling. Laughter and baby cries and teaching and shopping and counseling and chatting all mingled into one beautiful kingdom opus. Job training, a clothes closet, free childcare, English classes, a food bank, financial counseling, a small health unit and a dental clinic, family counseling, a pregnancy support center, legal defense advocacy, and a wonderful coffee shop—all declaring the same message: Philadelphia, Jesus is for you!

Luca then escorted his guests up the lefthand stairway to the second floor. "This again is Yushua's brainchild. Never seen anything like this anywhere before. It's all about social entrepreneurialism. We help catalyze new businesses for the purpose of employing those who are on the margins of society. The business community has really gotten behind all this."

Jimmy and Tom stood at the threshold and looked down the hall. Tom counted fourteen offices, seven on each side.

Luca walked slowly as he explained. "Now, we have a tough vetting process to get in here. Yushua personally screens each proposal. Equal to their business viability must be a passion to employ and advance the difficult to employ. We're only half full right now—seven companies have launched out of this space so far. But cumulatively, they employ over four hundred Philadelphians.

"Are these Christian companies?" Jimmy asked.

"Not necessarily, but they must abide by a common kingdom code of ethics. Five of our companies were started by Christ followers. But all the companies are full of employees who are part of our missional communities."

"They pay rent?" Tom asked.

"No, they don't. They donate a percentage of profits to the Freedom Center. That's how we keep the first floor running so well. Again, your janitor's idea."

Luca walked by a sign that said, *Rooted*. "That's a landscape company. They employ men and women after they're out of the prison system. They've got crews out all over the city."

They walked a few more steps to a door marked, *Cornerstone*. Luca laughed as he said, "I love this one. It's a high-end construction company. Finishing carpenters. The poorest of all in the city, many of them refugees, are doing the finest finishing work in Philadelphia's finest homes. They run the office here. They have a big shop down the street."

They walked a few more steps, and Luca said, "Let's stick our heads in this one." He opened a door marked *Fishtown Graphics, Inc*, and marched in. "Hey, y'all. Meet a couple of my friends from Atlanta—this is Tom and Jimmy."

The room had ten or twelve computer stations, all staffed by women of various nationalities.

A woman in her mid-forties stood. "Hi there, gentlemen. I'm Marcy," she said, holding out her hand.

Tom and Jimmy shook Marcy's hand and introduced themselves.

"So what have you got going on here?" asked Jimmy.

"We're a graphic design company," replied Marcy. "Our women here are building some of the best websites, logos, and marketing pieces for businesses in the state. We even have clients across the country, several in Canada and the UK, and even one in South Africa."

"Wow, that sounds great," said Tom. "Good that you can run things out of the center here, then."

"Absolutely," smiled Marcy. "There's no end to the possibilities. We've been able to connect in with the wider vision for Philadelphia Freedom, so, we just follow brother Luca's lead. Wherever they build a new Freedom Center, we expand our operations to that city as well."

Luca thanked Marcy and then escorted Jimmy and Tom back into the hall. In a hushed voice he said, "Fishtown Graphics counsels, trains, and employs women who have been exploited in the sex industry. Marcy loves the Lord, and she loves her girls. It's a room chock full of some of the most beautiful stories of God's grace that I've ever witnessed."

Jimmy's head was spinning. He had never thought of church in such a holistic way before. The idea of an hour of his clever sermons and Chip Bussey's music seemed like such a pathetic showing in comparison.

But Luca wasn't finished.

He walked them through a childcare company that employed victims of domestic abuse, a packaging company that employed the cognitively challenged, a home healthcare service that hired health assistants whose international credentials were not recognized by the state of Pennsylvania, and a coffee roasting company that hired immigrants with limited language skills.

Emotionally and spiritually overwhelmed, Jimmy and Tom stood at the end of the hall and said nothing.

"Something, isn't it?" Luca said with a wink. "Wait 'til we get to the third floor. We'll save that for tomorrow night."

"Can't wait," said Tom.

As they started walking down the two flights of stairs, Luca asked, "Sure I can't offer some Philadelphia Freedom hospitality? Hotels are pricey in the city."

"Thanks, Luca. Duane's actually covering the whole shebang. You should travel with a billionaire, brother," said Jimmy. "Makes everything way easier."

Chapter Twenty-Two

The Pope

"The pope called, and he wasn't in a good mood. Said that he and Mama are plannin' to visit next week."

Jimmy was sitting in the hotel lobby, staring blankly at the TV. His face had no color, and he looked visibly shaken.

Other than Christmas morning, Dr. Humphrey Alvin Norris never called his children. He was an important and busy man, so he left the more mundane family rituals to his wife. H. A. Norris had always been a force to be reckoned with, but over the past three election cycles, he went from being a Texas institution to becoming a powerful national figure. And even at the ripe old age of seventy-four, he was showing no signs of slowing down. Or softening.

"He's comin'?" Tom asked as if he hoped the answer would change.

"Yeah."

"Next week?"

"Yeah."

"When's the last time he visited?"

"Suppose it was when he spoke at that rally in the Mercedes Benz Center. But I had to go to him. He gave me a few minutes."

"That was a few years ago."

"Yeah."

"Why can't he just beam in from his cable news studio in the church?" asked Tom.

"It would be nice, but I guess not."

"So, what's he want?"

Jimmy paused and exhaled a slow breath. "Didn't say outright. Somehow he knows that I'm talking with Luca. Calls him 'the Marxist.' Said that he wants to make sure that my head's on straight."

"Oh."

Tom Butts didn't seem surprised at H. A. Norris' characterization of Luca. He had lived in that world before, and he knew how things worked. Staring at the worn hotel carpet, he quietly asked, "Did he call you when you resigned LifePointe, Jimmy?"

"No."

"Never?"

"Nope."

"Did he ask about APS?"

"No."

"But he knows about Luca. Strange."

"Yeah, he's got his minions. They're everywhere."

"Suppose so. Wouldn't surprise me if Berringer had his number. Does he know that we're here in Philly?" Tom asked.

"Dunno. Probably. He didn't say."

Tom paused again to gather his thoughts. "What can he do, Jimmy? You're a grown man. And you don't have to play political footsie to keep a congregation happy. He's got nothin' to hold over your head."

"We'll see, I guess," Jimmy said, unconvinced. "At least he's bringing Mama."

***

It was Monday night, and Tom Butts couldn't peel his eyes off the large wooden map that hung against the glass block wall.

"How many neighborhoods in Philly, Luca?" he asked.

"One hundred and fifty in the city. Another hundred suburbs."

"And how many neighborhoods have red pins?"

"Seventy-nine. That's what Santiago says. We should be in a hundred by the end of the year. A handful of suburbs, too."

"Holy cow. And all since the ice storm. That's unbelievable. Wouldn't it be great if we pulled that off in Atlanta, Jimmy?"

"Huh? Oh yeah. For sure," said Jimmy as he thumbed keys on his smartphone.

"Whatcha up to, brother?" asked Tom "You seem like you're in another world."

"Sorry. Just trying to figure out what's goin' on. Spoke with my brother Billy last night. He didn't know anything. Contacted some of my old Texas crew and heard something strange …" Jimmy's words trailed off.

"What's that?"

"Apparently some have him slated for a plush denominational job. Leading the National Integrity Commission."

"Really? They want him to become a lobbyist?"

"Well, you know, he loves hobnobbing with power. Matt Goertzen, who you know is connected, says that he's the most likely candidate. Said that they're looking for someone with 'moxy,' who'll call a spade a spade."

"Holy cow," Tom said for the second time in five minutes.

"Holy something, that's for sure."

"Well, we know he's not a tap dancer. Think he'll want a job like that?"

"Who knows. He'll have his mug in front of a camera more often so that'll be a seller."

Luca, who was quietly standing next to Jimmy, put his big hand on his shoulder and said, “You okay, brother?”

“I don’t know. It’s a weird place to be. Being the son of H. A. Norris ain’t a lot of fun most days. And I think that it’s about to get a whole lot worse.”

“I’m sure that I have no idea, brother. But listening to these last three minutes, I think I have a little better picture. I’m sorry.”

“Try the last forty years. Instead of a son, most of the time I felt more like a prop. I started out as a prop for the church. Then it was for the state. But now it looks like he needs his prop more than ever. And, unfortunately for him, it doesn’t appear that I’m the trophy he wants.”

“That’s rough,” said Luca. “A father’s blessing is no small thing. This is a time you’ll have to dig deep, my friend. Maybe talk with Yushua. You remember his story with his father? He had to work through some pretty deep things after that. He still struggles from time to time—a father’s wounds go deep. Ultimately, he came to believe that Jesus’ pleasure was the only blessing he needed, and he keeps struggling to stay there. That may be a bit of your struggle brother, but you need to know—Jesus is pleased with you, my friend.”

“Thanks, Luca. That helps. Really does. Guess I’ll just have to put on my big boy pants and grow up. A forty-year-old baby isn’t anything anybody wants to see.”

“You’ll be fine. Tommy’s there for you. So are we.”

“You bet, Jimmy,” said Tom. “’Sides, who knows how God might use this all. This may be our ice storm.”

Footsteps and laughter rose from the stairwell and echoed throughout Fatimah’s Floor. Joyful men and women and excited teenagers from Fishtown, Kensington South, and Northern

Liberties gathered around coffee and golden syrupy *kunafehs*, eagerly anticipating their favorite night of the week.

***

Good friends gradually trickled out of Tom's townhouse, one by one, until there was only Duane Harris and the Norrises left.

"Great evening, Jimmy," Duane said. "After our field trip to Philly, I've got a much better idea of where we're going. Think you did a super job painting the picture tonight."

"Thanks, Duane. I'm bushed though. And my folks are coming in tomorrow so we gotta run. Can never have something out of place. That's unforgivable."

"Jimmy, stay a quick sec?" Tom asked.

"Sure. What's up?"

Tom shot him a solemn look. "Want something to drink? Coke?"

"Ok …"

Tom led the way to the kitchen and motioned for Jimmy to take a seat at the breakfast bar. "Coke?" he asked.

"What's up, Tom?" Jimmy said with a note of apprehension.

"Well, I hate to break this to you, but it doesn't look like LifePointe is leaving things alone. Last night, after dinner, I got served a subpoena."

"A subpoena?"

"Yes," he said as he passed him the legal document. "I'm scheduled to be deposed as a witness for their lawsuit. And it's quick. The deposition is in two weeks. Up in Roswell in the law offices of Bell, McKnight, Arthur and so forth."

Jimmy's shoulders dropped as he reluctantly read the paperwork.

"So, Jimmy, I think that this could be a good thing," said Tom as he desperately tried to breathe some life into his friend.

"Yeah, how's that, buddy?"

"Well, right now they're only operating from rumor and innuendo. It's just a 'he said, she said' case. A very biased lawsuit with no real facts. My testimony will set the record straight. This will be a recorded proceeding and the black and white facts, which will all fall on our side, will be part of the record now."

Jimmy flopped the subpoena on the breakfast bar with a look of disbelief. "Think they're looking for truth, Tom? Seriously? Tell me that you're not that naïve. You've been around those jackals for how long? C'mon bro, they're on no mission for truth. They're looking to punish me. And it's not the 150K they're driving for. No, sir. They need to vindicate themselves before whoever's left over there. If they win the lawsuit, then they were right the whole time. Voila, Jimmy Norris is exactly the scumbag that they were always warning about."

"I guess," said Tom, not really wanting to concede his point. "But nevertheless, they're going to hear the truth from me. What they do with that moving forward is up to them."

Jimmy picked up the subpoena and gave it a second scan. "The seventeenth. A week from Thursday. Think we should have legal counsel there? Yushua maybe?" he asked as he passed the documents back to Tom.

"I'll shoot this over to him and see what he says. Maybe video conferencing him couldn't hurt. I'll see what he says."

Jimmy nodded.

"Don't worry buddy, we got this. Truth's on our side."

Jimmy nodded again, a little smaller this time. He quietly slid off the breakfast barstool and muttered, "I'm just so tired."

***

"Popemobile's landed," said Cindy. "Looks like they brought friends."

Cindy Norris watched through their front door's sidelight as her in-laws, Dr. and Mrs. Hershel and Bobbi Norris, escorted two strangers in dark overcoats out of their black airport limo to their front stoop.

"Who?" asked Jimmy.

"Two dudes. Security maybe?"

"Really? Things are gettin' crazier than ever. Sheesh."

When the doorbell finally rang, Jimmy walked with exaggerated slowness to the living room. "Let's let his eminence wait a bit," he whispered with a wink. "It'll be good for his character."

Cindy giggled and then whispered back, "He'll likely need therapy."

Thirty agonizing seconds and three doorbell punches later, Jimmy trotted heavy-footed to the door. "Well, would you look at who's here! Sorry, just finishing up something. You brought security?"

"James, Cynthia, delighted to see you again. It's been too long," said Bobbi as she moved in, arms extended for a hug.

"I missed you too, Mama," said Jimmy as he accepted the embrace.

Jimmy shook his father's hand and then waited somewhat awkwardly for introductions.

"Oh," Hershel conceded. "James, Cynthia, this is Tyler Pratt. He chairs the National Leadership Committee of our denomination; and William Gunderson, who chairs the Nominating Committee. They both hail outa Georgia here, so I invited them to come meet y'all."

"Meet little ole us? Gosh. Cindy, we must be more important than we knew. Am I running for something?"

Hershel, obviously not amused, cleared his throat and said, "James, may we come in?"

Jimmy escorted his well-dressed company to their modest living room. Hershel and Bobbi sat on the sofa while Pratt and Gunderson took the two leather recliners. Jimmy walked into the kitchen, carted out two wooden kitchen chairs, and he and Cindy sat down.

"How are the boys?" Bobbi asked. "Cynthia, those pictures that you post on the Facebook are amazing. Such handsome young men."

"They're doing fine, Mama. Thanks," said Jimmy dryly.

"And Cynthia, I just love how you're wearing your hair now. So stylish. Really suits you ..."

"Mama, can we get to the point?" interrupted Jimmy. "When's the last time you've visited? Eleven years? Twelve? And now you show up with the 'men in black' and ..."

"Enough!" bellowed Hershel. "You'll show your mother some respect."

"Honestly, Dad, if you sense any disrespect, it's certainly not intended for Mama," said Jimmy, not missing a beat. "'Cause I know how things work at the Norrises. I grew up under your roof, remember? I guess that this just ain't the long-lost family reunion we were hoping for."

"All right, if you want to get down to business, let's get down to business," said Hershel. "Ladies, is there something in the kitchen that needs your attention? Refreshments?"

"No, sir," said Cindy. "Kitchen's fine."

Knocked off guard once again, Hershel nervously cleared his throat, leaned forward, tented his fingers together, and started again. "We've got a problem in America. It's a spiritual problem. And it's getting worse by the day. Do you disagree?"

“I do not,” said Jimmy.

“And exacerbating this growing spiritual problem is a liberal elite that wants nothing more than the total annihilation of Christianity in America. They won’t be happy until every Bible-believing church is either closed down completely or so sullied and compromised that rainbow flags are flying from every steeple in the country.”

Hershel waited for some kind of affirmation from his son, but none came.

“And to make things worse, the liberal, leftist mainstream media are bananas. They’re out of control with their nonstop liberal propaganda. CRT this and CRT that. Everything to them is Critical Race Theory. And they’re rotting our country from the inside out. They want a country where nobody ever takes responsibility for their actions. Blame the system. There’s always somebody else to blame for their poor choices.”

Again, nothing but a blank stare came from Jimmy.

“Let me get to the point, son. I think I can help stem the tide. I think I have the tools, the background, the voice, and the righteous fire to stop the liberal elites in their godforsaken tracks. And some important people in our denomination think so, too. But I have a problem …”

Here it comes, Jimmy thought to himself.

“Let me be frank, son. My problem isn’t personal reputation within our tribe. I’ve spent a lifetime preparing for this role. My problem is you and your new friends.”

Jimmy gripped his knees more tightly, trying desperately to show no hint of emotion. “So, basically you’re saying that I’m America’s problem,” he said without breaking eye contact.

“Well, yes. Potentially. Can you imagine the heyday that NPR would have with you?” Hershel continued. “You, cozying up to that

CRT-pandering Lewis? My son, hanging around with that liberal Marxist …"

"Hold on a cotton-pickin'-minute, Dad," Jimmy broke in. "What in the heck are you talking about? You have no idea—"

"I know his kind," Hershel interrupted. "I know all about this Rev. Luca Lewis. I've seen his ilk and dozens just like him come and go. I didn't just fall off the turnip truck, son. Reverend Lewis and his kind have been peddling their 'liberation theology' since I was a kid. It's nothing but poison. And it's killing our country."

Veins started to bulge on Jimmy's neck which grew more crimson by the second. "Sir. Respectfully. You know nothing. Nothing. First of all, he's not a 'reverend.' He's an executive director of a YMCA. Second, I've known him for quite some time, and I've never heard him speak on CRT. Not once. Ever. Nor on your 'liberation theology.' Not once. What's more, I've never met a more Christ-centered, gospel-centered, kingdom-centered man than Luca Lewis. I don't know what dark pit you've been getting your memos from, but maybe get the real facts straight before you start slandering someone who knows more about Jesus and his kingdom than you'll ever know."

"Now dear, your father's just worried that—"

"Mama, I know exactly why my father's worried," interrupted Jimmy. "It ain't for me, and it ain't for the gospel. It's always been about pandering to his amped-up base."

"James," a silky voice came from the recliner closest to the window. It was Tyler Pratt. "Perhaps let me weigh in. You see, your father is important to the denomination. And that makes him important to the country. If he becomes the next president of our National Integrity Commission, he will have a powerful platform to influence Congress back toward a path of moral decency. You see, James, you need to see things in their historical perspective. I know that you envision good things coming from your association with Rev. Lewis ..."

"He's never been ordained. He's never been to seminary. And he works at the Y," Jimmy interrupted.

"All right. 'Mr. Lewis,'" he said, making quotation marks with both hands. "And, James, you may well be right—some good things might happen. Who knows? But if the small things that you accomplish, however good they are, stop the comparatively immense things that your father will set into motion, is that a trade worth making? Jimmy, you were once a preacher so think of it this way: would you want to give away America's birthright for a measly bowl of Pennsylvania pottage?"

"That's helpful, Tyler. Thank you," said Hershel. "You see son, there's so much you can't see that's going on. God has set up the dominoes. He has. It's him, not me. And who are you or me to stand in his way? You can see that, can't you, son?"

The ball was back in Jimmy's court and all eyes were on him. But he was offering nothing. Leaning back in his kitchen chair and staring out his living room window, he let out a deep sigh. A lifetime of memories flashed through his mind like a flickering newsreel. A myriad of disheartening recollections of loves given up in order to be a good son. He had given so much to his father. Given so much and received so little in return. His dreams. His ambitions. His passions. He sidelined them all to please his father. And now here he sat as a grown man. A father in his own right. A proven leader of men. And yet he was a son. A disappointing son. A small, insecure, disappointment of a boy now sitting in the all-consuming shadow of "God's anointed."

He let out another deep sigh.

As he was forming words of resignation in his mind, yet again bending to his father's dominant will, William Gunderson leaned back in his recliner, cracked his knuckles, and cleared his throat as if he were about to make a royal pronouncement. With a weaselly tone he said, "Besides Jimmy, we heard that you had some legal trouble. So, helping us could help you."

Jimmy straightened up. "Excuse me?" he said.

Gunderson continued, "Well we heard that you were being sued for breach of contract with your former church. LifePointe, wasn't it? Nasty stuff. Witness depositions start next week we hear. Tom Butts?"

Tears immediately began to form in Jimmy's eyes as his countenance changed. Only moments ago, he felt like a gladiator waiting to step into the arena, and now he felt like a broken and defeated prisoner of war. With erratic and unsteady inflections, he said, "You've heard about this, have you? I don't know how. *I* only got the news last night."

"Now, dear," said his mother. "You mustn't be melancholy. Being a Gloomy Gus never fixes a thing, you know that. Your father can help us here. He has a way with these legal things."

As she turned to her husband, nudging him for a response, Jimmy unhurriedly stood, took three steps, and then grasping the back of the kitchen chair with both hands, he said, "Mama, it's been awfully good to see you again. It has. Please give my love to the aunties. Cindy, mind showing our guests the way out? We shouldn't keep them. They have God's business to take care of."

And then he walked out the back door.

***

"Burgers ready in ten," Jimmy announced. "Half pounders. Cheese or no cheese, boys?"

As Jimmy maneuvered the small round meatloaves around his

grill, landing slices of processed cheese on every other burger, his phone buzzed. It was Tom Butts.

"Hey, Tom, what's up?"

Cindy, stirring the sweet tea, was listening intently to Jimmy's words.

"Yeah, sorry about that. Shoulda called. Been working from home the past few days."

Cindy continued to absentmindedly stir the tea as she waited for Jimmy to resume.

"Yushua? No, I didn't actually have to. Turns out that LifePointe is dropping the lawsuit. It's all over with. Sorry, brother, shoulda let you know. My bad."

Jimmy silently signaled for a tall glass of sweet tea.

"I'm not sure why they dumped it. I'm guessin' your eagerness to testify scared their britches off. Who knows with that crazy bunch?"

As Tom spoke, Jimmy scooped large spoon loads of ice into his glass.

"Oh, that went all right, I suppose. Never a picnic hanging out with my family. They didn't stay long, thankfully. But same ole, same ole, you know."

Jimmy, eager to change the subject, excitedly said, "Hey, buddy, I do have some good news though. Remember Darin Fletcher from Dallas? He's at The Oasis?"

"Yeah, him. Well, out of the blue, he called me the other day. His church has blown up. Six services a weekend."

Jimmy took a short sip.

"Yes, for sure. Anyway, his monstrosity of a church wants to invest in an inner-city project. Something that brings the gospel to a broken community in practical ways."

Jimmy covered the phone's mic with his thumb and whispered to Cindy, "More sweetener please, sweetie."

"Exactly, I thought so too. And apparently so did they. And they're wanting us to be their primary mission partner. We're talking long-term stuff here."

"I don't know. Word travels, I guess." Jimmy paused for a second, trying to think quickly on his feet. "Maybe Matt Goertzen said something after we caught up the other day. Who knows?"

"Truly is bizarre. Hard to explain for sure."

"A lot, Tom. A lot. Likely millions. He said, 'Dream it, sell it, and they'd write the check.'"

"Exactly what I was thinking. The Atlanta Freedom Center may be just around the corner."

Chapter Twenty-Three

The Partner

"I'm a bit nervous, actually. Can you believe that?" said Yushua.

"Well, he means a lot to you. And you haven't seen him in a long time," said Luca, who had become a few shades grayer and more than a few pounds heavier in the past few years. "'Sides, he is a dignitary."

"'His Excellency.' Crazy. That'll take a minute to get used to," said Yushua.

Over the years, Luca had heard Yushua's stories of Francis Murphy and the Mishqafa Refugee Camp countless times. And even though he had never had the privilege of meeting him, it was as if he were woven into the tapestry of their collective story. Certainly, there would have not been a Philadelphia Freedom or the subsequent multiplications of it in Baltimore, Harlem, Toronto, and soon, Tehran, without the faithfulness of Francis Murphy.

"Pretty big jump from running some refugee camps to becoming Canada's ambassador to the UN," said Luca. "Nice to see that somebody's promoting people with credibility, not just their pocketbooks."

"Well, he ran the whole shebang for a number of years," said Yushua. "I guess being in charge of the world's refugee system qualifies a person for the job."

Four Philadelphia city police cars were parked on the 2100 block of East Norris Street to ensure that there was a clear runway for the motorcade. Twelve uniformed officers, six on each side of the street, stood at attention awaiting the procession. The streets and sidewalks were impeccably clean. Not a wrapper or cigarette butt could be found. And the Philadelphia Freedom Center, which was required to close two hours early this day, had been polished from stem to stern.

"Here he comes," said Luca as he looked out the window of GroundWorx and watched three black Chevrolet SUVs round the corner, windows tinted, sporting both the Canadian and the UN flags. "Three armored trucks. We might need a bigger table, brother."

The motorcade pulled in front of the Freedom Center, and security officials from the two outside cars jumped out, scanned the streets, and then moved toward the center car. The driver and front passenger from the center car disembarked, surveyed the street, and then moved to the street-facing door of the black SUV. After a few seconds, a security official opened the door, and out stepped Francis Murphy. His hair was thinner and what remained was now a faded red. More of a light orange with a little gray at the temples. And he was dressed to the nines. His perfectly tailored dark blue suit drew attention away from his middle-aged spread.

Yushua, who was dressed in his favorite courtroom blazer, ignored all official consular protocols; bursting through the coffee shop doors in one hurried motion, he ran to the ambassador. "Your Excellency," he said, beaming as he smiled at his old friend.

"Yushua? Is that you, brother? You look so … so … so good!"

"Well, it's been many years since my imprisonment. Wounds heal. Scars fade. But how about you? Mr. Ambassador!" Yushua said, enunciating every syllable while holding both of his arms in the air.

"It's Francis, my friend. Always Francis for you," he said as he greeted his former "client" with a generous hug.

"Come, come. Let me introduce you to Luca Lewis. So much has happened since I left Mishqafa."

"I know more about him than you'd suspect, Yushua. My sister's kids are a part of Toronto Freedom. I get an earful every time I visit. Can't wait for you to fill in the details. This has got to be an incredible story."

As the two old friends walked toward GroundWorx, Francis asked, "Where's your limp?"

"You don't notice it?"

"No, not at all."

"Well, it's still there. Especially when it gets cold. And I've endured several winters here in Philly now, so I've seen my share of the cold. But I'm glad the limp is fading." They took a few more steps and entered the coffee shop. "Luca, this is the brother I have so often spoken of. Luca Lewis, may I introduce my friend, Francis Murphy."

Luca, appearing as formal as he could possibly manage, warmly but somewhat stiffly offered, "It is an honor, your Excellency." And then shook his hand.

"Francis. Just Francis. And can I say what an honor it is to meet you, Luca. I have heard so much about the movement. I told Yushua that my sister's kids are a part of things in Toronto. Heard that you were thinking of entering Tehran. And that piqued my interest."

"Coffee?" Yushua asked. "I make a pretty good cup. And we've got Yemeni beans."

"Does the King wear fancy pajamas? Of course," said the laughing diplomat, showing that his Newfoundland roots were not deeply buried.

Looking at a package wrapped in brown paper that was sitting on the table, Francis asked, "So, Mr. Lewis, that wouldn't be a bomb, would it?"

Luca laughed. "You'll have to ask the bombmaker after he finishes up with your coffee."

"Open it," said Yushua as a cloud of steam spewed from his machine.

Francis unwrapped the brown paper and then opened a white box to find a carefully folded navy-blue golf jacket.

"Do you like it? It's a large," Yushua asked.

"Yes. Large. That's perfect. Thank you."

"You might want to look at the crest," Luca interjected.

Francis unfolded the jacket to reveal a green, red, and yellow coat of arms embroidered on the chest with the words, *Quaerite Prime Regnum Dei.*

"Haven't seen this one in quite some time. My homeland's long forgotten this old coat of arms. 'Seek first the Kingdom of God.' Thank you, Yushua. I will wear this with pride."

"I still have the T-shirt," Yushua said. "It's a little threadbare. But it's framed and hanging on my office wall."

"Really?"

"Yes, sir. And it's been our movement's coat of arms from our very first days. We put it on almost everything to remind us of our prime directive."

Francis leaned back in his chair and stared at his new jacket. "That's amazing, brothers. Humbling."

"It's powerful," said Yushua. "I first saw the kingdom lived out in our secret communities in Yemen. Then I saw it lived among my fellow cellmates in prison. But it was you, Francis …" Tears began to form in Yushua's eyes as he struggled to gather his composure. "You taught me the Scriptures, Francis. You showed me the kingdom in God's Word. And from that foundation, I was able to understand my mentors' faith more fully. And from that foundation I was able to help my brother Luca carve out a path for others to follow. So much of this movement sits on the beautiful shoulders of faithful Yemeni martyrs. And Francis," he said, pausing to wipe his eyes with his palms, "it also sits upon your courageous and sacrificial investment into the life of a ..." He struggled again for control. "Into the life of a broken and discarded refugee."

Tears streamed down the ambassador's ruddy face. Several times he made attempts at composure, and each time he became more overwrought with emotion. He had seen so much in his lifetime. Much more than most people. And he had spent his life on behalf of others, giving it freely for the world's castoffs who simply craved safety for their families. For peace. He had given his life for the victims and orphans of other men's wars, to provide these precious sufferers with the simplest of things to survive. And on some days, it seemed worth it. So worth it. Some days. But most days, it seemed futile. Endless streams of endless suffering from endless wars. Nothing ever changed except the faces.

Luca handed Francis a few napkins.

"Thanks, brother. So sorry. A bit embarrassing. I'm not usually this delicate."

"Not at all," said Luca. "Standing in your sneakers I'd be doing the same. It's pretty amazing. God has let us—"

"Let us see," interrupted Francis. "You're so right, Luca. It is amazing. He's let us see. I've heard of it happening but can't say I've experienced it before. It's like God has let us have a peek under the curtain of eternity. Just a glimpse. We get to see how he has prepared everything for his kingdom. The past, the present, and the future. It's all a beautiful play that he had written before he put us on this earth. And when we obey him, we play a part. Just a small part. A small part in the most perfect story ever penned. And today I just got a little peek under heaven's curtain to see it."

"That's beautiful, Francis," said Luca. "It's the only life. And so many miss it. They're in church every Sunday and miss it. Sometimes I wonder if my papa … He's the one who inspired my vision. I wonder if he sees. He never got to look under heaven's curtain. At least I don't think he did. But I wonder if he can see things from his side. I hope so. He's my 'Francis Murphy.' And the two of you showed us a path that many walk on today."

"Cream?" asked Yushua.

"Yemeni beans? No way. I save the cream for Starbucks. Give it to me the way God intended," Francis said laughing.

Yushua passed out the coffees, lifted his mug into the air, and said, "*Regnum Dei.*"

Together, they toasted their common commitment.

"*Regnum Dei.*"

***

"Think we can get 'em all in here?" Tom Butts asked as he straightened a pile of brochures at the guest services kiosk.

"Hope not," answered Jimmy. "Nothing succeeds like success. Turn them away, and they'll want in all the more."

"What time does Philly land?"

"Three-ish," said Tom.

"Just Luca and Yushua?"

"They're bringing Santiago and the Irishman, too."

"Oh? Who's gettin' them?"

"I am," said Tom.

"Good. Thought so. Thanks. I'm heading there in a sec. Gotta be at ATL by eleven to pick up Darin."

"How many are Oasis sending? Seems like the numbers change every week."

"Few dozen for sure," said Jimmy. "Forty-five, I think. Enough to fill a bus. Their whole missions committee plus some of the retirees who came here on mission trips. They're comin' on a later flight this afternoon."

"So, you'll make the royal tour scheduled at six?" Tom asked.

"Yep. And we'll slay 'em at seven. Still have to polish up my message. Been out of the saddle for way too long. Can't believe how nervous I am."

"You'll kill it, Jimmy. You always do."

"You're kind. Okay, heading to the airport. Gotta make sure he stays happy with his investment."

"Six point eight million ain't nothin' to sneeze at," said Tom.

"Ain't that the truth—and I've got plans for a whole lot more," he said, rubbing his palms together.

By three o'clock, Tom had driven to the south side of Atlanta, parked in short-term parking, and positioned himself by the three ascending escalators at the South Terminal waiting for his party to arrive. Within minutes he spotted an unmistakable form.

"Luca! Over here."

Luca, Yushua, Santiago, and Campbell pulled their carry-on bags over to Tom who was wearing a bright red sweatshirt and standing by a bank of vending machines.

"Hey, Tom, wonderful to see you again. Been too long," said Yushua.

"Three years?" asked Luca.

"Probably. At least. Guess we've all been pretty busy," said Tom.

Campbell looked at Tom's sweatshirt and said, "Midtown Fellowship. What might that be?"

"That's what we're calling our church. We went back and forth for days before landing on that. Speaks to our location and our values. Jimmy's pretty excited about it."

"Oh," said Campbell. "Jimmy's here?"

"He's not. He's busy gettin' stuff ready for tonight. Gonna be a barnburner, we hope."

"Can't wait to see this building and what you boys have put together," said Luca. "Seems like we lost communication for a while."

"That's our bad," said Tom. "Thing's kind of got complicated around here for a while. That lawsuit from LifePointe, and then our partnership with Grapevine …"

"Heard a little about that," said Luca. "That's a big ole church. Y'all keeping honest? Lotta funky gravitational pull with an outfit like that."

"Check any bags?" Tom asked, ignoring Luca's question.

Luca shook his head. "Traveling light. Just here for the one night."

"All right, then let's head out, fellas."

The four Philadelphians were quiet as they headed toward Midtown in Tom's old minivan. Yushua, who was sitting by himself in the far rear seat, asked, "Is everything okay, Tom?"

"Sure. Why do you ask?"

"Just a strange vibe. Like you're not very happy that we're here."

"No, no, of course we're happy, brother. You guys started us off. We owe you a lot. Don't know where we'd be without y'all. That's why Jimmy wants Luca to share for a few minutes tonight."

After several minutes of silence, Santiago broke the tension. "I went online and saw your promo. That is quite the operation you've built. Three floors. Forty-five thousand square feet. Impressive."

"You know Jimmy. Never does anything halfway. A lot of it was patterned after your Freedom Center," said Tom as he pulled under the Holiday Inn overhang. "Okay if I drop you by the hotel? Have a few details at the church that I have to get nailed down for tonight. I'll be by at 5.45 to pick you up for the tour. Okay?"

"At the church?" asked Yushua with a raised eyebrow.

"Yeah, if you don't mind," answered Tom, seemingly unaware of Yushua's real question. "Lots of balls in the air right now."

Quietly, the four Philadelphia friends disembarked, left their carry-on bags with the desk clerk, and walked to a diner across the street.

Scooting over to the window side of a green vinyl booth, Campbell asked, "Something going on here that I don't know about, lads? Felt a bit of a cool breeze."

"It's been a strange season," said Luca. "These past few years, communication has pretty much gone from a one-way street to practically nonexistent. Been hard to get a phone call or email answered. Ever since they started getting help from Oasis, things have been kind of weird. Feels a bit like we're being kept at a distance."

Santiago, always the peacemaker, dropped his plastic laminated menu and said, "Well the main thing is that they're keeping things on track. Right? By their promo website, looks like they're going the right direction. Tom's probably just overwhelmed. Mr. Details and all. He's the one that has to keep the trains running on time."

No one commented, and no further word was said on the subject. Four cheeseburgers were ordered and eaten in unfamiliar silence. Other than some logistical inquiries and quick answers on their upcoming itinerary, the four friends ate without conversation.

Once all the forks were down, Luca broke the silence and said, "Well, best be heading across the street, I guess. He should be there anytime."

The four made their way to the cash register, Santiago paid, and then they headed across the street to the hotel. As expected, Tom Butts steered his minivan under the hotel overhang at precisely 5.45 p.m.

"Y'all ready?"

"You bet," said Luca.

And the four piled in and quietly made their way toward Midtown Fellowship.

***

Darin Fletcher was young, charismatic, conservative, and extremely well connected. Even though Second Baptist Church, Grapevine, Texas was started in 1923 by an itinerant evangelist by the name of Rev. William McCall, it wasn't much of a prize by the time Darin took the helm. A few dozen seniors, or "Q-tips" as Darin called them, sparsely speckled across an auditorium designed for five hundred. No one wanted this pulpit. The parade of pastors that preceded him hadn't been able to turn things around, so it had devolved into a preaching point for starving seminary students to grab a small stipend and a little bit of experience.

But Darin was twenty-seven with a freshly minted PhD, a stunningly beautiful wife who had been a finalist in a Miss Texas competition, a work ethic that knew no bounds, and a seemingly unending supply of energy. And as a former starting quarterback at Hardin-Simmons University, confidence was never in short supply. So, in Darin's mind, it wasn't a question of "if" Second Baptist would become the largest church in Texas. It was just a question of "when."

Under Darin, the church was renamed and rebranded to The Oasis, and it grew. In fact, it grew without the use of any of usual cheap gimmicks. There was no cable news studio connected to his study. There were no schmaltzy media stunts designed to grab attention. And there were no gratuitous building programs devised to generate momentum by portraying an outward facade of success. But they were always building something. One campaign after the next, feverishly trying to accommodate the never-ending stream of young families that wanted to call Oasis their home. Most every Christian celebrity, aspiring politician, and business mogul within fifty miles sensed God's call to be a part of the The Oasis family.

And what was Darin Fletcher's secret? Well, it wasn't really a secret. If you asked him, he'd tell you in a New York minute. It was simply faithful, gospel-centered, expository preaching. No glitz. No fluff. Just plain old-fashioned, good preaching. And he could outpreach anyone in Texas. And at every pastor's preaching conference, he proved it yet again.

With both of his hands full, trying to keep up with the demands of a burgeoning ministry, Darin did his best to keep out of denominational politics. Well, formally at least. But he was constantly being requested by the movers, shakers, and kingpin wannabees to endorse their positions, join their committees, or speak at their conferences. And as long as it didn't require an extended time commitment, Darin tried as much as he could to be accommodating. But, when Dr. H. A. Norris came calling four years earlier, he made an exception to his rule.

Four years into his "favor" to H. A. Norris, Darin Fletcher was unexpectedly impressed. He was told by others that Jimmy was not really a winner in the leadership department, but, in fact, he had pulled off exactly what he said he would. He had delivered the goods. Jimmy was now seated behind his desk in his minimalist, but expensively appointed office, within the new church building. Speaking to Darin on speaker, he began to pry for a kind word of affirmation for all his hard work.

"What can I say? I'm impressed," said Darin. "This is better than I expected. I like this better than our shop, I think."

"Couldn't have done it without you, brother," said Jimmy with an air of relief. "You know that. Y'all have been nothing but encouraging. Can't say enough to express my appreciation, Darin."

"Well, we think of you as 'Oasis Atlanta.' You're our Easternmost campus," said Darin with a warm smile and a wink. "So, what's on tap for tonight?"

"Tour at six, which we are a bit late for. Tom Butts is doing that anyway—he's awesome. Service is at seven. You got twenty minutes to preach. I'll do the same."

"So, you, me, anyone else?"

"We asked Luca Lewis to speak for five minutes. This three-floor concept was his idea originally."

"Luca Lewis? Your daddy told me about him. Isn't he a liberal? One of them 'social justice warriors'? Sure you want him speaking with us? Some folks will likely use that as ammunition."

"Nah, he's not a liberal," said Jimmy somewhat matter-of-factly. "People just don't understand him. He's got a good heart."

"Good heart or not, you're hitchin' my wagon to him. I'm not comfortable with that, Jimmy. I'd suggest you make an adjustment."

Jimmy sat thoughtfully for a few seconds, and then quietly said, "I can't, Darin. Not at this late hour. It isn't fair to him. Besides, Luca's a big part of things, and he flew in from Philly just for this."

The two sat in silence for several agonizing seconds, and then Darin, without blinking, looked into Jimmy's eyes, and said, "I believe you can. Jimmy. And you will. We don't have a choice."

***

The three dozen or so early arrivers from the missions committee of The Oasis, and the intrepid four from Philly were taking in the first-floor tour of Midtown Fellowship when Tom Butts received a text from Jimmy.

It read, *2 tight. Don't have room 4 Luca 2night. Find excuse to cut him.*

"Real nice," Luca said to Yushua. "They outdid us by a fair bit. Love the sports equipment exchange ministry. I'd never thought of that one before."

"It's a wee bit fancy for me," said Campbell in a hushed voice, not wanting the others in the small crowd that convened for the tour to overhear. "Everything is pearly white," he whispered to Luca. "Thought we were in an Apple store."

"Ah, it's fantastic," said Luca, shaking a finger. "They'll do amazing things from here."

Tom Butts was leaning against the food bank's glass doors and looking blankly at his phone. His face paling, he stared at his shoes and mumbled, "Luca ..."

"Yes? You okay, brother?" asked Luca.

"Um, yes, I guess."

Tom, giving no eye contact, awkwardly signaled to Luca that he had a private message to pass on. "I just heard from Jimmy that we're gonna run too long. The service that is. He's wondering if you might ..."

"Cut things short?"

"Yeah," said Tom. "Well, no. Not that so much. But maybe speak another time. Instead of tonight. Would that be okay, Luca? Later sometime?"

Yushua took a step forward, no longer pretending not to be listening. "Tom, you know that he was only going to speak for five minutes. You knew that, right? To be honest, that could be construed as insulting enough. Come all the way from Philadelphia for five minutes. But Luca kept reminding us to look at the big picture. But now you want to cut him out altogether? What is going on, Tom?"

Luca laid his big hand on Yushua's shoulder. "Now, brother, let's not jump to conclusions. Tom's got a good reason, I'm sure."

Tom's gaze never left his suede loafers. With flushed cheeks, he said, "I dunno, fellas. All I got was a text a few seconds ago. Said that we were short on time."

"From Jimmy?" asked Yushua.

"Yes."

"Figures," said Yushua.

Luca stepped beside Tom, put his arm around his back, and said, "It is no problem, Tom. We're just tickled to see what you guys have been up to. Aren't we, fellas?"

"Right," came unconvincingly from the Philadelphian trio.

"So how 'bout this tour?" asked Luca. "Ain't we ever gonna see the second floor?"

Tom took a breath, and then said, "Yep, follow me," and he led them down a corridor to the staircase.

The differences between Atlanta's and Philadelphia's first floor were mainly that of aesthetics. Even though Chantel had done a spectacular job, her work seemed amateurish by comparison. Here, frosted glass next to white glass panels, and stainless steel interspersed with black walnut cabinetry was the canvas for large stainless-steel letters that marked out the various ministries designed to serve the people of Midtown, Atlanta. The space didn't take a back seat to any of Atlanta's finest hotels.

But the second floor revealed more than just an aesthetic revision. In Philadelphia, Yushua had developed an administrative hub to multiply employment opportunities for those in the community who fell between the cracks. And his vision for a social entrepreneurial center had been enthusiastically embraced by business and community leaders alike. All fourteen spaces were now full. And they had a waiting list. But Midtown Fellowship had chosen to use the second floor as a revenue stream for real estate rentals. They rented offices to Christian non-profits for slightly below market rates. "First class offices for kingdom causes," was how Tom described the floor. "And some of the rent goes to support the ministries on the first floor."

Disconcerted glances shot between the Philadelphians.

"Ready to see the third floor?" asked Tom.

Most of the small crowd seemed impressed and eager to continue. Most, but not all.

As they walked up the stairwell, they came to a steel fire door. As Tom Butts grabbed the knob, he said, "Now this isn't the way most will come to the third floor. This is temporary. You'll see why in a minute."

Tom held the door as the tour group trudged in single file up the cement steps and into the large room. To the left of them was a construction zone partitioned by a wall of poly plastic. To the right was an auditorium filled with gray padded chairs, a large, elevated stage, a baptistry, and a frosted glass and walnut pulpit.

"We can seat five hundred here. And that's about it. But if you look on the other side of that plastic wall, you'll see what we're workin' on. See them escalators? They go to the ground floor. And down to the parkade. We've got the third and fourth floor of the adjacent office complex. The third floor will hitch another seven hundred seats to this place. And goin' up one to the fourth floor will be a state-of-the-art children's ministry space. We've got an option on the fifth floor, too. But so far, we haven't decided. So, without it, we'll be able to seat twelve hundred, plus another three hundred or so kiddos. And free parking all Sunday long."

By the hush followed by a smattering of quiet "wows" and "holy cows," the small crowd was obviously impressed. Tom spent a few more minutes describing audio/video technology and the satellite linkups with The Oasis, Grapevine, and then he broke for questions.

"Satellite linkups, Tom?" asked Luca. "What's that about?"

"Yes, Luca. To start out with, Darin's gonna preach. Video based. And then slowly, they'll bring in Jimmy. They're figuring fifty-fifty in two years."

A middle-aged woman in a red pantsuit raised her hand.

"Yes?" said Tom.

"Is that so Pastor Fletcher can build up the numbers? He's a wonderful preacher."

"I believe that's the plan, ma'am," said Tom.

Another hand raised. A bald man with wranglers, a button-down oxford, and cowboy boots asked in a flat Texas drawl, "Can this Jimmy fella preach? I mean, can he bring it like brother Fletcher? 'Cause if he can't, can't see how this'll work."

"Believe me, sir, Jimmy can lay it down," said Tom. "You've heard his daddy, right? Dr. H. A. Norris? Well, believe me, he's a chip off the ole block. Don't you worry about Jimmy. He can handle the pulpit like nobody's business."

Tom looked over his shoulder to see that the auditorium behind him was filling up. "Time for one more question? Anyone?"

Yushua Maalouf cautiously raised his hand.

"Yes, brother?"

"Tom, I'm a little confused … What happened here?"

"Excuse me?" asked Tom.

Yushua struggled to keep his composure while stringing together words that might form a coherent question. "What … happened Tom? What? How is this … different? Different from LifePointe? Better … different I mean. This doesn't seem different. Does it? Tom?"

Chapter Twenty-Four

The Kingdom

The sparsely appointed home was filled with the warm fragrance of freshly made falafels, smoked whitefish, and garlic roasted vegetables. It was one of a multitude of small, two-story concrete cubes that were constructed throughout Tehran in the years before the uprising and then the subsequent crackdowns of Ayatollah Khomeini. The area was filled with nondescript buildings that had been parged white with cement and had browned with the passing of time and countless dust storms. And like the sea of white and beige that surrounded it, the Hosseini residence failed to attract a second glance, but nonetheless, it was a safe and comfortable place that the family called home.

"Ten minutes, children," said a cheerful woman who was spooning golden falafels from a cast-iron pan onto a white ceramic plate. "Wash, wash."

"When is Papa coming home?" asked her seven-year-old daughter who was elbows deep in the kitchen sink. "I miss him."

"Soon, my darling, very soon. He has important work at the embassy."

"I want to be a translator when I grow up, Mama," said her ten-year-old brother, dressed in red shorts and a white and red football jersey. "Then I can be with the important people, too."

"You can be. But you must study hard. Your papa went to school for many years."

"But I don't like school," he said, crossing his arms. "School is too boring."

"Tsk!" she exclaimed. "You mustn't say such silly things. You don't want to become one of those ignorant radicals. You must go to school like Papa and be of some use to the world."

"Yes, Mama," he said in almost immediate resignation. "When is Papa coming home?"

"Your papa will be home later tonight, before you go to sleep. So, get all your schoolwork finished before he comes home, and we will have some chai with sugar and cinnamon together before bedtime."

The children quickly scurried to the table and found their places set with white plates, white napkins, and small glasses of clumpy white yogurt milk.

"Who wants to give thanks?"

The little girl's hand shot straight up, "My turn, Mama."

Like characters from a Norman Rockwell painting, the children sat straight on wooden chairs, clasped their hands together, bowed their heads, and expressed thanks to their Creator for his provision.

"Thank you. Extra cinnamon for you," their mother said with a smile and a little wink.

Together, the little family sat at their round Formica table, eating and laughing and sharing stories of football, classmates, and cinnamon chai.

"When can we go see Grandpapa's horses again?" asked the girl. "I love being at Grandpapa's farmstead."

"Not for a while, sweetie. We must wait for things to settle in their land. But we do have a surprise for you. But you'll have to wait for Papa to come home first."

"A surprise?" asked the boy.

"Yes. One you'll like. But you'll have to finish your schoolwork first."

The children wolfed down their dinner, helped clear the table, and then returned to attack their homework with a renewed sense of purpose.

With homework finished and the children dressing for bed with exaggerated deliberateness, keys could be heard jingling at the front door.

"Papa!" they said in unison as the door burst open.

Ashraf Hosseini was an educated Iranian in his late thirties. He was born and raised in Tehran, educated at the University of Tehran, and worked most all his life in the bustling metropolis of fourteen million. Except for a few short-term foreign excursions that were required in his diplomatic career, he was a true-blue son of Tehran. Ashraf was of average height, with short hair and an impeccably groomed beard, deep, piercing eyes, square jaw, and was always dressed with refinement. Though his mother tongue was Farsi, he spoke Arabic like a native, adequate French, and almost perfect English that was tinged with an Oxford burr.

He was born to a modestly wealthy entrepreneurial family who exported artisan Persian carpets to the European and North American markets. "Persian" was a relative term, and the Hosseinis soon learned that they could acquire carpets from almost any geography in the Middle East and call them Persian if they ascribed to a motif common in Oriental rugs that traditionally originated from Iran. Soon, the Hosseinis found themselves sourcing hand-knotted carpets from Iraq, Turkey, Saudi Arabia, Syria, and Yemen. And it was on one of these searches that brought the Hosseini family to a small Yemeni village named Bani Badi that was known for its fine Arabian horses. After several trips into the high country of Yemen, Ashraf's father, who rarely missed a business opportunity, convinced Ali Al-Khulani that he could make him wealthy by directly representing his steeds to European and American horsemen, cutting out all the middlemen who profited along the way. And true to his word, the Al-Khulanis increased their profits five-fold on every horse that they sold.

The good relationships between the Al-Khulanis and the Hosseinis soon fostered a romantic relationship between Ashraf and the beautiful Azima, the youngest of Ali and Fatimah's children. And after an appropriate courtship, there was a traditional wedding in Bani Badi, and a grand reception in the great city of Tehran, where the happy couple settled in to start their family.

"Chai, Papa?" asked the little boy. "Mama said we could have chai with sugar and cinnamon. Extra cinnamon."

"Yes, yes, let's go to the kitchen."

"How was your day?" Azima asked.

"Unbelievable," said Ashraf. "Do you remember me telling you of a university classmate named Farah? The one whose family was wiped out by the radicals."

"Yes."

"Well, while she was in England doing graduate work, apparently she married a Nigerian, moved to the US, and started some kind of coffee company. Anyway, my next assignment is to translate for her, which I don't understand because she's a native Iranian. Translate for her and for the Canadian ambassador to the UN."

He thumbed open his smartphone and read, "Farah Akintola and Mr. Ambassador Francis Murphy. Looks like we'll be together for most of the week. Nothing outside of Tehran. But there is no purpose or agenda listed. It's all very clandestine. Not sure what to make of it."

"Sounds intriguing," said Azima. "A UN Ambassador. This must be very important."

"Indeed. Important and very puzzling."

"Chai, Mama?" asked the little girl, squirming.

"Yes, yes, dear."

"And you have a surprise for us, Papa?" asked the boy.

"I do?" he replied as more of a question than an answer.

"Bani Badi," Azima coached.

"Oh, yes. Yes, I do."

***

As usual, the third floor of the Philadelphia Freedom Center was abuzz. But what was unusual this day was that it was a Sunday. On Monday through Saturday, district meetings were scheduled on this floor. The neighborhoods of Philadelphia were geographically grouped together, and their leaders convened weekly for equipping, reporting, celebrating, and team building. The large assembly area was the place where Luca Lewis and the lead team equipped, cast vision, and interacted with the district leaders and the leaders of the local missional communities. The glass-paneled meeting rooms that flanked both sides of the assembly area were designated for districts of missional community leaders to gather and report, repair, replenish, and advance. Monday through Saturday, Fatima's Floor was filled past capacity with excited disciple-making leaders who plotted together as gospel insurgents for a kingdom advance.

But this was Sunday. This was their day of rest. Other than hundreds of missional communities gathering to worship in homes, apartments, boardrooms, pubs, community centers, and coffee shops, Sunday was a quiet day at the center, by design.

But not this Sunday.

Luca worked his way through the crowd of district leaders with hugs and smiles, but noticeably was more reserved than normal—until he eventually managed to make it to the platform. Standing and facing the enthusiastic crowd, he quietly raised one arm in the air, and almost immediately the loud drone of laughter and spirited conversations faded into a quiet hustling of scurrying to find seats.

"Thank y'all for giving us this Sunday. We don't do this often, but when we do, you know that it is important."

The room was silent, and a heavy anticipation was in the air.

"You are our leaders. You are men and women that thousands of other men and women look to for spiritual guidance. You are the very backbone of this movement. You have proven yourselves as faithful and faith-filled disciples of our King Jesus. You have led missional communities to disciple their neighborhoods. Over the past ten years you have multiplied your missional communities into literally hundreds of other places across the great city of Philadelphia. And now you lead the leaders of this movement. Under your watchful care, our entire mission force gathers and then deploys into every imaginable crack and crevice of society, embodying the very good news of Jesus in themselves. You are the very heart and soul and sinew and muscle of Philadelphia Freedom."

Luca stopped for a moment, and with clasped hands and his face pointing to the heavens, he slowed his cadence even more, and then in almost a whisper he said, "And so it is you that I come to and ask for a sacrifice. And not a small one. Potentially, I am asking you for the biggest sacrifice that one can give on this side of eternity. I am asking for your life."

And if it were possible for a completely quiet room to become even more quiet, that is exactly what happened. There was a spiritual heaviness in the room. The kind that makes the air seem thick, as if you could cut through it with a knife. Trembling tears were forming in eyes everywhere, even though no one knew what Luca was planning. There was a solidarity of spirit among men and women and young and old alike that seemed to say, "Yes, Jesus. Yes. Now tell us where our 'yes' is assigned."

"It seems to us, your City Leadership Team, that God is unmistakably asking us to send our best to dangerous places for the sake of the gospel. We are being called to these places—not because they are dangerous, but because a door for the gospel is being opened wide. And we sense the Spirit is saying to our movement, 'Go!' And so, let me introduce some people to you. Some you know, and some you don't. But all of them are a part of this story. Duane, will you come up here and introduce yourself?"

A well-dressed African American man in his late forties rose to his feet and stood beside Luca.

"Hi. I'm Duane Harris. I'm from Atlanta. I am a layman from Midtown Fellowship—Jimmy Norris' church—some of you may have heard of it. Anyway, several years ago, Pastor Jimmy asked me to fly down here with him to see what y'all got going on. I was a pretty new believer at the time, but boy was I amazed. I'm a businessman, and I think that Pastor Jimmy might have thought that I could help y'all out. What a joke. You guys opened my eyes. You guys gave me a whole new picture of 'church.'"

"Tell us what happened," prompted Luca.

"Well, Yushua asked me to go to dinner with Mamadou and Farah Akintola. They were just starting GroundWorx Coffee at the time. They were not believers, but they had hearts that were warmer toward kingdom values than most Christian folks I knew, even though they had never met our King. I was really intrigued, both by their selfless business plan and by their sacrificial spirit. In the months that followed I made many trips here, as Yushua asked me to be their designated mentor. Every time I came, Farah and

Mamadou's questions were more and more about Jesus and less and less about business. I was really starting to feel like I was a few miles out past the last buoy—way, way out of my depth."

"Tell us about what happened next, Duane," Luca said.

"Well, one evening, at the coffee shop on the first floor, Mamadou asked me, 'Can Muslims like Farah and me have Jesus too?' What a question. I didn't know what to say. No clue. So I prayed, 'Jesus, help me help them.'"

Duane smiled at the memory and looked out at the crowded room of faces.

"And then, the Holy Spirit reminded me that Jesus didn't die for a religion, but for sinners. All sinners. So I said, 'No. No Muslim can come to Christ. Ever. It's impossible. Just like no Christian can come to Christ. Ever. Totally impossible. Only sinners come to Christ. Only people who understand that their personal or religious righteousness can never repair the brokenness of their sin problem. That's what Jesus' death and resurrection was all about. He didn't come to start a new and better religion in his name. He came to do what no religion could ever do. Not the Muslim one. Not the Christian one. He himself, God in the flesh, he alone could pay the price for our sin.'"

"Now you're preaching!" Luca said laughingly. "Then what happened?"

"At GroundWorx, on the first floor, at the back corner booth …" Duane pointed to the street, "Mamadou and Farah Akintola traded in their personal pride and their Muslim faith for King Jesus' life to be lived through theirs."

The room erupted with cheers and clapping and "hallelujahs" and standing high fives.

"Thank you, brother Duane Harris. Y'all, give him some big Philly love!"

More claps and cheers followed. A small cadre of brothers and sisters hugged him and slapped his back as he sat down once again on the front row.

"All right. Wasn't that good? And we're just getting warmed up. Mamadou, Farah, come on up. Oh, and Princess, too. Can't leave out our Princess!"

The Akintolas were familiar figures to those who were from the Fishtown area, but for most in this room, this was their first introduction. Mamadou wore a very traditional African styled shirt, straight cut and untucked, perfectly white, with white embroidering and pleats. Farah wore a ruffled herringbone jacket and pencil skirt, hair pulled back, and stylish boots. And Princess, who was now seven years old, still looked very much like a princess, dressed in pink taffeta and lace reaching to the floor.

"Farah, you're the President of GroundWorx, correct?" asked Luca.

"GroundWorx International now, Luca."

"Right. We'll get to that in a bit. So, tell us, what is the purpose of your coffee shops?"

"We employ the difficult to employ. We concentrate on giving refugees a place to start in the workforce. And so far, the majority of our management team were originally frontline baristas and cashiers. And then, Luca, we direct our profits to meeting needs in the communities where the coffee shops exist. Again, with a bias toward the needs of refugees."

"Isn't that beautiful! How did you become associated with Philadelphia Freedom, Farah?"

"It was Yushua Maalouf. I heard about his vision almost as soon as we immigrated from the UK and landed here in Philly. I was impressed with the idea of building a community of practical altruism, directly connected to social enterprise. He captured my imagination from the very first day. Mamadou and I were so excited when he told us we were going to be one of the first pilots for the second floor. Honored."

"And how have things been going?" asked Luca.

"Unbelievably. We have sixteen GroundWorx operating here in Philly. Another four by the end of this year. And then we are in Baltimore with five, Harlem with three, D.C. with four, Toronto with seven, and Montreal with four. Had a false start in Atlanta but think we might get things going there before too long."

"So, forty-three, if I did my math right."

"By year's end, Luca."

"And how many people have you provided jobs for?"

"Full time, we are employing 260 frontline workers. And twenty-one more here at HQ. With another two hundred-ish with part-time employment."

"So, 480-ish mostly refugees with jobs. Amazing. And before Philly and London, where were you born and raised, Farah?"

"I'm Persian. Iranian. Born and raised in the city of Tehran. My family was targeted and killed there when I was a graduate student in the UK."

"That's unimaginable pain for most of us to fathom, Farah. Would you ever want to go back to that place?"

Farah wasn't as quick to respond to this question. Looking at her boots, she drew a deep breath and said, "No. Never. Everyone that I loved was murdered there. And the killers still run the country. So, no. Definitely not. I would never want to go there again. But does Jesus want me to go there? That is another question entirely. And I think that the answer to that question is 'yes.'"

Luca put his big hand on Mamadou's shoulder. "How about you, Mamadou? What do you think of moving to Tehran?"

With a beaming smile, Mamadou shot back, "Luca, I was almost killed in Nigeria. Very close. And for only monies. Bad monies. I would be glad to die in Iran for Jesus. He is a much bigger treasure to me."

No cheers followed. Just silence. Farah, Princess, and Mamadou quietly stepped off the stage.

"'Glad to die in Iran for Jesus. He is a much bigger treasure to me,'" repeated Luca. "Thank you, Mr. and Mrs. Akintola. Thank you, beautiful Princess. You are teaching us all about the kingdom of God."

As the Akintolas found their seats on the front row, Luca shifted his feet as he gathered his thoughts. With a much slower and more thoughtful cadence, he said, "Lastly, let me introduce two people to you this evening. One you've never met before. And one that you know very well. Let's start with introducing you to a new friend. It's my distinct honor to introduce to you Mr. Ambassador Francis Murphy. Would you please join me, sir?"

Ambassador Francis stood and approached the platform wearing blue jeans, a blue oxford, and the golf jacket that was given to him by Yushua.

"Mr. Ambassador, you are Canada's ambassador to the United Nations, correct?"

"That is correct, Luca. But please call me Francis."

"Okay, Mr. Ambassador Francis," said Luca with a wry smile.

The room erupted in laughter.

Francis waved an arm to try to break in, and the room quickly quietened.

"Luca, I am an ambassador. Have been for almost forty years. For a handful of years I have represented Canada at the UN. Likely will for a few more. But the place that I ultimately seek to represent is not a temporal nation, but an eternal kingdom. Like you, and all my brothers and sisters in the room, I am honored to call myself an Ambassador of Christ, first and foremost." Once again, the room was alive with cheers, clapping hands, and thunderous "amens."

"Luca," Francis broke in, pointing to the crest on his jacket. "You see this coat of arms? It's the very symbol that accompanies your movement's logo. It's on the front of the building, I noticed. I see it in frosted glass on the panels beside us. And it's right here behind me, front and center. Not many of us read Latin anymore, but, church, what does it say in plain old English?"

Without hesitation, the gathering roared, "Seek first the kingdom of God!"

"Yes! That symbol is a long-forgotten coat of arms of my home province in Canada. Newfoundland. Perhaps once we believed it. But that would have been a time before I walked this earth. But you know what? God always has a people. He always has a remnant. An unlikely mob who dares enough to believe that his kingdom is the way that things should be. A people who run against the grain in order to show the world light and joy and peace and restoration. A people who are so Jesusy, so countercultural, that they scare the sacred pants off the pious and self-righteous. And you know what else, my Philadelphia family?"

"What?" was the instinctive response that came without hesitation.

"You are that people. You are that remnant. You are that Jesusy countercultural insurgency that is turning this broken-down world upside-right."

And then, in the quietness of the moment, Francis grabbed Luca's hand and raised it in the air, and with a strong voice, declared, "*Quaerite Prime Regnum Dei!*"

And the room thundered with the chant, "*Quaerite Prime Regnum Dei … Quaerite Prime Regnum Dei …*"

After a few seconds, when the Latin phrase had become quite unintelligible, Luca raised both arms with open palms to quieten his friends.

"Why is this coat of arms important to our movement, Francis?" asked Luca.

"I suppose it is because of young Yushua, or Omar as I first knew him. I was wearing an old T-shirt with the crest the day we met. And even though young Omar was running for his life, it became the subject matter of our first conversation. And in the refugee camp in which I concealed him, it became the very content of our lengthy talks. Young Omar had lived it. And I had learned about it. And together we wrapped the gospel's teaching around my theoretical theology. The kingdom of God, for me, for the first time, became both deeply theological and immensely practical. Young Omar, a six-month-old believer, did that to me. He wrecked me for 'church as usual.'"

"Well, I think it's safe to say that Yushua has wrecked a lot of us. In a good way." And then motioning to the front row, Luca said, "Yushua, why don't you come and join us."

Yushua stood. Streams of tears were running down his cheeks and dropping on the lapels of his navy sport coat as he made his way beside his old comrades. He no longer looked like the handsome young football player ready to take on the world. Instead, indelibly written on his face in scars and lines was the story of one who had suffered for his King, and who continued to faithfully follow his King into his mission, despite enormous personal cost.

Slowly, one by one, everyone in the room came to their feet. There was no cheering. No boisterous calls. Just a quiet clapping of the grateful hands of the men and women who wanted to express their deep love, respect, and thankfulness for their mentor, their guide, and their prophet. The one who taught them all so much about the forgotten ways of Jesus.

Rubbing tears from his eyes, Yushua attempted to respond to

this heartfelt tribute, "*Quaerite ... Prime Regnum ... Dei!* All glory to our beautiful, powerful, loving King!"

Luca, who himself was an emotional puddle, managed an "amen" as he wiped his eyes and tried to regain his composure.

"Francis," Luca said. "What is going on in Iran right now?"

"It's the most amazing thing, Luca. For a long time, across much of the Middle East, men and women who have no access to the witness of a Christ follower, or even a Bible, have been experiencing what has become known as 'Jesus dreams.' It seems that with no faithful witness coming to these poor souls, the Holy Spirit is leading them to search for Christ through various ways. This has been reported for some time now. Sometimes it is Jesus speaking Scripture that they dream of. Scripture that they've never before read, that points them to Jesus as the Messiah. Sometimes it is a dream of Jesus giving them instructions of where to go to find answers. Different dreams, but what is common is that they all point to Jesus Christ himself."

Yushua broke in, "This is true. I heard of this happening in Yemen. It didn't happen to me—there was a faithful witness for me, the man who gave me his name, the real O. G. Yushua Maalouf. But for many, this seems to be the beginning of their search for truth. And when they find Jesus, that's when they begin to pay a big price."

"Yes, Yushua, often a horrendously heavy price," agreed Francis. "But now, in Iran, there seems to be a disproportionate number of these reports. Sometimes it's an Iranian in a refugee camp outside his or her country. Other times it's reported among Iranian travelers. So, we can only imagine how many Jesus dreams are being dreamed among the people in Iran."

Luca stood with his eyes closed tightly as Yushua and Francis spoke. Without opening them, he lifted both arms high in the air and said, "Disciples of Jesus, this, this is our holy calling. This is what Jesus is saying to every blessed black, brown, white, and Asian soul among us. We have the answer to their dreams. We are not the answer. Oh, we know that all too well. But we have the answer. And the answer is our Lord and only Savior, Jesus Christ. And while these precious children created in the image of God are stumbling in darkness, we have the light. And we know that the light is a Person. While they are dreaming of light, begging for light, we are keeping it all to ourselves. But the Holy Spirit is saying to us, 'Philadelphia, no more! No more!'"

"And this is where we come in," interrupted Yushua. "Some of us will go. And some of us may not come back. We will go, and the Holy Spirit will connect us with those looking for their Savior. We will go and offer our lives so others can hear. And some of us will stay here and hold the ropes. But be careful my friends. Staying should never be the default position of a disciple of Jesus Christ. Those of us who stay should hear that instruction from God because Jesus' Great Commission clearly instructs us to go. So, we must ask ourselves, brothers and sisters, why is it that so many seem willing to go, but are planning to stay, rather than a more biblical posture of planning to go, but willing to stay?"

"And so," said Luca, "we believe that God is asking us to open a Freedom Center in the great city of Tehran. We will be sending six scouts next month to connect with some of Jesus' disciples in that city. They will prayerfully be able to determine how we can serve his persecuted people in their gospel witness. From the intelligence they will bring back, we will begin to enlist men and women from our movement here in Philly, and from movements in the other cities, to go and plant their lives among those beautiful, sacrificial, courageous people."

"Who are our scouts?" came a voice from the crowd.

"I'm glad you asked," said Luca. "We see in Acts 13 that the church in Antioch sent their very best into a missionary advance. We believe that this is the way of Jesus. So, we will send some of our very best. Farah Akintola will leave her daughter with Mamadou and go. Brother Duane Harris from Atlanta will go. Santiago Parra, our teacher, will leave Sophia in Maggy's care and go. And Campbell and Riona MacKay, our lead evangelists, will go. As will Yushua. And joining them will be our new friend, Francis Murphy."

"And it will be an honor of a lifetime," said Francis.

Yushua then moved between Luca and Francis, draped his arms over their shoulders, and said in almost a whisper, "*Quaerite Prime Regnum Dei.*"

***

"Ever miss the simpler days, Jimmy? The days before the pressures of syncing video conferencing with live presentations three times a weekend? When we used to work with Duane and the team and then come home to introduce our neighbors and co-workers to Jesus' people? You notice that none of them ever really made the trip to our new, bigger and better thing? A few of them show up every once in a while, but not often."

Jimmy looked up from his printed spreadsheets, took off his readers, and sighed. "Yeah, I do. Thought Duane would make it, but I guess APS is keeping him pretty busy. Kinda disappointing if you ask me."

"Well, Jennifer told me that Duane has picked up leading the Bible study at APS. More folks than ever are coming," said Tom.

"Really?" said Jimmy with a hint of disbelief. "That's incredible."

"Yeah, it is. Sounds like he's continued to keep in contact with Luca and the gang in Philly. Made a number of trips back there."

"Huh. I wonder what for?"

"Remember the Middle Eastern woman who started the coffee business?"

"Yeah."

"Well, Jennifer said that Duane led her to Christ. And her husband. So, Duane's been traveling back and forth mentoring them in business, and in Jesus, I suppose."

"Duane Harris? Our Duane Harris?"

"That's what I hear."

"That's unbelievable," said Jimmy as he leaned back in his chair and stared at the ceiling. "Wonder why he doesn't hang with us? We're right here in his own backyard."

"Dunno," said Tom. "Maybe he misses the simpler days, too?"

Jimmy shrugged.

"Anyway," Tom said, "we're coming up on two years since launch. Think Darren will let you preach anytime soon? Thought he said six months?"

"Yeah, I've been talking with him. He thinks it's too soon. Apparently, the feedback he's been getting from here is that nobody wants him to give up any Sundays quite yet. He thinks he needs more time to shore up the base. In his words, 'Things are still a bit too delicate.'"

"Feedback from who?" asked Tom.

"I dunno. His fanboys, I guess. There's no shortage of them."

"Well, that's the truth. How much more time?"

"I dunno that either."

"How long are you gonna stick it out? Jimmy, you're a gifted preacher. You should be back in the saddle. It's a waste."

Jimmy leaned forward in his chair with his elbows on his knees, stared at the carpet between his shoes, and said, "What else do I got, Tom? Not too many options out there for me. Fired from my last pulpit and been on the shelf here for almost three years now. Now my holy calling is to press 'play,' direct traffic on stage, and make sure the 'twenty somethings' in the band are in a good emotional headspace. Not really a resume that churches are clamoring for, I 'spect."

The two old friends sat quietly for a minute or two trying to avoid any semblance of eye contact; that would be too much at this moment. Jimmy's honest framing of their reality had caught them both off guard and sent them into a spontaneous melancholy tailspin.

"How did we get here, Jimmy?" Tom asked. "How'd we get right back here—back in the very same place?"

"I'm not sure, my friend. Practice, I 'spect."

"Maybe," Tom chuckled. "This is pretty much what we had at LifePointe, isn't it?"

"I don't think so, Tom. This is much, much worse."

Chapter Twenty-Five

The Apprentices

"Will it be another livestock auction?" asked a grizzled elderly man dressed in ill-fitting secondhand clothes, cradling a tiny cup of chai with both hands.

Ashraf Hosseini looked bewildered. "Livestock auction? What does this mean?"

Farzin Gholami, Ashraf's lunch companion, was one of the leaders of the Christian community in Tehran. A civil engineer by training, he was reduced to becoming a street peddler after being discovered as a disciple and subsequently imprisoned for six horrifying years. His neck, back, and shoulders now resembled the topography of the moon as he became a human ashtray for his tormentors' cigarettes as they "requested" names of other disciples. But he never broke. Not once. Now in his late sixties, Farzin Gholami was recognized by all disciples in Tehran as one of the elders of the city.

"Almost every year, disciples come from the West," said Farzin. "Most often from the US. They come to help the church of Iran, and they have good intentions. But the results of their good intentions are not always good. You know, as they say, 'The path to Gehenna is paved with good thoughts.'"

"Livestock auction?" Ashraf pressed.

"Yes, most often we are asked to gather the leaders of the communities in a place, and they are to 'share their vision,'" Farzin said, making quotation marks with his fingers. "What vision? Our Savior's Great Commission?"

"And the leaders from the West choose someone to support?" asked Ashraf.

"Exactly. It feels very much like a livestock auction. And it creates two sins among us: It tempts our brothers to tell stories that are not quite true, because support only comes to those with the best stories. And it creates a spirit of competition among us. Brother battles brother to be branded with someone else's branding iron. It's not right. We have many divisions now that did not used to be among us. Most have come from the auctions."

"I am sorry to hear this," said Ashraf. "I did not know. But I don't think that next week's meeting will be like that. The team that is coming is from many places: Iran, Yemen, Canada, Chile, Ireland, and the US. But I will make sure that this does not happen. I will talk to them before the meeting."

"That is good. Very good." The old disciple leaned back in his chair and asked, "How was it for you, brother? How did you find the Way?"

"Not so different from many in Iran," said Ashraf Hosseini as he carefully scanned the café for anyone too attentive to their conversation. "Like many in the university, I was attracted to the West. And I thought that the Way was part and parcel of a free and democratic secular society. I knew we needed change in our country, and I thought that the Way was part of the package toward a liberal democracy in our land. So, I began to explore …"

"Yes, yes," said Ashraf's companion, "I've heard of this many times. And how did you find correction in this?"

"Well, this becomes a very strange story, Farzin."

"I've heard so many strange stories since I've followed Isa, my brother. I doubt very much that yours will be the strangest. Tell me, please."

"I'm happy to, brother," said Ashraf as he lowered his voice. "It was really my wife, Azima, who helped me."

"She was a follower of the Way?"

"No, not really. Not yet. But she had experienced something in her country, in Yemen, that troubled her soul for many years."

"What was that?" asked Farzin as he placed his empty chai cup on the table and leaned forward.

"Well, she lost a brother and sister. Both on the same day. They went into the city for a doctor's appointment and then evaporated. Disappeared. The whole family was in a state of panic as they tried everything that they knew to locate them. They searched everywhere, but they couldn't find a single clue as to where they went."

"How old were they? Children?"

"No, no, Omar was in his early twenties. Fatimah was older, I think she was about twenty-five or twenty-six. Fatimah was very sick. She had been for many years. So sick she was about to die. So, Omar came home to visit her from law school, and suddenly she was healed. Azima said it seemed to everyone that it was a miracle. There was no other explanation."

Ashraf glanced around the café and then lowered his voice even further. "This is where the story becomes difficult to believe. I wouldn't believe it myself if it wasn't my wife who told it. Azima is anything but a fanciful storyteller."

"Well, what happened?" asked an impatient Farzin.

"My wife, Azima, who was several years younger than Omar at the time, was sitting on Fatimah's bed. This was perhaps one week after her brother and sister disappeared. She was distraught, inconsolable, weeping, when suddenly a child appeared. A little girl dressed in rags who was no more than five years old."

"An angel?"

"She didn't know. Her clothes were tattered and dirty, but her face shone—"

"Like an angel?" Farzin interrupted.

"Yes, I suppose."

"And then what happened, brother?"

"The little girl asked Azima to stand up. Azima did, and the little girl reached under the mattress where she was sitting and found a Bible. Well, pieces of a Bible, all taped together and then sewn with fishing line. We still have it."

"Did she say anything?"

"Yes, the little girl handed the Bible to her and then said the most remarkable thing. 'Isa sent me. Isa is sending Omar. Isa is with Fatimah. And Isa loves you, Azima. And Isa loves your family too.' And then she turned around, closed the bedroom door behind her, and disappeared."

"Did anyone else see her?"

"No."

"Is this when Azima became a follower of the Way?"

"No. This is when she became very confused. Her father saw little practical value in educating girls, so Azima's reading ability at that time was lacking. She knew that this was a dangerous book, so she hid it."

"Did she not tell anyone about this?"

"Until the week we were married, she had only told her mother."

"Did you believe her?"

"I believed that she believed it. But to be honest, I was quite skeptical at first. But she was so convinced. She begged me to teach her to read, and I was happy to do so. And the clever woman that she is, she picked it up quickly. And once she could read, she spent most of her time reading her little ragged Bible."

"Did her mother believe her story?"

"Yes, Azima thought so. As she told her the story, she had the feeling that her mother had a similar encounter even though she would never admit it. The only thing her mother ever said about the matter was, 'Say nothing to no one. Ever.'"

"So, how did you find the Way, Ashraf?"

"In our first year of marriage, while I was interning as a translator at the British Embassy, the deputy Head of Mission, Mr. Robert Langham, asked that I accompany him to an off-site meeting. I assumed that he was with the Way since he was British, and so I began to inquire about his faith."

"You didn't know much, did you, brother?" Farzin said laughingly.

"You're right, brother. I knew exactly nothing." He scanned the café again then said, "But Isa did. You see, Mr. Robert was part of the Way. And we were actually on our way to meet some secret community leaders. And after my third translation trip with him, I asked Mr. Robert if I could follow the Way with them."

"And Azima?"

"And Azima was waiting. For all those years she was patiently waiting. I came home that afternoon and told her about Isa's forgiveness, and she, without a second's hesitation said, 'Isa loves me, too.'"

"Was it her father?" asked Farzin.

"Was what her father?"

"Was it Azima's father who made Fatimah and Omar disappear?"

Ashraf tented his fingers as he thought out his response. "No one will ever say this, but I think so. There's something that's off with him. He's the most distant man I've ever met. He won't even allow anyone to speak of his lost children in his presence, which is strange when you think about it. And which will be difficult next week because they're coming to live with us in our little house, and we named our children Fatimah and Omar, after them."

***

The long, low, droning hum of the 747's engines was interrupted by the copilot's scratchy announcement. They would be landing in Tehran in thirty minutes. It was seventy-seven degrees Fahrenheit, the skies were clear, and the wind was coming from the north/northwest at eight knots. All in all, it was going to be a beautiful spring morning.

"Here goes," Yushua said with a measure of apprehension in his voice.

"It's been a while, hasn't it?" asked Francis as he began to organize his personal effects.

"Haven't been back on this side of the globe since you put me on that flight all those years ago."

"Quite a journey for both of us. God has blessed a Newfie and a refugee in some amazing ways, and I'm so glad that we're doing this next chapter together, Yushua."

"Feels really strange to think I am going to step out of this airplane, back into a country that wants to stop any messenger of Christ. I'm more rattled than I thought I'd be."

"I get it. I've been in Tehran three times in the last couple of years, but always primarily for a diplomatic purpose. And always with diplomatic protection. This is a first for me too in a long while."

"I remember how strange it felt to 'feel safe' when I first came to America," said Yushua. "I had been anxious for so long that 'safe' was an unnatural state for me. It took me months in Atlanta to actually believe it. And then so quickly I took that feeling of security for granted. I hope I remember to be consciously grateful when we return to Philly."

Ninety minutes later the scouting party had disembarked, cleared customs, and was standing by a glistening stainless-steel baggage carousel at the Tehran International Airport, awaiting their luggage.

"Got a text from Luca," Yushua announced. "He said, *Love you guys—and remember that you're covered.*"

Luca had arranged for twelve disciples to lift the scouting team up in prayer every half hour, twenty-four hours a day, seven days a week, for the two weeks they were scheduled to be in Tehran. They were instructed to pray specifically in two ways: for the security of the team, and for the spiritual eyes to see where Jesus was leading.

"Kinda puts a bit of starch in your ole britches, hearing that bit of news, doesn't it?" said Campbell. "I went from being a little nervous to being incredibly grateful in the space of a text."

"It is strange to be here," said Farah. "This was once all that I knew. Now I feel like an alien, a foreigner."

"You were built for this, Farah," Yushua said reassuringly. "It'll all come back to you. You intuitively will know how to relate to our brothers and sisters here. You're our Sherpa, and we'll be following your lead. Your story is in this land, and Tehran is in you."

"But Francis, Campbell, and Riona, on the other hand," said Santiago with a twinkle in his eye, "who happen to be among the whitest white people on earth … they may have a little more trouble convincing people that they're natives."

The group's laughter was drowned out by the sound of a buzzer announcing that the bags were about to drop. Sixty minutes later and the team had arrived at their hotel, persuaded the front desk agent for an early check in, unloaded their bags, and reconvened in the lobby restaurant for brunch. *Khagineh* was the order that everyone agreed on, after Farah's convincing recommendation. It featured a list of ingredients that together could not be anything but utterly delicious—saffron, ground cardamom, sugar, a lot of butter, and eggs.

"So, who, or what exactly, are we looking for? And how will we know when we find it?" asked the ever-logical Santiago. "It would be nice to have a bit of a profile so we can all stay on the same page."

"I understand where you're coming from, brother, but this will not be our way," corrected Yushua. "Any profile that we could draw up from our experience in Philly would likely cause us to miss God's plan for Tehran altogether. We will be navigating through some trusted relationships that our brother Francis has built, as we prayerfully seek the mind of Christ. We don't know what we don't know right now. But Jesus will guide us. I promise."

"Let me put it this way," Francis broke in as he leaned forward and spoke with a hushed voice. "Duane, would any missions committee in Georgia have chosen Luca Lewis to spark a movement in Philadelphia? Unlikely, don't you think? Nor would any group of pastors from Toronto have ever chosen him. It just never would have happened. But guess what? Jesus did. And the people in Philly could see it. So, there is no profile. There is only spiritual guidance. Guidance from our Iranian brothers and sisters, and from the Spirit of Christ."

By the way Santiago began attacking his eggs, it seemed that Francis' explanation satisfied his innate need for systems and control. No doubt, this was going to be a stretching experience for both his personality and for his faith. But also, a stretching, as most spiritual discomfort does, that would shape him more closely into the image of his King.

"God is doing something in this country that is special," Francis chimed in once again. "Even though the heat of persecution has been turned up, so has the activity of God. So, let me remind you again—we aren't coming here to start anything. We are coming to serve, encourage, and resource the kingdom warriors who are already here laying down their lives."

"Aye," said Campbell. "And when the stories of heroes are told, it won't be our names that are mentioned. That is not our desire. It's not for us to have another pin on the map that says, 'Look what Philly has done!' No sir. Our spot is simply to be some of the humble answers to the desperate prayers of his people. I'm sure that some will be very grateful for our help, but that will never be the story. The only story that will be told is the faithfulness of Christ and the faith of his church in Tehran."

"His church in Tehran ..." Farah repeated. "That phrase caught me a bit off guard. But of course, Jesus has a church here already. I hadn't thought of it that way." She paused for a few seconds and then pensively asked, "I wonder what it looks like?"

Duane Harris, who seemed to this point to be the most overwhelmed of the group, finally broke his silence. "Now everyone knows that I'm no expert here, but I'm bettin' it looks more like y'all in Philly than us in Midtown."

Then Yushua smiled, carefully folded his napkin and placed it across his plate, and said, "And if my recollections of the secret communities in Yemen are accurate, then perhaps a little more like heaven than we in Philly."

***

Tom Butts, sitting with his back to the door, was in his cubicle, thoroughly absorbed in his spreadsheets. Like every Monday, Tom had until 3 p.m. to have completed the inputting of a myriad of data fields from The Oasis' accountability processes relating to Sunday's attendance and giving. While Tom was fully engrossed in data, with his reading glasses precariously hanging on to the last knob of his nose, Jimmy barged in at sixty miles per hour.

"Tommy boy, guess where I just came from?"

"Jeepers," Tom said, clutching his chest. "You scared the pants off of me."

"Sorry, bro. But guess where I've been?"

"Where?" said Tom, unenthusiastically playing along.

"APS."

"Visiting Duane?"

"Well, that was my intention, but guess where he is?"

"I dunno."

"Guess."

"New York?"

"No, Tommy, no. Guess ..."

"Philly?"

"Close, but no. Duane is in Iran. He's in Iran with the Philly gang. They're setting up shop over there and he's a part of it. Jennifer filled me in."

"Holy cow. I wouldn't have ever guessed that."

"No kidding. Duane Harris. Can you believe it? Duane?"

"Well, kinda," said Tom. "I mean Duane always loved a big challenge. He dreams big. Remember how he used to talk about multiplying things here in Midtown? He had even bigger plans than we did. He was pumped. Well, at least he was, until this happened," as he gestured toward the administrative pit of cubicles. "Guess passing the offering plate wasn't quite enough to capture him."

"Yeah," said Jimmy as his smile faded.

"Hope they're safe over there," said Tom. "Iran ain't exactly Midtown."

Jimmy stared vacantly into the admin pit and said nothing.

"How long are they over there for?" asked Tom.

Jimmy, as if Tom's question had never been voiced, turned around and walked toward the door.

"Jimmy?"

"Sorry, bro. I've got my weekly call with Fletcher in an hour. I'm gonna get things cleared up." And then he left.

Fifty minutes later, Jimmy swung on his office chair, staring at the neglected books gathering dust on the chic floor-to-ceiling walnut shelves that surrounded his state-of-the-art adjustable desk, currently positioned in seated mode. Jimmy stretched his feet out on the desk and leaned back, rereading his contract of employment while chewing on a ballpoint pen.

"This ain't right," he mumbled to himself. "Other than my salary, he's kept no promises."

He looked up and saw Tom waiting quietly at his door.

"Yes?"

"Got a minute?"

"I'm not sure. Fletcher's a few minutes late already."

"I just wanted to pray with you before this call," said Tom in a timid tone.

"Not exactly in the prayin' mood right now, bro."

"I know, I just thought that—"

Just then, a ringtone playing the theme to "The Good, the Bad, and the Ugly," sounded from Jimmy's phone.

"Gotta get this."

"Should I go?"

"No." Jimmy motioned for Tom to take a seat. "Hello?"

The call started as usual. Perfunctory and insincere inquiries about family, which served as social lubrication to get to the meat of the call.

"Okay, bud, nickels and noses—I need your stats. How many did you run yesterday—all in?"

Jimmy, with his feet still up on his desk, lifelessly regurgitated figures from Tom's spreadsheet. It wasn't that he was embarrassed about Midtown's showing—Jimmy had unassailable facts to prove, that regarding the holy duality, he was overperforming. It's just that his heart wasn't in it. Hadn't been for a long time.

"Super. Man, you're doing really great. Couldn't be prouder of you, brother. Keeping the money flowing and the people comin', and we'll add those two new floors in no time."

When the call had fulfilled its reporting purpose and came to its customary conclusion, Jimmy cleared his throat and then said to his employer who was twelve years his junior, "Darin, got a few more minutes? I'd like to get some clarity on some things."

"Sure, buddy. What's up?"

"I was just reading my contract, and according to that, we should be on phase three of our transition plan. Phase three says that you preach Christmas Eve, Easter Sunday, and two other weeks mutually agreed upon. We haven't even fulfilled phase one. And I'm not feelin' much momentum that's moving this forward."

"Jimmy, you gotta be patient. We were building this plane while we were flying it. We didn't know exactly how to project this out. Neither of us have ever done anything quite like this before. All of our other campuses were takeovers. They were simple. They had no talent like you have, so we had to march in and fix everything. But we're building this one together. It's just taken a bit longer than we expected to nail everything down, but things are workin', aren't they?"

"Not for me, Darin. Not at all. Not for a long time."

"What do ya mean? You're doing an incredible job."

"No offense, brother, but a trained monkey could do my job. I am not at all fulfilled in my—"

"Hey bro," interrupted Fletcher. "Before you get too far, you best get your doctrine straight. This church ain't about you. This is the body of Christ we are talking about here. It's bigger than any one of us. We all have our role to play in his body. My role is to cast vision and feed the sheep. Your role is to implement the vision and care for the sheep. We have different assignments but ..."

Jimmy's furrowed brow deepened as he listened to the sermon. It's one he had heard numerous times before from Fletcher, and in fact, it was one that he himself had delivered on countless occasions. It was a reductionist version of the nature of Christ's body that he no longer believed, nor could stomach.

"Whoa, wait a minute." This time it was Jimmy's turn to interrupt. "You've just described IBM my friend, not the body of Christ. I used to believe all that drivel you're dishing out too, preached it myself for way too many years. But the big, hairy, unavoidable problem is, the sheep aren't gettin' fed by a sermon, nor are they gettin' cared for by a worship service. I don't care how slick everything is. And worst of all, the mission of Christ ain't gettin' accomplished through the business that we designed and fabricated and dubbed the body of Christ. This 'body' that we're building is mostly composed of parts that apparently are unnecessary for the mission of Christ. And we're happy if those wandering, disconnected body parts just show up once a month with some cash. What kind of a sick body is that?"

Tom's eyes were like saucers as he watched his friend blow up his career before his very eyes. His heart was pounding, he was sweating, he was anxious, and yet he was proud.

"You're not making any sense, Jimmy," said Fletcher. "Now, I'm just trying to follow your reasoning here. You're saying because you're not preaching, not fulfilling your gift, that this ain't the body of Christ? I'm assuming, by your reasoning, that if you were preaching, then this would be the body of Christ. This is troubling, Jimmy. Deeply troubling. You got some kind of messiah complex, brother?"

"Guilty," said Jimmy in a defeated tone. "Not for a messiah complex, but for a Judas complex. I am deeply ashamed to admit that I sold Christ's call for the thirty pieces of silver that you and my dear ole dad threw at my feet. Jesus had shown me a better way, a much better way. He gave me a living picture of his body, and I walked away from it for the safety and security of IBM church 2.0. I guess I thought I could influence things back to Jesus, but what a miscalculation that was."

"So, this is your resignation?" asked Fletcher.

"I guess it is. It wasn't my plan, but, yes, I guess so." Jimmy paused for a few awkward seconds, and then asked, "How many weeks do you need from me to hand things off?"

"None, brother. I'll find a new monkey tomorrow. Please be gone by the end of the day. I'll have your crap shipped to you."

Click.

***

Ashraf was a muddle of emotions as he pulled the white Peugeot 206 into the Beihaghi parking lot. "So, you're certain you can handle this? You know that this will change everything."

"I know, I know, my love. But what can we do? We can't turn our backs on them. It's too late, anyway—I'll make it work, I promise," said Azima.

"We will make it work, my love. All right, here goes," he said as he exhaled deeply. "Let's go get them."

The thick air smelled of diesel as they walked past dozens upon dozens of buses tightly sandwiched together waiting for their next voyage into the drylands. They pushed through the glass doors of the bus terminal and began to scan the crowd. And within minutes they found them. Slumping on blue plastic chairs next to a newspaper stand were Ali and Fatimah Al-Khulani, looking much, much older than they had remembered.

"Papa, Mama, you're early," Azima said as she trotted over to her parents with outstretched arms.

"Azima, Ashraf," Ali replied, nodding his head.

"Mama, how was your journey?" Azima asked.

"It was good. Comfortable. The foods were good. Very good."

"Wonderful. The children are so excited about your coming," said Azima. "How's the farmstead, Papa?"

"Bah, we sold the last of the horses to a Saudi," said Ali. "Nothing to feed them. And the rich man gave me a nag's price for my princes. I should have shot him instead."

Ashraf's glance to Azima said everything. This was going to be an interesting season for the Hosseini family.

The forty-minute drive back to their house was uncomfortably quiet. Questions were answered tersely with as few words as possible, with no comments or questions returned. As they pulled in front of their house, Azima pointed to a hand-painted banner that was taped to their front door. It read, *Welcome Grandpapa and Grandmama.*

"Look," Azima said. "The children wanted you to feel at home."

A tear spilled out of Fatimah's moist eyes and ran down her weathered cheek as she sat quietly and took it in. "It is so beautiful, Azima. Thank you. Oh, how I've missed you, my dear."

"We've missed you too, Mama. And so have the children," Azima said just as the front door flew open, and Omar and Fatimah came bounding down the sidewalk to meet them.

An hour later and the luggage was delivered to their new bedroom—which was formerly Ashraf and Azima's—the house tour was complete, and the expanded family had squeezed themselves into the small parlor for some sweets.

"How are the horses, Grandpapa? Do you still have Big Blackie?" asked Fatimah.

"No horses, child."

"No horses? None at all? Not even Blackie?" Fatimah persisted.

"No horses. None."

Omar and Fatimah looked confused, both from their Grandpapa's answer and from the coolness with which it was delivered.

"It's all the fighting in our country, child," Grandmama explained. "There's nothing to eat. Nothing for people, and nothing for horses. The fighting has hurt everyone."

"Papa told us that things were not good in Yemen," said Omar. "We pray for you every night. But I thought it was just bad in the cities, not the farmstead. I love your farmstead. It's my favorite place in the world."

The sincerity and kindness of little Omar broke through the hardened shell of his grandfather. As Ali looked at his grandson's innocent face, the smallest smile surprised everyone by appearing on his face. Omar smiled back. Ali then tapped his thigh twice, and Omar instinctively jumped on his knee. "Oomph," he feigned. "You're as big as a goat," he said with a laugh.

"Come here, beautiful Fatimah," Grandmama said to her namesake as tears flooded down her face. "I need so many hugs."

The afternoon was not at all like Ashraf and Azima expected.

The children were glued to their usually distant grandparents, and they were loving every minute of it. Especially, and most unexpectedly, Ali.

After dinner and some more sweets, Ashraf rose from the table and announced, "It's almost seven, and I must go to work. I have to translate for an ambassador from Canada and his delegation. Please excuse me, dear family, and enjoy your evening together."

"An ambassador. My daughter married a sheik? I thought a sheik would have a bigger palace!" said Ali, clearly in a better mood.

"Not a sheik, Papa, I'm a prince."

"A prince?" said Ali, this time not laughing.

"Yes, a prince. It was you who made me a prince, Papa." Then gesturing toward Azima he said, "By giving me your beautiful princess."

Even though the ancient city of Tehran was settled over seven thousand years ago, it was not always the cultural and economic center of Persia. It wasn't until the twelfth century, after the Mongol hordes attacked the heart of Persia's power, the city of Rey, that Tehran began to find its place in history. Fleeing refugees who survived the massacre of Rey found shelter in the tiny village of Tehran, and soon it became a prosperous trading center.

By the mid-sixteenth century, Tehran's natural forests, clear rivers, and bountiful hunting grounds caught the attention of the Persian emperor, who fortified the city with a wall boasting 114 towers. He created elaborate vineyards and gardens, built infrastructure and roadways, and set the city on its prosperous trajectory. But it wasn't until the Qajar dynasty of the late eighteenth century that Tehran was chosen as Iran's 32nd capital city.

From that time, Tehran rapidly expanded, as it continued in its founding tradition of being a welcoming recipient to fleeing refugees from various troubled spots from neighboring regions. The city's metropolitan area now covered over 750 square miles with over 2,100 city parks and was home to over 15 million souls. And Rey was one of its suburbs.

"Dang," said Duane. "This place feels like home. I keep thinking I'm back in New York."

It was an impressive city, and Farah couldn't be prouder to show it off. Farah herself, however, was almost completely concealed. Like every other teenage girl, woman, and mannequin in the city, her head and form were appropriately covered. Riona, who was not used to wearing a scarf over her hair, fussed with its hem.

"It is a beautiful city, and an important one," said Francis. "And its importance requires us to end the tour for now and meet our contact back at the hotel. We have work to do."

Within thirty minutes, they were warmly greeted by hotel staff and found their usual table in the lobby restaurant.

"Remember, code words," whispered Yushua.

"Aye," said Campbell with a little grin. "So we can meet the family and tell them about our Boss and the new neighborhood he's building."

Everyone laughed. Everyone except Yushua.

"Better dial it back," corrected Francis, catching Yushua's cue. "For the sake of our family here, we don't need to stick out more than we have to."

A distinguished looking man dressed in a dark blue suit, crisp white shirt, and perfectly formed blue tie walked to their table.

"Mr. Murphy?"

"Yes. Francis, please. And you must be Ashraf, I presume?"

"Yes. Ashraf Hosseini. It's an honor to meet you, sir. I assume that we dispense with official protocol? For your security? We probably shouldn't draw extra attention to you."

"Without question. We're all family here."

For the next hour, over a feast of lamb, rice, and vegetables, Ashraf grew in his appreciation of the team's purpose, and the team grew in their understanding of the "family" context. Employing the important code words became more natural, even for Campbell; and an air of admiration soon blossomed for their persecuted family, who every day risked everything for the sake of their Boss and his business.

"Any advice you should give us before we meet the others?" asked Yushua.

"Well, yes. One thing, I think," said Ashraf. "I've never been to America, so I don't know how the family is there. But I think some things are different. Different in a way that we don't want to see in our family."

"I'm afraid you're right, brother. There are a few things about our family that shouldn't be exported," said Duane.

"Maybe," Ashraf continued. "What you must understand is that the family here is small. And those outside the family are many."

"So far it sounds about the same," said Duane.

"No, you don't understand," insisted Ashraf. "Because we are so small, we must have good relations throughout our family. We must work together as a family. We cannot have one member of the family feeling superior—feeling like he doesn't need the whole family. Every member of our family is vital, but none are sovereign. Does this make sense?"

"I think so," said Santiago as he eagerly leaned forward clasping his hands together. "We generally see our 'families' in America as independent agents that make decisions based on what is best for that individual 'family.' You're saying that is not how it is here. You're saying that families here make decisions—"

"I'm saying that our families are not independent," interrupted Ashraf. "They're interdependent. They're not sovereign nor autonomous. They have a Boss. They all have the same Boss. And that Boss doesn't give out competitive and contradictory orders to the many families. His orders bring the families together, into his business. One simple plan. One great commission. One business. And it is necessary for all the families to participate in that mission together."

"Well, isn't that a novel idea," quipped Campbell. "Suppose we can learn something for Philly? I think we might be as guilty as any other 'family' when it comes to independence. Maybe more so than some."

"You're not wrong, brother," said Yushua. "And we'll have to discuss this when we get back. But for now, Ashraf, what advice would you give us for the meeting?"

Ashraf drew a deep breath, and then gently spoke. "I mean no offense and no disrespect, but I was asked to say this by a city elder: please do not divide the families. Don't pick out one or two to bless. Every year, groups fly in and do exactly that, and every year, we're further behind because of it. You see, nobody used to make a living from the family business. But some were taught, taught by well-meaning teams like yourselves, that if they did what you asked, they could count on your support. So, one by one, many families have become sovereign—well, not really sovereign; they are owned by families in the West. And one by one, they've moved out of fellowship with the other families in the city to compete for more brothers. They had to compete, because 'their' family now must financially provide for their living."

The dinner ended, and Ashraf graciously excused himself after explaining some logistics for their upcoming summit. The team sat quietly around the table and reflected on what had just happened.

"So, who's the teacher here?" asked Riona. "Sure doesn't seem like us."

"We've got something to learn, no question about that," said Yushua. "But we also have something to give. That's why our Boss brought us here."

Francis, who had been largely silent up to this point, stretched his back and said, "And perhaps, just perhaps, this interdependence of families that we're learning about goes much beyond a city. Perhaps the global family has something to teach us."

"Yes, yes," said Farah. "And perhaps interdependence means that our mission in Philly," and then she corrected herself, "I mean, our Boss's mission in Philly, requires the families of Tehran."

Chapter Twenty-Six

The Bedouins

"I've got the evening, honey, the whole glorious evening."

"Been a while, hasn't it?" Chantel asked as she ripped open envelopes.

"Way too long. Bills?" asked Luca.

"What else comes in the mail? And our gas bill, I tell you what . . ."

"Don't you worry about it, sweetie. Go grab the couch. I'm cooking," Luca announced as he dropped his briefcase on the mudroom bench.

"You are? What are we having?" she asked with a big, beautiful smile.

"Barbeque," he said, waving a brown butcher paper package. My papa's pork steaks to be specific. Double sauced. Picked up some nice thick ones at Frenchy's."

"I tell you what, Sanders is going to be ticked; that's his favorite meal."

"Is he working?"

"Yeah, he picked up a couple extra shifts at the restaurant. He won't be home till past ten."

"The boy's got moxie, I'm proud of him. Maybe you'll save him a small one, honey. Maybe?" Luca said with a wink.

"You go tend to your fire, and don't you worry about what I eat, Mr. Lewis."

Luca laughed, and then headed directly outside.

He arranged a full bag of charcoal briquettes, stacked two high and covering the full bottom of his papa's old Oklahoma Joe. Like a company of little square coal soldiers in perfect formation, Luca followed his papa's methods to the letter. A quarter quart of lighter fluid later, and the fire was on. There was nothing left for Luca to do now but wait for them to start to ash up.

As Luca rested on a wicker patio chair that faced his backyard, he thought about nothing. Not about the Y. Not about Philadelphia Freedom. Not about the team in Tehran. Not about his family. In fact, his deepest thoughts at that moment were about pork steaks. And moments like that were rare.

Rare and fleeting.

"Your phone is ringing," shouted Chantel. "It's Jimmy from Atlanta. Want me to get it?"

Luca sighed, and then said unenthusiastically, "Yeah."

"Jimmy," Luca said as heartily as he could manage. "How are things in Bible central?"

"Ha!" Jimmy coughed, as Luca's greeting caught him unexpectedly. "More central and less Bible, I'm afraid."

Luca chuckled and then went straight to the point. "How can I help you, brother?"

"Not exactly sure, Luca. Just thought I might sound some stuff off of you. I really value your perspective."

"You value my perspective. Well, that is interesting. I'm not sure I realized that."

"I know, I know," was the response that came from a less self-assured version of Jimmy Norris. "I know, and I am sorry, Luca. I'm not sure what's wrong with me."

After several seconds of awkward silence, Luca asked once again, "How can I help you, brother?"

"I'm an idiot, Luca. A coward and an idiot. A fool."

"I have no rebuttal for you so far, Jimmy. Tell me what's going on."

"You know what's going on. I got scared. Scared of doing church in a way where I wasn't really in charge. Scared of my father. Scared that I'd fade away into obscurity."

"You still scared?"

"I am. But in a different way. Now I'm afraid that I've missed my one chance to be a part of something special. Afraid that I have wasted my life."

"Midtown Fellowship isn't special?"

"Oh, so not, Luca. It's worse than what we had at LifePointe."

"Dr. Fletcher didn't let you preach?"

"You saw that comin', I guess?"

"Had a hunch. Stage lust is a tough addiction for some folks to shake, and I was skeptical that he would want to share the spotlight."

"Yeah," was all Jimmy could say.

"So, you gonna quit?"

"Already done that, and he's already replaced me with a twenty-four-year-old intern from his church in Texas. Took him two whole days."

"Got tired of waiting, did you?" asked Luca.

"No, it wasn't that. It was Duane Harris."

"Duane?"

"Yeah, I went to visit him at APS and heard that he was in Philly with y'all. Ticked me off a little, to be honest. Then I heard he was going to Iran with y'all. That didn't feel good either. That really stung. And then Tom Butts woke me up. He said Duane Harris wasn't interested in our mission because our mission was too small of a thing for him. That's when the penny finally dropped for me, Luca, because I wasn't interested in our mission either. Hadn't been for a long time."

"Well, I must say, I think that Tom sized up Duane about right. He's growing like a weed because he's doing what he was built for. So, what's up Jimmy?"

"I need you to be honest with me, Luca. I need you to shoot straight. Where did I go off track? I mean, how did I make such a mess of things? I've basically been fired twice, and I'm no closer to figuring out church than before I met you."

"What do you think your problem is?" asked Luca.

"I dunno."

"Come on, Jimmy, let's be real. What's really your problem? Why aren't you getting it?"

"I'm not sure. Is it that I'm too programmed with the wrong ideas? Been doing church a certain way for most of my life. Can't break out of the box?"

"No," Luca said flatly.

"Maybe 'cause I've never really seen the real deal modeled up close? Never had a mentor?"

"Try again, Jimmy."

"Gosh, I don't know, Luca. Is it because I'm too weak to stand up to all the dark forces that were trying to blow me off track? Too weak to stand up to my father?"

"You're getting colder now, Jimmy."

"Well, you tell me then, Luca! You tell me! Why am I such a pathetic loser?" Jimmy was now sobbing, weeping as only a man who has lost all hope can. "Luca … I don't know what to do … I'm so lost …"

"Perfect," said Luca. "Those might be the most honest words I've ever heard come from your lips, my friend. Perfect. Because only a lost man can find his way to Jesus. And this has been your battle, Jimmy, I've seen it. You think that the church is a means to an end. And you are the end. Your reputation, your upwardly-mobile climb, you, you, you! But you see, Jimmy, you're not the end. It's never been about you. And your church isn't the end, either. Jesus' eternal kingdom is the only true end. And when you and your church are squattin' on Jesus' throne, it's a powerless, idolatrous, disgusting thing to see. You see, Jimmy, the body of Christ isn't a place or a time—it's Jesus working his will and his ways through his people. All of his people. Jesus gets his way in his church, or it's not his church; it's yours. It's just that simple. So, what's your problem, Jimmy?"

Luca waited as Jimmy formed various sounds and syllables, but no understandable words came. "It's okay, brother, take your time. We're good," said Luca.

After several failed attempts, words started to slowly flow. "I've been saying the right words, but my heart has been far from those words. I've been looking for a silver bullet. A shortcut. Looking for something that would get me back on top. It sounds so awful, I know how it sounds, but it's true. I'm a traitor, Luca, that's my problem. That's what's wrong with me."

"Ah, and there it is," said Luca. "You're a traitor. A weaselly, treacherous usurper of Jesus' throne. So let me ask you another question. Does Jesus forgive traitors, Jimmy?"

Jimmy offered nothing.

"Can Jesus use a traitor, Jimmy?"

Again, nothing but silence.

"Maybe we should ask Peter? Yes?" Luca poked gently. "That's probably enough for now, Jimmy. Want to talk in a few days?"

"Sure, okay."

"All right, buddy. But until then, do me a favor, would you?"

"Okay."

"Think about the end that you desire the most. You're in a good place now, brother. Stay there for a while. Just sit there. Bring your heart close to Jesus, so close that your heart has no will of its own. Think about the end that you want the most. And then let's talk."

Luca stood, slipped his phone into his front pocket, and walked to his Papa's old Oklahoma Joe. The little coal soldiers that once were red hot and sitting in perfect formation were now reduced to a powdery mat of cold, white, useless ash. Luca could see the irony and smiled.

"Honey?"

"Yes?"

"How do you feel about Olive Garden tonight?"

***

The avocado green taxicab inched slowly alongside a sea of yellow and green, carrying fares to work, shop, and explore Tehran's bustling business district. Dangling on a red lanyard from the rear-view mirror was the driver's credentials. Muhammad Madani, driver number 5730, appeared to be more of a street brawler than a chauffeur, but his incongruous soft-spoken demeanor soon put even the most skittish passenger at ease.

"Do you have business at Shandiz Mashad?" he asked.

Farah, who sat between Muhammad and Yushua, returned in Farsi, "Yes, we will be meeting some associates there for dinner. Have you eaten there before?"

"No, too expensive for a simple taxi driver."

"Oh dear," said Farah in English. "I hope we have not chosen a place too posh for our friends."

Francis, who was sitting in the backseat between Campbell and

Duane answered, "We will be honoring them. Ashraf was clear that we would be paying. We have the whole upper room to ourselves, and Ashraf assured me it will accommodate our needs. It'll be fine, Farah."

"Okay, thank you," said Farah as she let out a breath. "It's been so long since I've been among my people, and I've never been with my 'family' here before. I'm a bit off my game, I'm afraid."

"Are you here seeing family or business associates?" Muhammad questioned in perfect English.

"Umm, yes. Both. Some of my cousins are in our business," Farah answered, visibly shaken. "I have been away for many years."

"These are not your family, are they?" Muhammad gestured to her ethnically diverse companions who were traveling with her.

"No, no. These are my business associates from America. We have business here in Iran. Coffee. They wanted to meet my cousins while we were in Tehran."

"I see. Very nice friends," said Muhammad with a big smile.

The paying occupants of the green cab sat in silence as the car slowly crept its way through traffic toward Shandiz Mashad; each more painfully aware of the risk they were potentially putting Farah's "cousins" in. One wrong word to the wrong set of ears could have horrific ramifications to those who faithfully represented Christ in one of the world's most difficult places. And the gravity of that realization now weighed heavier on their shoulders.

"Here we are," said Muhammad in English, pointing to the meter.

"Thank you, sir," said Farah in Farsi as she pulled a fistful of rials from her purse. "Keep the change please, Muhammad . You've been a wonderful help."

Farah's associates all offered a generous "thank you" as they disembarked and made their way to the restaurant's doorman who immediately ushered them to a well-dressed maître d'.

"We have a 7 p.m. reservation. GroundWorx," said Farah.

"Ah, yes. Your guests have arrived. They're waiting upstairs. Allow me."

The maître d' escorted them through the restaurant to the back wall that led to a glass and steel staircase, and then up the stairs to a room dotted with a dozen white round tablecloths.

"Here you are. I trust you will enjoy your evening."

"Thank you," said Farah. "It is a beautiful room."

A small crowd of about twenty men who were standing in three or four groupings halted their conversations as they looked at the foreigners. Some were smiling, some were not, but all were measuring their hosts.

"Welcome, brothers, welcome Farah," said Ashraf Hosseini as he broke from the crowd and made his way to the Americans, giving warm handshakes to all. "We are so blessed to have you come and be with us."

Francis responded in surprisingly good Farsi with, "It is our honor. Thank you all for joining us this evening. May our fellowship be sweet and may it honor the One true God."

Most in the room seemed surprised and somewhat pleased to see a redheaded foreigner speaking in their mother tongue. Heads nodded and murmurs of approval resounded in the room.

Yushua took a step forward and said in near-perfect Farsi, "Yes, I join my colleague Francis in thanking you for meeting us today. We are all in the same business, and we all have the same Boss. And in that spirit, we come to you this evening not as supervisors, but as servants. We want to learn from you as to how the business goes in Tehran. And if we have some tools that could help the business, our Boss wants us to freely share them."

Again, the men seemed startled to see someone whose facial features were obviously not Iranian yet spoke so well in their language. Stern faces started to soften, and smiles began to emerge on faces that seemed undecided only moments ago.

“It is so good to be home,” said Farah, smiling and clasping her hands together. Her features, accent, and the way she carried herself immediately told this gathering that she was from Iranian wealth. “It has been many years since I have been home in Tehran, and so much has happened since I left. My family was eradicated, and I became a refugee—but it was in that struggle I found my true purpose. Now I join you in the business. And they join us as well.” She gestured behind her. “Santiago is from Chile, Campbell and Riona are from Ireland, and Duane is from America. All of us, your servants.”

Smiles tempered with an unexpected amazement grew on the faces of the men. They had endured and humored numerous such gatherings over the years, but the posture of these foreigners was decidedly different. There was no sense of smugness or superiority lurking under a thin spiritual disguise in these visitors. Instead, a spirit of true humility and admiration was what they unconsciously projected. And even though all were very aware that a UN Ambassador was in their midst, there was not an inkling of pride shown by the visitors. Respect, admiration, and solidarity was the only message being conveyed.

An elderly man in a rumpled gray suit stepped forward and began to speak in Farsi. “My name is Farzin Shah,” Ashraf interpreted. “And I have been in ‘the business,’ as you say, for over forty years. Like many in this room, I bear the marks of the work on my body and in my spirit. I am now called an elder of the city, even though I know I limp in many ways—physically, emotionally, spiritually …” his voice trailed off as his gaze cast to his feet. “But I must say something. Something I don’t think that you understand in America. Here in Iran, we are one ‘business,’ as you say. We have only one ‘Boss.’ And we do not want to be divided. We do not want to be separated from one another by you showing some favor and some others not. Together we are the body. And when separated, the 'business' is not helped—it is impeded. And so, please, I beg you, please do not divide the body in Tehran. Let us decide whether your tools are helpful, and if they are, let's make them available to all." He paused a second or two and then said, "I hope that I have not offended you, because I see our 'Boss' living in each of you."

"You have not offended us, dear brother," said Yushua. "You have spoken a truth we needed to hear. A truth we need to rediscover back in our homeland. And I think that whatever gift we might give you in the future, it will be a small thing compared to the gift you are giving us right now. So, thank you for speaking a truth that we needed to hear for our business back home. And please help us to honor your request—we have much unlearning, much repenting to do before it becomes a natural way for us."

"Ameens" resounded across the room as a spirit of camaraderie now fully replaced the air of suspicion that was there only moments before. Ashraf directed all to sit—one "guest" at each table—and each was to share about how they saw the business going.

After four courses and about ninety minutes of lively discussion, Ashraf rose from his table and thanked all for coming. One by one the brothers hugged one another, hugged their new friends, and made their way down the steel and glass staircase.

"That went so much better than I expected," said Ashraf. "I will meet with the elders tomorrow evening to see what our next step should be. But thank you, thank you for your humble posture. My brothers did not expect it—and it made all the difference."

"How could there be anything but humility in us when we know the price that these dear saints pay for following Christ?" asked Yushua.

"It is not as common of a response as you might expect, Yushua," said Ashraf. "In fact, they're conditioned for an entirely different attitude."

"That's sad. 'Tis a shame," said Campbell.

"You're right, brother. Embarrassing if you ask me," said Santiago. As he put on his jacket, he asked, "So, what's next, Ashraf? What should be our next steps?"

"I will meet with the elders tomorrow night and see. They will pray and decide."

"And so, we …" prompted Campbell.

"And so, you," said Ashraf, "are invited to come to our house for lunch tomorrow. We don't have a large house, but Azima and I would love for you to join us."

"Azima?" repeated Yushua, somewhat startled. "That would be a rare name in Iran, wouldn't it?"

"Yes, for sure. My bride isn't from here. I met her as a young man when I traveled for my father's carpet business."

"Really? Where is she from?" persisted Yushua.

"Azima's family is from Yemen. A small village in the mountains near Dharma."

"Dharma," said Yushua, looking surprised. "Her family made Persian carpets?"

"No, no. It's a long story, but the short version is that my father helped sell her family's horses to high-end breeders in Europe and the US. Beautiful Arabians. We ended up learning the horse business and then …"

Yushua took a step back, tried to speak but couldn't. He sputtered and slurred but nothing intelligible came out. His eyes were wide, confused, dazed, curious, and angry. His pulse raced as his clammy face grew pink and white and red all at once. Ears ringing, the room began to spin.

As he reached for the back of a chair to steady himself, Francis grabbed his arm. “Yushua?”

***

Jimmy clicked his ballpoint pen over and over while staring blankly at the phone that sat on his patio table.

“You gonna call him soon?” asked Tom. “’Cause you ’bout wore out that pen.”

“Tough call to make, Tom. Not sure he’s gonna like it, and even if he does, it means going back to the beginning.”

“Actually, way before the beginning,” corrected Tom. “It’s going back to a place where I don’t think we’ve ever been. Ground zero. Call him, Jimmy.”

“Gaaa, okay.” Jimmy flicked through his phone, found what he was looking for, and pressed down with his thumb. “Here goes ...”

“Hello, Jimmy.”

“Hey, Luca, thought I’d reach out. You got a few minutes?”

“Sure, brother, what’s up?”

“Lemme put you on speaker phone, got Tom with me. Is that okay?”

“Sure. Hey, Tom.”

“Hey Luca, been a while since we’ve talked.”

“Sure has, Tom. Are you doing okay?”

“Think so. You?”

“Fine, fine. So, what’s up, fellas?”

Tom looked at Jimmy as if to say, “Get on with it!” Jimmy paused, and then leaned forward until he was inches away from his phone, and said, “Uncle. Luca, that’s our decision. Uncle.”

“Say what?”

“We give up, Luca. Tom and I. Our wives, too. We give up. We all give up. You know how you said I should get my heart into such a condition that it has no will of its own?"

"Yes."

"I'm not sure, but maybe I've gotten there. Gotten there for the first time in my life. Every decision I've made in my life, I've made with an agenda—what will be best for me, my career, my finances, and on and on. It's always been me, myself, and mine. But I want to make a different decision right now. A decision that is biased by a different agenda: what is best for Jesus' kingdom."

"Well, that's progress for sure, Jimmy. So, what's the decision?"

Jimmy took a deep breath, exhaled, and then shaped his lips to form the most difficult sentence of his life. "I want you to take me, Luca. Take us. Take us all. We want to move to Philly and unlearn what we know. Unlearn and repent. We need new minds. Before I can learn something new, before we can learn something new, we must unlearn and blow up what we thought we knew. I haven't …" Jimmy corrected himself. "We haven't been able to accept Jesus' teachings of his kingdom because they didn't fit our religious forms."

"So, 'Uncle' you say? What does that mean to you—exactly?" asked Luca.

"I don't, I mean, we don't know. I think what we're saying, Luca, is that our history shows that we need to be rewired. Reworked. And we have to unplug ourselves from the system that we know in order to learn a new way. We need to understand repentance, and to do that, we need you, and your people. We need you to disciple us."

"And who's paying for this rewiring?"

"We don't want to be a burden, Luca. We will find jobs. Join the community—not as experts but as novices. And maybe in time we can be of some use to y'all."

"Okay, Jimmy. Okay, Tom. Under a couple of conditions."

"What's that?" asked Jimmy.

"If it is really 'Uncle' that you're sayin', I need you to do one more thing, Jimmy, to prove to yourself that this is true repentance. I need you to call your daddy and tell him so. I don't need you to tell him off, but I do need you to tell him what you're doing, and why you're doing it. I don't 'spect he'll understand, but you've got to put your hand to the plow and not look back, for once in your life. You've looked back too many times before. Your daddy has some kind of hold on you that makes you shrink back from Jesus' kingdom. Can you do that?"

"Honestly, Luca, that is my next call. Needed to make sure that we were good first."

"Good, good. Tom, I got something for you to do as well."

"Okay," Tom said hesitatingly.

"This isn't for me, Tom; this is for you."

"Okay."

"Tom, you can't come. You need to stay in Atlanta. You need to discover how much Jesus loves you, my brother. Discover that he loves you—apart from Jimmy. You need to hear his voice speaking to you, and through you. You are more than a loyal friend, Tom; you are a hand-chosen priest by Jesus Christ himself. You are a good man, Tom Butts. One of the best men I know. But you can be more than that, much more. You can be dangerous for his kingdom. But as long as you're Jimmy's ole faithful sidekick, that'll never happen."

Silence was Tom's response. Tears welled up in his eyes and spilled onto his full cheeks and ran down his neck.

"Tom?" nudged Luca.

Nothing, only more silence. Tom sniffled and snorted and finally managed to gain enough composure to voice a question, "What should I do in Atlanta, Luca?"

"Ask Jesus, Tom. And maybe you and Duane Harris can pray about that one together. Tom … ?"

"I'm sad," said Tom, "but I know that you're not wrong. It's been easy to live in Jimmy's shadow—but easy ain't necessarily living, I get that. I'll do this, Luca. It's a sacrifice in some ways, and freedom in other ways."

"Sacrifice and freedom are two sides of the same coin, aren't they, Tom? I'm proud of you, brother. Dangerous Tom is what I'm callin' you from now on. Dangerous Tom Butts. Jimmy, you good?"

"Yes sir. I'm sad too but agree with Tom—you're not wrong. I liked having Tom in my corner but never really thought how the shadow I was casting was keeping him from becoming a kingdom warrior himself."

"Okay, friends," said Luca, "this has been one call I won't soon forget."

"Me either," said Tom.

"Ditto," said Jimmy. "Not in a hundred years."

After they disconnected the call, Jimmy and Tom sat quietly for a few seconds, rehearsing in their minds what had just taken place.

"Are you okay with this, Tommy?"

"I am. I know it sounds kinda weird, but I'm sorta excited. It's like I'm a kid going out on his own for the first time."

"That's good," said Jimmy. "Hey, brother, I'm sorry for hiding you in a corner, not letting you stretch and grow."

"Shush, Jimmy. It was my choice. I liked being in your corner—it was safe. But until Luca mentioned it, I never knew that 'safe' was keeping me from Jesus. My fault, not yours."

The two old friends hugged with a new and deeper sense of love and respect for one another. They knew that these next few weeks before Jimmy moved would be a fleeting season, and in some ways, they really didn't want things to change. But things would change, and it would be good. After a minute or two, they sat back down in their patio chairs and looked up at the night sky.

"Clear night, isn't it," said Tom.

"In so many ways, Tom. In so many ways."

"Well, I guess I better go and break the news back home," said Tom in a foreboding tone. "Not sure how this is gonna go."

"I can imagine," said Jimmy as he thumbed through his phone. "Mind staying a few more minutes? I think I'm gonna need you in my corner one more time."

"Hello, Daddy ..."

***

The cab chugged past row after row of white concrete apartment complexes, each one more unremarkable than the last. The only distinguishing characteristic that separated them was the era of their last white paint job. White upon white, interrupted only with green splashes of oak, beech, linden, and hornbeam trees. From a distance, it was breathtaking and fitting for a prized painting in any number of gift shops. But only from a distance.

"Valiasr Road is next. 16581, correct?" said the cabdriver through a smudged perforated plexiglass partition.

"Yes, thank you," said his nervous passenger.

The taxi came to a stop in front of a rowhouse complex, and Yushua tipped the driver generously.

"Thank you, boss."

"Thank you, Ahmed," said Yushua as he closed the door and apprehensively strode to the front door and rang the bell.

Ashraf answered with a broad smile. "Yushua Maalouf, are you feeling better? I hope it wasn't food poisoning—you looked so bad."

"I'm fine, thank you, brother. Something didn't agree with me, but all is well."

"Where are Francis and the others?" asked Ashraf. "I thought they were joining us?"

Yushua, ignoring his question, craned his neck around the entrance way, to see if he could see Azima. Nothing. "Your wife is not home today?"

"She will be home before long. The children have a half day at school, so she went to pick them up."

"Children? How many?" asked Yushua.

"We have two, a boy and a girl—and they keep us busy, brother. Do you have children?"

"No, I've never married. Maybe someday," said Yushua. "Your wife's name is Azima, correct? A Yemeni from Dharma?"

"You have a good memory. You were so sick when I was speaking of her, I'm surprised you recall those details. Yes, she is from a farmstead that was in the mountains of the Dharma region."

"And they raised Bedouin Arabians?"

"Exactly. Beautiful animals—honestly, some of the best in the world." And then Ashraf held for a second. "Did I mention Bedouins? I don't usually get that specific."

Yushua, ignoring his probe, pressed forward. "And how long have you been married?"

"Um, fourteen years. Almost fifteen."

"That is good, brother. That is a worthy accomplishment. And is Azima good with the fact that you follow Isa?"

"Yes, absolutely. She loves him, too. We have followed Isa for almost all of our married years. God has been gracious to us."

"And how did Azima become a disciple?" pressed Yushua as the interrogation continued, and then quickly added, "And you too, of course, brother?"

As Ashraf started to answer, the sound of laughing children could be heard approaching the door.

"Here they are," he said as he rose to unlock the door.

A boy, eleven or twelve years old, skipped into the parlor wearing a blue and white school uniform, and on his heels was his sister, perhaps seven or eight, who immediately ducked behind his brother when she saw the stranger.

"Papa, is this one of the men from America?" asked the boy who struggled to stand erect while his sister clutched onto the back of his school jacket.

"Yes, yes, this is Mr. Maalouf. Mr. Maalouf, this is Omar. And hiding behind him is our brave daughter, Fatimah. Come say 'hello' to Mr. Maalouf, children."

Omar walked forward, towing his sister behind him.

"Pleased to meet you, Mr. Maalouf," Omar said, politely extending his hand.

Yushua reached his hand out and clasped Omar's but said nothing. He stared at the boy's face, and the face of the little girl that was peering out from under Omar's armpit, but he offered no greeting. Tears were forming in Yushua's eyes as his top lip began to quiver.

"Are you okay, mister?" asked Omar.

"Yes, sorry," Yushua sputtered. "You're such handsome children. So big and strong and healthy. Fatimah, you look just like your beautiful mother."

"You've met Azima?" asked Ashraf in a disconcerted tone.

"Yes," Yushua said, as he wiped his eyes and nose with his shirt sleeve. "Where is she?"

Troubled by the substance and manner of Yushua's answer, Ashraf still managed to maintain his diplomatic decorum and politely answer his question. "She'll be here in a minute; she's just helping her parents out of the car."

And as quickly as warm loving emotions washed over Yushua, a cold wave of anger suddenly overtook and smothered his blissful mood.

"Her parents are here? They're here in Tehran? Staying with you?" he asked sharply, sounding more like an accusation than an inquiry.

"Yes," Ashraf answered uneasily. "The famine and civil unrest in Yemen forced them off their land. They will stay with us for a while."

Suddenly, voices could be heard coming from the open front door. Azima's voice was soft and sweet, encouraging and full of life. The old man's was its opposite. Cold, flat, weak. And the old woman's was, unlike her former czarina self, quiet.

"Azima, meet our guest from America. The ambassador could not come, nor the others, but we are honored to have Mr. Yushua Maalouf with us."

Azima, who was distracted by her parents' slow descent into the parlor, offered a hand and a quick glance to Yushua. "Pleased to meet you, Yushua."

"Likewise, Azima. It is so good to see you."

"Please excuse me for a moment. I must help my parents to their room for a nap."

Yushua watched a version of his family pass in front of him. An unfamiliar version. His sister looked somewhat the same to him but older, much older than he expected, appearing more like his memories of his mother than any remembrance he had of her. And his parents, as they shuffled around the corner toward the hallway, seemed like entirely different people than the ones he once knew. He had forgiven them so many times before, and yet anger toward them would still surface at the most unexpected times. Forgiveness for his parents, especially for his father, was a constant battle and not a singular event. Yet as he watched this old couple ambling to their room for a nap, his anger mysteriously lifted. Instead of resentment, sadness and regret descended and filled its spot. So much had been taken from him—he had now lived almost as much of his life hidden from his family than embraced by them. So much was taken from him, so much was taken from them all. This feeling of sadness and regret was not an unfamiliar emotion for him—it often came after the work of forgiveness. But this was a different kind of sorrow. For the first time, it wasn't directed to his own loss but to that of his parents.

Why do I feel such empathy for a father who killed his children? he wondered. This reaction was strange and unfamiliar and mostly unwanted.

"So sorry for being such a rude host," said Azima as she walked in and started straightening the sofa pillows. "This is all new to my parents. They've only been with us for a couple of days."

"Azima," Yushua said.

"Yes?"

"Azima. Don't you remember me?"

She squinted as she gazed at her unfamiliar houseguest, and yet as she took him in, her countenance slowly shifted toward wonder and astonishment. "Om—" she stopped herself.

"Azima, it's me."

"Omar," she whispered, pressing her hands against her face. "It can't be," she said, as her legs gave out, and she landed on her knees.

"Yes, Azima, it's me … Omar."

"But you, you, you, and Fatimah …" Tears streamed down her face as something she dared not believe came true. "I knew, Omar, I knew. I had a dream or a vision or a heavenly visitor. The little girl said that Fatimah was with Isa, but that Isa sent Omar …"

Ashraf stared from his wife to Yushua with his mouth open.

He'd thought there was something strange about the way Yushua had been acting, but he couldn't quite believe what he was now witnessing.

"Yes, sister. I saw our sister Fatimah die. She was shot with many other disciples in Dhamar. I was imprisoned and the visitor, the little girl, rescued me from the prison, and said that Isa was sending me."

"And I thought that I was all alone," Azima said as she stood with unsteady legs to hug her lost brother with an embrace that had to somehow make up for all the lost years.

"All alone?" said Omar. "What do you mean by 'all alone'?"

"You and Fatimah disappeared, Omar, and then less than two weeks later, our older brother, Ali …" More tears trickled down her cheeks as she shut her eyes tightly.

"Yes, what about Ali?"

"We found him in the stables. He …"

"He killed himself, Yushua … I mean, Omar," interjected Ashraf, sparing his wife from having to say the terrible words out loud. "He hung himself."

"Our house was so empty. So empty …" Azima said as her thoughts drifted. "So, Omar, Isa sent you to the United States?" she asked while wiping her face with her apron.

"After some time in a refugee camp, yes, he did. I have been in the US for nearly fifteen years."

"Working for Isa?"

"I think so. Things started out differently than I expected, but Isa had a perfect plan. It has been an amazing journey, sister."

Azima walked to the fireplace and opened a wooden box that sat on the mantel. Reaching inside it, she pulled out the tattered and taped and hand-sewn rag of a Bible.

"Remember this one, brother?"

She handed it to Omar. Omar gently opened it and looked at the worn pages that he had memorized. He thought of his days with Fatimah by the brook as together they dreamed of Isa's kingdom. He thought of the courageous disciples who were butchered alongside Fatimah. He thought of his suffering in prison, and of his dear fellow prisoners who gave him everything they had. He thought of Yushua and Francis and Luca, each who showed him so much of Isa's kingdom. And now he thought of Azima, and Ali. And of his father and mother. Overcome with emotion, he collapsed on the floor and wept.

"What happened?" said Ali Al-Khulani as he hurried into the parlor. "Why is this man crying? What happened?"

Azima helped her brother to his feet and wiped his face with her hands.

"Papa," she said, "this is your son, Omar."

"Don't be foolish, daughter."

"Papa, look at him. Look past the scars and the crooked nose. Look at him."

Ali Al-Khulani took slow, uneasy steps toward his son. Squinting through his eyeglasses, he focused on the stranger's face. And then, just as with Azima, his expression wondrously softened. He touched Omar's face with his old, weathered hands, and then gently whispered, "Son?"

"Papa," Omar whispered back.

"Where have you been, my son? Where have you been for all these years?"

"You do not know, Papa?"

"No, how could I? I looked for so many years, but I gave up looking. We thought you were dead."

"Someone killed Fatimah and tried to kill me. For so many years I thought it was you, Papa."

"Me? Why would I kill my children?"

"Forgive me, Papa, I don't know. It was someone who knew our family. The executioner had our family picture from our parlor."

And then Ali Al-Khulani lifted his face to the ceiling and closed his eyes tightly, and with tight lips and trembling hands, he reached for his wallet. With shaky, thick fingers, he carefully unfolded a yellowed piece of lined paper.

"I've never let anyone see this before. I was always afraid to believe it was true. Read it."

Omar read it to himself. More tears ran down his face. "Oh no. Oh no," was all he could say.

"What does it say?" asked Azima.

Omar took a long, deep breath and then exhaled slowly. "It says, *I am so sorry, Papa and Mama. I never meant for things to go like this. It should be me and not them. It's all my fault. Please forgive me. Ali.*"

Silence hung thick and heavy in the parlor after that. No one spoke. No one moved.

After several minutes, Ali Al-Khulani refolded the note and placed it back in his leather wallet. He sat down and looked at his son.

"Tell me, Omar, my son, where have you been all these years?"

"I've been living in the United States, Papa."

"The United States. And what have you been doing there?"

A shaky voice coming from the hallway interrupted Omar before he could form an answer. It was Fatimah Al-Khulani Sr., Omar's mother, who was lifting her calloused, weathered hands to the ceiling. "Omar, my Omar …" She struggled to speak through her tears. "Ali, it's our Omar. He has been serving Isa. Isa al-Masih sent our good boy. And our beautiful daughter, Fatimah, is with Isa now. This I know."

Epilogue

"Thanks for coming over. I really needed this," said Chantel, twirling her necklace. "Isn't it amazing to think about all that's happened because of this little piece of jewelry? I wear it every day as a reminder."

"It changed my life. Totally changed my life. The 'little man' has become everything to me," said Brenda. "I cannot imagine how I would be dealing with this cancer as a single mom without Jesus and our church family."

Chantel reached across her kitchen table and clutched Brenda's hands. She looked into her eyes and said, "Sweetheart, we are here for you. You and Rhonny both. And whatever comes, you'll never be a single mom—because we will always walk with you, and you know that our Jesus will never leave your side. Not ever."

Brenda sniffled and smiled, brushed away tears with her thumbs, and said, "Thank you, Chantel. You and Luca mean the world to me. I better go though; I need to be back when Rhonny gets home from school."

"Of course, of course. Please be sure to give that precious girl a big ole hug from her auntie Chantel."

Chantel walked her longtime friend to the door, and after warm farewells, went into the kitchen and pulled three loaves of freshly baked bread out of her oven. She placed them on wire racks on her kitchen counter to cool, and then picked up her journal and curled up on her favorite chair by the window. Her heart was so full, and so she did what was most natural to her. She worshipped with a grateful spirit.

With her readers perched on the bridge of her nose, she stared out the window and thought about the life they'd lived since meeting Brenda. It had been just about fourteen years since Luca had purchased the necklace from the jewelry shop down the street. She thought about the Mt. Pisgah Bible study that she tried to revive, and the hardness of the people's hearts. She thought about the ice storm, and all they learned through it about belonging and believing and then behaving. She thought about Campbell and Riona, Santiago and Maggy and Sophia, and Yushua and the powerful ways that they had impacted her family. She thought about their excitement and then their disappointment with Jimmy and Tom—and how they were now back in their lives, this time on more solid ground.

And then her thoughts drifted to her late father-in-law, Pastor Lewis—the one who first saw this beautiful kingdom vision they were living. He was the one who saw with the clear eyes of faith, and then spoke bold faith into the hearts of a few. A small remnant. But he never got to see the fruit himself. *Papa would have loved Brenda*, she thought. *She is living proof that he was right all along.*

And she looked at the brown recliner and thought about her husband. The man of her dreams who became so much more to her than she had ever dreamed. *Papa would be so proud of Luca. The boy who never "fit in" in church is now leading a global disciple-making movement.* And then she beamed as she looked out at the driveway. *And he'd just love that Sanders is driving his ole Olds.* She closed her eyes in wonder as she soaked in God's grace that had been so generously lavished on her family. "Thank you, Jesus," she whispered.

Grateful tears ran down her face as she crossed her legs, opened her journal, and began to write:

> *It seems that God is never truly finished writing our stories. He stretches and grows us into fuller beings, molding us into the very image of Jesus through both our successes and our failures. If we allow him. Sometimes he pushes us further and deeper into community with those around us, while other times we must leave the comfort of what we've always known to become who we were always meant to be. For this one thing I learned to be true: following Jesus means that we never stay the same.*

She reread her words and immediately thought of Jerome and Choyz and Kofe and Angelica, and then Tom Butts. Men and women who had so much to give, and yet who spent so many years waiting on the sidelines. With those faces in her mind, she wrote:

> *There are those of us who find solace in hiding in the shadows of others, forgetting it is our own blooms that need the sun. We must remember that our Father had good purposes for breathing his life into ours, and with that breath of divine redemption, we are grafted into a body that has no unnecessary or extraneous parts. And so, there is not one of us who is not in need of walking into the light we have, as we are tenderly guided by the reassuring timbre of his gentle voice. For it is in that walk of faith that we can truly experience his pleasure.*

Chantel paused from writing, and once again stared out the window as she replayed the whole Atlanta ordeal in her mind. It had left scars. Yushua, and Luca, and Tom, and now Jimmy. They were all wounded by other leaders who viewed themselves as indispensable to Jesus' mission. Leaders who, in many ways, saw themselves as the very focus of the mission. And then she clicked her pen again and continued to write:

There are still others of us who burn under the light of too much sun, forgetting that sometimes we must allow others their moments to shine. The warmth of the spotlight, for some, has become both their security and their identity. And in the process, they have recklessly seized Jesus' mission as their own. But when we stop and look to our left and our right, we will always see a greater body ready for their turn; one that has been patiently waiting for us to equip and nudge, rather than entertain and ignore. But for this, we must first loosen our grasp, acknowledging that the mission has never been ours.

Chantel closed her eyes and smiled, offering another prayer of thanksgiving for the words she had been given and the reality of seeing them beautifully lived out through the people of Philadelphia Freedom. What a staggering difference it was from all the empty years they had endured at Mt. Pisgah. Her heart swelled with gratitude to her heavenly Father for his patience and grace, and for the courage of a few who would dare to seek a better kingdom.

And then she wrote:

And then there are those, like my husband's sweet papa, and Luca himself, and our amazing Yushua, and even Jimmy and

Tom, who have been both burdened and blessed. Who have seen and who cannot unsee. Who have craned and stretched and peered above the colorless and indistinguishable haze into the heavenlies, and for whom that blissful visage always, always remains. To these, it has become an indelible and enduring revelation that cannot be easily dismissed.

And for Chantel, these words expressed exactly the way things were. For when she saw a better way, there was nothing appealing about what she had known. And although the narrow way was a much more difficult road, it was only on this path where she experienced the wonder of Jesus' kingdom being revealed around her. Much like giving birth to Sanders, pain and blessing were two sides of the same kingdom reality.

And the pain was more than worth it.

Grateful tears ran down Chantel's cheeks, as images of broken lives wondrously restored ran through her mind like an old newsreel. Though sometimes, when she was in the midst of the valley, she honestly wondered about the cost. But deep down, even in her darkest days, she always knew the cost was worth paying.

Squinting through thankful tears, she wrote:

And for our family, and for Yushua's family, the blessing of sight became a burden. A true burden. And the burden of that revelation, in the end, though often appearing more curse than gift, was indeed a blessing of the highest order. A blessing for many. And like fire in our bones, our determined obedience has illuminated a greater, more eternal story, and we have all found our fitting place within it. And though it was never easy, it has always been altogether good.

Chantel smiled a beautiful smile as she sat alone, gazing out of the window. Her beaming face glowed as she remembered the stories that Jesus had rewritten in so many lives. And as she reflected on those stories, her heart instinctively shifted to the ones yet to be written.

And with pen in hand, she began to intercede.

"And I lift up Jimmy to you, Father, and Tom, and their families, and the countless others just like them. Those whose next small step is known. Those who have experienced the bewildering grace of our gentle yet persistent Revealer—that they might demonstrate their true belief through yielded obedience."

And then she looked out her window and down her busy street. Though Jesus had done so much, it was only the beginning. It had to be. There was so much more following of him to do. His kingdom needed to find a place in so many more homes in her neighborhood. And so, before walking outside to deliver freshly baked bread to her new neighbor across the street, she wrote: *But for us, what is unknown and uncharted and undiscovered is the wondrous and eternal story that awaits to be written on the other side of our next step.*

Chantel clicked her pen and flipped her journal closed and then set it down on the arm of her favorite chair. She stood and took a small step toward the window, closed her eyes, and felt the warmth of the sun streaming against her face. Her heart was so full and peaceful and at rest, and without uttering a word, she lifted her face in a spontaneous attitude of worship. So much unmerited favor had been showered on her family. She had seen more than her pastor and father-in-law had ever described from Mt. Pisgah's pulpit or even spoke about around their family dinner table. She had seen more than her husband had ever expressed as he painted his beautiful pictures of their future in the hearts and minds of so many hungry disciples. And she had even seen more than her own spirited imagination had ever dared to revel in as she dreamed of what could be. She had experienced a different kind of church. One with the power to turn an upside-down world upside-right, as Jesus got his way in yielded life after yielded life. She had seen, firsthand, the *body of Christ* looking and behaving like the *person of Christ*.

She had seen Jesus' kingdom.

And once you see …

Acknowledgments

Pastors Jack Conner and Henry Blackaby: thank you for showing me at a young age what Jesus' church looks like when the kingdom of God is her sole ambition. You helped me see in a way that I could never unsee—nor would I want to.

Laura, my beautiful bride and co-conspirator: thank you for your willingness to walk by faith through many seasons and adventures—your walk with Jesus always inspires me. Thank you for selflessly allowing me to burn the candle at both ends for the months it took to write this novel. I love you.

Pastors, church planters, and missionaries from the global church: thank you for your patience with us in the West. My life has been enriched and altered by the testimony of your faithful and courageous witness. This is your season in history. You are our teachers. We are beginning to see.

Anna Robinson and colleagues at 100 Movements Publishing: you are a unicorn in the publishing industry—your purpose drives your passion. Your passion for Jesus' kingdom made this novel better. I have nothing but the utmost respect and admiration for you and your team.

Alan Hirsch: you have helped many see that the person of

Christ and the body of Christ should bear a far greater resemblance. Thank you for your friendship and prophetic voice. Your life's influence in this story is evident.

Connie Taillon, Barb Kennedy, Peter Roebbelen, Brad Klinck, Daniel Yang, Tony Lynn, David Nickerson, Vance Pitman, and Brian Bloye: thank you for your helpful feedback in the writing process—it really made a difference.

And my much older and wiser sister, Cathy Yinger, who also grew up under Pastors Jack and Henry's influence, and who, with her husband, Ken, have given themselves away to Jesus' kingdom in foreign lands: thank you for your heavy lifting on this project. You've been my teacher for as long as I can remember.

What Did You Think of *Once You See*?

First of all, thank you for reading *Once You See*. As you probably noticed, the story's themes have long captured my heart, and as a result, the writing of this novel was at times both emotionally excruciating and spiritually exhilarating. The power of story, in my opinion, is a much too neglected medium in helping us see and feel a better future.

So, I hope that the story added value in as much as it helped you see and feel the substantial difference between a church centered on itself, and one centered on the kingdom. If so, it would be incredible if you could share this book with your friends and family by posting to Facebook, Instagram, and Twitter.

If you enjoyed this book and found some benefit in it, I'd personally like to hear from you and hope that you could take some time to post a review on Amazon. Your feedback and advocacy will be the most powerful way to help get the message out.

Gratefully,

Jeff Christopherson

Discussion Guide

Thank you for taking the time to read this story and to engage in discussion with others. My hope is that we all continue to rediscover the original design of Jesus' church so that the body of Christ might more closely resemble the person of Christ. Such a profound shift will require us to move away from a Sunday-centric primacy to becoming an interdependent community, devoted exclusively to Jesus' redemptive gospel mission.

In the story's scene where the prisoners are ministering to one another, we begin to see a beautiful picture of Jesus' church. Day by day, they prepared one another for faithfulness through the suffering they knew was coming with each knock on the door. Hussein Nazari's last words, "I am ready sir," give us a poignant picture of the power of Jesus' community in preparing our faith for the inevitable tests, trials, and temptations that come to our lives. It seems we are most like Jesus when we find ourselves surrounded by his people and propelled by his priorities.

I have had the joy of meeting Christ followers like Hussein and Yushua; people who have experienced the body of Christ in the microwave of intense persecution; disciples of Jesus who have had extraordinarily little to unlearn about the nature of Jesus' church because there was no margin for lesser things. Meeting these faithful giants has served to humble me and, like Luca, revealed some of my own wrong motives, and, like Jimmy, showed my own selfish desire for an easier way. I am different because of people like Hussein and Yushua. And I want to be.

There are no heroes in this story but Jesus. It is true that Yushua had extraordinarily little to unlearn, and Luca had less to unlearn than Jimmy. But what they had in common is that they all needed others to gain a truer perspective. So, this novel, and the discussion that follows is for all of us Yushuas, Lucas, and Jimmys. For wherever we start from, we only make spiritual progress when, through mutual interdependence, Jesus becomes the hero of our story.

So, it's no accident that Duane was led to Jesus when Jimmy was going through difficult and disorientating spiritual growing pains. In a similar way, Christ will most profoundly impact others as you share your true and imperfect journey with them.My hope is that in these discussions, you'll find ways to minister to one another.

So, let's all unmask. Let's be truly honest. And let's allow the most authentic version of ourselves to be seen by a few trusted others. For in this humility, we make room for the grace of God to recalibrate our aspirations toward the eternal purposes of Jesus' kingdom.

With great appreciation,

Jeff Christopherson

Jeff Christopherson

About This Discussion Guide

How to Use This Discussion Guide

As you continue your journey toward revealing the kingdom of God in your own life and leadership and within your faith community, this Discussion Guide can be used in three different contexts:

- As a pastor, in a learning cohort alongside other pastors
- With a church leadership team
- With your small group or missional community leaders within your church

You can use this resource as a personal study, but it will work most effectively in a group setting within a transparent community. As we come to know Christ and his ways more fully, we will desire to constantly reform our practices so that our lives fulfill what our minds understand.

However you choose to engage in this process, please set aside ample time to pause and deeply reflect on what God is saying to you. Completing the work isn't the end goal. The objective is to gain a richer, more Christlike life, leadership, and church. Such a kingdom assignment requires intentionality and space to breathe in order to settle into your priorities and practices.

Once you have completed the Discussion Guide, if you would like more support and training on this learning journey, then please get in touch and find out more information about a Learning Lab, which will help you embrace this change alongside other church leadership teams.

Please email info@movementleaderscollective.com for more information.

Overview of This Discussion Guide

The Discussion Guide is divided into three sections:

Section 1: Name the Status Quo

If you want to go on a journey of change toward a preferred future, you have to know where the journey starts. If I am attempting to get to Chicago, whether I start in Los Angeles or Baltimore has a huge impact.

This section will help you begin with the personal challenge of naming your status quo—not the aspirational self-talk but uncovering and owning the cold, hard reality in which you find yourself.

The questions will help you evaluate the current thinking and praxis of your church or ministry. Spend some time completing this exercise at the beginning of your time together, or individually before meeting. Then share your responses and discuss them with each other.

Section 2: Take the Journey

This next section outlines five areas of focus for you to use as you meet with others in a discussion group. Each discussion covers one of the five stages of change: *Discover, Unlearn, Repent, Relearn* and *Follow.* (The three middle stages of Unlearn, Repent, and Relearn are based on the *Movement Journey*, created by Movement Leaders Collective.[1]) This will help you to understand the journey you will travel to bring about transformation in both you and your church. Below is a brief description of what each of these five stages entails:

- **Discover**—Receive God's truth afresh as it is revealed to you

1 See https://movementleaderscollective.com.

- **Unlearn**—Embrace the gap between your mindset/ behavior and God's truth
- **Repent**—Realign your mindset and behavior to God's truth
- **Relearn**—Begin to embody and express God's truth that has been revealed to you
- **Follow**—Live out these truths in your life, leadership, and community

As you work through each of these five stages, you will start by reflecting on the whole book (all seven temptations), but these five stages can also be applied to each temptation individually. As you move through the process, you will begin to focus on one or two of the most significant temptations for yourself and your church. However, it's important to keep all seven in mind. After you have completed the Discussion Guide once (increasingly focusing on one or two areas), you can then go through the Discussion Guide again and apply the five stages of change to any one of the other seven temptations that are particularly relevant in your context.

A journey of change for a church or for a leadership team must be embodied rather than simply remain conceptual. This will mean that you, as a leader, will need to personally embrace and embody this *metanoia* (changed mind)—as you cannot ask others to go where you have not gone yourself. So, as you journey through the second section, it's important to think *personal* before *professional*, and as you consider the changes that need to be made, think *me* before *them*.

This section will also aid you in beginning to imagine or reimagine a preferred future—the greener pastures that lie on the other side of the valley of the shadow of death (Psalm 23). It is important to have a compelling vision of where you are going in order to help you traverse and persevere through the valley. As you engage with this section, do not just think of *what* needs to change but also *why* it needs to change, and what it might look like for that kingdom imperative to be fully expressed in your context.

Begin by focusing on one of two areas where you can start to bring change. This intentionality and focus can channel your prayer, effort, camaraderie, and perseverance toward genuine and lasting transformation. And as you begin to experience breakthroughs, you will develop the testimony, faith, and muscle memory to begin to embark on a lifelong journey of change.

As the old adage goes, "A rising tide lifts all boats," so transformation in one place will also bring changes in the other areas.

Section 3: Share your Learning, and Learn Alongside Others

This section briefly outlines an opportunity for you to share your learning with the wider church and to learn from others on the same journey.

Section 1: Name the Status Quo

This exercise will help you to gather a baseline of your current thinking and action in each of the seven temptations so you know where you are starting your journey.

Look at the Kingdom Corrective statement for each temptation, and simply circle a number on each of the seven continuums as a snapshot of your current reality. The more honest you are with your circle placement, the more you will be equipped to bring about change in yourself and your church. Remember, this is not an exercise of religious condemnation but of inviting God's grace-filled conviction.

1. **Philosophicalism**: "We are a Bible-believing people."
Kingdom Corrective Statement: *"Biblical belief demonstrated through practical obedience is how we characterize genuine orthodoxy."*

Not true/ never expressed ———— sometimes true/ expressed ———— fully true/ expressed

0 1 2 3 4 5 6 7 8 9 10

2. **Professionalism**: "We have a gifted pastoral team."
Kingdom Corrective Statement: *"We are mobilizing everyone in our church to be a disciple-making disciple."*

Not true/ never expressed ———— sometimes true/ expressed ———— fully true/ expressed

0 1 2 3 4 5 6 7 8 9 10

3. Presentationalism: "Our worship is inspiring, and our preaching is strong."
Kingdom Corrective Statement: *"We are the functioning body of Christ in community 24/7 instead of directing the bulk of our energies toward Sunday."*

Not true/ never expressed		sometimes true/ expressed		fully true/ expressed

0 1 2 3 4 5 6 7 8 9 10

4. Passivism: "Everybody is welcome."
Kingdom Corrective Statement: *"We are actively looking for lost sheep and joyfully embrace inconvenience and disruption in our personal comforts to engage non-believers."*

Not true/ never expressed		sometimes true/ expressed		fully true/ expressed

0 1 2 3 4 5 6 7 8 9 10

5. Pragmatism: "We are one of the fastest growing churches."
Kingdom Corrective Statement: "We *choose to measure growth in terms of city-wide gospel impact rather than relative comparison with other churches, our brand awareness, or the size of our attendance."*

Not true/ never expressed		sometimes true/ expressed		fully true/ expressed

0 1 2 3 4 5 6 7 8 9 10

6. Partisanism: "We love our country."
Kingdom Corrective Statement: *"Our highest and exclusive loyalty is to the eternal kingdom of heaven—not a temporal nation, nationality, ethnicity, or political ideology—and we happily lower any allegiance that could become a gospel barrier."*

Not true/ never expressed		sometimes true/ expressed		fully true/ expressed

0 1 2 3 4 5 6 7 8 9 10

7. Paternalism: "We train pastors around the world."
Kingdom Corrective Statement: "*We have a humble learning posture, believing that Jesus' church is expressed in a globally diverse mosaic that includes every nation, tribe, people, and language.*"

Not true/ never expressed				sometimes true/ expressed					fully true/ expressed	
0	**1**	**2**	**3**	**4**	**5**	**6**	**7**	**8**	**9**	**10**

As you review your results, try to make this an act of prayer and reflection that is expressed in community with others. Your communal discernment will sharpen the picture of reality.

The reality you see now shapes the journey ahead. Now that you have your baseline, you can embrace the journey of change in all seven troubling temptations, but the next step is to use Section 2 to identify one or two areas to intentionally, prayerfully, and strategically embark on the journey of change.

Section 2: Take the Journey

You are about to walk through the arc of change that will take you down and through the valley of the shadow of death, toward the greener pastures (Psalm 23).

As you work through these five discussions on the five stages of change, keep in mind the whole book and all seven temptations. Use the seven temptations as the backdrop of your learning.

Once you have done this, you can work through these five stages in one or two troubling areas of temptation.

At the end of each list are emboldened "reality check" questions, to help focus your reflection and discussion on your own reality and preferred future.

Discussion 1: Discover

This discussion focuses on the issues that the characters in the story discovered about church, what the Bible teaches us about church, and the key themes for you and others within your church to discover together.

Story

- Describe Yushua's experiences of church, first in Yemen and then in North America. What are some of the most striking contrasts?
- Discuss how Luca's father's church, Mt. Pisgah, measured success. What was missing?
- What parts of Jimmy's and Luca's church experience seemed least like the church we see recorded in Acts?
- Which of the three main characters (Yushua, Luca, and Jimmy) can you relate to the most?

- **Reality check:** ***How do these learnings apply to the reality of your own church, and what needs to change in your current context?***

Bible

- Read Acts 2.
- Discuss some of the key priorities of the newborn church.
- Which elements were the responsibility of the people, and which were the responsibility of the Spirit?
- **Reality check:** ***Which priorities of the early church are present in your current reality of church? Which priorities would you like to be present in your future?***

Discover

- Read over the Seven Temptations of the Western Church (on page 437).
- Reflect on your most troubling "Status Quo" results from Section 1 of this Discussion Guide.
- **Reality check:** ***What are one or two that seem to be quite healthy in your church? Why do you think that is? What are the one or two that you seem to struggle with more than others? Why do you think that is?***

Pray

- Listen to each other.
- Listen to God's prompting.
- Pray for one another.
- Pray for your church.

Homework

- Before the next discussion, reflect on your results in prayer and discussion with one or two other trusted Christ followers.
- Reflect on the Scriptures associated with the one or two weakest areas you identified.
- Reflect on how your behaviors could change in order to move toward a more Christlike expression in this area of temptation.

Discussion 2: Unlearn

This discussion focuses on the aspects that the main characters in the story needed to unlearn and what the Bible teaches us about unlearning. From there, we will look at key themes for you and your church to unlearn together.

Story

- What were some of the ingrained habits that Jimmy needed to unlearn about the body of Christ? How well did he do in the unlearning process? Why do you think that was?
- What do you think his trajectory would be after he left his father's shadow? How might the future-story of his faithful friend, Tom Butts, pan out? Why do you think that might be?
- What things did Luca need to unlearn about church? How well did he do?
- What did Yushua have to unlearn? How well did he do?
- **Reality check:** ***How do these areas of unlearning apply to the reality of your own faith community? What areas do you as a leader and as a church need to embrace unlearning?***

Bible

- Read Galatians 1.
- Describe some of Paul's critique of the Galatians.
- What unlearning did the Galatian disciples need to concentrate their attention on? Why might these be difficult lessons for them?
- Why is unlearning so difficult?
- **Reality check: *Which elements of Paul's critique and affirmation need to be internalized as unlearning in you as a leader and in your church?***

Unlearn

- Focus on the one or two temptations you've identified as the weakest areas for you and your church. Very specifically, what practical unlearning needs to take place in those areas?
- Focus your prayer, reflection, and discussion on the Kingdom Corrective statement for those two temptations.
- What various phrases do you repeat, and what decisions do you make that demonstrate how this temptation manifests in your thinking, speech, and action? (Be as specific as is helpful.) Write them down.
- **Reality check: *What decisions are you making, and what conversations are you having that are working against you? (Consider the behaviors that are feeding the temptation and holding you in unhealthy mindsets and habits as a church.)***

Pray

- Listen to each other.
- Listen to God's prompting.

- Pray for one another.
- Pray for your church.

Homework

- Study the list of various phrases you repeat and the decisions you make. Jot down some notes as you reflect.
- Pray through the list, asking for God's conviction and clarity as you embrace the unlearning he has surfaced.
- Reflect on how your language could change to move toward a more Christlike expression in this area of temptation.

Discussion 3: Repent

This discussion focuses on the issues the characters in the story needed to repent of, what the Bible teaches us about repentance, and key areas where you and your church can begin practicing repentance.

Repentance, or *metanoia*, literally means to change our mind. By God's grace, the Spirit convicts us to change certain mindsets or ways of thinking, and as a result, we believe and behave differently.

Story

- What are some examples of repentance (or changed minds) that we see in the characters of Luca, Jimmy, and Yushua?
- What does the unexpected discovery that Yushua makes about his brother giving him over to the police, when he is reunited with his family, reveal about our flawed need for justice?
- Jimmy had some great learning times and then often fell off the wagon once again. Each time, Yushua, Luca, or Tom

was there to challenge him to relearn and repent. Describe some of those times.

- **Reality check:** ***In the area of your most troubling temptations as a leader and church, what change of mind*** **(metanoia)** ***is required to realign yourself to Jesus' mission and Jesus' ways?***

Bible

- Read Colossians 3.
- What is it that Paul challenges the Colossians to put to death? What does he challenge them to put on?
- What is the role that the believer plays in this putting on and putting off? What is Christ's role?
- **Reality check:** ***Which elements of Paul's critique and affirmation need to be engaged with in repentance in you as a leader and in your church?***

Repent

- Look over the list of phrases and decisions that you wrote down in the previous discussion that relate to the two temptations that are the most troubling to you. Read them aloud, confessing them as sin before the Lord and each other.
- As the group reads and repents, proclaim the gospel of forgiveness on each other.
- Read aloud the Kingdom Corrective statements, and begin to rephrase them in your own words.
- If you have capacity, repeat this process for every one of the seven temptations.

- **Reality check: *Practically, how does what you have read aloud and sought God's forgiveness for become a cultural change in the behaviors of your life and the life of your church?***

Pray

- Listen to each other.
- Listen to God's prompting.
- Pray for one another.
- Pray for your church.

Homework

- Write down some practical ways that the Kingdom Corrective statement for your most troubling temptation can become a place of repentance and your greatest re-learning opportunity.
- Create an accountability plan for how you will turn and walk toward the future God is calling you to live into in this area of temptation.

Discussion 4: Relearn

This discussion focuses on the ideas that the main characters in the story had to relearn, what the Bible teaches us about relearning, and the key themes for you and your church to begin to move into relearning.

Story

- What were some of the ideas that each of the three main characters in the story relearned about being the body of Christ? About Christ? About themselves?

- What aspects of the kingdom of God did people around each of the three main characters begin to emulate?
- How did the three main characters grow in their dependence on Christ? On Christ's body?
- **Reality check:** ***Where do you as a leader and as a church need to embrace and embody relearning? Specifically, what new spiritual muscle-memory does relearning require?***

Bible

- Read 2 Peter 1.
- What are the qualities that Peter calls believers to grow in? What is the believer's role in these activities, and what is God's role?
- **Reality check:** ***Which of the qualities that Peter calls upon do you need to newly express as a leader? As a faith community? Which of these qualities are currently absent or weak within your context?***

Relearn

- Look over the notes you made as homework from the last discussion about the Kingdom Corrective statement in your weakest area. Read them aloud as if Peter were encouraging you to grow in these things.
- As each person reads, affirm them in what Christ is calling them to.
- Discuss specific actions that you may be considering based on your relearning opportunity. What is God calling you to do with what you are relearning? Invite input from each other.

- **Reality check: *Practically, how does what you have read aloud and affirmed become real in the behaviors of your life and the life of your faith community in the coming days and years?***

Pray

- Listen to each other.
- Listen to God's prompting.
- Pray for one another.
- Pray for your church.

Homework

- Draft on paper a plan of how the areas of relearning might become real in the mindset and behaviors of you as a leader, in your small group, and across your church community.
- Strengthen your accountability intentions for how you will make the plan become reality over the coming weeks and months.
- Share your plan with two to four trusted voices who are part of holding you accountable and praying for you as you embark on the journey of change.

Discussion 5: Follow

This discussion focuses on how the main characters in the story learned to follow the Spirit of Christ, what the Bible teaches us about walking in the Spirit, and the key themes for you and your church to begin to follow and move into obedience.

Story

- What changes did Luca, Jimmy, and Yushua make to how they led ministry, based on their relearning?
- In your own imagination, how might Philadelphia Freedom have changed some values based on the learnings brought home from the Iran team? What might have happened in Philadelphia?
- In what ways were you surprised by how the three main characters followed the leading of the Holy Spirit?
- **Reality check:** ***What one faith step do you sense the Holy Spirit is challenging you to take in your leadership? What might stop you from taking that step?***

Bible

- Read Luke 24 and Acts 1.
- Describe the ministry hand off Jesus set up for the apostles.
- Who was the ministry to be led by?
- What would the Great Commission have looked like without Pentecost?
- **Reality check:** ***Practically, and very honestly, how would your ministry as a leader and as a church be different with or without the power and presence of the Holy Spirit?***

Follow

- Read aloud the actions you wrote down since the last discussion, and review the plan you made as homework after the last session.

- Discuss among the group some specific changes you believe the Holy Spirit is leading you to stop doing or start doing.
- **Reality check:** ***As you are honest as a group, what are the challenges that will stop your plan becoming real, embodied, and actioned?***

Pray

- Listen to each other.
- Listen to God's prompting.
- Pray for one another.
- Pray for your church.

Homework

- Begin to act on the plan that God has led you toward. Hold each other accountable, and uphold each other in prayer.
- Celebrate small victories and first steps, and be honest, prayerful, and accountable in the places of early battles or struggles.
- As you see initial momentum, remind yourself of all seven temptations, bearing in mind their potential to hinder your progress and create dangerous pitfalls.

Section 3: Share Your Learning, and Learn Alongside Others

No singular church has all the answers, and every church has valuable learning to share with others.

Please get in touch to share testimonies of change, learning from your context, and any coaching or support needs you have as you embark on this journey.

If you would like further coaching or support to help implement the changes you've discussed and read about, please **email: info@movementleaderscollective.com to engage with a Learning Lab journey, where you can learn alongside other churches in the change process.**

Seven Temptations of the Western Church

(with biblical references)

1. Philosophicalism: "We are a Bible-believing people."
Kingdom Corrective: Essential to a sincere belief in the inerrancy and infallibility of God's Word is an assumption that calls his disciples to become a Bible-obeying people, and not merely intellectual stakeholders of theologically orthodox positions. We understand that true orthodoxy affirms that biblical belief is a *verb*—doctrines that we humbly live and practice—rather than a *noun*—theoretical precepts to which we philosophically subscribe. Therefore, we choose to measure spiritual maturity and doctrinal integrity with the benchmarks found in our everyday obedience to God's Word.

Scriptures: Luke 6:46, Luke 11:28, John 14:21–23, John 15:14, 2 Timothy 3:16, James 1:22–25, James 2:19, 1 John 2:3–6, 1 John 5:3, 2 John 1:6

2. Professionalism: "We have a gifted pastoral team."
Kingdom Corrective: The gospel is every disciple's calling—not just a chosen few. Because of this, we seek to multiply Jesus' disciples by developing and deploying the body of Christ into a diverse and infinitely reproducible co-vocational mission-force. Therefore, our vocational leaders see their primary assignment as equippers and multipliers of Jesus' disciple-making insurgency.

Scriptures: Luke 19:11–27, Acts 18:1–3, 1 Corinthians 4:12, 1 Corinthians 9:18, Ephesians 4:11–13, Colossians 3:23–24, 1 Thessalonians 4:10–12

3. Presentationalism: "Our worship is inspiring, and our preaching is strong."
Kingdom Corrective: We are the functioning body of Christ in community, not a well-tuned Sunday service. Though we value the weekly gathering of believers for corporate worship and biblical instruction, we also understand that Jesus' purpose for his body cannot be contained in that hour. Therefore, what we most highly prize, publicly celebrate, and consider as our ultimate act of worship is preparing the entire body of Christ as sacrificial servants for Jesus' 24-7 mission and his imminent return.

Scriptures: John 4:24, Acts 2:46–47, Acts 13:2, Romans 12:1–5, 1 Corinthians 12:12, Ephesians 4:11–16, Hebrews 13:20–21

4. Passivism: "Everybody is welcome."
Kingdom Corrective: We actively search for lost sheep—not hope that lost sheep look for us. Therefore, we happily inconvenience our personal comforts and disrupt our religious preferences for the

sake of effectively participating in Jesus' selfless and courageous search and rescue mission.

Scriptures: Matthew 4:19, Matthew 5:14, Matthew 28:19–20, Mark 8:35, Mark 10:29–30, Luke 15:3–7, John 20:21, 1 Peter 2:9

5. Pragmatism: "We are one of the fastest growing churches."
Kingdom Corrective: The kingdom of God is our only goal, and not the advancement of our individual brand. Because of this, we choose to measure growth in terms of city-wide gospel impact rather than excelling in a competition for an evaporating market share of the evangelically predisposed. Therefore, for the kingdom outcome of gospel proximity, we prefer to selflessly invest in united efforts of gospel collaboration rather than pragmatically contending for our own interests.

Scriptures: Matthew 5:1–12, Matthew 16:24–26, Matthew 23:1–12, Mark 8:35, Luke 15:1–7, John 12:24–26, John 17:1–26, Romans 15:5–7, Ephesians 4:1–6

6. Partisanism: "We love our country."
Kingdom Corrective: While national patriotism and political perspectives are normal and necessary for healthy and functioning democracies, our highest and exclusive allegiance is to the eternal kingdom of heaven—not a temporal nation, nationality, ethnicity, or political ideology. Therefore, we voluntarily lower all secondary allegiances so that our earthly perspectives might not become a stumbling block to the life and death mission of Jesus' church.

Scriptures: Joshua 5:13–15, Matthew 4:8–11, John 13:34–35, John 18:36, 1 Corinthians 1:11–13, 1 Corinthians 3:1–4, Galatians 2:20, Galatians 5:13–15, 1 Timothy 2:1–4, Titus 3:1–2, 1 Peter 2:17

7. Paternalism: "We train pastors around the world."
Kingdom Corrective: We have a leadership that maintains a humble learning posture, holding to a sincere belief that Jesus' church is expressed in a globally diverse mosaic that includes every nation, tribe, people, and language. Therefore, we engage global diversity with a gospel-centered posture that eradicates any hubris of geographical or cultural superiority by seeking to both learn and assist in ways that honor and edify the body of Christ wherever it is found.

Scriptures: Matthew 8:5–13, Luke 4:24–27, Acts 13:1, 2 Corinthians 8:8–9, Philippians 2:1–11, 1 Peter 5:5–6, Revelation 7:9

Bible Copyright Information

ESV

p. 107, "And he gave the apostles, the prophets …" (Ephesians 4:11–12).
p. 175, "I therefore, a prisoner for the Lord …" (Ephesians 4:1–16).
p. 224, "To equip the saints for the work of ministry …" (Ephesians 4:12).

NIV

p. 102, "Blessed are the poor in spirit ..." (Matthew 5:3–12).
p. 222, "As the Father has sent me…" (John 20:21).

NKJV

p. 222, "You have heard that it was said …" (Matthew 5:43–44).

Made in the USA
Columbia, SC
03 September 2023

22435670R00278